THE CULLED

On the roof, I puked again. The throbbing in my ear was jacking about with my sense of direction, and it didn't help when the moonlit city put itself together bit-by-bit inside my topsy-turvy bearings.

I was so far west of the park I could see the tiny fishing punts on the Hudson, beyond the tangle of docks and quays spread out below me. Taller buildings rose to my left and right – faint lights glimmering inside where innocent scavs struggled to get by with some semblance of a *life*.

It was actually sort of beautiful. If it hadn't been about a mile in the wrong direction I might have paused to appreciate it.

There were no roofs to leap across to here. No secondary stairways to scamper back down.

And, if I'm honest, no energy to go on. The thing inside me curled up and went to sleep, exhausted, and left me alone. Only human. Outnumbered and outgunned.

Trapped.

"Fuck." I said.

Footsteps up t

Time for the e

D0830409

An Abaddon Books™ Publication
www.abaddonbooks.com
abaddon@rebellion.co.uk

First published in 2006 by Abaddon Books™, Rebellion Intellectual
Property Limited, The Studio, Brewer Street, Oxford, OX1 1QN, UK.

Distributed in the US and Canada by SCB Distributors, 15608 South
Century New Drive, Gardena, CA 90248, USA.

10 9 8 7 6 5 4 3 2 1

Editor: Jonathan Oliver
Cover: Mark Harrison
Design: Simon Parr
Series Advisor: Andy Boot
Marketing and PR: Keith Richardson
Creative Director and CEO: Jason Kingsley
Chief Technical Officer: Chris Kingsley
The Afterblight Chronicles™ created by Simon Spurrier & Andy Boot

ISBN 13: 978-1-905437-01-6
ISBN 10: 1-905437-01-3
A CIP record for this book is available from the British Library

Printed in the UK by Bookmarque, Surrey

The CULLED

Simon Spurrier

Abaddon Books

WWW.ABADDONBOOKS.COM

CHAPTER ONE

Somewhere over the Atlantic, with a canyon of heavy clouds spilling open below like a hungry gullet, I decided enough was enough.

"Fuck it." I said.

I'd moved three times already. Like a trail of cheap Pollock imitations I'd converted the aisle-seats of rows one and two into sticky red monuments to my own mortality, and already First Class Reclining Lounger 2B was streaked with enough congealing blood to saturate the upholstery. I felt a lot like I was dying, and if not for that boring old voice spitting from the back of my mind – *don't you fucking give up, soldier* – the idea might even have seemed alluring. The pain killers we'd lifted from the storage lockers at Heathrow appeared to have achieved exactly squat – except maybe enhance the growing desire to puke – and try as I might to sit still the ugly little 'O' of puckered gore just below my left shoulder was refusing to clot. It dripped and oozed, and soaked through everything I wore, and got into places I'd rather it didn't. Last time I took a piss in the cubicle behind the cockpit – door missing, safety lights plundered years ago – I looked down and for one horrible second thought I'd caught a stray in my undercarriage. Even the relief at disproving *that* theory hadn't occluded the pain.

So. The decision crept up slowly enough, but lacking for any idea of what sort of reception committee we'd get at LaGuardia, I couldn't put it off indefinitely. I chewed my lip for a while, munched philosophically on a thought-displacing can of dog food from my pack and decided to have a dig.

They teach you self-triage in the first year of training,

but it's rudimentary stuff. The basic attitude is that if you get wounded on a mission you've already fucked up the whole 'covert' gig, so what happens to you afterwards is entirely *your* problem. I remember the staff medic they sent over from the MOD squinting thoughtfully at the roomful of grunts ranged out in front of him, with an expression that said: *Oh, you poor bastards.* He spent two weeks lecturing us on sterilisation and euthanasia policy, and when he got to the part about bullet-removal simply sighed over his clipboard and said:

"Just make sure you're dosed to the *gills*."

Sir, yes sir, etc etc.

I stood up, refusing to concede to the shakes in my legs, and made my way forwards. The pack we'd loaded with tranqs and stimms – and every other bloody thing we could find – sat in the co-pilot's chair next to Bella. From the glassy eyes, and beads of sweat tangled in her hair, I guessed she'd been staying awake care of amphetamine pick-me-ups, and she barely looked round as I rummaged for a cocktail of my own. She'd come through the firefight at Heathrow unscathed – mostly by hiding behind me – and looked like she was taking the piloting pretty seriously. Knuckles white on the control stick, breath laboured, lower lip creased where she'd bitten too hard. The amount of empty vials scattered on the floor, I hoped she didn't give herself a heart attack before we hit the tarmac at the other end.

Hit. Bad choice of word.

I found a stack of hypoderms marked 'Bliss' – stylishly bound with an elastic band – and shrugged. Since the whole 'End of the World' shtick a veritable smorgasbord of crazy narcotics had bubbled to the surface – repressed military Perf-Es, street drug mixtures and DIY chembrews – and who the hell was left to say what they all did? But

'Bliss' sounded better than 'infected screaming agony', so I told myself *side-effects be damned* and yanked one out of the bundle.

The elastic band snapped and stung me on the cheek. Very fucking macho.

"Might be out for a bit," I grunted, hoping Bella hadn't noticed, unwrapping a hypo and ambling back to the cabin. If she heard me at all, she didn't answer.

I took time setting myself up. Despite the engine's growl and the unsettling *bong-bong*s of warning instruments from the cockpit, the empty plane was an eerie sort of place. Like a dried-up river, or a morgue without a corpse, you take away the thing that makes something what it is – in this case the passengers required to make this thing more than just a big flying cigar-tube – and all that's left is a hollow promise.

Oh, and a wounded man getting shitfaced on 'Unknown Drug X', with an unsterilised pair of tweezers and a roll of nylon twine set aside.

I took it easy with the dosage. No telling what's normal, what's an OD, what's instant death. The candyfloss comfort came up like a warm bath, sliding along each limb in turn, and for a second I worried I'd spiked myself with some barbiturate crap that'd put me to sleep before I'd even poked into the wound. But then it hit my brain like a slap, airburst an embarrassingly orgasmic sensation into my crotch and told me – over and over, like a scratched vinyl playing in my ear – that everything was going to be okay.

Seriously good shit.

I was already jabbing about in the exposed muscular layers of my upper arm before it even occurred to me I should be in agony. I guess that in some abstract sense I *was*, but like watching a bad film through the wire-caged windows of the TV shops they used to have on Tottenham Court Road, it was a distant and silent sensation; and it didn't take much to turn around and focus elsewhere.

Don't you fucking give up, soldier.

Sir, no sir, etc etc.

When it came out, grinding against something I'm pretty sure was bone, trailing strands of half-congealed blood like cobweb threads, the bullet was an unimpressive little thing. For the amount of pain it'd caused, I was half-expecting an AMRAAM sidewinder with barbed fins, so the amorphous blob of iridescent snot that emerged was curiously disappointing. I *plinked* it down on my foldout meal tray, squirted a thick loop of military-issue antiseptic into the crater and got to work with the twine. The whole thing was a botched job – I knew that – already oozing pus and still refusing to stop bleeding, but in the absence of an emergency unit, doctor, nurse, or person with the slightest clue what they were doing, it was a work of fucking *art*.

I tied the last knot, broke the cord with my teeth, slapped an antiseptic dermal pad over the top and wound a thick strip of torn cloth round it several times.

Then I stopped, felt smug, allowed myself a moment or two of self-satisfaction and passed out.

Maybe the 'Bliss' was mildly hallucinogenic. Maybe I was delusional from loss of blood and suppressed pain. Maybe the sleep deprivation was getting to me and screwing with my thought process.

Or maybe I've just got a lot of nasty shit clogging up my imagination.

Whatever the reason, slumped there in my seat aboard an empty 737, thirty five thousand feet above the Sargasso

Sea, my unconscious brain shat a kaleidoscope of blurred irrelevance: contradictory and clashing symphonies of half-remembered experience. I felt sick.

It felt a lot like rewinding through my own life. It felt a lot like viewing my history in cinematoscope vibrancy, except with DVD extra features and a meaningless musical track, on a TV screen with the colour mixers fritzed to shit.

It took a while to stabilise (whatever meaning *time* had) and when the psychedelia surrendered and the ugly memories came into uglier focus, I would have done anything to wake myself up – except that when you're asleep you don't *know* it. The human brain's annoying like that.

It all went in reverse. It jumped about and skipped important stuff and generally confused the hell out of me. I don't know for sure, and Bella wasn't much good for paying attention right then, but I'm guessing I scrabbled about inside the cabin like an epileptic sleepwalker. Should have remembered to buckle-up.

In my head, I was back in London, running and panicking, and—

Chattering rifles, out in the darkness. Muzzle flash behind the slats of scripture-daubed blast-shields and swabs of knackered concrete cracking open as strays struck the earth.

Heathrow. It'd gone downhill since the Culling Year. Planes stood like dead sentries; plundered for glass or metal, listing at strange angles where tyres had punctured or wheel columns had snapped: all marks of whatever violence had first swept through the compound five years before.

Back in the centre of the city, the random aggregate of survivors and raggedymen I ever actually spoke to had dismissed such scars – everywhere you looked – with a shrug and a philosophical grunt.

"Cullin' Year," they'd say. As if that covered – and excused – every anarchic sin, every thoughtless act of destruction that went along with a city entering self-destructive free-fall. All the looting. The thieving. Murdering. Raping. Burning the shop fronts, clogging the river with car wrecks, hoarding tinned foods, slaughtering police horses, coughing and stumbling and spitting blood from lungs on the verge of liquefaction.

Waiting for the nukes that never came.

The Culling Year. It was a crazy time.

Here and now in the airport, the devastation was all that much harder to ignore. The precision of the planes, the carefully mapped elegance of the compound: all distorted, broken, salvaged and left to withdraw behind bristly weeds and the slow creep of rust. The violence had ended years ago, but its effects stood untouched, like alabaster monuments to the insanity of an entire population.

Over my shoulder, the gunfire faded out. I kept running, dragging Bella along by either her coat or her hair – I hadn't stopped to check – and headed for the one aircraft that was patently undamaged: repainted in the garish blue of the Apostolic Church of the Rediscovered Dawn.

Neo-Clergy. Currently trying to kill me.

Somewhere, out between the hungry darkness of the airstrip and the humming lights strung up around the tower, someone shouted. A rasping burst of biblical condemnations, to cover the clattering of clumsy hands reloading rusted hardware. Even further away, booted feet raced towards the racket with the sort of haste one learns to associate with hardcore well-trained military types,

*and I reminded myself with a groan that most of the
barracks emptied their survivors into the Church during
the year, with the casual abandon of men swapping one
institution for another. I wished the shouting voice would
shut the fuck up.*

I was a heretic, apparently. A defiler, a philistine,
a walking abomination, a devil fit only for immediate
destruction and above all else a sneaky motherfucker.
I recognised the dulcet tones of the same fat monk I'd
'befriended' earlier that day – playing unscrupulously on
the hints of his sexuality he'd betrayed in coy glances and
coquettish gestures – then unceremoniously clubbing him
over the head with the stock of a rifle when he turned to
fetch me some water.

It was a way in, anyway.

And then Bella was shrieking something behind me –
"the bag! the bag!" – and as I turned to assess what was
going on, the Kalash' opened up again. Something dull
and hard happened to my left arm, and I was pirouetting
in my place without meaning to.

"Oh." I said, wondering why cracked concrete was
pressed against my cheek. "Oh."

And Bella screaming, and the engines of the aircraft
powering up with a whine, and the throb of more guns,
and pain and confusion and drugs and more blood than
I've ever seen before, and—

Bong-bong.

The aircraft, flying itself, chiming out warnings about
who-knew-what.

I half-opened my eyes; a fissure of light strong enough
to spot the curved steel struts of underchair braces, the
lifejackets stowed in wire compartments beneath each

one, and an ancient packet of dry roasted peanuts. Empty, of course.

Back in the present.

You're on the floor, soldier.

Addled thoughts turned over lazily, wondering how long I had before the hostess came and told me to get up, whether I'd barfed on anyone's hand luggage, whether I could ask someone to get me a coffee. I think reality would have asserted itself pretty soon after that, if the Bliss hadn't flexed in my veins again.

Another proto-climax, building in my groin. Another rush of shivering oddity, and the most distant reports of pain in my left arm, before—

The signal.

This was before Heathrow. Shit - this was the reason for Heathrow. This was before the Neo-Clergy and Bella and all that.

This was lying alone on my palette, stretched out in the corner of Comms Room 221A, in the eastern wing of the Vauxhall Cross SIS building. Dozing, staring out at the river and wondering at all the other raggedy survivors, curled up in tube stations and mall stockrooms, clustered round oil drum fires and squabbling over rats and pigeons.

I wasn't smug at my own warm little womb of safety – not exactly – but it came close.

London was ugly before the Year. Afterwards, it was...
Different.

Let me tell you: a city looks strange without lights. At night, the sky is black and star-pebbled, just like anywhere else, and if you've lived in London any length of time you know that's wrong. The sky should be yellow-green. Blazing with light pollution, oozing out of the constant clouds. It was like The Cull had stolen the very colour from the sky; flattening all that was civil, all that was advanced. Look at the world now, it said:

Eco-friendly, yeah. But not much fucking fun.

Curled there in my room, mind empty, chin resting on a heap of stolen pillows, it was a well practiced thought process. Five years into this dismal new reality, and there was nothing much left to say about it.

Nothing new to get excited abo...

The signal sparked the consoles to life with a neon-storm and a chatter of code, and I jumped like I'd been electrocuted. Down to reserve power, the building wouldn't even let you switch the bloody dimmers on, let alone the systems. There must be some kind of automated kicker, powering-up for the duration of an incoming signal. Clever.

Five years, they'd stood silent. Consoles growing dusty, covered in tinned-soup spillages and stolen porn, or whatever other luxuries I'd plundered on any given day. For five years the antennae on the roof – concealed ingeniously within blocky, deco architecture – had stood inert, listening to a silent spectrum.

Five years I'd slept in the same room, getting by, scavenging up and down the riverbanks by sunlight, creeping back at night like a bear to its den. I'd always ignored the others who'd adopted the same routine. Old administrators or low-level secretaries, I guess, lucky enough to remember the entry codes to let them in, but never getting past the divisional checkpoints inside the central lobby. All automated. All closed.

But not to me. Not to senior personnel.

Up here there was still the ghost of power. Low-level illuminators at night, self-sealing doors. Solar panels on the roof, I think, though I'd never found them. There was even a functioning vending machine down in the armoury, though the coffee tasted like plastic and the tea frothed with mouse shit. Still, here was safety. Here were sealed doors built to shrug-off a missile-strike, a tunnel beneath the river to the heart of bleak, deserted Whitehall and all the accoutrements of my old life.

Files. Computers. Weapons.

And now a signal.

I thought it was a joke first of all, but that was daft. Who amongst my friends – and there were never many of them to start with – had the means, let alone the diseased sense of humour?

Nobody. Nobody was left. Nobody senior enough to know the codes, nobody who knew how to tap-in up here. Not since the Chief choked on the mushy debris of his own lungs and the two surviving directors were mobbed en-route to a Cobra meeting. Since then, camaraderie amongst ex-employees had been pretty low on the agenda.

The code chattered away like a chorus of angry crickets, transferring to the flickering screen in unbroken columns; flashing green as each security clearance was challenged, negotiated, allowed.

And then a word, immersed in the stream of data.

It scrolled by so quickly I almost missed it. Eyes wide, I convinced myself I was mistaken, and ignored the prickles of sweat wriggling out of my forehead as I hunted it down again.

There.

++PANDORA++

My stomach lurched. Something happened to my heart that felt a lot like a black hole opening in my rib cage. I staggered, I think, because suddenly I was sitting down with my hands out, pressed on the edge of the desk like a safety-bar holding me into the carriage of a rollercoaster.

The word raced past again, bottom to top, a pixellated burst of... of what?

Choirs of angels, rays of light, divine intervention. Who the bastarding hell knows? It wasn't possible, but there it was.

And then the final security clearance was offered, the linkage was established, the vocal channel opened with a greasy pop, and I was listening to static.

And someone breathing.

And a voice that said: "Are... Are you there?"

I recognised it.

"Oh." I said. It was all I could manage. It came from the one deep-buried part of me that – alone – was able to function in the face of this revelation. The rest of my brain was a stunned fish, flapping on a pier, waiting for a rock to pound it to paste.

"Oh..."

And then the reserve power died, the channel closed, the screens winked to blackness one by one, the lowlights perished and the great black silence rolled in to gobble the building like never before.

I remember losing it. Just a little.

I remember storming and breaking things and snarling. I remember the blood so thick on my mangled knuckles, from beating on the walls and the consoles, that they dripped across the carpet. But most of all I remember the feeling swelling up inside me; the feeling I'd forgotten, cast off like a dead skin all those years ago. The feeling that said, loud and clear in the base of my skull, wrapping iron knuckles around me, straightening my posture and giving me no room to argue:

Don't you fucking give up, sold—

Something touching my face.

I came out of the delusion/flashback far quicker this time, and with the scream of engines abusing the edge of my consciousness I remembered where I was without much preamble. It felt like I'd managed to pull myself up into another of the plane's chairs – still as groggy as fuck – and, nylon be praised, the blood had stopped trickling down the inner edge of my arm. I wondered how long had passed.

Somewhere an alarm was whooping quietly, a polite emergency. I almost laughed at the idea, and decided, with a half-hysterical chuckle, the drug was still in me.

Concentrate.

I felt another light touch, a gentle *something* brushing against my lips and, with sluggish realisation, tried to form words.

"No, Bella..." I mumbled, struggling to open my eyes. "S'not... s'not *likethat*..."

The plane seemed to shiver. She touched my lips again.

"*Toldyou*..." I slurred, aware of the spittle hanging off my chin and the cotton wool dampening every movement. "I'm not... not *innarstd* inthatshit..."

Then my ears accustomed themselves to the whine of the plane (higher pitched than before?), filtered it out like layers being peeled clear, and picked up the mantra of garbled words hammering out of the distance, lurking beneath.

"...fuck..." it hissed. "Fuck fuck fuck... oh god fuck no... what's... what's... oh, fuck..."

Bella. Still in the cockpit. In trouble.

So who's–?

I rammed my eyes open, combat conditioning superheating every instinct, muscles tensing from head to toe... and wished I hadn't. My senses shortfired, adrenalised my fragile waking mind, and kicked the last vestiges of the Bliss into action. It came on like a storm of white noise, wrapped under and over everything I could see and hear and touch, and my last impressions before I slid under for a third time were of a tangled, tentacled *thing* stretching down towards me from above, brushing sensually against my lips.

Air mask. Emergency procedure. The plane's in trouble.

Shit.

Alarms and swearing and airquakes, adjustments to fickle impermanent gravity—

A siren raced past outside. Two, maybe three weeks ago I would have bothered to get up and check what it was. Police, fire, ambulance, mountain-sodding-rescue?

Now there wasn't much point. They were all ambulances.

*This was... before. At the start. This was before The Thing went airborne, before the mass graves and gasmasks, before they firebombed St Mary's and sent out the A-Vee body carts with the speakers and the flamethrower turrets ("...deposit all corpses upon the pavement... do not approach this vehicle... deposit all corpses upon the...").
This was at the very beginning, when the hysteria hadn't had time to get going, when people clung to their fragile little hopes of stability, when no one had quite figured out how bad things were going to get and the brass were playing it cool. No need for alarm, blah-fucking-blah.*

This was five years before I got the signal.

I slumped into an armchair, alone in my flat, listening to the alarm dopplering its way into the distance, and swirled the ice in my drink. For some reason the tinkling of cube against glass put me in mind of the street café in Kabul – tanbur and sarinda music, heavy scent of melon-molasses in shisha pipes – where two months before I'd broken two of my fingers.

I winced at the memory. Getting old, maybe. The mark's guards had soaked up both clips of hollow point .22, and in the end I had to choke the poor bastard to death as he did his best to prise my fingers off his windpipe.

Krak, krak, gurgle.

Don't you fucking give up, soldier.

Sir, no sir, *etc etc.*

I took a sip of scotch. Glanced around, gloomy.

The flat wasn't up to much, if I'm honest. A smattering of CDs on shelves, expensive but unnecessary gadgets to sharpen kitchen knives and open wine bottles, an aquarium with no fish (who'd feed them?) and a double bed that was rarely double booked.

I believe "unlived in" is the phrase.

Sometimes I'd feel inclined to pluck shirts and socks – fresh – out of the drawers in the bedroom, and drape them artfully about the place, like they'd been thrown off or forgotten about. Designer slobbery, for Christ's sake. How tragic was that?

Well it was all going to change, and there was no avoiding that. I glanced at my watch and took another sip, wondering why the removal van was so late, and fidgeted.

Another ambulance, another streetside-dirge for the slumbering city. I think even the throb of a helicopter (air ambulance, sure as eggs are eggs) passing somewhere in the background hum of London.

On the TV a BBC anchorman was busily disseminating the day's developments.

"...and was joined by the health secretary in re-issuing his assurances that all possible efforts are being made to contain and counter the epidemic. When challenged by protestors on the alleged withholding of public inoculations, the prime minister appeared visibly shaken; assuring members of the press that viable treatments could not be issued until scientists understood more about the nature of the disease.

"In a parallel incident, the Pentagon was today sealed off as protestors converged upon Washington, DC demanding action against soaring cases of infect..."

I hit the 'standby' stud like it had offended me.

Another ambulance, outside. Sounds of people arguing in the next flat along.

Someone coughing in the room above. Not a good sign.

I was woken up an hour later – unaware I'd even fallen asleep – by a shrill double-bleep from my mobile phone. A text message. I flipped the oyster-lid open, spotted the name in the 'Sender' register and hurried to open the message, feeling a vague sense of unease that I could neither shake nor explain.

SOZ. It read. CHANGE F PLAN.
BIN CALLED IN.
MAYB 2 WKS?
U WAIT?

I stared at it for about an hour. Like watching a football replay, hoping against hope you'll spot something you missed last time, hoping it'll all turn out differently.

"Oh." I said. To myself. To the invisible fish in the tank, maybe. Maybe just to the phone, which kept switching off its illuminated display every time I left it alone. "Oh."

Another ambulance went past.

And I woke up for absolutely the last time in the blood-streaked shuddering cabin of a hijacked Boeing 737, feeling like a volcano had taken a shit in my skull, wondering why everything was rushing backwards and forwards.

This time, it really *was* Bella. Gripping me by the moist rags that passed for my clothing. Shaking me back and forth, so the base of my skull rebounded over and over off the plasticated upholstery of the seat.

"...know you can *hear* me, you *fuck*, you *wake up*, you *wake up*, you..."

I mumbled something inarticulate. Her vocal barrage didn't stop, just shifted gear like a machine heading straight for burnout.

"...we're going to *die*, you prick, we're going to *crash*! The *gear*, okay? It didn't *deploy*! Bloody autopilot's taking us *down* and, fuck, we're going to *die*..."

I wondered if I had enough time to take more 'Bliss'.

CHAPTER TWO

I've always had a thing about landings.

Before The Cull, before the streets filled with dead/dying/hoping-for-death bodies, before the survivors realised what was going on, before the public accusations and riots and whirlwinds of violence and lynchings and general bad shit, I was a frequent flyer.

Under less sinister circumstances I would have built up enough air-miles to take me as far as Jupiter, but when every flight is accompanied by a new passport, new name and new identity, it's difficult to keep track. In my line of work, there wasn't much by the way of perks. Not that it mattered much. Not any more.

The point is, I'd been on enough journeys to know the routine. The sudden gees of the take-off run, the misery of getting a seat next to the toilet, the Sod's Law ratio of passengers in the neighbouring seat (normal people to weirdoes, 1 to 3).

And every time, at the culmination of every tedious stint, after hours and hours of staring glumly at the inner surfaces of a brightly lit tube, when the captain's voice crackled in hidden speakers to announce the imminent touchdown, *every time* my stomach took a little lurch.

I know all the arguments. I've *had* them all. Usually with the weirdo next to me.

"...still statistically the safest way to travel..."

"...more likely to get hit by a bus than..."

Blah blah *blah*.

Call me a pessimist, but there's something about the image of 40,000kg of tightly compacted metal and plastic descending at catastrophic speed towards a strip of rock, which is not – let us be quite clear about this – renowned for its *softness*, that does my head in. There's something about 200-plus people strapped together in a cylinder with fins, undertaking a controlled stall in mid-air, that gets my palms a little sweaty.

Paint me irrational.

Five days before I woke up from the Blissout in the cabin of a doomed 737, with Bella shaking my head and telling me we were going to *die*, she and I had been making plans.

Talking it through, sat in a burnt-out pub in a burnt-out street on the outskirts of Heathrow, eating feral rabbit and an optimistic harvest of wild berries. Bella had told me about autopilots. I'd only found her the week before and we were still getting used to each other. To me she was someone with piloting experience, too dosed out of her head to care about the hazards, with her own private reasons for wanting to get Stateside. I didn't waste any energy caring what they were. Not then. It meant she'd help me without needing payment, cajolement or threats. Bonus.

To her, I was just the gun-toting psycho that'd get her aboard.

"Thing is," she'd said, picking blackberry pips out of her teeth, "an autopilot can do pretty much everything."

"You what?"

"S'right." She waved a dismissive hand. "I mean... obviously you need a *real* pilot too. Keep an eye, re-plot, react to shit. But basically the auto's doing the tough stuff. Following the course, regulating height and speed, all of that. If it weren't for the takeoff thing I figure they would've got rid of the crew altogether, given a year or ten." She scowled, adding the silent:

If not for The Cull, I mean...

Still a common thing, in conversation, talking about

22

the future like there still *was* one.

"The takeoff thing?" I repeated, confused.

"Yeah. Don't ask me why. Trainers never explained it, and I was only on the course three weeks. Needs a human touch, I guess. Too many variables, too much left to chance."

I nodded, faintly relieved. The idea that each time I'd taken off in the past my life had been in the hands of a glorified calculator hadn't sat well.

Until:

"Hang on. *Only* takeoff?"

Bella had smiled at that. She'd cadged a cigarette off me earlier (I don't smoke, but currency's currency) and now she lit it carefully, tar drawling lazily past her teeth.

"Only takeoff."

"Then... the landing's... ah..."

"Yep." Another evil little grin, blowing out smoke like a squid venting ink, then a shrug. "Not *always*. Most pilots'll do it themselves. Matter of faith, I guess. But say it's raining, or there's mist on the runway. Hit some buttons, sit back, Bob's your uncle."

"Fuck."

"Yep."

"So when we, ah..."

"Heh heh."

She had a pretty laugh, all things considered. She was far more prone to sniggering nastily, which got on my nerves, but still. It's not like there was much to laugh about.

"When we fly," she said, "you can bet your last soggy Marlboro I'll be using the auto as much as I can. Trust me, it's the more reliable option."

Needless to say, this conversation had not filled me with confidence.

At around a thousand feet, with the alarms hitting an unbearable crescendo and a visible gash of smoke rising past the starboard windows, the full stinking reality of the situation leeched its way past the Bliss hangover and punched me between the eyes.

I was flying aboard a plane belonging to a notoriously unforgiving sectarian movement, which hadn't been properly maintained or serviced in five years, which had an unknown quantity of fuel in its reserves, a terrified junkie at the controls who'd never progressed in her training beyond a computerised flight simulator, and a catastrophic amount of damage to part or parts unknown of its undercarriage.

And it was being landed, single-handed, by a geriatric computer.

"Oh fuck." I said. "We're going to die."

Bella stopped shaking me.

"S'what I've been trying to *saaaaay!*" she screamed, eyes bulging.

For a moment or two we stared at each other, with nothing but the irregular whine of the engines and the spasmodic whooping of alarms between us. Then we burst into laughter.

Adrenaline does funny things.

Bella's laugh didn't sound all that pretty just then.

As near as I can tell, the auto brought us in on target.

I wasn't watching closely – the seat I'd buckled myself into was set some way back from the cockpit on the grounds that if things *did* get ugly the further forwards one sat the uglier they'd be – but in snatched glimpses through the open doorway I could make out the distant scar of what might be an airstrip, burnished in the bronze light of the afternoon, bordered on one side by a blurry haze of outbuildings and on the other by a bright mirror of water. To me it seemed to be directly ahead and low on the horizon, which I can only assume is the best place for an airstrip to be.

Bella sat next to me, singing freaky little nursery rhymes, refusing to talk.

Listing vaguely to the right, even through the muddy soup of my senses (ironically the pain from my arm had returned to full strength long before my instincts had), I sat grimly prepared for the wingtip to clip the tarmac, shearing off the entire thing and sending us cartwheeling – trailing fuel and smoke – like a colossal Catherine Wheel.

Or maybe the tail would dip, and we'd ricochet up like a throwing knife on the backspin, somersaulting up and over until the cockpit nosed into the rock like a blunt javelin, shattering every surface and filling the cabin with atomised glass.

Or maybe the starboard engine would blow on impact. Maybe we'd know nothing about the crash at all except an exquisite burst of fire; a supernova to shred every window, every seat, and every fragile little bone in our bodies.

Maybe we'd hit a building.

Maybe we'd over-fly the runway and bury ourselves, full tilt, into the mass of service yards and hangars cluttering the distant reaches of LaGuardia. Maybe we'd topple down into the mid-island water, venting bubbles as the dark swarmed up around us.

Maybe we'd...

Oh, fuck.

Having an imagination is never a good thing in a desperate situation.

"...in the tree top... when the wind blows, the cradle will..."

"Bella?"

Distant bushes through the windows at the edge of my vision.

"...when the bough breaks, the cradle will fall..."

"Bella – shut the *fuck up*..."

The horizon bobbed into view on both sides. The tarmac came up.

"...down will come b..."

Kroom.

Sparks. Alarms screaming like abandoned babies.

Everything shuddered. A backblast of air funnelled down the cabin from ahead, peppered with glass and stone, and my neck twisted so hard I yelped in shock. Grass and distant buildings snickered past outside the window, but not in a straight line. We were curling on the runway, half-deployed landing gear screaming and twisting in protest beneath us, rolling us sideways, careening in a cloud of molten metal and whirligig embers. Spinning off the tarmac.

A sudden moment of weightlessness, and pain all across my midriff as the seatbelt bit. From the corner of my eye I saw Bella rise into the air, pancake-spreadeagle on the ceiling with a cockroach *crunch*, and then back down, nutting a headrest and flipping, upside down, onto her side.

No seatbelt.

Shit.

A bone jarring shudder, and crippled metal twisting with an operatic screech. Through the window beside me, lost behind a grid of contradictory smoke-trails and fluttering debris, I could make out the arrowhead of the wing tilting backwards and up, shearing itself off as the plane barrel-rolled into its slow skid. It ripped clear with a terrifying lurch, sprayed fuel which ignited immediately, and shattered itself magnificently across the tarmac like a neon waterfall. The metal of the fuselage – four seats in front of me – buckled with a shriek, shattering all the glass down the left side and vomiting smoke into the cabin. Everything went black and toxic, and even through the acrid fog and my own desperate coughing I could hear the battered impacts of the plane's death throes. It snarled and groaned its way across the last of the runway, ripping gouges of rock with an angle-grinder roar, then dipped with another lurch onto the grassy rough. Bella groaned somewhere in the murk.

Time started to return, piece by piece. Sparks drooled.

And – slowly at first, but gathering speed as inertia surrendered to the shifting weight – we rolled. Landing gear comprehensively AWOL, single remaining wing arcing up and over the fuselage like a shark's dorsal, ceiling bowing and sagging then snapping straight as it took the strain. My seat swapped verticality for an abrupt horizontal, lifting the whole cabin like a theme-park ride, sharp-edged seatbelt constricting me again.

The second wing slapped at the ground with a bowlike shudder and snapped off. Like some cylindrical juggernaut the fuselage rolled across it, breaking apart at the seams as it went.

Inside: tumbling chaos.

Debris dropping then lifting, blood rushing to and from eyeballs, hands swapping between lap and forehead.

Bella flapped like a dying fish, *thud, thud, thud*, off ceiling and floor with each new rotation. If she was still alive, she didn't look it. Nothing much I could do to help.

We seemed to be slowing down.

Then something detonated behind us. The all pervading jet-whine of a long-lost engine maxed out with a painful hiss and – *oh fuck oh fuck* – striated everything, inside and out, with shrapnel. Metal was punctured. The craft rocked and shunted forwards, heat-blast roiling back from the mangled tail, and hacked at the rags of my bloody clothes. Something stung my knee. My face bled. What few windows remained exploded like froth on a wave, and I had the fleeting impression of singed grass surfing past the shattered porthole as we rolled again. Something sharp and long punched itself through the metal beside me, coming to rest a scant foot from my side: a shattered stanchion from the rough beside the runway, picked up like a thorn.

And finally, like a great engine throbbing itself into dormancy, the airplane came to an appalled halt; listing on its back like a clapped-out whore, waiting for another bout. Smoke plumed on every side, and the quiet crackle of flames tugged at my punch-drunk consciousness.

"Shit." I said.

And Bella's inert body – half resting on the back of a chair directly above my head – surrendered to gravity, flopped in mid-air with a boneless kick, and impaled itself on the jagged spike in the wall.

I don't think I'll ever forget the sound it made.

The first instinct was to get out.

All that Hollywood bullshit about fuel tanks spontaneously going up like Krakatoa – long after the crash – could be safely ignored. The second engine had fallen silent shortly after the mad tumbling stopped, killing with it any obvious danger of explosion. But the irrational panic remained like an ember in my guts, and the fires already lit were plentiful enough to be scary. With the smoke gradually thickening and the slippery cut across my forehead leaking into my eyes, I thrashed about to get to the seatbelt buckle, finding a sudden unshakeable *need* to be away from this bastarding plane.

Away from Bella's limp little body. Staring straight at me.

Don't you fucking give up, soldier.

Sir, no sir, etc etc.

It was stealing over me by degrees that I'd *done* it. I'd got to the States. I'd fucking *done* it.

And yeah, there had been sacrifices and hardships. Yeah, there had been pain and chaos and untidy scrambling. Yeah, there had been death.

But you don't do what I used to do, for fifteen years, without seeing some or all of that at some point. You don't get to slink like a shadow between the raindrops, killing and cutting behind the scenes of a hundred and one foreign powers, without learning how to bottle it all away. Screw it up into a venomous little ball and dump it, derelict and forgotten, somewhere in the poisonous wastes of the unvisited mind. Anything it took to get-on-with-it. Mental conditioning. Emotional disconnection. Whatever.

I'd got to America. Nothing else mattered.

Though, to be fair, the victory was soured somewhat by the attendant uncertainty of what I'd find out there. Five years ago, before the news-shows stopped broadcasting and the emergency radio fell silent, before the Internet became an unchanging frieze – dying piece by piece as humming servers across the world sputtered out – it had looked like the US had not fared well.

Certainly they'd caught a nuke or two.

Listen: it turns out nothing brings out the aggression

in a population like a shared disaster. If you believed the projections they made back at the start – and I did – the AB-virus took out 93% of the world's population. That's fifty-nine billion people, for the record, bent-double with the pain, spitting mangled clusters of alveoli out of their lungs and into their mouths, bleeding from eyes and ears and arse, dying by fractions.

You hear that?

Fifty. Nine. Billion.

It's a bigger number than I can imagine – and that wasn't even the end of it.

There was a time – perhaps a month or two – when the governments and networks and lines of communication were still nominally functional. Stripped down, understaffed, kept afloat by the efforts of men and women who'd watched nine out of ten of their colleagues drop dead, who'd been left blinking in the glare of responsibility with no clue, no hope and no idea.

I guess it was inevitable some stupid fuckwit would start throwing accusations.

The AB-virus was manufactured, they said.

Biological weaponry, they said.

State-sponsored terrorism hiding behind pandemic disaster, they said, and they pointed fingers and found 'proof', and let the tension escalate. The news was all but dead by the time the missiles dusted off, but we heard about it. Even in London.

I like to think nobody targeted Britain because our diplomatic status was untarnished, our potential involvement in any biological assault was laughable, and our impartiality prevented any accusations being aimed at us.

Yeah. And pork-chops come with wings.

No, we were spared because there were no wankers left

in Whitehall to stick their heads over the parapet and join the row. No one left to contribute to the growing worldwide squabble. No one left to press Big Red Buttons.

After the Cull, any poor fucker left in charge was either lynched by the mob or ran and hid. It was a very British way of dealing with disaster.

It was also, now, half a world away.

I drew myself painfully through the interior of the destroyed plane and tried to anticipate. From the heat and glare ebbing through the largest of the ragged rents in the fuselage it looked like a pleasant day, which was something of a novelty after five years of acid rain and London skies.

I threw a last look back at Bella – hating myself for not having the energy to lift her off that spike; for not pausing a moment longer to at least close her eyes. But no... that same feeling of being bottled-up; trapped in a cage. Waiting for *something* to come and get me.

It's a cliché, but you don't get any good at what I used to do without letting your instincts guide you. That and the fact that, in my line of work, there was *always* something coming to get me.

Logic suggested the Neo-Clergy would be nearby. This was, after all, their plane. It was also *their* route, plotted ahead of time into *their* autopilot, landing us (for want of a better word) at *their* chosen destination. They could be relied upon to take exception to the way I'd treated their property.

I probed a hand into the pocket of my coat, seeking reassurance.

Still there.

Good.

But what else to expect? A nuclear desert? A

radioactive wasteland haunted by the insane and the dying? Cancerous wildlife staggering on tumourous legs, lurching up to feast on the new arrival?

I'd been to New York once before. It didn't sound all that different.

I'd stowed the supplies pack in a luggage locker near the cockpit. Working my way forwards, past twisted seats and dangling airmasks, it was easy enough to retrieve. But as I tried to heft it onto my shoulders, grunting under my breath, it occurred to me exactly how weak I was. My head rushed for a split second – the legacy of the Bliss – and I staggered, overbalancing awkwardly.

"Bollocks!" I hissed, falling onto my arse.

It saved my life.

A stuttering burst of semi-auto rang out from somewhere behind me, clawing a neat geyser of shattered plastic and fibrous insulation from the ceiling/wall above my head.

Exactly where I would have been.

I dropped and rolled, textbook fast, before my brain even caught up. A chatter of gunfire followed – I guessed from the same source – shaking the air like a giant fan and tugging on my raggedy coat as it ripped a hole in the trailing edge. I swatted out the singed fabric before it caught light, finding myself hidden by the padded shield of a sideways seat, and let the adrenaline take over.

Identify the enemy.

"Where the *fuck*," a voice shouted, NY accent thicker than a sergeant's skull, "are the *kids*?"

Ah.

The kids.

"I can explain!" I shouted, keeping the terror thick in my voice. "Just... just don't shoot me! *Oh god oh god.* It wasn't me! They sent me to tell you!"

"Who sent you?"

"T-the..." *Think fast.* "The Bishop! There was a problem! W-with the kids, I mean. They wanted me to explain, s-so they..."

"What problem? Where the *fuck* are they?"

Get a direction. Zero-in.

"*Answer* me! Where *are* they?"

Further along the cabin. Standing in the aisle. Must have climbed in through the missing tail.

Alone?

"Please, I... I just... *oh god*..." I knocked out my best sob. I hammed it up like a true thesp. I poured every false fear into that gurgling pitiful little voice, and when the figure appeared slowly on the edge of my vision, creeping forwards with his lips pursed, it was set in a posture of laughable unwariness. His gun was lowered.

He rolled his eyes when he saw me, cowering and shivering in bloody rags with snot pouring off my nose.

And the Oscar goes to...

"Pull yourself together," he said, a fraction softer. "Now tell me who the fuck you are or it's..."

I moved faster than my own senses could register. Mental conditioning. Third year training. Biological reactions: without thought or judgement. Zen disciplines with chemical catalysts: reaching down into the subconscious, switching off your abstractions and *dis*tractions, becoming something less and more than rational.

Letting the body take over.

"Hng." he said.

I took out his jugular and carotid with a single sweep of the hunting knife I'd been carrying since Heathrow. More blood, soaking through my coat.

Doesn't matter.

I pirouetted downwards whilst the poor bastard was still wondering where I'd gone, wondering why his voice had stopped working, wondering why only gurgles arrived in his mouth where there should be angry, demanding words.

Three stabs to the ribs. Two directly between intercostals, the third glancing sideways off the breastbone, snapping something with a greasy *pop*, then sliding in as soft as you like.

Stepped back.

Considered a fourth stab upwards from solar plexus, decided it wasn't needed.

Retreated to my cover behind the chair and waited with animal patience for the human parts of my brain to come back on line.

Start to finish, it took about six seconds.

The man stayed upright for another five as his body worked out it was already dead.

He hit the puddle of his own blood like a belly-flopping pig, jerked once or twice, and went still.

I wiped the knife clean on a sleeve and cleared my throat.

There didn't seem to be anyone else around.

CHAPTER THREE

Interlude

The man had opted to change his name for the duration of his mission – not that he'd had a lot of choice. It was that or put up with the Sachems nagging him for the rest of eternity.

A week ago he was Rick. Today he was Hiawatha. Go figure.

He gunned the Honda along the main street of a picturesque everytown, enjoying the growl of the old engine – still a perfect melody, despite its hiccups and occasional coughs – and selected a sidestreet at random. Nobody on the sidewalks. No curtains twitching or faces peering over tumbledown walls. Nobody here to see the Mighty Hiawatha passing through.

He supposed he ought to be honoured. It was, after all, a name dredged from the deepest troughs of tribal heroism – belonging first to the great warrior/prophet who reconciled the squabbling nations. Hiawatha – the original – had been friend and brother to the deific Great Peacemaker; a glorious ancestor-totem in his own right and the illustrious architect of the first Great Confederacy. Four hundred years later and the white men still insisted on calling the Union of Five Nations by its insulting handle – the Iroquois – and never gave it another thought.

Ignorance and arrogance. So said the sachems, anyway.

(Cue dull lectures about the Confederacy's 'invention' of democracy, its influence on the US's own constitution, and a hundred-and-one other details, hopelessly out of date, that the clan mothers and their chieftain pets

meme-repeated every time anyone was dumb enough to ask a vaguely cultural question.)

Iroquois meant 'Rattlesnakes'. The clan mothers hated it.

Rick (née Hiawatha) rather enjoyed the description. It appealed to the youngster inside him, a sinister sort of moniker to match the leathers and war paints the Tadodaho had given him. Certainly it had more character than the title the Confederacy gave itself – 'Haudenosaunee': the people of the long houses. Not exactly a name to strike terror into the hearts of one's enemies, particularly when most of the 'long houses' these days were Winnebagos.

Rick let the bike drift to a halt before an imposing building at a crossroads. It looked like maybe it'd been a courthouse or something grand and prestigious – long ago – but a glistening plastic sign announced its more recent owners to be RAY N' JAKE, this being their GENERAL STORE.

Bless.

Rick listened to the engine rumble itself away into silence, wondering if anything was left inside the boarded-up building. His stomach gurgled. He'd have to start worrying about fuel soon too. Either that or stay stranded out here in ghost-town suburbia forever – and a more hellish prospect he could not imagine. He pocketed the keys, and swung himself down onto the sidewalk, flicking his long double-braid out of his eyes. Everything seemed quiet. An overgrown sign – hanging off its rusted pole on the far side of the street – let him know he'd strayed into the curiously-named town of Snow Hand (this on a day of glorious sun and only minor QuickSmog), and asked him to drive carefully.

He smirked.

On the subject of misinformative names, he also found

it tricky these days to refer to the ubiquitous enemy (i.e.: assholes who persisted in calling the Haudenosaunee the 'Iroquois') by such a simple term as 'The White Man.' It seemed ridiculous. Some of his best friends inside the tribe were white, genetically speaking, and the council had supposedly granted them just as many rights, freedoms and opportunities as its trueblood members. It never ceased to amaze Rick that the 'new' tribesmen – who had eagerly joined the Confederacy since the Cull and were mostly paler than an anaemic goth – seemed utterly untroubled by the constant bitching about the goddamn 'white man'.

It was like they'd resigned from their own species.

Lucky bastards.

His silent perplexity brought a little smile, unbidden, to his face. He was remembering the last night before he left his home-village to embark on this ridiculous trip, and his good pal Leicester (formerly a whitebread bank clerk, now a hunter-scavenger with the Kanien'kéhaka lodge), smoking an enormous hash pipe. The dumbass had actually started griping, perfectly serious as only a raging pothead could be, about the 'Pale-Skinned Devils.'

Rick still found himself sniggering at that one, a week later.

Snow Hand's unremarkable environs looked unlikely to yield much by the way of food or fuel. Small white and green houses, clad in sycamore and aluminium, nestled into the wooded hills on every side. Pretty much all the trees were dead, Rick noticed, which didn't help the sense of cloying not-quite-rightness. He'd stopped in enough places up and down the I-80 in the last few days to know this was hardly a rarity. Maybe some weird effect of the fallout had taken its toll along the eastern face of the Appalachians. Maybe a lack of rain, or just too much fucking sun, or something in the QuickSmog or... or whatever. The forests round here were dead. Not his problem.

Rick squared up to the door of the general store, not letting the little gang of crows squatting on its roof startle him. They – or others like them – had been keeping pace with him for a good fifty miles now, perhaps hoping he'd spontaneously drop dead. It didn't bode well for his hopes of finding food.

The wide window outside the shop had been comprehensively boarded up: first with planks (long since desiccated and crumpled), thereafter with an increasingly desperate array of corrugated iron, chicken wire and a long lost car door.

Impregnable. Ish.

"Hello?" Rick called out, casually drawing a feather-pocked crowbar from his saddlebag, not entirely sure if he wanted to be heard. A fat cat, long since gone feral, glared impudently at him from a weed-choked driveway across the street. He shrugged. At least if there was nothing in the store he might find some lucky tins of pet food somewhere. Or...

He wondered how easy it was to skin a cat...

He had a half-hearted attempt at prising open the door – fat chance – then quickly and efficiently scrambled up the boarded window like a squirrel up a tree, coming to rest on the ledge of an upstairs window, scaring the choir of nosey crows from their holier-than-thou vantage. Iron bars, of all the luck, bisected the window, but the wood was so ancient and the plaster sealing the cavity so rotten that a few hefty swats with the crowbar and some hot-faced brute force was all it took to gain entry.

The way Rick saw it, the harder it was to get into one of these dismal places, the more likely it was there'd be *something worthwhile inside. He slipped in, silent as death, gripping the crowbar like a samurai sword.*

Whoever had occupied Snow Hand five years ago – Pale Skinned Devils no doubt, ha! – had either died or moved on. Same as most places. Uprooted families, the dead going unburied. Back at the start, when people began to die and the Government said conspicuously less and less about it every day, people had clued-up quicker than the suits had expected. Something big, going down, being kept quiet.

Maybe the townsfolk had even seen the flare-flashes in the night, out across the southeast horizon, as the Sovs or the Saudis or whoever-it-was took out Washington like bleach on a stain. That's the sort of thing that'll kill your community spirit, deader than disco.

Snow Hand. Some of them went east to NY, probably, and no doubt died there. Some went west, over the hills. Probably died too.

Some of the lucky ones maybe fell in with the Haudenosaunee, to stay alive and count their blessings and get on by.

(Yeah, the uncharitable voice of rebellion grumbled inside, just so long as they respected the goddamn old ways and didn't rock the fucking boat.*)*

Rick checked the rooms of the first floor on automatic, adrenaline burning away like a barely-noticed light. Nothing. Not unless you could eat a child's rat-nibbled dollies, or run a Honda on the contents of a cologne drawer. Taking it as read that the place had been looted before it was still no surprise to find jewels and gold stashed away, untouched in makeup cases and bedside drawers. Who was going to steal something so useless, after all?

He shouldered the crowbar and made his way downstairs,

into the store, sighing as his thoughts turned back to the tribe, wondering what would happen if he just turned around right now and headed home. Fuck the mission. Fuck the Sacred Duty.

Back in the Haudenosaunee, the sachems – forever peering cautiously over their shoulders to check the matriarchs approved – had told him all the 'Nationalistic Crapola' (his phrase, not theirs), all the white man/red man dogma, all the 'Them-and-Us' bullshit: it was a state of mind. The Confederacy had found its place and its path in this topsy-turvy post-Cull world, and anyone who made the effort to stand in their way or interfere was designated 'The White Man' – whatever their skin tone. Simple as that.

Rick would have gone on to point out the flaws in this terminological morass – mainly that it was fucking stupid – except at this point in the conversation the sachems generally parroted the same trite platitude that inevitably cropped-up in the answer to any challenge to the status-quo:

"If it was good enough for the ancestors..."

At the bottom of the stairs he could see the interior of the front door. A heavy-duty lock – well oiled, well tended – had prevented his entry from outside. Hmm.

Actual *skin colour, the Confederacy maintained, didn't matter in the equation any more. How could it, when at least half the modern Haudenosaunee were as Caucasian as they came? They'd been welcomed into the tribes with open arms (altruism or smugness? Rick secretly wondered) and taught the interminable lessons of the past. What mattered, the matriarchs croaked, was not the identity of those practicing the Old Ways, simply that they* were *being practiced.*

Pushing open a connecting door into the service area,

Rick reflected gloomily on how eagerly the new white Iroquois had embraced the lifestyle, the ceremony, the trappings of something culturally genuine. He'd been hearing the same old stories all his life – born and bred on a cockroach-infested reservation – and couldn't remember it ever filling him with the same sense of childlike glee and religious satisfaction as Leicester and the others. Smearing their snowy skins with ash and paint, eschewing modern clothing – and there was plenty of that about, since the Cull – for old style jerkins and deerskin rags.

Somehow, deep down in the (plentiful) ocean of his immaturity, Rick had felt betrayed. Jealous, even. How dare they, these interlopers? How dare they show up out of nowhere, join the tribe, and get twice as fucking much out of it as he did?

The problem was this:

He'd spent all his childhood, all his years of education, all his earliest years of adulthood, trying so hard to be white. How dare the world roll on its head? How dare every bastard suddenly want to be Iroquois!

The shop smelt of dust and cigarettes, with the faintest tang of ancient alcohol. He pushed through a mildewed bead curtain into the storeroom out the back, and paused to yank cobwebs out of his hair.

Whenever he was in a really bad mood, Rick tended to call the white Iroquois 'Tourists'. He'd call the quaint little village-lodge a theme park, and loudly offer to take photos of fat Yankees wearing branded ethnic costumes for a mere $5. Then he'd caper about trying to sell make-believe hotdogs, or guided tours of the casino complex cunningly disguised as a wooden longhouse.

Last time he pulled this routine, one of the Sachems had beaten him so hard he'd had to sleep sitting up for a week... but it had been worth it, just for the look on everyone's face.

The point was... The point was, it was all such a joke! The Confederacy existed – thrived! – because its way of life worked. *In this twisted devolving excuse for a world, it worked. It worked because its infrastructure remained when everything else collapsed. It worked because it created ties that didn't rely on material benefits or familial ancestry. It worked because it was a shared equalitarian society that would only – could only – function when everyone was progressing together.*

Rick was confident about this. He'd been studying social sciences when The Cull began.

That put a stop to that.

The point, the point, the point. The point was there *were reasons for the good old Injuns to swap places with the Pale Skinned Devils as the most stable and viable community, and none of them had anything to do with the old stories and religions and myths. Running and dancing round fires, throwing clods of earth, chanting and smoking and yadda yadda yadda.*

Theme park stuff.

Worse still, despite their voluble claims to the contrary, the council simply weren't playing it as fair as they said. Otherwise how in the hell did he, Rick, a so-called 'pureblood' Onundagaono – who had never given a shrivelled racoon's cock for the history or religion of the Haudenosaunee – been chosen for a sacred role any number of the white tribesmen would have happily killed to fulfil?

It was, in a word, bullshit.

They'd given him three gifts before they sent him out. That was a headache, too. Sort of mythic: three fabulous tools for a bold knight to take on his quest. Scant goddamn consolation for being thrown to the wolves, in his opinion.

It wasn't like any of the gear was even worth much.

From the matriarchs who ran the Confederacy from the sidelines, the bike. XR650L Honda street bike with mismatched tyres, scavenged engine parts and highly unreliable homemade saddlebags. A clapped out piece of shit, by any other name, but they'd been so proud as they wheeled it over. Rick remembered being mystified. The lodges had access to much better gear than that, but the womenfolk had stared at him so earnestly, puckered faces intense, and warned him of dire misfortune should he desert the vehicle.

Don't you lose it, they'd said. *Don't you leave it behind.*

Great.

From the sachem council, smiling toothlessly, nodding and gurning, he'd received a packet of the sickly weed the old bastards smoked relentlessly in their shanty lodges. Rick would've appreciated that one, at least, if the stuff in question wasn't notorious amongst the Haudenosaunee as having some... strange properties. No one knew where the old men grew it (certainly not in the same carefully-cultivated beds as the dope the youngsters raised), or what they added to it, or how it worked. But it did... things.

Given that they'd sent him on a holy mission, Rick had been quietly astonished that they'd thought it was a clever idea to give him two ounces of dried Brain Death for the ride.

And finally, from the Tadodaho, a tiny bundle of fabric, with something hard at its centre. Rick had been a little more positive about this. He and the Tadodaho had always got along; the old man was alone in all the tribe in being prepared to listen to Rick's gripes and answer them – patiently, infuriatingly, correctly. Rick had fumbled open the fabric wrapping with excited hands to find...

A needle. A silver sliver of metal, like a sewing-pin.

"Should come in useful, that," the Tadodaho had said, nodding sagely. Rick had felt like the victim of an awful joke.

And now, days later, he could feel the same package, bundled-up in his back pocket. He gripped it vaguely through his leathers, blinking in the low lighting of the dusty store and glancing around himself with the trailing vestiges of his mental tantrum retreating.

He let his jaw hang open.

He'd never seen so many guns in his life.

An hour or so later – or so it seemed – in the upstairs bedroom full of mouldering dollies and toys, Rick awoke to someone shouting.

Footsteps on the stairs.

Not a good start.

Ungumming his eyelids carefully, the afternoon sun did its meagre best to piss a few half-hearted rays through the QuickSmog, between the mouldering frames of the upstairs window, and onto his face.

"Fuck..." Rick mumbled, wiping dribble off his chin. He hadn't meant to fall asleep.

Looking back over the tail-end of the dream he'd been woken from, he supposed he must have been vaguely aware of something coming; the grumbling tone of an engine, the creak of the General Store's front door: all incorporated into some rapidly-diminishing abstraction involving tomahawks painted white, flocks of shrieking crows with heads like hash pipes and a fat cat telling him, in the Tadodaho's whispery voice:

"If it was good enough for the ancestors..."

Well, thanks. Thanks very much, oh glorious old ones. Now he was good and fucked.

"Ram?" the voice snarled from halfway up the stairs, chain-smoker-deep and alcohol slurred. "Ram? That you? Where'd you get that pieceashit fucking bike, man? Looks like it got squirt straight outta the junkyard's prick!"

Rick visualised his battered ride. The voice had made a pretty fair assessment.

The footsteps on the stairs sounded, now that he thought about it, heavy.

He lifted himself upright as quickly and quietly as he could, still half asleep, and considered his options. None of them looked good.

After finding the cache of guns – pistols, rifles, Uzis, grenade launchers, shotguns, two dusty old mortars and a gargantuan shoulder-rocket hanging off the wall – he'd put two and two together and come up with a single word:

Collectors.

Out here, outside the major cities, in the great field-strewn swathes of American Nowhere bisected and fed by cracked freeways, the Collectors were everywhere. Rick knew only too well who the mercenary bastards worked for, gathering up supplies, weapons, drugs, and...

–he thought of the tribe, whittled-away little-by-little–

...and other things.

But Collectors were just collectors. That was the point. As long as you had nothing they wanted, as long as they weren't on some big-assed spree, they'd ignore you.

As long as you were over 18.

As long as you weren't red-skinned.

Shit.

Back in Fort Wayne, and across all the lands of the Haudenosaunee, every day was a spree. But out here things were quieter. Right? Out here, surely, the Collectors *wouldn't* know *about the Blood Anomaly...*

On the other hand, if some psychotic biker got home to his secret stash of hardware to trip over a sleeping Injun, it'd be fair to expect he's gonna be pissed.

Rick had therefore placed himself in the upstairs room at the front of the General Store, exactly where he'd climbed in, stolen shotgun in hand. Just a short rest, he'd promised himself. There'd been no food or drink anywhere inside, and whilst an armoury groaning with enough hardware to take out a war party could only be considered an exciting find, it didn't go far to re-enlivening the flesh. He'd sagged like a nosebag to the floor beside the window, eyes already heavy.

He'd see anyone coming a mile off, he'd told himself. He had an easy exit if some asshole tried sneaking up, and he'd always been a light sleeper. If something woke him, he'd have plenty of time to react.

Yeah, right. And in the meantime some vicious sounding colossus had pulled up outside, come in through the front door (which meant he came here frequently, which meant he knew about the guns, which meant he almost certainly had one), and come stamp-stamp-stamping up the stairs to find Goldilocks eating his porridge.

Metaphorically speaking.

"Ram! Fucksakes, man! You bin shootin' my shit again I'll kick your a...."

The door burst open. Something vaguely bear-like – but somehow smart at the same time – reared in the entrance, a silvery covering shimmering. Rick barely had time to see it, let alone react intelligently, but somehow the shotgun was levelled and his finger was on the trigger while sleep was still fogging his thoughts.

In the spilt second or two before the muzzle roared, he realised the behemoth was human. Facial hair like a dead orang-utan pasted to his head, narcotically unfocused beetle-eyes peering out beneath red-weed eyebrows; a ridiculous bowler-hat perched jauntily atop the thatch. The creature's frame was encased inside an enormous silver puffer-jacket, covered in bright strips of cloth and fluttering pendants; pinstriped office-pants that looked utterly out of place but glaringly showcased tiger striped shin guards and gym socks; goth-spec boots like they'd been dragged off an astronaut in mourning, and – ironically the last thing his eyes fell upon – an outrageously fucking massive machete.

The man looked like a Vietnam vet who'd got a job as a taxman, then gone cuckoo one day in a camping gear shop. It was a lot to take in. Rick didn't even bother.

"Hey!" the man grunted, eyes briefly finding focus.

The shotgun took his right hand off.

Rick was no stranger to firearms but he yelped quietly at the shotgun's kick and staggered backwards, fighting to line-up the second barrel. The grizzled creature barely slowed: fist reduced to a frothing stub of congealing paste and dangling tendons, machete shattered and bent out of shape, hurled away in an expanding cloud of meaty lumps and bony shards. From somewhere inside the crippled mess an artery squirted feebly.

"You're not Raaaaam!" was the freak's only concession to shock or pain. Even with half his knuckles popping greasily beneath his booted feet, he kept coming.

Totally and completely, Rick decided, out of his skull.

A paw wrapped around the barrel of the gun and yanked it, hard. A wad of sparks and smoke roared somewhere underneath the giant's armpit, knocking a head-sized hole in the plaster behind him and sending Rick jerking backwards again. The gun was wrenched out of his hand, swivelled expertly in the man's remaining fist like a baseball bat, and swatted him across his cheek. Despite the flashes of light and building pain – getting sharp quickly, now – Rick felt that this was somehow unfair.

"I... I shot your fucking hand off..." he muttered, as if trying to remind the roaring monolith above him. Somehow, at some point, his face had got itself stuck to the floor.

Above his head the shadow of the shotgun moved backwards and up; wooden stock brandished like the head of some arcane mace, ready to pulverise his skull. It almost seemed like too much bother to try and roll aside, but with a sort of half-hearted fatigue he flopped onto his back, curled his head downwards, and held his breath.

The stock bounced off the floor, above his scalp, with a thud.

Rick stared groggily upwards, peering through the misty haze of arterial ejecta, and kicked the bear as hard as he could right between the legs. This was all happening to someone else, of course: as disassociated from reality as the dream with the tomahawks and crows. Rick fought the urge to laugh.

Real or not, sheer overwhelming damage seemed to be slowly catching up with the giant. The groin trauma had done what no amount of shock or blood loss had managed: making him stagger, wretch, then topple to his knees with a sharp crack. The shotgun – empty – skittered away into the corner, and Rick felt himself, as if from a whole world away, pick himself up and dust himself down.

"Raaaamm...?" the stranger warbled, flopping onto his side like a greasy mudslide, squeezing at the pulsing abortion that had once been his fist, trying to stop the bleeding. Rick stared down at him – at his froth-flecked lips and buzzing eyeballs – and decided that whatever the guy was on, he wanted some.

In fact, an unpleasantly guilty sensation was stealing over Rick like a fart in reverse: he'd broken into someone's home, wrecked their window, stolen their gun...

...and then shot them when they caught him red handed. Not exactly the type of criminal ignobility you'd expect from someone carrying the name of the Mighty Hiawatha.

"A-are... are you okay?" He mumbled, feeling ridiculous, to the sobbing colossus.

The creature focused on him on the third attempt – spasmodic eyeball rotations calming for an instant or two – and scowled, sweat and grease dappling his scarlet forehead.

"You're not Ram." He said, surprisingly softly.

"Uh. No. No, I'm not. Look, I'm really s..."

"Where's Raaaam?"

"I don't know. Who's Ram?"

"Raaaaaymond."

"Oh. I see. I..." A vision bobbed into Rick's mind: the glittering plastic sign dangling just outside the window. "S-so, uh... So you'd be Jake?"

The fat man's eyes became suddenly still, brows bunching together. "Jake?" He said.

"Yeah."

"Jake's dead. I'm Slip."

Rick coughed, wondering if he should perhaps offer some sort of medical care but wishing he could be a million miles away. Instead, scrabbling about for something to say – anything! – he blurted:

"What, um. What happened to him?"

"Dead."

"Yeah, you sa..."

"Screwed-uppa mission. Let the kiddies getta wayaway. Bosses inna Ay-pos-tol-ic-Church got pissy. Blamed him, *see? So I fucked him inna eyes."*

"Um." Rick cleared his throat. "What?"

"Pulled 'em out. Best bits. Juicy. Likealikealikea lychee, Ram says."

Oh yeah. That was the other thing.

Collectors.

Weren't too fussy where the next meal came from...

"You... uh..."

"Sucked 'em out. Et 'em. Fucked the holes. Fucking catamite Jake asshole. Fucked him good, heh heh heh."

The weird thing, Rick discovered, was that it was a relief. Accidentally blowing off someone's hand who'd just been trying to protect their property would've tested even his powers of conscious amorality. Discovering said mutilatee was a cannibalistic psychopath took the edge off the guilt, and the confirmation that his unintentional victim had been dealing with the Neo-Clergy was enough to leave Rick positively elated. It was all he could do not to spit on the guy's bristly jowls as the blood pumped out of him and his life rustled away.

He went downstairs, feeling a little dazed, and helped himself to as many guns and as much ammo as he could carry.

He went outside.

He went back inside and dumped the shoulder-launched rocket, cursing under his breath. It turned out 'as much as he could carry' wasn't as much as he thought.

He went outside again, and stared at his bike. The clan mothers had been quite specific.

Don't you lose it, *they'd said.* Don't you leave it behind. It'll only bring you grief.

The cat was still glaring at him from across the street, reminding him of his dream and the withered-faced old Tadodaho whispering about the Ancestors.

"Fuck that." Rick said, out loud.

Then he threw a stone at the cat, slung a leg over the monstrous Harley Davidson trike his would-be murderer had kindly left parked beside the Honda, and gunned his way back towards the I-80 with the purr of a zombie tiger.

He had an appointment in New York, and he intended to meet it in style.

CHAPTER FOUR

Back in London, every Sunday, if you had the time and the inclination and something to barter your way inside, you could watch a little entertainment. Of sorts.

John-Paul Rohare Baptiste, basking in directed light: a beacon of divine purity in white robes and towering mitre, marked with the simple scarlet 'O' of his order.

Offering prayers. (Ranting, if you ask me, but then I'm not the target audience.)

Performing miracles. (Staged, if you ask me.)

Evangelising, enthusing, speaking in tongues, convulsing in communion with angels, dribbling and shrieking. Reading snippets from the bible, sometimes. Sometimes from other books, as the whim took him. Standing stock-still, like a rabbit in the headlights, as his underlings snuck into frame and proclaimed, accents Noo-Yoik thick, that the "Holy Spirit has come upon him..."

Nobody else seemed to find that as funny as I did.

The man was as mad as a stoat, in my professional opinion, not that anyone ever asked. This, after all, was entertainment. This was, in some dimly understood part of the survivors' 'society', one last link with the past. Media. Broadcast signals. Something civilised...

This was back in London. All over the UK as far as I could work out. Christ, all over the whole world, for all I knew.

They called it The Tomorrow Show.

The luckiest people – scratching out a survival in the

suburbs, or holed-up in automated offices like me – had the remnants of electricity. Enough to plug-in for the requisite one-hour session every week, entranced like a spectator at the advent of the moving image. It felt like that, sometimes. Like something that had become mundane – the broadcast of sounds and shapes – had rediscovered the awe of its inception.

No one expected there to be TV in the aftermath of The Cull. It was almost magnetic.

Other people pilfered rusting generators from abandoned worksites and derelict studios, summoning the juice required to bring their equipment to life, be it knackered B&W antique or plasma screen treasure. They'd set up in debris-covered squares and graffiti-pocked warehouses, charging the great crowds who gathered to gawp in food or fags or favours, to squint up at the fuzzy image and await the broadcast.

Every Sunday, at four o'clock in the afternoon (that's eleven EST), it came on. Since The Cull London had become a silent city anyway, but never more so than in that crystalline moment before the show began. Breaths held, fists clenched. I guess not many of them had been overly spiritual before it all happened, but having the word of God disseminated directly into your eyeballs still beat hunting pigeons and scavenging in the underground. No contest.

"Abbot!" they'd shout, as the crowds gathered. "Abbot's on! Trade tickets! Tins, meat, fresh water, fags! Abbot Baptiste on soon!"

I'd been to a few, down through the years. Just out of interest. Just to see what all the fuss was about, maybe even (whisper it) just to be around other people.

It was always the same routine. They'd flick the switches one minute before four. Hush fell, and eyes *focused on that bright oblong of swarming white noise, like a blizzard in zero-gee. Time dragged, and before you knew it people were muttering, trading worried glances, adrenaline overflowing. Is he coming? Have we missed it? Has something gone wrong? Oh, Jesus, pray for him! Pray for him to come! Don't let him desert us!*

Idiots.

Bang on four: the signal. A test card marked with a spectrum colour-check, enclosed in the same scarlet circle that decorated everything the Neo-Clergy ever touched, and that included the clothes of their audience. A ragged cheer from the crowd, a tinny burst of recorded organ music, and there he was.

Smiling. Serene. Wrinkled like a geriatric prune. Wobbling mitre slipping down over a frail brow, nose classically aquiline, chin jutting proudly from the abyssal folds of a robed collar. I always thought he looked like an albino vulture. Like a friendly old granddad with a secret perversion. Like a war criminal, trying to fit in.

Saying so out loud probably wouldn't have gone down well.

The sermons always began the same way. Push hard into a close-up – friendly eyes and soft smile filling the screen – slip into a vague soft focus that could have been intentional or technical inefficiency, and let the old goat speak, deep-south drawl sincere and stupid, all at once.

"Blessed," he said, "are the children."

"*Where*," the voice roared, loudspeaker whining with painful distortion, "*are the children?*"

"Please!" I shouted, bracing myself against the ragged tear where the plane's tail had parted company with the fuselage. "I... I'm hurt! I'm bleeding! I need help!"

"The fucking *children!*"

Too much to hope the despairing nobody routine would work twice in a row. This was going to get messy.

In snatched glances, staying low against the tortured edges of the fuselage, I figured there were ten men out there, give or take. Wafting through haze-coated patches of burning fuel and smoking debris, creeping forwards like sodding commandos assaulting a hostage siege. The tail was the obvious way in, but there were others. Smaller rents in the metal walls, the shattered panes of the cockpit, up through the sagging crater halfway down the cabin, leading into the gloomy luggage hold; now resting on the horizontal.

I was, to put it bluntly, screwed.

"You come out!" the loudhailer squealed, changing tack; the speaker's voice gratingly high and delivered in uncomfortable bursts. "You get your ass *out*! Mister! Arms *high*!"

Diversionary tactics. Keep me standing here at the rear, trying to buy time, whilst the kamikaze crew popped in somewhere else. *Subtle.*

I hefted the dead man's rifle and checked the setting. The wasteful idiot had it on a three round burst. Quickest way to prematurely empty your clip.

He'd been sent in on point, I guessed. He and his mates stationed at the airport, waiting for flights from who-knew-where-else to disgorge their cargo and head back home for more. London, Paris, Madrid... Where else had the Neo-Clergy set up base?

"You got ten seconds! Ten, asshole! You hear?"

Oh yeah, the cargo...

No wonder they were pissed off with me. Not only had I fucked their plane, I didn't stop to load-up with the usual freight.

Blessed are the Children...

I caught an ugly mental image of the same spinning, whirligig plane crash – sparks and metal storms spiralling in every direction, smoke venting like haemorrhaging blood – albeit packed to the gills with terrified youngsters. Crying out for parents they'd left in London, screaming and sobbing as windows shattered and shrapnel spun. Never quite making it to the 'rediscovered dawn' they'd been promised.

"That's seven fucko!"

Yeah, yeah.

The man I'd killed lay at my feet, a deflated skinbag oozing congealing fluids. I'd dragged him all the way down from near the cockpit, and with a raging narcotic hangover and some major blood loss issues, it hadn't been much fun. From what little I could see of his gung-ho colleagues, through the murk and smoke of the crash site, they were dressed the same: grey robes, black army-boots, heads shaved with military precision and M16A2 semi-automatic rifles clutched lovingly to their chests. I guessed the Apostolic Church of the Rediscovered Dawn got its fingers into the military on *this* side of the Atlantic as easily as the other.

The dead man had a scarlet ring tattooed around his left eye. It made him look lopsided. Sinister and ridiculous, all in one.

The loudmouth on the speaker got down to 'five'. It was a fair bet they'd punch in through the front and sides of the wreck shortly before the countdown finished. *Take the sucker by surprise.*

That's what I'd do.

Time to go to work.

I picked up the dead man, arms looped under his shoulders, and pressed my head into the small of his back. His lungs wheezed somewhere deep inside, more bloodpaste gathering on his lips. I folded myself carefully onto the floor (formerly the plane's left flank) and arranged the stiff so his cloak covered the more obvious extremities of my body. Something warm and damp dripped onto my chin.

Lurking in the lee of a battered service area, where hostesses had at one time heated their plastic meals and bitched about unruly passengers, I was nothing but a shadow beneath a corpse. I rested the gun against the guy's hip, flopped his sleeve across its stock, and curled a finger beneath the trigger guard, waiting.

The combat conditioning folded in again, running it all in slowtime, making an abstraction of everything, highlighting details. I was getting sick and tired of the insides of this fucking plane.

A whisper of cobwebbed aggression moved deep down in the calluses of my old brain. I was a caveman with an Armalite semi-automatic rifle, and a shield made of meat.

The grin came up unbidden.

"Two!" the loudspeaker snarled, voice dripping impatience and (the conditioning told me, senses tuned to a level far subtler than any I could detect alone) genuine fear.

They're not used to this.

Too fucking bad. *I* am.

Somewhere in the shell of the plane, noises dampened by the corpse's weight, glass shattered and booted feet struck the felt floor. In fuzzy half-vision, glimpsed in the acute angles of the robe, I could make out figures crawling sideways from the breached hold, slipping down from fissures in the fuselage further up the aisle, creeping forwards from the cockpit.

They had their weapons held ready, but too low, too

macho, too seen-it-all-in-movies. They kept stopping and starting, listening for threats, fighting to keep the shakes out of gloved hands. They poked into every corner. They paused when they got to Bella and talked in a low whisper-murmur that no self-respecting covert op would touch with a bargepole.

A pair of booted feet stopped near me.

"Fucker got Garson..." he said.

Moron.

I relieved him of his face with shot number one. Not easy to aim from underneath a dead guy, but it did okay. Caught him broadside of the ear, flipped him back, shouting. Skull-flecks and a popped eyeball. I put another one in his chest somewhere, just for good measure.

Let the grin widen a notch.

Pushed poor old Garson out the way.

Sighted down the aisle. With care. No rush.

The others were panicking. Reacting to the gunshots, looking for targets. Shouting, arguing, crouching in that idiot combat-posture that looks like constipation. Narrow space, men standing one behind the other. No room for covering fire.

Begging to be killed.

One shot at a time. Nothing flashy. Aim, fire, aim, fire, aim, fire.

Muzzle flash, serpentine smoke. Quiet clods of blood and flesh, knocked astray from pale robes, like melons beneath sledge hammers. One guy got off a shot in return, but desperate, off target. A convulsive squeeze, like preemptive rigor mortis.

There were eight in all. Four down already; dead or disarmed. Three more diving for cover (I caught a fourth as he fell, once in the ribs, again in the leg) and shuffled myself upright. Let Garson tumble to the floor, slippery.

Kept firing. Kept the other arseholes ducked down. Got lucky and caught one on the foot. He hadn't hidden from sight. Watched the boot fragment like a leather mine, his gun tumble away.

I was shouting, I realised. An unintelligible rush of animal sounds and half-formed words. *Speaking in tongues.* Heh.

Behold the Holy Spirit, coming upon him...

I kicked Garson through the mangled tail, letting him spoon outwards onto the tarmac like a man tripping on the edge of a cliff. Kept firing. Started shuffling back into the fuselage.

Outside the plane, whatever was left of Garson was ripped to shreds, silenced munitions plucking frayed tatters off his robes like feathers from a pillow. A trigger-happy sniper, then, somewhere out on the airport side of the strip; getting overzealous. Probably the same guy with the loudspeaker.

Moron.

Two guys left inside. I kept firing. Deliberately off-target. Let them think I didn't know where they were. Let them sweat. Let them pluck up the courage to—

"Asshole!"

The first one came up like a gofer from a hole. Pistol in each hand – fucking cowboy – shouting and cursing like a trooper.

Which, let's be quite clear, he obviously was not.

He got off a couple – misses, obviously – and went back down with an expression of ultimate bewilderment. The top half of his head was missing.

Good shooting, soldier.

I stopped firing. Stayed ready. Knew exactly where number eight was.

I could hear him crying.

"Oh god..." he kept saying. "Oh god oh god oh god..."

I wondered, distantly, if he was playing the same trick I'd played. Get me off guard, then turn with a savage smile and a slicing edge.

No.

The subconscious analysis came online. Bone-deep, beyond thought or effort. Animal instincts peeling back layers of information with scary accuracy.

No, he's terrified. It's in his voice. He knows he's going to die.

I considered letting him live. Just a kid, probably. Some speccy troll inducted into the Clergy sometime since The Cull. Looking for strength in numbers. Never imagining he'd wind up huddled against an economy-class aeroplane seat, on its side, with a psychopath who'd just gone through his hardass pals like a flaming sword.

Poor little bastard. I almost felt sorry for him.

Then I remembered why I was here, remembered the signal and the five long years, and the pain and the mourning, and the deep dark voice—

Don't you fucking give up, soldier!

—and I stepped forwards and shot the little rat through the top of his skull, so his brains slapped out of his jawline like snot into a hanky.

Sir, no sir, etc etc.

Outside the plane, beyond the sputtering of tiny fires up and down the runway, everything was still. Somewhere distant a couple of seabirds cawed, reminding me – with an ignorable spurt of melancholy – of London. But otherwise, *nothing.*

I lurked, vaguely combat poised, and stared out across the landing strip; torn and pocked by the plane's passage.

It shivered here and there with a faint luminosity where fuel had spilled and ignited, like a fiery reflection of the calm waters stretching away beyond. The idea of sprinting across the tarmac – strafing to confuse the bastard sniper who may or may not still be out there somewhere – and diving into the swampy morass held a sudden and unshakeable appeal. I imagined the water washing away the filth and blood that had soaked my coat; all the congealing gore that had spattered me moments before, as I moved up and down the plane with one of the cowboy's pistols, putting an end to the moans and pleas from the monk-soldiers I'd wounded.

No time for last words, no gloating, no fucking power trips. Just step-up, barrel-between-eyes, look away, squeeze trigger.

The lecturers used to call this ruthless mercy.

Second year of training. Major Farnham Dow presiding.

"It's easy – piss-easy," he'd said, *"to feel sorry for someone you've clipped. He's lost everything. He knows he's for it. He's going to... to blub and piss himself. He's going to ask for mercy, if he can. Talk about his family, maybe. Whatever.*

"The point is, the only reason he's not dead is because you missed with the first shot. It's your mistake, soldier, not his. And it doesn't change anything. Does it?

"You think he wasn't trying to kill you too? You think he'll renounce a lifetime of violence if you spare his life? Dedicate himself to charitable-bastard-causes? You think he won't shoot you in the back, if he still can, when you walk away?

"No. Don't be so fucking stupid! A wounded enemy is just a dead enemy who doesn't know it yet..."

Rationalising it and doing it were worlds apart.

I'd exited through the luggage hold, scampering across perpendicular support-struts and cargo-webbing, heading for the chasm of shattered steel and twisted, solidified slag where the forward landing-gear had been rammed upwards into the guts of the plane, tearing a long scar in the fuselage. The exit opened onto the sea side of the strip, away from the airport buildings and – I hoped – the sniper. I spent a good five minutes at the opening, darting glances left and right, sneaking out to check the roof of the wreck and retreating once again. Nothing. Either he didn't have a bead on me at all, or he was waiting for me to come out to play.

I fucking *hate* snipers.

I stepped out and stayed out. The air smelt of salt and ash; an acrid cocktail that seemed to ride on the light breeze rippling over the waters. The feel of sunlight caught me unprepared, a warmth I'd forgotten in the perpetual greyness of London. Ever since The Cull – ever since the bombs fell, half a world away – England's Pastures Green had become 'Mires Grey'. I once spent half an hour with another survivor – I forget his name, but he was a talented rat catcher – rambling informatively about skyburst radiation and the fucking Gulf Stream. Used to work for the Met, he said.

I tuned out thirty seconds in.

Quite how all this enabled LaGuardia airport, squatting on the watery edge of New York like a growing patch of mildew, to enjoy unbroken sunlight and cloudless skies was quite beyond me. I felt like I'd just arrived at Disneyland.

I let the desire for a dip in the water ebb away; put off by the kaleidoscopic blobs of oil smearing the surface, and the brown tint to the shoreline. With more scratches and open wounds than I cared to think about, it would be less a bath and more a proactive infection.

Enough time wasting.

I edged my way along the length of the fuselage, pressed against the sagging underside in the shadow of the plane's girth. At the cockpit I paused and shouldered the fully-loaded rifle I'd liberated from another of the Clergy goons, and clambered up onto the pitted slope, wincing as I put a little too much weight on the wounded arm. It had started bleeding softly again; one or two of the messy stitches popping open. I swore under my breath and tried to ignore it.

Dangling there like meat on a hook, staying low, I could peer through the shattered panes of the cockpit and take careful stock of the flat killing-ground beyond, spread out on the left side of the wreck.

Wide, regular, empty. No cover.

Shit.

Halfway between the edge of the still-flaming debris field and the distant airport buildings – clustered like toys around the distinctive inverted-lampshade of the control tower – a series of ramshackle sheds and lean-tos had been erected, improbably sturdy, in a rough semicircle. Cables and joists held them in place, stretched out like a high-tension big top built of plastic and wood. A railed gantry ran along their tops, marked at each end with a conning tower plated with corrugated iron. I squinted through the haze coming off the fuel-fires and made out a big sign, graffiti-texted inexpertly and tacked to each end of the rail, hanging down across the front of it all.

I felt an eyebrow ruck upwards.

The sign read:

WELCOME TO THE NEW DAWN

...along with all the usual scarlet circles, colourful highlights and other assorted Neo-Clergy bollocks. The whole compound set up looked like it'd been made out of pipe-cleaners and bogrolls at the local school, then scaled up a couple of hundred times.

It was painted bright blue.

It was all a bit pathetic.

I could see the sniper now, through the chinks of shattered glass and mangled instrumentation of the cockpit, standing in full sight on the gantry. He had a loudspeaker slung on a cord across his shoulders and a seriously sexy scope-rifle cradled in his hands, at a guess an M82. I'd only even seen them in pictures.

Shit.

Above a pair of wide sunglasses – tinted ruby-red – a stupid sort of flat-cap was set jauntily on his scalp, somewhere between a beret and a devotional *kippah*, and his robes were several shades whiter than those of his dead colleagues. So:

The boss.

I tried to get a bead on him, squinting along the barrel of the M16, but at this range I might as well blow snot. He had his back to me, leaning down over the rear of the railing to point and shout at someone below, hidden behind the sign. There seemed to be an argument going on, and in his apoplexy the twat-in-the-hat was stamping and waving his fists in a full-on tantrum.

A violent growl picked up from out of nowhere – an engine, gunning hungrily – and a blocky shape emerged from behind the compound. Fat and square, grinding along slowly. For one awful moment I thought it must be a tank. Some ultra-rare military surplus these insane godbotherers had maintained for years. But no, it was far weirder than that.

It was a school bus, thick flanges of corrugated iron hanging down to protect its tyres, painted the same lurid blue as the buildings and marked with the same great scarlet 'O's on either side. The windows were blocked-up – padded by what looked like dozens of Kevlar jackets marked 'NYPD' – and the front windshield protected by a heavy-duty wire mesh. I couldn't see the driver. I couldn't see who or what was inside. All I could see was this surreal shape lumbering towards the plane, towards me and my complete lack of preparation, and the fucking stupid 'destination' inside the little window above the front:

SALVATION (ONE WAY)

I felt like shooting at it on general principle.

The vehicle took a wide arc around the plane's tail, circling behind the wreckage, shunting its way through lumps of flaming debris with the impunity of something big, impatient and impervious. I dropped quickly down from my shaky vantage and squirreled into the recess beneath the drooping camber of the cockpit, the first vestiges of panic rising inside. When it drew alongside, the driver would have to be blind not to see me. What precisely was I supposed to do *then*?

It didn't take a genius to work out what they were up to. A lazy recon around the perimeter to get a good look at the side they couldn't see from their hickledy conning towers. To flush me out into the open, if I turned out to still be alive.

With the sniper on one side and an armoured vehicle on the other, it wouldn't be hard work to catch me out, pick me off like a flaky scab.

I breathed deep, letting the conditioning guide me. Thinking like a machine.

Only viable place to hide now was back in the bloody plane, which I'd just spent half an hour trying to get *out* of. I considered crawling back. I even tensed, ready to hoist myself out from my pitiful cover and up through the shattered cockpit windows, probably lacerating myself all to hell in the process, but still... It was better than n–

The bus stopped.

Its brakes squeaked quietly as it drew to a halt beside the knotted cavity of the missing tail segment, far off to my right. I could hear voices arguing inside. A hatch flapped-open near the rear and a robed figure leaned out. I froze.

The man tossed something, underarm, into the plane's tail.

"Go!" He shouted, presumably to the driver.

The hatch slammed shut and the bus moved on.

"Oh fuck..." I whispered.

The tail bulged. The whole wreck shuddered, scraping deeper into the dry grass. Round the corner of my cover, too far out in the open for me to see clearly, flames and tumbling lumps of metal arced high overhead, shattered fragments of blue-painted hull spiralling in orbital contrails of sparks and smoke, to bounce and break on the tarmac.

A few bits and bobs *pinged* cutely off the bus. It didn't seem to mind.

They thought I was still inside. It didn't much matter much, either way. Inside or out of the wreck, with the 'Cult Of Unfair Destructive Hi-Tech Gadgetry' around I was as good as mince.

Think, think...

The bus cruised gently forwards, cornering the rear of the plane and pausing beside the next gaping rent in its fuselage, a third of the way along its flank. Again, the hatch flipped open, and like some surreally casual picture – a guy in a park pitching a ball to an overeager dog – the goon flipped another grenade into the wreck.

The bus moved on.

This time the detonation blew off an emergency exit door, straight upwards like a rocket, to tumble over and under back down again. More spilled fuel caught fire as the debris mushroomed out, and for the second time I felt a wave of weakness and nausea passing over me. Everything seemed to go grey.

Fuzzy.

Meaningless.

Not now!

Blood loss. Hollow prickles of heat up and down empty veins...

I–

Don't you fucking give up, soldier!

I brought the rifle up to my shoulder. This time the bus driver would see me. This time they'd be too close. The grenade would blow out the front of the plane, erupt through the cockpit like a great pulsing embolism, crushing and breaking and burning me all at once.

The brakes squealed.

The hatch flipped open.

The goon wasn't looking out, bending back inside to shout at the driver, hands curled snugly around the baseball bomb, ready to throw.

I heard:

"...fucking opinions to your*self*, grandpa, and let the *real* men do the..."

He pulled the pin.

I shot him.

The hatch flipped closed, bloodhaze wafting down and out. The grenade sill inside.

The unseen driver shouted.

I pushed myself deep into the recess and curled into a ball.

The bus's arse blew off like an overfilled balloon, smoke swallowed the sky, pulsing waves of weirdness sent me flopping like a boneless doll with vomit on my chin, and everything faded to white.

CHAPTER FIVE

My first worry was that my eyes weren't working properly.

Okay, so I'd just woken up. No need to panic yet, maybe, but the training and conditioning went *deep*, and the first thing you learn is *be aware*.

Know everything.

Cover the angles.

Right.

I had the vague idea I'd passed out from loss of blood. There was something about a... a bus? A plane? What the fuck? Maybe I was still hallucinating.

Maybe this hazy curtain obstructing everything I was seeing was just an effect of my traumatised mind, or something cloudy dripping in my eyes, or... or whatever.

Assume a worst case scenario.

Sir, yes sir, etc etc.

So: Major damage following oxygen starvation to the brain, leading to sensory corruption and an inability to effectively continue.

Solution: Abort mission.

I remembered where I was. I remembered the plane crash and the gunfight and was even starting to piece together the thing with the bus when the biggest puzzle-piece of all dropped into place: I remembered why I'd come here.

The Signal.

'Inability to effectively continue' wasn't an option. 'Abort Mission' could, pardon my French, fuck off.

I mentally nutted the worst-case scenario and tried out a little optimism for a change. When I twisted my head to glance at the floor beneath me – I was lying on my right shoulder, aching from my own weight – the cracked tarmac of the airstrip came into perfect and unobstructed focus. It was only when I looked further afield that my vision became obscured, as if the horizon was playing hard-to-get.

"Stay still," someone croaked. "Nearly done. Can't finish-up if you keep moving."

My skin prickled, and it took a moment or two to realise why. I was half naked. Lying on a mangled runway surrounded by debris and fuel, unable to see anything past a few dozen feet, in nothing but my underwear.

"H-hey..."

"Dammit! Stay *still*." A wrinkled hand – dark brown knuckles and a pale palm – dipped briefly into my field of view and gave me a chastising flick on the forehead, not doing much for my sense of security. I felt my whole body rocking a little, as if a dog had got hold of my left sleeve and was tugging it from side to side, though I wasn't wearing anything and consequently had no sleeves.

It was all very odd. There was no pain.

I poked my tongue around my mouth, half testing for the taste of blood, half summoning the strength to speak, and eventually tried: "What are you... uh...?"

"Sorting you out." the speaker said. His voice was hard-accented – African-American, New York sharp – with an inbuilt semi cackle that turned every statement into a grandfatherly demonstration of humouring the kiddies. I felt vaguely patronised, and couldn't work out why.

"And how," I said, failing to focus yet again on the murky distance, "are you doing that?"

"Minor transfusion, first up." The voice sounded matter-of-fact about this, despite the subject. "About the only good damn thing about The Cull. Everyone's a donor, see?"

"Blood?"

"He's a quick one!" I got the impression the guy, whoever he was, was squatting behind me. "Yeah, blood. Which is to say: you were seriously lacking for the stuff, pal."

"A-and you gave m... From where?"

"No need to worry 'bout *that*."

I silently begged to differ, but the same tugging sensation from my left shoulder was distracting my attention and the voice – an old man, I'd decided – wasn't finished.

"Then it was tidying up, see? I mean... who made this damn *mess* of your arm here?" There was a quiet *tap-tap-tap*, and I imagined a finger poking the skin next to the bullet hole – though again I felt nothing. "Might as well have poured a quart of mud in the hole and closed it down with knitting needles."

"I... I did it."

"Done it yourself?" The voice went quiet for a moment, then whistled softly. "Well... maybe that's different. Still a fuckin' mess, mind."

"You've... You've sorted it?"

"Yep. Anitsep, new stitches, new dressing." He paused, considering my voice. "Limey, huh?"

"But I can't feel it. My arm."

"Lived over there myself, for a time. Nice place. But for the weather."

"I said I can't fee..."

"Yeah. That'd be the anaesthetic."

I started to blurt: *Anaesthetic? Where the fuck did you get th–*, but my thought-process shifted rails with an inelegant *clang* and ran up against a far more obvious quandary.

"Why?" I said.

"Why what?"

"Why are you doing all this? What's going on?"

"*Ah.*"

The syllable was pronounced with the sort of enigmatic significance that said:

More to follow.

There was a heavier tug on my left side, executed with a certain amount of rough finality and a breathless grunt – "There!" – and then a coarse hand rolled me onto my back. I felt a little like a turtle inverted in the sun, unable to lift myself upright. Not that I'd tried yet. I was far too busy staring up at my benefactor, wondering if I was still asleep and hadn't realised.

"Evening." The shadow said. "Name's Nate."

He was an older man. I think. Five years since the Cull it was already difficult to say, hard living took its toll on some worse than others; youngsters quickly hardened, faces became taught, lines (not *laughter*, obviously) gathered at corners of eyes and mouths. Plus fallout, starvation, exposure, injury. Who could say? My best guess put this guy at sixty, but he looked older and acted younger. His skin was a uniform teak that gave his face an unreal quality every time he smiled. Perfectly white eyes and teeth lighting up like bulbs set into a dark sculpture.

"Nate." I repeated. He grinned.

He wore a strange getup, like he'd spent all his life pilfering clothes of a vaguely uniform bent. Tan and khaki camo combat trousers (sorry, *pants*), a pale blue shirt with an NYPD insignia stitched into the lapel and an outrageous jacket – dark blue, festooned with gold pips and double-buttons – which it took me a moment to recognise as an Union Army antique. I figured he'd looted it from some re-creation society or fancy dress store, though admittedly – thanks to scuffs, stains and frays – it did *have* a century-and-a-half-old look about it. Its effect was simply to add to the overall impression of a uniformed nutter, driven to steal anything vaguely official-looking like a magpie hording shinies.

I resisted the urge to salute.

This curious attempt to look authoritative was undermined somewhat by the accessories he'd chosen: bright red sneakers, a white New York Mets baseball cap and a vivid yellow belt with the most enormous buckle engraved with the legend:

POP BITCH

There was a dead guy sitting next to him.

Nate followed my glance and his grin faltered a touch. "Ah," he said again.

The corpse was one of the Clergy-soldiers, though I didn't recognise him from inside the plane. He didn't have a hole through his face, for a start.

His grey robes were blackened and singed, spattered with blood and dirty water, and the patches of his skin I could see were just as soiled: peeled back in moist red welts or incised totally by razor-like fragments of shrapnel. One of his arms was hanging off at the shoulder by a few threads of gristle and a notched bony core, and his head was so tattered the scarlet tattoo around his eye was barely visible at all. He sat slumped, semi-upright, against the tangled remains of the same armoured school bus that prowled my recent memories. It reminded me, surreally, of a novelty firework: its front-end all but untouched; the remnants of its length blown-to-shit so totally that their remains barely made any physical sense at all.

The dead Clergyman had been the guy inside. The grenade chucker.

Nate coughed, embarrassed.

A thin rubber tube meandered from a grimy canula thrust into the corpse's wrist, out onto the floor where it coiled once or twice towards me, then vanished beneath the edge of my exhausted peripheral vision. I didn't want to turn my head to confirm it, but I had a pretty good idea where it led.

It was full of blood.

"Not like he needed it..." Nate said, a little surly. "And I disconnected *plenty* of time before he died."

Well that's okay then.

Nate fussed beside me – lifting up the other end of the transfusion tube and waggling it like a glove puppet – and then started tidying away the various equipment he'd scattered on a mostly clean blanket beside me. Stitching needles, bloody rags, sealed packs of military-issue sterilisers and antiseptic pads, and a roll of off-white bandaging that'd come partly unrolled and scampered off along the oil-spattered tarmac.

The horizon still hadn't come into focus. I was starting to worry.

"Why can't I see properly?" I asked, finding that I could control my body – just – but was so exhausted it hurt even to think about moving.

Nate scowled for a minute, confused, and peered around us. If I'd had to guess, his expression was one of someone who'd just spent hours saving a stranger from bleeding to death, only to discover they were already vegetative in the brain department.

"Can't *see*?" He said.

"It's... it's like a... a blur. Like... Near-to things are okay, but the further away stuff gets..."

He looked at me like I was a retard.

"Well *that*," he said, "is what's sometimes called *fog*."

Even despite the panicky relief, I still had some headroom for feeling like a fuckwit.

"B-but... but it was perfectly clear when the plane... when it..."

"Well, that's New York for ya." He waved a dismissive hand, gazing out into the wall of soupy white. "It's called the QuickSmog Eff-Why-Eye."

"Eff...what?"

"Eff-Why-Eye. For Your Info. Sorry... Guy gets sorta used to talking in letters, hanging around with the grunts, you know." He hooked a thumb towards the slumped body and shook his head. "Soldiers and monks, Jeez-us! Nary the twain should meet."

I struggled to hang on to a single thread. Nate was the sort of guy who could hold three schizophrenic conversations at once, leaping from tangent to tangent like a monkey on speed. There was a shielded intelligence simmering away in those eyes, too, hiding behind the accent and the daft clothes, but watching everything. Paying attention.

"QuickSmog." I repeated, bringing him back.

"Yeah, yeah. Guy I knew one time told me it started right after the camel-jocks zapped out DC. 'Cause, you know, I wasn't stateside back then. Never saw the lightshow. But yeah, QuickSmog... Comes in quick, goes out quick. Just like that. No rhyme or reason. Doesn't seem to do much harm, though if you ask me right now it's a good thing."

"How come?"

"You kidding? Fucking great plane wreck, burning to shit... sending up a pillar of smoke higher'n a pothead's prick." He grinned. "And with your robe-wearin'-pals here gone away, nothing to stop the scavs from coming to take a look."

Scavs. Robe-wearin'-pals. Camel Jocks zapping DC.

One fucking detail at a time.

Know everything.

Cover the angles.

"There was a sniper... a-and a driver. Guy in the bus. He dead too?" The effort of talking was becoming appalling now; even as the sensations started to return to my numbed arm the rest of me was screaming for rest.

Nate sniffed, wiping a dewdrop off his nose.

"Well now," he said. "Your sniper up there, that's a mean pieceashit Cardinal name of Cy. Near as I can tell he wasn't milit'ry before The Cull, so I guess something pretty damn nasty musta happened... Man's fucked in the head but good. Gen-u-ine psycho. *Heh.*" Nate spat on the ground. "High-up too. Maybe take over from the Abbot some day. See, Cy's in charge of bringing the freight from the airstrip back to the city. When the bird comes down all wrecked-up like that, and all the kids missin', he knows straight away his neck's on the line. That's how come the Choirboys went in so hard. Cy wanted to have a... a body, whatever. Like: 'yeah, the airport's fucked and we didn't get the Brit tithe, but I caught the guy who did it...'"

"Me?"

"Right. Only he didn't. And then you come out killin' every motherfucker left and right, and Cy starts to figure maybe he should stop worryin' what his boss gonna say, and start saving his ass. So he sends out the bus, all packed-up with grenades and shit, to keep you busy. Maybe even kill you, if he's lucky." He nodded towards the shattered school bus. "Soon as old Bertha went kablooie you can bet your ass Cy was hightailing back for the city in the Outrider."

"Just a diversion?"

"Right. Couple of... sacrificial lambs, you might say. Told to go *die* so Mister-Hat-Wearin' *fuck* gets to breathe another day. I figure he'll spend the whole journey wondering what to tell the boss. Ask for reinforcements – my guess. Be back here... maybe a day and half? Suggest you get yourself gone by then, huh?"

"And the driver?"

Nate grinned again, and leaned further over. Deep in the shadows of his left eye, all but indiscernible against the blackness of his skin, I could make out the long curve of a scarlet tattoo.

A half circle.

I stiffened.

He waved a set of keys playfully above me, then tossed them over his shoulder.

"Not much left to drive now."

"You're... you're Clergy too?"

He chuckled to himself, lifting up a bundle of something ragged and stinking which I first assumed was a dead dog, and then realised were my clothes.

"Not really," he said. "Not any more."

An hour later, Nate and I sat in the alcove beneath the front wall of the shanty-compound, hiding from the wind, listening to the great Welcome sign flapping above us. The QuickSmog had surrendered to a sudden squall that darted up with no obvious warning, phasing away into the dark.

Out across the waters encircling the airport, the distant smudge that was the northern reaches of the city faded by degrees into darkness. I'd expected – stupidly – the same neon jungle I'd seen in every film, the same speckled star field of glowing tower blocks printed in every guidebook. The same scene of candle-like serenity glossily reproduced on the cover of the city map I'd plundered from a bookshop in Covent Garden, and sat studying for days and days back in Heathrow, as Bella and I planned the journey. It was still in my pack, that much-thumbed map; not that I needed to look at it any more. I knew all its lines, all its labels, all the red blotches marked on its surface...

But no. From a distance the post-Cull city, just like London, was a haunted place; an inky nothingness flecked here and there by the fragile, sputtering lights of nestled survivors, and the brazen fumes of miniature industry.

Nate had moved me into the shadow of the blue compound's corrugated walls, across the grass and away from the wreck, as soon as I'd been strong enough to make the journey, bracing me with one arm and lugging my pack with the other. He said it would be best to get away from the plane before true darkness fell. The local scavengers would be slinking in to take a look at what had caused all the commotion, and it was all too easy to get caught up in the scraps and squabbles as they fought over the spoils.

I got the impression he wasn't talking about coyotes and wild dogs.

Now, on the cusp of night, the air was getting cold and the view growing grim.

The plane still flickered. *Things* moved in the smoke.

Nate said he was a 'trustee'. He said this meant the Clergy sort of employed him, but didn't expect him to do any of the shit stuff. No evangelising, no indoctrinating, and definitely no acting self-important about the Church's self-assumed manifest destiny in ushering in the New

Dawn of Civilisation.

Actually, what Nate said was: "...those dress-wearing assholes couldn't get me down with that bullshit even when they *were* poking guns in my back" – but he meant pretty much the same thing. "Eventually," he said, "they figured I was worth more alive, tried asking *nice* instead of just *demanding*. We've all been getting by just fine ever since."

Until I showed up and slaughtered your mates.

Until your boss ran off like a robe-wearing pussy, and left you behind.

Until you decided to keep me alive rather than kill me whilst you had the chance.

Hmm.

The whole issue of *why* he'd helped hadn't been entirely covered yet. I'd taken a bottle of supermarket vodka out of my pack to share with the guy – I figured it was the least I could do – and he was sinking it like a fish. I ought to have felt more grateful, I suppose.

Instead...

Those old instincts. Those old voices.

Know everything.

Don't you let yourself owe anyone anything.

Sir, yes sir, etc etc.

Nate said he'd been a little... *uncooperative* when Cardinal Cy told him to drive out onto the killing-strip just to keep me busy. He said he'd kicked up a fuss at the idea that he should go throw himself into the jaws of the wolf, whilst said Clergyman ran like a custard-coated cockerel. Nate said he'd protested vehemently at the treatment, that he hadn't signed up as a trustee just to forfeit himself to let some vicious little prick live, and that he'd entered into a considerable argument with his fellow sacrificial lamb when ordered to play kamikaze.

He said eventually the guy chucking grenades out the back had to hold a gun to his head just to get the engine started.

That explained why he wasn't in any hurry to rejoin the Clergy. Traitor to the cause. Coward. Deserter. Blah-blah-blah.

Fine.

It *didn't* explain why he'd gone to so much trouble to keep me alive afterwards.

I asked him.

"More rat?" he said, ignoring me with a bright grin, hacking away at something small and furry with a skinning knife.

I nodded and lifted an empty skewer off the makeshift fire, and jabbed at the slimy morsel he held out. Second only to pigeon.

Over by the plane dark shapes crossed in front of the dancing fires, like inky puddles of moving shadow.

"Still a lot of guns aboard." I said, tense.

And Bella's body.

Nate said the scavs wouldn't be doing any shooting. "Relax," he said, and passed me the vodka with only the tiniest reluctance. He said that whatever the scavs found, they'd present immediately – with all due ceremony and cringing deference – to their bosses in the Klans. He said that if any of the poor fuckers dared waste a single bullet, and word got back to their bosses, they'd be in the hunt pens or skewered on territory poles before they knew it.

I asked him what the Klans were.

He smiled and bit into his rat.

The wind got colder.

Nate said he'd been a doctor, once.

"Kind of," he said.

He said he'd been born in the Bronx and miseducated

in Harlem, and but for a lucky seduction in a downstate disco would've wound up still there, scrabbling for cash and crack. He said that twenty years ago – or so – he got lucky with a rich white chick who fell for his unmistakable charms and took him along to England when her company reassigned her. He said she paid through the nose to set him up. He said she enrolled him in night school to finish his basic, then community college, then – pushing harder – medical training. He said every step of the way he worked his balls off, because it turned out he could handle failure and addiction and crime and poverty, but the one thing he couldn't handle was seeing her disappointed.

It was all a bit 'soap opera,' but I didn't like to break the flow.

Nate said he flunked the final exams so bad he would've done better to leave the question papers blank.

"Morphine addiction," he explained, staring off into space.

And that, he said, was that.

"Couldn't you resit?" I asked, picking out rat bones from between my teeth. "Get cleaned-up, try again? Seems a bit late in the day to go throwing it all away."

"Yeah." he said, and his voice was quiet. "Yeah, you're right there. Except Sandra – that's the lady, the... the one who took me over there – she sorta caught me with my pants down."

"Ah."

"Yeah. With her secretary."

I looked away, unsure whether to cringe or snigger. "Ah."

When I looked back, Nate's expression was... well, sad – obviously – but something else too. Like the face an exec gets when the deal falters at the last meeting.

Like the face I used to see on missions, when the grunts and agents round me realised it'd all gone to tits, and people were probably going to die, and it just *wasn't fair*. Like... frustration, maybe. A sense of annoyance at circumstances beyond one's control.

Which is sort of weird, given that it was all his fault.

Something dark flitted through the shadows outside the circle of light cast by the fire. Nate stared at it for a moment, utterly untroubled, and spat into the flaming logs.

He said – the story rumbling on as if uninterrupted – that the money dried up pretty quick after that. He said he only realised how much he'd appreciated her (and/or her cash, depending on how you wanted to interpret it) when it was too late. Sandra cleared off, heartbroken. He let things slide. His Visa hiccupped and lit-up alarms on a Home Office computer and before he knew it he was Nathaniel C. Waterstone of no fixed abode, with a deportation warrant next to his name and a brand new shiny heroin addiction to support.

I coughed as politely as I could, aware that this man had just sewed me up. "So when you said you'd been a doctor..."

"Yeah." He shrugged. "Kind of."

He looked away and sighed, as if he could see all the way across the Atlantic from where he sat. "*London*, man. Docklands, Tower Hamlets, the East End. Plenty of places they pay good money for a guy knows what he's doing with needles. Someone... *unofficial*. You know?"

Nate said he'd been a backstreet sawbones. Mob cutter. Bullets removed, knife wounds cleaned, bodies disposed: no questions asked. I guess I believed him, mostly.

He had an honest face.

Out across the roughage bordering the airstrip, somebody

yelped. There were voices out there too – masked by the crackling of our little fire, muttering and arguing. More shapes darting in the dark.

"Scavs." Nate shrugged.

I kept a hand on the M16 and asked what would happen to the bodies of the men aboard the plane. I didn't mention Bella. I wasn't sure why, at the time, but I know now. Even then, sitting with Nate in the cold, the scratching at the back of my head was gearing-up...

Something about him.

"Depends." He said.

"On what?"

"On what Klans they're with. Mostly they'll just... steal clothes, leave the bodies. Coupla tinpot tribes up west got a thing for fresh meat, way I heard, but no way we'll get that shit down here. Guy I knew once – you'll like this – said you go through Ess-Eye these days – that's Staten Island, you know? – you're a... *heh*... a goddamn moveable feast. They got crossbows and *arrows*, man, he says. They got fuckin' *spit roasts*, and I don't mean like in no porno.

"Up here, nah. Nah. Civilised, man. Welcome to Queens."

His grin lit up his face. With Nate, you never knew how serious he was being.

I asked him again to tell me about the Klans. He chuckled and lit a cigarette.

When The Cull started, he said, and folks started dying in the streets of London, he was holed-up with a gang of Albanians. He said up 'til then he'd been passing from group to group – Triads, Afghans, Jamaicans, even the old-school suit-wearing Pie and Chips brigade. He said these Kalashnikov-waving psychos took him on as a kind of examiner: checking the girls they ferried-in from the continent, making sure they'd last in the massage parlours and interactive peep-booths. Nate said he'd never stared at so much pussy in his life, and there came a point where it sort of stopped having any attraction.

He said at around the same time, he decided to go cold turkey.

He looked away again.

I got the impression there was more to it than that. But sitting out there in the cold with a fresh bandage on my arm and a half-digested rat inside me, listening to human filth arguing in the dark over guns and knives and all the other shit I'd left behind on the plane, I didn't have the heart to probe.

The thing was, someone almost certainly made Nate give up the skag. Maybe someone helped him, nursed him through it, whatever. I don't know. But the thing about Nate was, the thing I could tell within seconds of meeting the guy; he wasn't the kind who made decisions. Not on his own. He wasn't the kind to lead the way.

"Was eight days into the detox when the... the virus, you know? When it got as bad as it got. I had me a... a tee-vee, little one, in the room. News shows, back to back. Bodies on the streets, hospitals over flowing. Pretty much all the Albanians dropped right there. Spat blood, hit the deck. I'm telling you, man, the *stink*... Rest of them upped and gone. Tried to get home, maybe. Everyone's got a family, huh?"

He sighed.

"I tell you, man... I was scared. There's me, pissing outta my ass, shivering, puking, all that shit, immune system *fucked* to hell, and the end-of-goddamn-times *plague* outside my door. Just about gave up."

I remembered too. London. Chaos. Panic. It was weeks before they could tell why some people survived. Why most didn't. Revealed little by little on garbled TV shows and home-printed leaflets, in that spasmodic time before the media gave up the ghost.

"But I survived." Nate said. "Fuck, yeah. Came out clean."

And so did I.

What I remember most is, the *unfairness*.

I suppose I always felt I was lucky. Due a fall, surely, but there I was, winning a lottery I never even bought a ticket for. Outside there's priests and nurses and charitable souls rotting on the pavement, and here's me – he's a fucking *killer* – breathing clear.

It didn't seem right.

It's a weird thing, feeling guilty for being alive.

"Anyways," said Nate, flicking a chunk of wood onto the fire from a stack beside the corrugated wall, "that put the cap on doctoring."

He said he'd wandered in London for a year or two. He hinted he'd done his best to help where he could – triage, treatment, tidying – but I guess there was always a price.

Nate didn't exactly radiate selflessness.

After two years the Apostolic Church of the Rediscovered Dawn was up and running. I remember that too. The Abbot broadcasting his miraculous sermon every Sunday, the crowds gathering, the scarlet tattoos and chanted prayers.

The robe-wearing creeps strolled straight out onto the charred remains of the world stage, and declared that they alone – as an entity embracing values of community, integrity, intelligence and of course *faith* – could sweep aside the horrors of the Cull and work towards a new, restored civilisation.

They said that they alone could overcome the 'inertia

gripping humanity' and rebuild, recreate, re*start*!

Those.

Arrogant.

Fucks.

They came to London and spread the word. I ignored them.

They said for most people it was too late. The world they'd known was long gone. They said the people could console themselves with living as best they could, embracing Jesus, making the most of their lives in the rubble. They said devoting oneself to the Neo-Clergy was the only expression of purity and hope for the average man.

But for the children... For the children there was so much more. Innocent, unsullied by the calamities of the past, not responsible for the sins that had visited the Cull upon the world. For them the future was clear. So said the Clergy.

They must build a new dawn.

So the priests came and got them.

At gunpoint, sometimes. But mostly they didn't even need to threaten, mostly it was parents waving goodbye, smiling, proud of their contribution to the world, and that was the worst thing of all.

The church ferried the kids off in blue-painted planes, and ignored the tears and shrieks, and told everyone, *everyone* involved:

Be grateful.

They were going somewhere better, the Clergy said.

Sitting there in the cold, listening to Nate's story, my eyes plucked at the huge banner above me. I shivered.

"They brought them here," I grunted, shaking my head. "The kids. Didn't they?"

Nate nodded.

"Why? What do they *do* with them? Where's this... this fucking *new tomorrow*?"

Nate shrugged, took a slurp of water from a screw cap cantina, and carried on with his story like he'd barely stopped to breathe.

Nate said the Clergy found him on the streets of London. They'd heard he was a doctor. They said they might have a need for someone like that. They might even raise him up to a state of grace. Besides, they said, he was already American.

They had two conditions:

"Number one," he said, "they told me I got to have faith. I told them if they gimme a job and food and somewhere warm to sleep, I'll believe whatever the hell they want.

"And number two, they said I gotta go back to New York."

He stopped, and looked for a second or two like he wasn't going to continue. It was strange to see. Nate's natural state was 'droning', and every time he stopped to stare off into the darkness with those spotlight eyes it was... disconcerting. "So you came back," I said. "And did what?"

He looked at me for a second – proper eye contact, for the first time – then away again. Someone screamed playfully out by the wreck.

"Same as before, more or less. Ironic, huh? Just like the Albanians. Checking over the produce when it arrives. Making sure it's fit to travel. No sickness, no frailty. Clergy only wants the best."

"You inspected the kids?"

"Right. Shit, I was in *charge* of them. Clumsy old guy with a friendly face and a dumb costume. Made jokes. Patched up cuts and scrapes. Told 'em all everything would be just fine. Drove the bus into the city, came right back for the next batch. London, Paris, Moscow. Planes comin' in from all *over*."

"So you're the ferryman to the New Dawn?" I said, trying out a little sarcasm; seeing how the old man would react.

Know everything.

Check the angles.

He smiled, a little too slowly, then nodded. "I like that." He said. "Yeah, I like that."

Something rustled nearby. A spreading whisper of cloth and feet. My hand tightened on the M16, eyes scanning the shadows, but Nate waved a laconic hand in my direction and grinned.

"No need, man."

Not reassuring.

Something oozed out of the dark. Something hesitant and filthy, matted and feathered down each flank of its raggedy form. Something that broke-up as the firelight caught it; separated down by degrees into an aggregate. A crowd of people.

Staring, all as one, at the meat roasting over the flame.

They came into the light like a single entity, scuttling on far too many legs. They looked – *random thought here* – like extras from the set of a war film: recognisably human but coated in the makeup department's finest emulations of soot, dirt and dried blood, scampering with that expression of people who don't know what they're doing or why they're doing it. Several had fresh wounds – nicks and cuts from knives and teeth – and eyed each other warily.

The ones at the front carried themselves with a seniority based on whatever Byzantine pecking order was at work, clutching in their dirty hands stolen guns, scraps of clothing, bundles of chemical ephemera and all types of other salvage taken from the plane. One was holding a seatbelt buckle, smiling with the smug expression of someone who'd outperformed herself. Another one – a young man – had Bella's jeans slung over his shoulder.

The M16 felt good in my hand.

Let it go, soldier.

Sir, yes sir, etc etc.

"Well, then..." said Nate, reclining back against the compound wall with as much disinterested ease as he'd shown before the darkness disgorged them. "What can we do for you?"

I think I half expected them to speak in grunts and moans, if at all. They looked so devolved, so fucking *prehistoric*, that at that point it wouldn't have surprised me if they'd dropped down and worshipped the 'Great Fire Makers'.

It sounds arrogant, now I come to say it. I mean... why should they be any less coherent than me? Why should their five years of hardship and filth be any less dignified than mine?

"We smelt the rat," a tall woman said, near the front. She reminded me of someone, and a shiver worked its way along my spine.

Shut that shit down, soldier. Job to do.

Nate shrugged. "And?"

"And we thought maybe you'd trade."

Nate shook his head. "No trades."

"But... *see*?" The woman plucked a plastic drinking beaker out of a raggedy pack, brandishing it like a jewel. "Good, see? Perfect for trading, that is. See what I've g..."

Nate's voice hardened a little. His face stayed the same. "No. *Trades*."

The scavs flitted a few awkward glances back and forth, then the tall woman's eyes went sneaky. Heavy-lidded and intense, like a child conspiring to do mischief.

"We could *take*..." she said, quietly, acting nonchalant.

Nate chuckled to himself.

"You could," he said. "Yep."

The scavs shuffled, shifted their weight from foot to foot. Here and there a blade twinkled in the firelight, and my heart twisted in my chest: speeding up, blurring time.

Endorphins washed down me.

Muscles tensed.

An old man shuffled to the front, dark blue sweater decorated with stripes of white paint, and I watched him with the targeted eye of a predator.

"What Klan?" He wheezed. "Mm?"

"I'll show you mine if you show me yours." Nate ginned. The M16's grip was warm now, heated by my own palm.

All at once the scavs twitched; a great roiling ball of motion, and without a single conscious thought I was lifting the gun and reaching for the arming bolt and...

Nate's hand sat on the barrel, holding it down. He gave me a look, shook his head, and grunted towards the scavs. They hadn't been attacking at all.

They stood brandishing themselves, like a medical examination taking place *en masse*. In each case the proffered elbow, shoulder, arm, stomach, neck or ankle was decorated by a small mark. A burnt branding-scar in the shape of a smiling face, eyes like double-arches above a mountainous nose, with a pair of satellite ears protruding on each side.

"Mickeys," said Nate. He gave me a doting smile, like an old man discussing the merits of different chess pieces, and said: "Respectable Klan, that."

"Trade now?" The woman said. "Or we'll help ourselves."

"What Klan?" the old man whispered, hopping from foot to foot. "What Klan what Klan what Klan?"

Nate tilted his head back, letting the fire chase away the shadows beneath the brim of his cap. The scarlet semicircle seemed to *blaze* on his cheek.

"*Clergy...*" went the whisper. A fearful susurration rushing around the crowd. "*Godshits...* Choirboys... Fuckin' *Clergy...*"

And then they were gone.

Nate and I sat in silence. Eventually I coughed under my breath and asked him, third time lucky, if he'd tell me about the Klans.

He gave me a funny look, smirked quietly, and said:

"Shit, man. What you think I bin *doing*?"

CHAPTER SIX

The Consolidated Edison Power Plant facility, directly off Astoria's 20th Avenue, was a continental wedge of pipes, cables, depots, spinal chimneys, blocky storage tanks and stark structures like geometric skeletons made from girders. All of it pressed up against the same polluted, watery banks as the airport. There was something undeniably sepulchral about it. A knotted tangle of hip-like joists, vertebral chains linking moving assemblies, and skull-like containers that had long since lost their sheen.

Nate had brought me here at first light, when I'd told him I needed transport.

He hadn't asked me why. He hadn't asked me what I was here to achieve.

Hadn't told me why he was tagging along.

Hmm.

Standing outside the power plant, it was plain to see the whole place was inactive. Rusted to fuck; plundered for raw materials, stripped apart in a million acts of petty vandalism and selfish salvage.

There was red bunting dangling above the concourse as we stepped off the street – giving the whole thing an air of ludicrousness – and the corrosion-melted gates slumped awkwardly, reminding me of reclining figures watching the world go by. The health and safety signs above their heads had been neatly crossed through with red spray paint, and someone had erected a billboard above the entrance, which read simply:

WHEELS

. I felt someone staring, that same old prehistoric instinct, and glanced around, with hairs prickling, for the culprit. Only when I looked directly up did I find him: a dead head, sockets empty, skin tattered, lipless jaws set in a timeless grin. This grisly voyeur sat mounted on a telegraph pole; cables stripped away and its solid girth painted in stripes of tar and red paint.

"The fuck does *that* mean?" I said, nodding up at it.

"Territory marker," Nate mumbled, smoking a straw-like cigarette. One of mine. "Black and red means this is En-Tee."

I gave him a blank look. The acronym thing was starting to piss me off.

"Neutral Territory," he grinned, pointing further into the plant's network of alleys and avenues, all festooned with the same black and red flags and bunting. "No Klan business."

"So the dead guy...?"

Nate shrugged, drooling smoke. "Maybe picked a fight. Got outbid, tried to pull pecking rank. Who knows? Maybe just an unlucky schmo inna wrong place when someone wanted to make a point. Folks that run the En-Tees don't take kindly to rule-breakers. They can afford to enforce, y'see?"

Like so much that poured from his mouth, Nate's casual explanations mixed the common sense with the bewildering. Pecking ranks, territory markers... it was all the stuff of just another drug-dream. A revisit to the malleable memories and landscapes of the Bliss trip. But still, I wasn't *entirely* in the dark. I'd spent much of the morning at the airport dozing and thinking, listening to the old man snore, picking his brains about the Klan-system whenever he deigned to wake.

If I understood one tenth of what he'd said, during the

Culling year, New York – not to put too fine a point on it – had gone straight to hell. He'd painted a picture of streets clogged up with empty cars, skeletons tangled along sidewalks. Of the military running out of control with water cannons and teargas. Of riots like full scale wars and whole blocks burning to ash on the grounds of a single suspected infection. He hadn't been there – he was still in London at that point – but leaving aside the narrator's propensity for hyperbole it still wasn't easy listening.

What *was* certain was the Klan system. In a weird sort of way, despite everything, I was impressed by it. It was easy to see how it must have started, and at the back of my mind – beyond the doubts and disapprovals – it seemed like the most natural thing in the world. Like some new species released onto the savannah, frightened herds running together; accreting like shit flowing into a bowl.

Strength in numbers.

Pack mentality.

The oldest instincts in the book.

The way Nate told it, the Klans all had their origins in different places. Maybe some grew up round whichever politicians survived the Cull and got lucky, outside of Washington when the nuke skyburst. You can imagine that happening, maybe. Little guys in suits, standing on stone steps, kicking up a fuss. Like you used to get in Hyde Park, like Speakers' Corner every Sunday. Angry men and women on stools and ladders, spouting fire and brimstone. Since the Cull, they would have been *Kings*.

Still... It's a big step from there to gang colours, to skin brandings, to closed territories and aggressive expansion and nightly raids and sallying-forth and midnight skirmishes and blood in the gutters...

The night before, as Nate explained this stuff, as I told him I just didn't *see* rational people acting so dumb, sinking so low, he stopped with a grin and said:

"Desperate times, man."

The main driveway along the interior of the power plant took a sharp corner, every inch of the way draped in swatches of fabric and makeshift adverts. Most carried the names of food stalls and barter points (promising FARE TRADE, WIDE SELECSION, ALL SCAV CONSIDERD), branded in each case with iconic images of bygone snacks; hotdogs, burgers, bagels. I found my mouth watering at the memory of such extravagant-seeming meals, and asked Nate what the stalls *really* traded.

"Rat." He said, not looking around. "It's all rat."

Some of the Klans, maybe, came up from less obvious sources. Lantern-jawed drill sergeants discovering they had no country left to fight for, nobody left to shriek at, no way of draining off the dynamo-level testosterone. Civic leaders, celebrities, lawyers. The local bloody postman. It didn't take much, back at the start, to be the centre of a pack; to let something comfortable and secure grow around you. Maybe some of those putative mobs – coalescing and running together – could even claim they'd formed their miniature little states for all the right reasons. Nate told me one of the Klans, back at the start, was called the 'Thin Blues.' Bunch of NYPD grunts, he said, banding together, facing down the chaos. He said that to start with they even had a decent stab at maintaining the peace; driving about, making arrests, shooting looters. He used the word 'altruistic', which sounded weird when he said it, and tricky to take seriously.

He said it didn't last long.

He said ever since then, the Thin Blues had been one of the *smaller* Klans.

Inside the industrial sprawl of the Con Ed facility we reached a checkpoint, where two enormous blokes in black clothes and red bandanas stood divesting everyone of weapons. A small queue of raggedy scavs had formed, and beyond the canvas-draped checkpoint I could see the peristaltic movement of large crowds, deeper inside the facility. It made me nervous. In London, the only time you saw that many people gathered together was for the Abbot's sermons, and just *thinking* about those left a bad taste in my mouth.

I watched the guards frisking and checking, allocating each person a number to be used in recollecting their guns and knives, and tilted my head towards Nate.

"What Klan are they?" I asked, nodding towards the muscular goons.

"Right now," he said, "no Klan at all. Neutral Territory, remember? They're being paid to keep it that way."

As if to reinforce this point, the guards commanded each entrant to display his or her Klan marking. Elbows and shoulders were silently brandished, knees held out, necks craned, and I caught a few fleeting glimpses of the squiggles and meaningless icons depicting each different group. In every case the guard quickly tied a black rag, plucked from a filthy basket, around the scar; hiding the brand from sight.

"Neutral." was all that Nate said.

We reached the front of the queue and caused something of a commotion. For a start, Nate's branding could hardly be covered with a simple piece of rag – unless he was prepared to submit to blindfolding, which he wasn't – but it was the nature of the mark itself that really got them riled. They kept exchanging looks, clenching their jaws, wondering out loud if they should fetch the 'Em-Bee'.

More fucking acronyms. Nate seemed to be enjoying

all the consternation.

He'd explained it to me last night, the instant that the scavs he'd called 'Mickeys' scuttled off into the dark.

"The Neo-Clergy," he said, "the mighty New Church, the holier-than-thou warrior priests of the New Dawn were really just another Klan."

Oh, a *big* one, to be sure. The biggest. The de-facto rulers of New York, whose powerbase gave them an administrative control over all the others, but still...

It hadn't seemed possible, somehow. How could something so mundane, so *seedy*, as this feudal mob have spread across the devastated world to make its claims of ushering-in a new future? From angry thugs to architects of tomorrow.

According to Nate, the Apostolic Church of the Rediscovered Dawn started out as a band of raggedy-arsed bastards calling themselves The Choirboys. They had no particular defining features – besides a reputation for being twisted little shits – and would have languished in obscurity had they not encountered the man named John-Paul Rohare Baptiste.

No one knew much about him. No one knew where he'd come from or who he'd been. All they knew was that he shouldn't be alive, and he proved it to them over and over again, with tests and samples and nothing-up-his-sleeves, just as he had continued to do every week on his detestable fucking TV show.

The Blight should have *got* him. He should have been Culled.

But he lived anyway.

Under his guidance, and the fluttering banner of his self-declared divinity, the Klan swelled like a tumour. It came to the point they could have challenged and annihilated any other group they chose, but they *didn't*. They simply tuned out from the power struggle, announced that their intentions had transcended the merely territorial, and elected themselves into a position of magisterial arbitration.

Nowadays they monitored the others, like proud parents adjudicating the play fighting of toddlers. They formalised the squabbles and scuffles, they leant their backing to whichever Klans they favoured, they provided weapons and drugs (their most valuable currencies), and in return they demanded The Tithe.

Oh yeah...

The Tithe.

"Every child above age five," Nate had said the night before, like reading from a scripture written inside his eyelids, "and below age eighteen, to be inducted into the Ay-Cee-En-Dee."

That's Apostolic Church of the etc etc.

They'd spread the good news across the oceans. They'd conquered the airwaves when all other frequencies had fallen silent. They'd taken responsibility for the future when all the starving, dribbling politicians and leaders and generals left behind could not, and then they'd made it their business to take charge of the children.

They'd made the people *want* to give up their own kids. And they were just another New York *gang*.

I found myself wishing I'd taken a little longer with the fuckers inside the plane.

Eventually, loving every minute of the guards' continuing bewilderment, Nate dug from his pocket a tattered eye patch and covered over his half-tattoo. He looked like he'd done this sort of thing before. The goons all but fainted in relief; apologising with twenty shades of uncharacteristic pomposity and explaining that members of 'The Great Klan' so rarely visited the Mart, they were unprepared. It's one of those sights that sticks in the mind: two seven-foot yetis fawning and scraping over a scrawny old git dressed like a tramp with a uniform fetish. Nate clucked and swaggered along the concourse.

The guards turned to me and let the panicky hysteria fade from their grizzled faces. They took my gun, glancing at it with suspicious eyes that said *how inna hell did you come by this, little man?* and told me to show them my Klan marking.

"Ah." I said.

The way it worked, Nate had told me, was that you had your Klansmen, and then you had your scavs. The scavs were like livestock. Their loyalties determined by whichever mob happened to rule the territory in which they'd chosen to eke-out their lives. Some went wherever their Klans went, or chose the most profitable or benevolent of regimes to nuzzle up to. Others were just spoils, like land taken in territorial scuffles; unceremoniously re-branded as the occasion required.

It sounded feudal. It sounded fucking *stupid.*

"Why don't they just *leave*?" I'd said, in the airport, as Nate explained. "Why don't they just *rebel*? There must be thousands of them."

"They do." Nate shrugged. "All the time. Not a day goes by there ain't a little... revolution, uprising, whatever. Chaos on the streets, every fucking night. But here's the thing: you want a way to share out scavenged shit, or food, or whatever you got? Klans're the only way."

"Bullshit."

"Not bullshit. Good sense. And if not good sense then natural-fucking-order." He'd licked his lips, waving a hand as he hunted down an example. "Let's say you're a... a young girl, right? Only just escaped the tithe. No parents. No weapons. No friends or food. Who's gonna stick up for you? Who's gonna make sure that shitty squat you found to sleep in don't get raided, or burnt down, or torn-up by some crackhead rapist? Huh?"

I'd shaken my head, unable to bring myself to agree, but I could see what he was getting at. Just.

"And what if you're *not* helpless?" I'd said. "You've still got to... toe the fucking line. Join up, act like a piece of *property*, get branded like a sodding *cow*."

"Yes you do. Yes you do. But the only way is up. And what happens when you impress one of the hotshots, huh? Or maybe cosy-up to the Klanboss? Or kill someone in the communal bad-books?"

I'd shaken my head again.

"Promotion." He grinned. "Become a Klansman. Free to carry weapons. Free to roam. Work your way up. Maybe one day challenge for the top spot."

"And if you fuck up?"

His voice had gone quiet, all but lost behind the crackling fire.

"Then you out on your ear. And you better hope you can take care of yourself, or else find someone who can."

Talking about himself, again. Just like always.

Nate said the Klansmen wore gang colours, and let their brands heal over. They got to carry weapons and administer internal justice and expand territories and all the other bullshit war games you can imagine. They played at being generals, gladiators, law enforcers and conquistadors. They got all the best gear. They had first choice of any scav, ate the best pickings, collected on debts, upheld the Klan's integrity and generally acted big.

I told Nate I was shaking in my boots. I'm not sure if he knew I was joking.

Back to the power plant.

"I don't have a brand." I told the guards.

"You ain't a scav?" One of them ran his eyes up and down my pitiful clothing. "*Look* like a scav."

"Fully paid-up Klansman." I said, smiling, knocking-out my best US accent and still managing to sound (in my head, at least) like I was taking the piss.

I was.

"Yeah?" The guard said, looking like he'd already had a bad day and couldn't be arsed with it getting any worse. "What Klan?"

I thought for a moment, smiled sweetly and said:

"The Culled."

They let me through, eventually, and as I passed him by the biggest goon grumbled, half-hearted.

"No Klan business inside."

I grinned and told him to perish the thought.

As we passed the checkpoint and wound our way further into the facility, I caught Nate staring at me, like some freakish version of a pirate, uncovered eye twinkling.

He'd been carrying my pack since the airport – to spare my shoulder, he said – and now he unslung it carefully onto the floor, staring at me with a curious smile.

I wondered for the fiftieth time what he was hoping to get out of all this. Out of helping me. Out of saving my life and bringing me here.

Call me cynical, but Nate didn't strike me as the sort of guy to do something for nothing.

"Take another cigarette?" He asked.

He'd earned it. Of course he had.

Currency's currency.

"Go ahead."

But as he dipped his hands inside the pack they moved

with a speed and confidence that betrayed all kinds of stuff, if you're a paranoid bastard like me. If you know what you're looking for.

Familiarity.

Confidence.

Avarice.

When he saved my life, when he made the choice to attach himself to me rather than kill me, as I lay with a dying man's blood pulsing into my veins, he'd had hours and hours to go through the bag. Was that it? Was that all there was to him staying with me?

He'd seen the goods and wanted to earn his share?

No. No that made no sense. He could have just let me bleed out, let me die there on the runway, then taken it all for himself.

What then?

That same scratching. That same itching *something* at the back of my mind.

Something not quite right.

Something not adding up.

"Nate."

"Mm?" He said, sparking the cigarette.

Just ask, dammit...

"Why are you helping me?"

The air smelt of salt and car fumes. For a long time, there was silence.

He watched me. Eyes unmoving.

"Thought we'd established that." He said, slowly, as if I was being ungrateful. As if I'd told him I didn't *need* him.

"Try again." I said, gently.

He sighed. Pursed his lips.

"I walked out on the Clergy, pal. Saved my own skin when I shoulda... shoulda died like a martyr. That's what they expect. *Thoughtless obedience*, you understand?"

"So?"

"So if they catch up with me, it's... It'll be..." He looked away, face fearful, and coughed awkwardly. Another long suck on the cigarette, calming his nerves.

"Anyway," he said. "I seen you in action."

"And?"

"I kept you alive, raggedy-man. Now all you got to do is return the favour."

And it was an explanation, I suppose. It made sense. It all added up.

And underneath it all the dark voice in my mind, shouting:

Don't you fucking give up, soldier.

Don't you get distracted, boy.

Don't you let things slip.

Sir, no sir, etc etc.

Nate was helping me. Because of him I was healthy enough to carry on; to get the job done; to go after it like a flaming fucking sword. Everything else was just dross. Everything else was just peripheral shit that didn't matter. Who *cared* why Nate was helping me? He'd given his explanation. Now *move on*.

Except, except, except.

Except that as Nate dropped the cigarettes back into the bag his hand paused – a split second, no more – next to the battered city map with its New York scrawl and red ink notes, and his lips twitched. A fraction. Just a fraction.

Then he caught me staring, and closed up the pack with a friendly smile, and led me further inside the power plant.

I took the pack and shouldered it myself.

"How you feeling?" He said, as we walked. "Got your

strength back? Lot of blood you lost, back there."

Reminding me. Keeping me indebted.

Not subtle, Nate.

"I'm peachy." I told him, a little colder than I'd meant.

Basic training, year two:

Call in favours. Get people good and beholden. Make friends. Make the fuckers owe you one.

But don't you let yourself owe anyone anything. You hear me, soldier? Don't you get yourself in arrears. Don't you feel obliged to take care of anyone.

People are parasites, boy. They see something strong, they clamp on.

They slow you down.

They complicate shit.

"Just peachy," I mumble-repeated, morose.

CHAPTER SEVEN

By then, the TV broadcasts were getting random.

The signal itself was okay. Would continue to be for another year or two, up until the power died and the generators sucked dry on fuel and all the diehards up at White City gave up. By which time barely anyone had a TV left working anyway.

But at the start, loud and clear, picture-perfect, 100% dross.

Mostly it was repeats. A computer governed the scheduling, I guessed, to cover holes and overruns. Endless episodes of Only Fools and Horses, long-gone seasons of Porridge and The Good Life, a smattering of game shows whose contestants won or lost years before. Friends reruns, over and over and over and over, and anyone who gave a shit waited in vain for an episode called 'The One Where Everyone Dies of an Unknown Flesh-Digesting Virus.'

No one was making anything new. No documentaries about the present emergency. No one had the time or energy to programme the channels.

Everyone was too busy staying alive.

This was at the beginning. This was during The Cull itself, as The Blight swept the country, as the infrastructure gave way like a dam made of salt and all the comfortable little certainties – advertising, street-sweepers, hotdog stalls, the Metro newspaper on the underground, discount sales, pirated DVDs, free samples in supermarkets, full vending machines – all the little frills you never fucking noticed, just slowly...

...went away.

Except the news. Sometimes, anyway. "God Bless the

BBC!" People would say, as they passed in the street, tripping on bloody bodies and dead riot cops. Sometimes days would piss past with nothing – no bulletins at the top of the hour, no "we-interrupt-this-antique-comedy-to-bring-you-breaking-news" – and out in the rain all the uncertain crowds who couldn't work out why they weren't coughing and dying like everyone else were all anxiety and confusion, waiting beside the screens. But once in a while... once in a while.

I imagined a skeleton crew, struggling on bravely at Television Centre; sleeping and living in its ugly bulges just to get the word out. I imagined them feeling pretty good about themselves, like the fireman who goes above and beyond to save a crying kid, like an artist who doesn't sleep for a week to get the right tones, the right shades, the right effects. Like the soldier who keeps going, who never gives up, no matter what.

In a civilised – and I use the word with the appropriate levels of irony – world, news is just another commodity. It so rarely affects you. It so rarely intersects with the sheltered, blinkered universe of your real world. It's just another entertainment. Another distant work of fiction (or as good as) to be picked apart and discussed in the local boozer, over tea or coffee, sat on the train, wherever.

The Cull changed all that. The Cull made it so everyone was living the news, all the time. Suddenly all the people – the quiet little nobodies who called themselves 'normal' and never made a fuss – knew what it was like to be a native of Baghdad, or an earthquake widow, or a disgraced politician. Suddenly they all knew what it was like to switch on the box and hear all about themselves, their own world, their own shitty lives, discussed in the same autocue-serious tone as every other dismal slice of bad news.

It must have been a weird sensation.

(Not for me, though. I'd been making the news for years, one way or another. And I mean 'making'. Some weeks it felt like foreign affairs correspondents would've been out of a job but for me and mine, though they didn't know it. And no one ever said my name.)

On this particular day, the eagerness to receive fresh information was stronger than ever. All throughout the blistered wastes of London, little knots of people had formed – their clothes not yet raggedy, but getting there; their faces not yet malnourished and gaunt, but getting there – to crowd around flickering sets in front rooms and electronics shops, tolerating the dismal repeats on the off-chance of a new bulletin.

Two days ago, they'd mentioned the bombs falling in America. Rumours of atomic strikes, attacks all across the world, missiles going up and tumbling back down, EM pulses like technological plagues and supertech 'Star Wars' defences misfiring; farting useless interceptors into lightning storms and spitting heat seekers into the sea.

When they'd made that *announcement* – a couple of days before – it had been tricky to know how much was confirmed and how much was fabrication. Concocted, one suspected, by the dishevelled creature sat behind the news-desk, staring in terror at the trembling camera. It was difficult to imagine the usual BBC specimens – bolt upright, faces slack, Queen's English spoken with a crisp enunciation that bordered on the ridiculous – stammering and coughing quite so much as the nervous girl huddled behind her sheaf of papers, as she told an entranced London that nuclear Armageddon was right around the corner, then sipped carefully at her water.

It had been a tense couple of days, since.

I sat it all out in the flat. It had changed since that gloomy day when I got the text, when the removal guys failed to show up, when the ambulances streaked past one after another. Now the fish tank lay smashed on the floor, the CDs were all off the shelf in a heap, a couple of pot plants were turning slowly brown with their stalks broken and roots unearthed, and the front door sported a few splintered little holes where I'd shot it – for no reason other than to let the neighbours know I was armed.

I'd had a tantrum or two, that's all.

The phone hadn't rung. There were no more text messages. Nothing.

Oh, and, PS: nuclear bombs may be about to fall.

Not the best week of my life.

The point was, on this day, when the catchphrase comedy was blissfully interrupted and the serious little NEWSFLASH screen cut-in without announcement or music, pretty-much every poor beleaguered fucker in the entire city leaned a little closer to the set, and held their breath.

It was a new face behind the news desk – even younger than the last one, with an untidy mop of hair and a thick pair of glasses that reflected the shimmering blue of the autocue off-puttingly – and he cleared his throat agonisingly before beginning.

What he said had nothing whatsoever to do with bombs.

"Good afternoon," he said. I almost laughed. "A UN-sponsored team of researchers based in the United States have today released a statement regarding the unknown sickness that is now estimated to have struck two thirds of the countries of the World, and shows no sign of abating. Despite the poor quality of the signal, agencies still in

contact with the BBC across the Atlantic have confirmed it to be genuine, though its source is as-yet unknown.

"According to the report, the disease targets particular biological conditions with a precision formerly unknown in medical science. Referred to by the unnamed author of the report as the 'AB-Virus,' the infection – which is airborne and requires no physical contact to transmit – attacks red blood cells at an unprecedented rate; causing muscular, respiratory and cardiac failure within days."

A cut-rate graphic appeared on the screen: a crude image of eight identical human silhouettes, in two rows of four columns. Headers across the top of the table read A, B, AB and O, whilst the rows were marked with simple mathematical symbols for positive and negative.

"Oh shit..." I whispered. The penny was beginning to drop.

"Each person," the voice continued, settling into a sort of cod-documentary narration, *"possesses one of four distinct types of blood – known as phenotypes. These are characterised by the various protein markers, or 'antigens', upon the surface of each red blood cell. So, people of phenotype 'A' have A-antigens,"* here the first column of the table lit-up in lurid yellow, *"and people of phenotype 'B' have B-antigens. Those whose blood-type is 'AB' have antigens of both varieties, whilst those with no antigens at all belong to phenotype 'O'."*

In each case the strip of yellow highlighting clunked its way along the table. I felt like I was watching one of those godawful educational videos they used to crack-out in biology lessons at school, with the unconvincing sexual metaphors and the pulpy innards of rats and frogs.

"The practical effect of this system is to determine what blood-types are safely viable for transfusion into medical patients. Patients of blood type 'A,' for example, cannot

*be safely given blood of any phenotype containing 'B'
antigens and vice-versa."*

The voice drew a breath. It was hardly compelling
viewing, but I didn't envy the poor bastard delivering it.
It was like 'Doomsday-By-Boring-Science.'

I guess even then, at the back of my mind, knowing as
I did that I hadn't felt a twinge of sickness, and being all
too familiar with my own medical stats, I knew what was
coming.

"The categorisation is further complicated," the voice
droned, "by the presence in most people's blood of a
further protein marker: the so-called 'rhesus' antigen."
Here the entire upper row illuminated, like a bad version
of a Connect-Four game show. "Any person with Rhesus-
positive blood cannot viably donate to those with Rhesus
negative blood, whose bodies contain natural antibodies
to defend against the antigen."

I caught a sudden mental picture of filthy people all
across London, clustered into makeshift bomb-shelters,
trading bewildered glances and muttering "Wassefucken'
talkin' baht?"

The newsman continued, a little shakily.

"The UN report makes it clear that the virus, once
contagion has occurred, will specifically target red blood
cells bearing antigens of any type. So any person of
phenotypes A, B, or AB; or of Rhesus-positive blood, is
susceptible to infection."

On the screen, the little graphic changed, a crude red
'X' appearing upon each and every cell within the table,
except for the last one.

"Subtle." I said to nobody.

The camera cut back to the guy behind the desk. He
looked tired, and someone had nipped-in to yank off his
glasses during the off-screen monologue, so now he was

squinting comically at the autocue.

"If the report is correct," he said, "less than seven percent of the population of the United Kingdom – those of phenotype O-Negative – are safe from infection."

He coughed quietly, glanced off-camera for a moment, and then licked his lips. He knew what was coming.

"The report ends... The report ends with a summary of the research team's attempts to develop a treatment for the 'AB-Virus'. Viewers... Uh. Some viewers may find the following audio file disturbing."

I laughed again, bitter.

"Yeah..." *I said.* "Yeah. Because telling nine-out-of-fucking-ten people they're going to die isn't at all disturbing, mate, is it?"

The poor kid was up out of his chair – face crumpled in disgust – before the image even blurred away into a bland red screen with the astin 'UN RESEARCH REPORT.'

A man's voice – American – came out of nowhere:

"As to our findings regarding the... ugh... the... hnh..." *A thick bout of coughing broke through the signal; ugly sounds of spittle flying and phlegm being swallowed, which lapsed by degrees into silence. Machinery and murmuring voices sounded quietly in the background. The voice started again, dry and uncomfortable.* "—the treatment of the virus. We've... We've found nothing. No way to stop it. It obeys all these... these rules we don't understand, but even so... every division is a... a new strain. You treat one – kill it, even – the next one's different. It... hnnk... it can't be sto..."

The voice broke off again, the coughing far uglier this time, interrupted with staccato grunts of pain and short curses. It softened slightly – the speaker moving away from the microphone – but the obvious pain of the fit was hardly diminished, and I found myself wincing in sympathy.

And then everything changed.

It was only quiet, but I heard it. There's no doubt. No fraction of uncertainty in my mind.

It was barely audible. It rose out of the background hubbub and the storm of coughing and wheezing dominating the signal, but oh God I heard it. I know I did.

"Lie him down!" A new voice said. Tinny with distortion and distance, but somehow resonant and deep nonetheless. "Get him down! And switch off that fucking micropho..."

The signal died.

The news programme stopped.

The repeat episode of Only Fools and Horses *picked up where it'd left off, with canned laughter roaring out of the box.*

Out on the streets of London, a low moaning, building through sobs and cries of horror, was growing all across the steepled skyline.

In my flat, I shot the door six more times, drank half a bottle of vintage single malt, and went out to start a fight.

That night – the night that London tore itself apart – I could take my pick.

Someone tried to rob me. Emphasis on the *tried*.

Give the little punks their credit: they had a system. Probably been pulling this shit every day for months, and if it weren't for the fact I clocked them as soon as I saw them, it might even have worked.

Somewhere inside the heart of the Con Ed power plant facility, a broad plaza had been cleared. Intestinal pipes and tanks dragged aside, buildings burned and shattered, the whole roughly-square patch razed to a cracked-concrete wilderness.

It *heaved*.

The weirdest thing was – and I didn't realise this until later – there were no kids. It seemed natural enough to expect them, somewhere amongst it all. At the heart of the colourful crowds, at the source of the excited shouts and squeals, amidst all the bodies squashed together or dashing through scant open spaces as they blossomed and filled. It was pandemonium. It was human convection in a tattered blend of colours and sizes, pushing and jostling and grunting, haggling out loud, or simply standing tall to yell offers at top volume.

But no kids. In all of New York, just like London: no kids.

"Wheels Mart." Nate said, leaning idly against a rusted pipe and lighting another of my cigarettes. "You want transport, you find it here." His eyes narrowed, almost imperceptibly. "Where we going anyways?"

I ignored him and let the sensory overload knock me about, letting my instincts adjust, taking stock.

A hundred and one aromas gusted past – not just the usual filth and stink of too many unhygienic people – but the smoky promise of meat and stew, served diligently by a long row of low stalls, to the colossal queues of hungry customers. Prices were written in arcane barter-notes: weighing cigarettes, ammunition, items of clothing, canisters of fuel and recreational narcotics against the value of ratburgers, dog food gumbo, home-grown potatoes and (*fuck me, the smell!*) freshly baked bread. My senses kept trying to tell me I'd died and gone to heaven.

All around the outer perimeter of this bustling plaza

other stalls were erected, bartering all manner of curious products and scraps of salvage. So wide was the square – and so thick with people – that I couldn't even make out what the distant stock *was*, though a tent near me held nothing but live chickens and shrieking budgerigars in small wicker cages, and something that looked troublingly like a parrot was turning on a spit over a barbecue. There were no weapons visible anywhere, except those clutched by the small groups of black-clad guards lounging about on walls and turrets around the enclosure, keeping half an eye. The distinctive shriek-scream-grunt of pigs rose from a muddy morass behind another section of the crowd, and most audible of all – over the top of everything else – was the growl of engines. Dozens of them. From all quarters of the mart fumes coiled upwards like greasy fingers, and at regular intervals a fresh cavalcade of bikes throttling, cars backfiring and heavier vehicles rumbling to life sounded above the mêlée.

The crowd was thickest at the centre, where a tall man in a wide-brimmed Stetson dangled uncomfortably from a series of cables and harnesses above their heads, waving arms and shouting out what I first mistook for unintelligible nonsense. The crowd seemed to be responding in kind – hands raised, necks craned, roaring out and waving bits and pieces of tatty scav every time the pendulous showman wobbled overhead.

It took me a while to realise he was running an auction.

"Four an' five!" He was wittering, almost too fast to catch, "four-and-five, pack of burns, pack of burns? Pack of burns! Anna piglet! Raise me? Best scoot inna house, here! Vespa, onlythabest! Raise me? Raise me?"

The crowd hollered – everyone shouting all at once – and the MB ("Master've bids," Nate grunted) dangled about like a string puppet, pointing fingers, taking offers, and promising new barters. A shiny chrome moped sat on a plinth beside the crowd, guarded by four serious-looking guards.

"Pack of burns?" I asked, flicking Nate a look.

He shrugged and brandished his cigarette, then scowled and looked me up and down.

"You wanna try lookin' any *more* like a goddamn *tourist*?"

I realised I'd been blocking the causeway. Sticking out like a sore thumb with my bulging backpack invitingly obvious, bolt-upright and fascinated where everyone else was either rushing about like their arseholes were on fire or leaning, just like Nate, against whatever item of sturdy ephemera they found. There were two correct states of being inside the Wheels-Mart: involved or not involved, and neither one involved any sense of wonderment.

Paying attention; taking an interest; having a bag full of unknown goodies. These were one-way-tickets to getting noticed by someone.

My 'someones' emerged from the crowd to my left, and I knew what was coming immediately. Two young men – early twenties at a guess, maybe even tithe-dodgers – scrapping and squabbling, rolling in muck, dirtied fingernails clutching at torn rags. They sprang and locked again, snarling like ferrets, tripping each other in their clumsy aggression then scrambling upright for a renewed attack.

It was all very convincing.

Except for the glances.

The tiny sideways squints in my direction.

The subtle eyes that told me everything I needed to know.

One of them drew a knife, circling in suddenly to thrust

inwards towards the other, who rolled aside theatrically and yanked his own shimmering little shiv out of the hem of his boot. The pair closed again, their angry wrestles and desperate stabs bringing them – as if by magic – stumbling towards me. Choreographed to perfection. Messy and fast and unpredictable, and as authentic as it gets, but *I* knew.

The body language.

The stance.

Nate was watching them with some interest, I noticed, completely taken-in; face a slack mixture of disapproval and distance. Even some of the crowd – studiously nonchalant of all other things – were twisting to watch the brewing carnage. Everyone was ignoring me, never considering it might all be for my benefit. One or two punters even started calling out encouragement to the fighters, making wagers and shouting advice, whilst others scanned the crowd for the nearest guards.

"No Klan business!" A woman hissed, trying to break them up. The young men shoved her away and kept circling around each other, knives hooking hilt-to-hilt, then twisting back and forth inside one another's guard. Vicious. Personal.

Always heading right for me.

By the time they dropped the pretence and pounced – both at the same time, unlocking from their fake pugilism like a bear trap in reverse, knives outstretched on each side like scissor blades – I was already moving. Diving beneath the double-stab, rolling awkwardly across the backpack and flicking out one orbital leg: roundhousing the first punk – a freckled beanpole with bright purple hair – off his feet. The other darted-in with a snarl, catching a straight-handed chop to the side of his tattooed neck and – as I vaulted upright from the ground – an angry, unsubtle head butt on the bridge of his much-pierced nose. To be blunt I think he was dead from the neck wound already – he bloody should have been, the way I hit him – but I was angry. Sue me.

He went down without a word.

The purple-haired geek got up slowly, shaking his head to clear the fuzz, and backhanded his knife into a downward slicer. I picked up his mate's shiv – dropped from one spasming hand – and grinned at him; letting my body tell him how calm I was, how much I wanted him to rush me, how much I was *urging* him to come take me o...

His eyes flickered, just a millimetre, to one side.

Cold sweat. That sinking feeling.

Third guy behind me.

Two for the diversion, one for the strike.

Clever.

I sidestepped a fraction early. I figured the attack was imminent, but I left the fucker with too much time to angle his swing. Still, if it's a choice between denting my skull with a heavy tyre-iron or missing by inches and instead swiping the fabric along the top of my pack – tipping me over like a sleeping cow – I'll take the latter every time. I slash-stabbed blindly with the shiv as I stumbled, snarling from somewhere deep inside me that wasn't entirely rational; feeling a tug and a tear and a spatter of warmth, rewarded with a scream. The breath exploded out of me as I thumped to the tarmac on my back, crushing the kid with the pierced face for a second time and sending something sharp punching through the top of my pack; digging me in the nape of my neck.

This Johnny-come-lately sneak-up-behind-a-guy arsehole – an enormous man with a braided beard and a pair of lensless glasses – staggered and moaned, squirting blood from an arterial gash on his thigh. He'd dropped the tyre iron at some stage, but as the purple-haired youth closed in on me with the knife the giant swatted him on the shoulder, held out a bony paw for the blade, and dropped down to finish me himself.

Something small and red appeared between his eyes.

The back of his head came off, and for a second or two he looked startled; as if his brain was still feeding him waves of shock and uncertainty, despite being scattered in a semicircle across the mud. A gunshot echoed across the crowd – like a guest arriving late for a party – and everyone jumped.

"Fffff..." he managed.

The kid with the purple-hair took off.

Without being entirely conscious of it, sitting upright in one long fluid movement, I felt my arm extend, left eye closed, fingers releasing. The shiv – a curled tooth of flat steel, easily palmed beneath gloved fingers – spun off into space; a shuriken that caught the weak light as it whispered.

It hit the punk at the base of his skull, just beside his left ear. It looked like it went deep, and when he sagged to the floor – arms quivering, legs bending back on themselves – he wasn't in any rush to get back up.

There's a lot of blood in a scalp. It clashed with his hair.

It dawned on me slowly that a lot of people were staring. Several of them were wearing black clothes and red bandanas, and were going to great lengths to elbow their way through the crowd in my direction.

A shadow fell across me.

"Stay the fuck there," it said, poking the two dead punks near me with a smoking rifle.

My guardian angel, I guessed. The one who blew off

the giant's head.

From below, it looked a lot like a tattered, hunchbacked ogre.

Its voice was actually kind of sexy.

CHAPTER EIGHT

Her name was Malice. I figure she was probably 'Alice'
– maybe 'Melissa' – at one time, but the whole gung-ho
nickname thing worked pretty well for the mercenaries
the Wheels-Mart paid to keep the peace, and they were
never happier than when striding about, calling out each
other's ridiculous handles across the braying crowds.

Spuggsy.

Moto.

Tora.

Nike.

And so on. I pretended to be impressed as they
introduced themselves. Pumped up and black-clad in
every case, moving with that familiar 'I'm-a-hard-bastard'
confidence you see in mercenaries the world over.

They'd propped me up in a canvas shelter off to one
side of the auction (still noisily ongoing through the tent's
doorway) and now Malice was staring at me, more-or-
less-alone, with her arms folded. Nate stood behind me,
dabbing at the cut on my neck. I think he was enjoying
being part of the attention. Light through the tattered
canvas ceiling dappled the interior of the room, making it
seem busy and claustrophobic, and it was almost an effort
– in amongst the extremes of brightness and shadow – to
focus on Malice's eyes.

She was the blackest person I'd ever seen in my life,
and she was so beautiful it hurt.

"So," she said, voice guarded. "Guess we owe you
one."

"Why's that?"

"Took out the three Goddamn amigos back there. They
been causing trouble few weeks now. Coming in off the

water, we figured."

"Happy to oblige."

She smirked unconvincingly.

Malice wore the same black threads as all the other guards (though it would be unfair not to mention how the baggier parts of the ensemble crinkled as she moved, hinting at what was going on underneath) and the same red bandana – in her case folded into a bright sweat-band around her crown. Her hair was shaven away to that not-quite-stubble length – like the velvety patch on the tip of a horse's nose – which so few women can pull off, but makes the ones who can look so ball-rupturingly sensational.

Malice looked like she had a hunch on her back. A big one.

Once in a while the hunch – hidden away beneath black veils – gurgled to itself.

The kid, she told me, was a fraction over a year old. Malice never mentioned the father, so I figured he was long gone or dead. It (I never found out a name, or a gender) stayed quieter than any baby I've ever known, and seemed perfectly untroubled by its mother lugging about a high-powered air-rifle and a sweet assortment of other popguns. Once in a while Malice jiggled in a strange sort of way, rocking the wicker harness the baby was huddled inside, as if she knew when the sleepy sprog was on the verge of waking up without even having to look.

Every time she jiggled like that it looked like she was giving me the come-on.

"Who are you?" She blurted, just as the silence was getting uncomfortable.

I shrugged. "Just a customer. Just passing through."

She shook her head. "Uh-uh. I saw the way you took

out them rats. You're ex-mil, pal. Showed in every move. Special forces, maybe. SEALs. Whatever it is you Brits got..."

Not even close, honey.

"Does it matter if I am?"

Her eyes narrowed. "Yeah, it fuckin' *matters*. Some psycho stalking 'bout in my Mart."

"I didn't start th..."

"And the only ex-mils round these parts're with the Choirboys."

Aha...

I frowned. "Clergy, right?"

She spat on the floor, as if disgusted by the very name. I started to like her even more, and wondered just how highly the universally loved Neo-Clergy were *actually* regarded...

I held my palms out – like showing her I had nothing to hide – and pointed to the distinct lack of scarlet tattoos on my eye.

"I'm not with the Clergy."

Her eyes darted to Nate. In the cover of the tent he'd flipped-up the pirate eye patch like a pedal-bin lid, making him look like a astonished panda. "But your pet here?"

Nate 'tsk'd through his teeth and waggled a finger. "Ex." He said. "Ex, sugar."

She just glared.

"He's officially retired," I said, flipping Nate's eye patch back down with a quiet slap.

Malice spat again. "No such thing."

The silence stretched out. Malice started pacing a little, left then right, keeping her eyes fixed on us all the time.

I drummed my fingers on the arms of the chair, creating every impression of disdainful boredom, and whistled quietly. My neck felt tight, like Nate had stuck a monstrous plaster across it, and I hadn't had a chance to find out what had caused the wound yet. I was sort of glad I couldn't see.

Outside, the fast-talking MB sold a battered BMW to a man with three piglets of his very own, who'd outbid a guy with a portable power drill and a book of jokes.

Mostly the vehicles were cheap, in 'who-gives-a-shit' money terms, but I guess I shouldn't have been surprised. When 93% of the world shuffles off the mortal slinky there are a lot of jalopies left rusting in empty driveways. The way they saw it, the black-clad personnel of the Wheels-Mart were just agents. Middlemen to cut out the tedious business of finding, breaking into, hot-wiring and maintaining vehicles. The klans sent their scavs along to buy the best of the pick, and as long as everyone kept themselves polite, self-serving, and oh-so-very-neutral, the whole system worked.

Until someone who stands out shows up. No one likes a guy who rocks the boat.

I got the impression Malice and the other guards were mighty twitchy. Ready to snap. Ready to kill.

And they didn't like the Clergy.

Hmm.

After long, boring minutes had passed, I cracked my knuckles nastily and said:

"So. You going to let us get on with it, or what?"

Malice made a show of ignoring me, pulling off that same weird rolling motion, hip-twitching as she soothed the baby.

I stood up.

"Or do you guys make a habit of pulling this shit on anyone who does your job for you?"

She smiled, and this time I think there was at least

a glimmer of genuine humour in there, no matter how guarded it was.

"You want a *job*, limey? That it?"

"Fuck no."

"What, then?"

"Want a set of wheels."

"Going somewhere?"

"Yep."

"Want to tell me where?"

"Not really." I shrugged my tattered coat back on over the top of Nate's bandage, and threw Malice an impatient stare. "We able to do business here or not? 'Cos if it's less of a timewaster I'm quite happy to go stand in the crowd and shout at the wanker on the wire."

Her nose wrinkled thoughtfully. "You got currency?"

"Apprehending known villains not good enough?"

"Covers fuel costs, maybe. World don't turn on good deeds, pal."

"Too fucking right."

I picked up the pack the thieves had been after and brandished it for Malice's inspection, oozing all the business-like cool in the world.

"Ten cans Pedigree Chum," I said, letting the bag spin on its straps. "Six packs of cigarettes. Two bottles Jack Daniels, one bottle supermarket-brand vodka. One tin powdered milk. Three cashmere blankets, only the best will doodle-do. Two packs condoms." (Malice's eye met mine, lightning-speed) "Three vials amphetamine, six sachets barbiturate tablets, eyedropper full of acid, an eighth of Moroccan woodbine – if you believe the dealer – and five hypos of some weird mil-shit called 'Bliss'." I smiled sweetly. "Take your pick."

Nate coughed, awkwardly. Malice was staring at me with an ironic eyebrow, like she was trying not to laugh.

I became distantly aware of a quiet noise, like:

Spitaspataspitaspata

The pack was leaking. A few jagged shards of glass – half a vodka bottle and the angular rim of a JD litre – had torn their way through the fabric in several places, and their wasted contents were puddling on the floor. It looked like a lot of other shit had fallen out too. Somewhere outside, in the thick of the crowd.

"Ah," I said. "Bugger."

This minor calamity seemed to adjust the atmosphere somehow, as if by demonstrating that I wasn't *quite* as cool as I'd made out, I'd taken the sting out of Malice's suspicion. I'd like to say I'd planned it that way. The woman even smiled openly once or twice – her posture relaxing for a beat – as we rescued what we could from the doomed offerings.

The alcohol was all gone and the cigarettes reduced to a soggy mess, stinking of whisky. Nate (self-elected expert) declared them to be utterly worthless, then pocketed them quietly when he thought I wasn't watching. The blankets were stained but useable, the dog food and rubbers untroubled by their liquor soaking, and the drugs – which I'd hoped would be my most valuable bargaining chip – had alternately dissolved, shattered, fallen out of the pack, or dribbled away. Two of the Bliss hypos remained, along with a single vial of 'phets and the baggie of skunk. Nate kept moaning quietly under his breath every time we found something else ruined or missing, like he'd had it in his mind that the longer he stuck with me, the more of my stash he was liable to inherit.

I wondered vaguely if the drastic losses were enough to make him stop following me round. To break the debt.

I let the thought go, for now – content to let things carry me, trusting my instincts – and poked about in the miserly little stash we'd rescued. Five years of misery and starvation since the Cull, and the 'drugs problem' had mutated mysteriously from 'There's Too Much', to 'There's Not Enough'. It's hard to take the moral high ground when you've watched your friends die, when you've spent all day chasing ornamental ducks along stagnant canals, when you're freezing to death and when someone's offering you a quick and easy way to escape.

'Just say no?' Fuck *that*.

Just say *gimme*.

If fuel was gold in this mean-arsed new world, then hardcore narcotic stimulation was platinum.

"Not going to get you much." Malice shrugged. "How far you gotta go?"

"How about you show me what you've got?"

She shrugged again – the baby hiccupped – and gestured towards the rear door of the tent.

I stepped outside and felt my neck prickling. This is the same feeling all men get, when they step into a room full of gadgets, or fast cars, or big guns.

Set back from the main square, on an adjacent street between black painted walls of corrugated iron and criss-crossed walkways manned by gun-toting guards, Malice led me through rows of cars, vans, pickups, SUVs, motorbikes, bicycles and – shuffling nervously against the rope walls of a makeshift paddock – a trio of horses. Amidst the dozens of wheeled contraptions the whinnying livestock was about the only means of transport in the place that hadn't been radically altered in some way, and even they'd been daubed with crazy patterns in black and red branding paint. On everything else clashing colours and crudities were smeared along every chassis, windows were shattered or missing, innards had been comprehensively plundered. It would have been faintly depressing – like a scrap yard refusing to give up the ghost – had it not been for the special area, roped-off with its own guards. Inside its boundaries everything had been augmented, streamlined, *changed*. I gazed lovingly at steel roll-bars, wheel-covers in three types of mesh, hulking nitro canisters wedged inside passenger seats and ten different variations on the theme of 'heavily armed.'

Pintle mounts poked like miniature SAM-sites from the roofs of jeeps and spot-welded AVs. Swinging hatches – just like on Nate's old school bus – replaced side-doors and load containers, whilst several cars sported a sneaky set of exhausts below the rims of the front doors, to blast flames at the touch of a button at anyone dumb enough to try getting inside.

I wanted to *play*.

All of them were painted black and red.

"What're these?" I asked Malice, barely able to control the drooling.

She smirked. "Rentals."

"And how do you make sure the customer brings them back?"

"Oh, that's easy."

"Oh yeah?"

"Yeah. We go with them."

At the far corner of the section my eye fell on something. Something big and angry-looking. Something spiky.

I nearly fell in love.

"The *Inferno*," said Malice, following my eye. "Cute, huh?"

It had been a fire truck once, though to be fair it bore about as much similarity to its previous incarnation as a shark to a diving bell. It was... *sleek*, which was an adjective I'd never have picked to describe a fire engine before. 'Like a speeding brick', maybe, but never *dangerous.* Never *predatory.*

Progressive layers of sheet-iron had been built-up from a sort of conical crest along the truck's nose, like the scales of a dagger-like fish. Below its new snout a shallow dozer-scoop clamoured with spikes and barbed wire, whilst wide flanges protected the windshield above.

All four tyres wore heavy swaddles of chains, canvas padding, rubber coils and thick iron rims, and a set of spares were lashed carefully beneath a wire and sheet gurney on the left flank. Halfway down the truck's 30-foot length an angle-poised turret reclined its muzzles towards the sky, its firing position enclosed on all sides by a low balustrade of welded plate steel. At one time it'd been a water cannon, easily hitched to a tanker truck and fired in great arcing loops. Now it had been modified. Converted in ways I couldn't easily see, so the central cannon stood surrounded in a clutch of cables, secondary devices and dangling controls. I think I picked out a Mk19 grenade launcher amongst the oily barrels, which told me everything I needed to know.

You did not fuck with the *Inferno.*

Secondary and rear-angle tertiary gunmounts were placed further along the vehicle's spine, each one protected by small forests of steel jags and corrugated shields. The whole thing was painted as black as sin, except the rims of the wheels and the hood above the windshield, which stood out in vibrant red like the belly of a Black Widow.

It was something of an effort to form words. "How many... does...?"

"Four crew. Five if you want the big guns out, but that's extra. Room for as many passengers as can hold on."

"And how much... ah. How much would it cost to...?"

She stared at me. She wasn't smiling.

"A lot more," she said, "than you've got."

So that squished *that* one.

Long story short: I ended up embarking on my perilous quest on the back of a fucking quadbike, which sputtered and farted every time I throttled it, and it cost me everything I had except a single can of dog food, a sodding cashmere blanket and a packet of condoms. Malice said I'd got myself a bargain, and filled the whiny little vehicle up for free.

I settled into the driver's seat – feeling pretty good, letting the engine tick over – and turned to thank her for her help. She was already walking away, disappearing into the tent, and the last I saw of her was her baby staring at me owlishly from her shoulders, dribbling with a smile. I sighed, wondering what I felt.

Attraction? Loss?

Guilt?

Nate was staring at the quad with a sort of disgusted fascination. I sat back in the seat and folded my arms. *Let him choose*, I thought, feeling nasty. *Let him ask.*

"So, *ah...*" he shifted from foot to foot.

Then *tsk*ed.

Then started clambering on.

"Whoa, whoa... hang on..." I waved him off. "You're coming just like that?"

"Too damn right."

"But, you're... I mean..." I gaped, earnestly astonished. It felt a little like a limpet had attached itself to me, and no matter how long I held it over the fire it wasn't going to let go. "You don't even know where I'm headed!"

I watched his face.

There. There it was again.

The hesitation.

The eyes flicking to the pack on my back, then away

again.

"Don't matter." He said, forcing a smile. "I'm game."

"And if I wanna go on alone?"

"Then I remind you how I saved your life."

"But..."

"And I *add* – seeing as how you're bein' so hardass about it – that my price just went up. I get bodily protection, plus one blanket, one can dog food."

"You want all my shit *too*? For *what*?"

He smirked, white teeth electric beside me.

"Travelling medic." He said. "Keep you outta trouble."

And then it was too late, and he was perched on the pillion and pointing ahead like a general giving the order to advance, and that was that.

Good, I tried to tell myself. *He's a resource. He can help. He knows the area.*

But always the itching. Always the uncertainty. Always the suspicion.

What's your ulterior motive, doc?

And even deeper than that, drummed-in at a genetic level, the angry lectures splitting open my head; a tac-command feed direct into my skull.

Don't you let yourself owe anyone anything. *You hear me, soldier? Don't you get yourself in arrears. Don't you feel obliged to take* care *of anyone.*

"Oh, hey," he grinned. "And throw in them rubbers, too."

My train of thought derailed itself in a blur of disbelief. "*You* want condoms?" I gaped.

He seemed vaguely affronted. "Damn straight! You think I wanna be a daddy aga..."

He stopped himself, mouth open, then blinked once or twice and started over; coughing his way through the hesitation. "You think I wanna be a daddy, *my* time of life?"

I stared at him for a moment, wondering what to say, how to react, then shrugged and tossed him the rubbers.

"Fine," I grinned. "Clean me out."

He scrambled onto the saddle's pillion like a scarecrow mounting a horse, and I gunned the bike along the Mart's central promenade with a fierce sensation of freedom, letting the customers still pouring in take responsibility for not getting run down. Even so, as I stopped to retrieve the rifle and pistols I'd lodged with the goons at the check-in, there was something grinding in my mind. Cogs interlocking, memories grinding. Something about Nate. Something he'd said, maybe.

Something not quite right...

We churned through the Mart's main gates, bobbing uncomfortably over untended tarmac and roadside debris, and took a sharp right. Nate leaned down and shouted over the roar of the wind.

"What I said!" He called, voice hoarse. "Earlier on! About the Clergy!"

"What about them?"

"About... About what if they catch up to me! They... They got these... what's it called, man! Jesus-Cross!"

"Crucifix?"

"Yeah! Right! They got a shitload! All ready for any motherfucker pisses them *off*!"

Visions of medieval tortures and Inquisitorial nastiness slipped through my head. I kept seeing that scene from *Spartacus*; the main road flanked on both sides by crucified rebels, and saw me and Nate swinging in the breeze. "Oh yeah?" I shouted. "Where's that?"

"Midtown, man! Manhattan! Biggest territory there is! Centre of the fucking universe!"

I let the quadbike bring itself to a trundling halt, feeling the engine die-down, forming words carefully.

"What you doing?" Nate blurted, prodding the quadbike. "Is it busted?"

"No, no, it's... *ah*."

"What?"

I tried to grin. Failed.

"Well, it's just... you'll never guess where we're headed."

CHAPTER NINE

Interlude

Raymond – or Ram – caught up with Rick somewhere in the city suburbs. The first he knew about it was a speck in his single remaining wing mirror, gathering size as it tore toward him at top speed.

At first he thought nothing of it. He'd seen little of anyone during this last leg of the journey, but the few people he'd spotted were enough to relax his nerves, where before he would have stiffened and fled from anyone. Out here, beneath the ever-changing sky (one hour burning bright, the next choked with fog, the next boiling with turbulent clouds; but always on a scale that seemed somehow too big, defying the eye) his only company were the occasional figures distantly glimpsed across the hills, tending fields or felling dead trees. Once or twice he'd even passed vehicles, always heading west. Mostly monstrous pickups and HGVs crammed to the gills with filthy-looking people, who stared at him with dead eyes as the trike gunned by, manoeuvring awkwardly around the abyssal potholes and gaping cracks that striated the roads. Some of these travelling groups were surrounded by little clusters of motorbike outriders, who glared suspiciously as they hurried all other traffic off the road. Each time he saw them Rick stiffened, expecting more silver-jacketed Collectors, imagining Slim's bloodless body stretched-out in the hardware store back in Snow Hand.

None of the bikers so much as looked at him.

Other trucks bristled with quills like porcupines: men with rifles and swivelling arms-mounts, suspicious of everything that moved. He wondered who they all were, where they were all going, what they did all day long – then promptly forgot them as soon as he reached the next corner.

He was in a slightly fragile state of mind.

The I-80 was an endless grey snake, cracked and mud-drenched, pocked with deep wells and unexpected fissures that crept-up on the unprepared traveller, wending its way through hills and fields of green and brown. Here and there old heaps stood and rusted – breakdowns that no one ever bothered to tow clear – and only the twittering of unseen birds, and rabbits scampering for cover, disturbed the hypnotic progress of the tarmac serpent.

Rick was beginning to relax about the Harley too. At first it had seemed an unnecessarily flashy addition to his equipment: a mid-life-crisis on three tyres. It roared like the end of the world every time he gave it some throttle, and along with its dayglo paintjob in yellow and red, it conspired to be the absolute opposite of 'inconspicuous.'

The clan mothers would not have approved.

On the other hand, it was fast. It was far sturdier than the Yamaha, and in odd moments between small towns he'd begun to fancy he was riding an armchair; hovering across forests and lakes. With the stolen shotgun strapped across his back and a veritable cornucopia of other weapons stashed in the saddlebags, he kept seeing himself in some tacky Schwarzenegger moment. Crashing through flaming debris with a pithy one liner and a minigun blazing.

In fact, Rick – née Hiawatha – kept imagining himself and his environment in all sorts of outrageous new ways. This had something to do with the boredom of cross-country travel, something to do with his natural imaginativeness, and a lot to do with the enormous quantities of the sachems' weed he'd been smoking since his run-in with the colossal bear-like sodomite who attempted to kill and eat him the night before.

He figured he owed it to himself.

He'd spent the night in a mid-sized town called White Deer, two hours or so down the interstate from his fateful encounter with Slim in Snow Hand. The place had been mostly deserted, but a pocket-sized population had set up a sort of commune around the central square, and Rick was too exhausted and too nervy to risk breaking-in somewhere else. He traded one of the 9mms and a box of ammo for a comfy bed and two pouches of dried rabbit, and even got a bowl of vegetable soup into the bargain. The people were polite, eager to please, but ultimately empty. He could see the terror in their eyes; the way they kept looking back and forth from him to the Harley, to the bulging saddlebags.

At one point a little girl appeared – precociously smiley – and asked him if he was a Collector come to take her away to the bad men in dresses. He was about to tell her "no" – to tell the whole goddamn town he was nothing to do with the fucking Clergy, or any other troublemaking scum they might be afraid of – when her mother swept her away with a dozen fearful glances over her shoulder and a muttered warning for him to "stay the hell away from her!"

Point taken, he kept himself to himself after that: got as stoned as is it physically possible to get, sat staring at a fire with all the usual bullshit thoughts of spirits and voices that he only ever got when he 'wasn't himself', and cleared off in the morning before the sun was fully up.

Two hours down the road, he passed a place called Kidder. There were three bodies strung-up on builder's scaffolding beside the turnoff; old and dried-out, almost skeletal now, dangling by their wrists on sharp cords

of barbed wire. A spray-painted plaque below each one
declared their crimes to the passing world.

THIEF

MUSLIM

INJUN

Each Tag had a scarlet circle sprayed below.
Rick decided against visiting Kidder.

He paused only once during the morning – another
narcotic stop, to top-up the fuzziness that had insulated
him from the terrors and confusions of the night – and
now as he flew along the ridged spine of the grey snake
road, sweeping in lazy arcs from left to right, his mind
wandered in all the beautiful, empty places the Sachems
would have been proud to lead him.

Endless valleys of sound.

*Broken wildernesses, with great gnarled trees standing
lonely on ancient barrows.*

*Horizon-spanning herds of buffalo (or at least, great
shaggy monstrosities with horns like scimitars, which
is how – never having seen one – he imagined buffalo
must look), oozing across grassy plains and moaning,
deep down where sound stops and feeling begins, to each
other.*

*Ghost-dancers, capering from side to side, seething and
hissing as the chalk-dust coating their dusky skin dripped
away with their sweat.*

They were singing a song, he could tell. All of them. The
landscapes, the buffalo, the trees, the dancers. He'd never
learned the language of his people – too busy playing
the white kid, turning his back, ignoring the Tadodaho's

patient sermons – but somehow he understood. Deep in his bones, it made a sort of sense. In his back pocket, the silver needle wrapped-up in its rags became a tuning-fork: humming a single note of crystal beauty that shivered all through him, connecting him to the world, to the sky, to the Song.

It was a hate-hymn, he understood, to drive the bad ghosts away; shrouded and tattooed, with their dusty god and their scarlet demagogue.

The sky was talking to him. The grass was tugging at his leather legs, whispering in great wind-driven susurration, and the boughs of an ancient vine – sagging over the Interstate as he drifted by on the back of the magnificent thunderbird – told him to "watch out, boy... watch out..."

It was a heavy-ass dream-vision, and the matriarchs would have been proud – it just wasn't very good timing.

Something slapped him in the face; waking him from the foggy dreamsleep to find grasses and leaves fap-fap-fapping against his chest and head, and the trike scrambling – almost on its side – along the verge at the edge of the interstate.

"Fuck!" he yelped, waking up in a hurry. "Fuck!"

He wound his way back into the centre of the road, negotiating more potholes, gulping for air and promising himself to stay awake – even considered getting rid of the remaining pot – when the black speck appeared in the mirror.

It got big quick.

And yeah; at first it didn't worry him. The relaxing tendrils of the smoke soothed away all his tension and he even found himself giggling, without quite knowing why, at the swiftly growing reflection. Just another biker, he figured – travelling even faster and more recklessly than him – soon to sweep-past on his way to the smoking blot on the horizon that would, eventually, become New York. Descending from the hills, the city was a spillage of brown and grey paint, washed-through with QuickSmog graffiti and chalk dust scribbles.

"Haha!" It was hard not to laugh. Not just at the other biker, oh no: at everything.

Everything was good. Everything was funny.

"Haha!"

In fact, so vast and smudge-like was the endless plain of industry and smutty air on the eastern horizon, that Rick's narcotically liberated consciousness completely forgot about the pursuing rider and went flashing off down a million new tangents, to get wrapped up in wonder at the patterns a smoking chimney made against the sky; the curious sweep of a green park amidst the urban sprawl; the flight of a bird overhead; the—

The roar of another Harley.

The flash of a silver jacket in his mirror.

Deep inside, at some cold rational level untouched by the cloying comfort of the drug, Rick was screaming and shouting in half-grasped terror. But outside, on the surface of the chilled-out shell containing him, he did nothing but giggle and make lion roaring sounds under his breath, trying to out-growl the approaching bike, trying inwardly to wrestle himself into some semblance of conscious control.

Swearing over and over that he'd never smoke dope again.

He watched a tiny flash-flicker in the mirror, like a speed camera shuttering open in his wake, and shouted "Say Cheeeeeese!"

At this distance, squinting carefully into the fly-spattered mirror, he could just make out something long *and cumbersome poking at odd angles off the rider of the other chopper, and a corkscrewing contrail snarling-up the air between them.*

The rocket launcher.

Fuck.

"Haha!"

He would have died, but for his sluggish reactions. The idea of swerving furiously to his left gripped him by lazy degrees, so that when finally he twisted the forks of the trike's front wheel a whole second had already passed. A vicious grey blur – venting heat and smoke – squealed past him like a localised earthquake, directly beside his left ear. Right where he would've been if he'd managed to get his act together sooner and swerve.

"Whup!" He shouted, half drooling in bowel-voiding terror, half whooping with stoned elation.

The rocket dipped down a second or two ahead of Rick, then nothing but smoke and fire-flash and a bilious black-red-grey dome bulging up and out, and tentacles of soot and shrapnel curling down like the branches of a willow, and he was heading straight into the dark heart of the fireball and—

—and this time he swerved with a little more presence of mind, banking the trike through the blind heat and soot on the rim of a seething crater, gunning his way forwards with his eyes closed, his hair singeing, and no goddamn idea where he was going. The Schwarzenegger stunt shit suddenly looked pretty fucking ridiculous in his mind's eye.

By the time the smoke was out of his face and pouring off the bike's tyres, the other guy was almost on him; tearing an unconcerned hole in the wall of black smog and shouting something, deep and vicious, that Rick couldn't understand. In momentary glimpses at the speckled reflection he could see the rocket launcher was gone – hurled casually onto the verge the instant it was empty – and now the slumped character was crouched low over the handlebars of his reptile-green chopper like a ghost riding a lizard, free hand filled with a compact, matte-black machine gun, long silver jacket flapping in his wake.

Rick yanked the shotgun off his back and hoped he looked like he knew what he was doing. Riding one handed was all very well, and maybe he'd even be capable of firing a loaded weapon with the other, but doing both simultaneously whilst harried from directly behind by an indistinct psycho was quite another matter. He struggled for a second or two to twist and aim, almost hit an abyssal pot-hole, and swerved once again with a shriek.

The world blurred past.

The machine gun chattered somewhere over his shoulder, driving him low against the saddle, and for the second time he found himself driving blind. Miniature craters blossomed all across the tarmac below and before him, and something whined angrily as it ricocheted off some hidden part of the trike. Rick hoped it wasn't anything important, then remembered he wouldn't have known one way or the other anyway.

He was still finding it sort of tricky not to laugh.

The other bike drew level. Glancing to his side, Rick could see his attacker clearly for the first time – and wished he hadn't looked.

Ram wasn't a big guy. He was wiry and pale, with greasy red hair that hung in bedraggled knots over the front of his sweaty, pointed little face. He put Rick in mind of a rat. A compact and bundled package of lank fur and corded muscles. Not the fastest or the strongest critter out there, maybe, but corner the little bastard in *the wrong place and it'll turn and fight and won't ever give up.*

Ram had a look like he always *felt cornered.*

Rick shouted "Rrrrrraaaaabies!" Because it seemed sort of appropriate.

"Killed... fucking... Slip!" the gangly creature snarled, eyes blazing, tweaking his bike's course to be perfectly parallel to Rick's own, then raising the machine gun with theatrical slowness, yellowing teeth bared.

He wore a head guard, of sorts. A football helmet with its visor removed and a pair of rotten, curled horns – ripped from the head of a ram – affixed on each side. And a bowler hat glued to the top.

To Rick, despite the whole 'impending death' thing, the dribbling psychopath looked for all the world just like Princess Leia, complete with currant-bun haircoils on the sides of her head. Rick found this screamingly funny, and started laughing.

Then he stopped, and started to whimper.

That made him laugh too.

It was all pretty pathetic, but at the very least it made Ram pause in tightening a finger over the machine gun's trigger, fascinated by a piece of prey manifestly even more insane than he was.

Rick closed his eyes and waited.

And waited.

And then there was music, and voices, and rustling.

Abruptly he seemed to be half-asleep again; like a sudden wave crashing against his mind, prising open his eyes and altering everything in the subtlest ways. The world was still just as it had been, Ram was still riding there beside him, gun pivoting upright... but somehow everything was different. Everything was fluid and glacial, shimmering with a sort of hard-edged light that *came from nowhere, and went to nowhere. Maybe it was the shadows, or the shape of the sky, or—*

The music, again. The chanting voices with their hymn of hatred. The grass rustling and the buffalo lowing. The Tadodaho surrounded by the oldest Sachems, and the clan mothers – the true leaders – huddled in cloaks beyond the light of the tribal fire.

Another dream-vision, nuclear-bomb-bursting open in his pot-fuelled preconceptions.

The great spirit, the Earth-Initiate; the trickster coyote and the turtle-man.

Thunderbirds circled overhead, every wing beat a new calamity, every eye-flash a splinter of lightning to stab at the ground.

"We told you," one of the matriarchs hissed, peevish, "to stick with the fucking Yamaha."

Rick giggled. In his limited experience, dream-visions rarely cussed.

"No time for that," the Tadodaho croaked, folded-up in a bat-like shroud of leathery cloaks and feathered cords, hard-lined face bisected by sharp slashes of black paint. "Look."

He nodded out of the dream, and Rick stared past the hazy walls of his own subconscious back out into the real world, like a drive-in movie for his own skull. The moans of endless buffalo herds changed tone discreetly – modulated downwards into a synthetic blare, and became the panicky blast of a truck's horn.

Further along the freeway, a mile or so ahead of Rick and Ram's helter-skelter rush, there was an HGV oncoming. It had ducked through a splintered section of the central reservation to avoid a black mass of rusted debris on its own carriageway, and was now occupying two third of the road directly ahead of Rick. Just like all the others;

crammed with stained workers and glaring guards, horn
screaming over and over.

There was room to get past; but not much. And Ram's
bike, tearing along solidly at Rick's side, wasn't budging
an inch.

Rick flicked a glance across at the horned freak. His
face had changed. He was smiling, twitchy and vicious,
and victorious, gun raised but not fired. He'd spotted the
juggernaut. He knew fun when he saw it.

"You hold!" He shouted, eyes watering. "Killed Slim, you
fuck! You hold your line! You chicken that motherfucker
out, or I shoot!"

Rick giggled, despite himself. At least the psycho was
giving him the choice.

A blast in the brain or a head-on collision. Tough call.

The people in the truck's container were waving arms,
roaring at him to move, to shift out the way, to fucking
clear the r—

The walls went back up, and the music carried him
away again.

In the dream, the Tadodaho wasn't troubled. He eyed
Rick – no, not Rick; Hiawatha – warmly, and said
something that no one else could hear. The birds in the
sky laughed and sang and rushed together. The trees bent
down and doubled-over, chuckling so hard their trunks
creaked and the ends of their branches snapped. The
Thunderbirds roared their amusement and the grass... the
grass just rustled its quiet titters into nothingness.

It was all a big goddamn joke. Hiawatha smirked, then
started to giggle. It had never been like this, before. Oh,
shit, he'd been stoned a million times. He'd tried to... to
commune with the fucking spirits as often as any of the
Haudenosaunee. But always he'd felt like a fraud; like
peering-in on something from the outside, like he was

trying to be serious and spiritual about something deeply stupid.

"That's just it," one of the Sachems said, head inflating like a balloon. "Who told you to be so damned serious?"

They all started laughing too.

The road ahead glowed.

A patch – nothing more – of purple fire and green smoke, with a knot of make-believe birds circling above it, igniting on the tarmac ahead. It wasn't real. It shifted and shimmered, changing directions and breaking form. It was on the far right of the highway, pressed up against the verge, like a patch of spilt oil, set alight by a passing rainbow.

Hiawatha laughed, and the world laughed too.

He understood.

The walls dropped down, the dream passed, and he was awake again. The world still streaked-by. Ram was still shouting at him to hold his line, to smear himself against the truck, to do himself in, to get dead, to make up for Slim, to just–fucking–die!

Slowly, without even looking, Rick angled the trike towards Ram. Ten seconds or so, maybe, before he hit the truck. A gradual drift, tectonically slow, towards the psycho, closing the gap between the choppers.

The machine gun poked against his cheek.

He smirked, imagining himself. Racing at top speed, bike-to-bike, with a gun to his head.

"Arnie," he whispered to himself, "eat your heart out."

"You get back over there!" Ram snarled, so close that even the wind couldn't diminish the force of his voice. "You get back or I'll shoot, I swear to Jesus, and when you're roadkill I'll fucking do you in every goddamn hole you got, boy!"

The distance to the truck was swallowed up. The

massive vehicle was slowing, braking hard, but it didn't matter. He'd still hit it. There wasn't room for both bikes to pass.

The glowing mirage passed at the edge of the road. The birds shrieked. The trees groaned. The buffaloes snorted and rutted and screamed in the night, and—

Rick jerked the trike, hard, to the right. The gun-barrel dug in to the meat of his cheek, the choppers locked briefly then parted, sparks spat, Ram shouted, and then they were separating out, jerking outwards: Rick straight back into the path of the truck, Ram slinking outwards towards the verge of the road, smirking and laughing at Rick's dismal attempt to push him aside.

He was too busy laughing to notice the enormous pothole at the edge of the interstate.

The dream cleared totally. The coloured smoke and fire that had marked the cavity vanished, and the birds dissolved into the air.

Ram's bike nosedived, and made a noise a lot like:

Klut.

The front wheel dipped against the edge of the pothole. The forks crumpled. The rear segment flipped upright – a green horse bucking – and Ram sailed, asshole upright, out of the saddle and onto the tarmac, to scream and grind his filthy leathers away, tumbling and skidding.

Rick swerved perfectly into the vacated space, and braked hard.

The truck rumbled past, horn moaning into the distance.

Silence descended bit by bit, and the last thing to shut the fuck up was the roaring in Rick's ears.

Ram lay on his back, breathing shallowly, a bloody trail of skidmarks marking his slide across the floor. His face was half gone. His bike was a crippled mess, lodged and broken in the pothole's leading edge, and Rick took his time – feeling strangely dispassionate about everything – to siphon off the remains of its fuel into his own chopper's tank.

He felt like he'd seen the 'real' world, and this bland reflection of it was trivial by comparison. He gazed out to the east, and for the first time noticed that same purple-green haze, like an echo of the bright fire inside his dream, hanging above the endless city. Showing him where to go.

"...get you..." Ram whispered. "F-fucking... fucking get you..."

"You don't even know who I am."

"Tell me," the rat-like freak snarled. "Tell me who. Find you." There was blood trickling out of his mouth where he'd bitten his tongue.

"I'm Hiawatha," said Hiawatha.

Then he drove into New York, and stopped only once en-route for a smoke, just to keep the dream fixed in his mind.

Five hundred miles west, in a place that was once called Fort Wayne, the Tadodaho glanced around the circle of assembled Sachems – faces masked in the smoke-thick air of the Dreaming Lodge – and the shrewd-eyed women-folk standing behind each one, and nodded. The communal pipe at the centre (it looked like it had been carved out of a single piece of wood in the shape of an impressive bear totem, but in fact was a resin cast of a completely meaningless sculpture made in Taiwan in 1998) gave out the last few sputters of smoke and died, its usefulness complete.

"He's through." the Tadodaho said, leathery skin

crumpling as he smiled sagely. "Be in the city in a hour or two. Get the war party together. We need to get to the meeting place."

"Now?" One of the others said, peevishly.

The Tadodaho pursed his lips, then shrugged.

"Weee-ell... Soon, then. Who's for a beer?"

CHAPTER TEN

The air in the tunnel was almost tropical. Damp too, musty, like you'd get in a cave whose only visitors were incontinent foxes and a less hygienic class of beetle. Indistinct *stuff* – unexpectedly cold in the muggy darkness – dripped on my head, and in the gloom I had to force down the shivers and keep telling myself *it's just water, it's just water.*

The lights had died long ago – shattered lamp heads good now only for rat holes and bat-roosts – so Nate and I revved along the barren tube slowly; relying on the quadbike's stammering headlights and the fluttering flames of tiny hammock-dwellings, strung-up in odd corners and service-nooks. The clapped-out engine sounded painfully loud, and more than once I saw pale faces eyeing us from the shadows, squinting at the sudden brightness then burying themselves back beneath nest/beds of rags and cardboard.

"More scavs?" I asked Nate, unnerved by the feral look of these troglodytes.

He shook his head. "Flips. Worse'n scavs." Their eyes caught at the light as we streaked by. "No Klans, no homes. Mostly they're... outcasts. Crackheads, maybe. Some loonytoons. Lot of folks went nuts, straight after The Cull. Happens, you know? Happens when you see your whole family puke up their lungs."

I shivered and shut the thought away.

Passing us by with their pale faces streaked by moisture, slack jaws mumbling, they put me in mind of salamanders. Fat, grub-like, nocturnal.

"The Clergy don't mind them being here?" I asked, eyeing yet another scarlet 'O' marked on the outer wall of a corner ahead. Someone had even formed a crude crucifix out of bicycle reflectors, which sat in the centre of the circle and *blazed* in the onrushing light. I felt like a dart, arcing towards a target.

Behind me Nate shrugged, as if to say the Clergy had far more pressing things to be *minding* than a few reprobate squatters.

Signs of the ownership of the Queens Midtown Tunnel were all around us. Even before we'd entered it, back on the other side of the East River, the territory markers had stood in long rows down either side of the approach-road; brittle white and topped in each case by a wide scarlet ring.

Three heavily-armed goons had stood on the outer perimeter of this abstract border. Two men and a woman, each wearing nothing but arctic camo trousers and braces, jointly conducting a heated discussion with a shambling host of raggedy scavs. Some of them were pointing at us.

"Mickeys," Nate had grunted, voice muffled. I noted with narrowed eyes how the tallest of the men – a swarthy giant with arctic white hair and livid red rank-stripes scarred onto his shoulders – broke-off from the argument to glare as we rumbled by. It wasn't until we'd passed beneath the tunnel's arch that I realised Nate was hiding his face.

As the tunnel roof had closed over us, our last sight was of a carefully hand-painted sign, hanging above the on-ramp, which read:

AND HE SHALL FIND THE KINGDOM OF HEAVEN

"Yeah," Nate had spat. "One way or the other."
Back in the dark, a quarter hour or so later, I swerved

to avoid a lump of congealing debris – a much-rusted car wreck, probably, and considered the tunnel roof above us. Back in London, a year or so after The Cull, I ventured down into the underground, just to see. Back there the place had been busy; thronging with communities trying to stick together, trying to stay warm. But the effect was the same. In the lightless depths you started to think…

About all those thousands of tons of rock and soil and water pressing down above your head. About ant colonies in zoos – with walls made of glass – and thousands of thoughtless creatures going about their business in the arteries of the earth.

The Queens Tunnel was kind of the same, except this wasn't an artery. It was a vein; sluggish, deoxygenated, blue with worthless blood. Nate pointed ahead to another sharp turn and we cruised towards the faintest glimmerings of light – an illusion of day, always lurking beyond the next corner. Nate said this was the route he took whenever he was bringing kids from the airport. He said he knew the way like the back of his hand.

I asked him how many people *really* knew what the backs of their hands looked like.

He ignored me.

I was glad of his knowledge anyway. The number of rusting obstacles and dangling patches of ruined tunnel were prodigious, and without his instructions we would have collided with something straight away.

I asked him again what happened to the kids when they'd been delivered. Did they grow up to become priests? Did they go off to some secret place to begin building the future?

I couldn't see his face, but it took him longer than usual to answer.

"I told you," he said. "I don't know."

The tunnel cornered and re-cornered in defiance of all obvious directional architecture. I'd been under the impression it joined Queens to Manhattan with the minimum of fuss, directly across the strait, but evidently its sinuous course took us deeper into the island, below the knot of blocks and stores of Murray Hill, before curving back on itself to spit us out into the daylight up a debris-strewn ramp shadowed by overarching blocks. The muggy humidity retreated, and it would almost have been a relief to enter the sunlight had the QuickSmog not slunk back during our time underground; covering the blunt buildings of Midtown in an unsettling, gloomy whitewash. Over my shoulder the distant peaks of the financial district were masked – just the ghostly suggestion of needles penetrating the earth – and every street corner had become a cheap special effect.

Just as before, the Clergy markings were everywhere. Territory poles, graffiti-tags of scarlet and red, banners strung across empty streets. An enormous mural showing a smiling John-Paul Rohare Baptiste regarded us from the gable-end of an apartment block. For some reason I couldn't have found it any more menacing, even had the grinning Abbot been clutching at an AK47 or wearing a balaclava like the terrace-markers in Belfast. He just radiated... *wrongness.*

The whole place was *still.* Static. No distant movement, no scavs, no dogs, no rats. Even the birds hadn't bothered to hang around, and from the empty horizon to the north – Central Park, I guessed, beneath the level of the rooftops – to the haze-choked shadow of the Empire State that rose above us over our left shoulders, the whole uncomfortable place more than deserved its epithet:

Hell's Kitchen.

After the communal degradation of London, and the

noise of the Wheels Mart, it felt a lot like the surface of the moon. Silent as a graveyard, with its own vacant atmosphere and a sort of giddying gravity; like nothing was real and would all spin-away into the universal haze at any moment. I let the quad trundle to a stop at an intersection, and morosely scanned the skyline.

"There." Nate said. "Manhattan."

I'd expected something busier. Some sectarian commune, perhaps, filling the entirety of the midtown district, swarming with children abducted from across the ravaged world. I imagined a glowing paradise. An industrious enclave of forward-thinking radicals, blocks wide, staffed with the young and the enthused, building and *re*building, working hard on the civilisation of tomorrow.

What a load of old bollocks.

There were cars, frozen in time, bumper-to-bumper. Dead tyres and shattered windows. Skeletons slumped in front seats, or curled in skinless patterns on the sidewalk. Here and there fire-damage had blackened a rusty hulk, or scoured a section of street of its rough surface. Flamewagons, I guessed; burning the bodies of Blight victims, trundling by five long years ago.

Newspapers flapped. Colourful litter sat like bright decorations speckling the rusting, filthy morass.

The sun was sinking to the west. It even made the whole thing sort of beautiful.

I asked Nate where everyone was, and caught myself whispering. He glanced around at the rooftops, sniffed noisily, then shrugged.

"Two answers to that."

"Oh yeah?"

"Yeah. First one is: all holed-up. Central office. See, your Clergyman, he's not a regular Klanner. No scavs and Klansmen, like that, no no no. This crew, they got the clerics, the soldiers, the pilgrims, the trustees." He tapped the tattoo on his face, eyes grim. "Whole different hierarchy. Besides, these fucks got more on the mind than the usual. Territory. Drugs. Guns. Whatever. These assholes got faith. Whole worlda complications."

I glanced around again, unnerved by the quiet. I slipped off the quadbike and rummaged in my increasingly empty pack, producing the battered city map and unfolding it carefully. "So... they don't mind strangers strolling about up here?"

"Ah, well... There's that '*mind*' again. Do they *mind*? Yeah, yeah, I figure they do. But they ain't gonna do anything about it until someone raises a hand. Then you better believe they'll go Krakatoa on your hairy white ass."

I looked up from the map, trying to get my bearings.

"My arse isn't ha..."

"Not the *point*. Point is, depending on whatever the fuck it is you're *doing* here, as long as it ain't to do with pissing off the Clergy, we'll be fine."

There was something strange in his eye. I pretended not to notice and rotated the map, staring off into the east.

Nate cleared his throat.

"So?" he said.

"So what?"

"So *are* you?"

"Planning on going up against his nibs there?" I nodded at the smirking mural on the wall. "Nope. None of my business. Couldn't give a rat's tit, mate. I'm just here for some information."

Nate looked relieved. I glanced down at the heavy red ring marked on the map's surface, then back at the eastern horizon, feeling an unexpected shiver of anticipation.

Then I folded the booklet away and clambered back onto the quad, suddenly remembering something.

"You said there were *two* answers."

"Yeah. Yeah, I did. Answer number two is: they're all around us."

And he was right. I could feel it. Eyes peering out of the shadows, regarding me from half-boarded windows on either side, squinting from rooftops. I couldn't see anyone.

That just made it worse.

I gunned the quad towards 42nd street and turned a sharp right, winding my way north-east in a series of step-like diagonals, working hard to create the impression I knew what I was doing. Nate had gone quiet. On the horizon a shape swarmed slowly out of the haze. A blank slab of stone – vast and wide but skinny along its third dimension – like a cereal packet built to colossal proportions.

Nate seemed to be fidgeting, suddenly, throwing looks in all directions. I still hadn't told him where I was headed, and certainly not *why* I was headed there, but as the brooding shadow of the building loomed ever nearer, I guessed it was pretty obvious.

I should say something to him, I guessed. Ask him if it was safe. Ask him his opinion.

But:

Something not right...

Something not right about him...

Something to do with his story, with his name, with London...

It was the same old confusion. The same old contradiction between the information supplied by my senses – that Nate was easy to trust, a fun guy, a diamond in the rough – and my instincts; which grated against some tiny snippet of subconscious knowledge and made me wary.

But then, I'd been wrong before.

Eventually he leaned forwards on the saddle and called out over the noise of the quad's angry little engine, voice thick with trepidation despite the volume.

"You remember I told you how come none of the robe-wearin' fucks're on the street?" He called. "All in the... the Central office, right?"

"Yeah?"

He pointed at the black building.

The quad roared. The buildings blurred-past, the black monolith got bigger.

"Oh," I said. "Fuck."

"And now, his holiness Abbot John-Paul shall demonstrate yet again the miracle of his bein', that those who do not believe may be enlightened, and those sons and daughters who cleave already to the bosom of our great community may be strengthened further by his diviniteh!"

Deep-south accent. Nothing better for delivering a bit of sermonising showmanship.

The tragic thing is, when the robe-wearing bastard said the word "bosom" I glanced round the fringes of the crowd to make eye-contact with some likely-looking kid, to titter conspiratorially at the naughty word.

But there weren't any kids. Obviously.

That was the point.

This was back in London. This was maybe two, maybe three years ago. This was one of the few times I let curiosity get the better of me, and went to see The Tomorrow Show.

Standing in a knackered old warehouse somewhere in

Docklands, with a crowd gathered round a snazzy plasma screen TV, I couldn't help remembering midnight mass at Christmas, as a kid. Standing there with the family, heads bowed, singing carols...

Even then, I was old enough to know what I believed and what I didn't. Even then, that same sense of awkwardness, of hypocrisy, of toeing the line of something you don't believe in. That same half-formed urge to leap up and slap the vicar, and start shouting at everyone to think, to open their fucking eyes, to stop being so stupid!

I was young. What can I say?

But yeah, the same sensation. Huddled with the TV crowd on a Sunday, zombie-like expressions fixated on that square of flickering light, drinking every word the announcer said. That same sense of not belonging, as everyone around me listened with an alien devotion to the words of John 'look-at-the-size-of-my-bloody-hat' Paul Rohare Baptiste, and his crew of evangelising loudmouths.

That day the broadcast was stronger than usual – the signal more pronounced, the flickering of the screen less intrusive – and the gathering was determined to eke every last iota of information and holiness out of it that they could get.

"The miracle" They wittered around me. "He's going to do it! He's going to do it!"

Oh yeah...

The Miracle.

He performed 'The Miracle' maybe once a month. We'd all seen it before. Even so a little thrill went through the crowd; the fortifying knowledge that their faith was not only being reaffirmed, but positively vindicated. They saw this shit as proof of the Abbot's divinity, and despite all my carefully-polished cynicism I couldn't help but be a little impressed. Oh, yeah, the routine was full of holes, any number of cheats and camera-tricks to muddle the results, but still... It was something about the faces of all the people on-screen, marvelling and gasping in astonishment. You could fool the camera, maybe, but it was a hell of a lot harder to fool the geeks in the studio.

"Hallelujah!" shouted one of the guys in the crowd. Probably a Clergy plant.

It began like it always began, with the announcer bringing two smiling young acolytes into frame. Both were under 18 – a girl and a boy – either so utterly indoctrinated into the church that their beaming smiles were natural symbols of their contentment, or so doped out of their skulls that they didn't care at all. They wore the same dull grey cassocks as everyone around them, with one notable exception; they each lacked a left sleeve, exposing their bare arms to the shoulder.

"Brother James, Brother Tilda." The announcer introduced them with a smile and a swagger, leading them to a white desk inside the same old dusky studio. Three Petri dishes sat waiting, empty, next to a sophisticated microscope with a cable-drenched camera affixed to its viewing column.

The announcer smiled at the camera, mumbled a prayer with his eyes closed, then pulled a trio of sealed hypodermic needles out of a recess in his cloak.

The crowd shivered again.

"Both these fine young acolytes of the Rediscovered Dawn – bless their souls, lordah! – got 'emselves blood type 'O-negative'. Same as us all, brothers and sisters! Same as everyone alive on this good green earth, created and Culled by Him Above!"

He jabbed a needle into the girl's arm, drawing out a puddle of blood with practiced speed. He then thanked the girl, made the sign of the cross between her and himself, and waved her out of the camera's frame. The syringe was emptied into the first Petri dish, and the whole process repeated with "Brother James."

"Now," said the preacher, placing a tiny swab of Tilda's blood on a glass slide beneath the microscope and brandishing the syringe containing James's like an old West sharpshooter. "Since both these wonderful sons and daughters of Je—sus have the same blood types, it's no trouble at all to mix 'em together." He smiled ironically. "All you doubters out there – that ain't faith, people, that's science!"

The crowd laughed on cue.

The image shifted to a microscope view. A uniform expanse of red blobs, so tightly-packed together on a field of bright light that they could almost be mistaken for a solid block. Red blood cells.

The tip of the needle shunted into view like a clumsy freight-train, skimming layers of Tilda's blood aside in its haste. I wondered abstractly if there was some deliberate rationale behind choosing acolytes of different genders; some discreetly sexual overtone in the public mixing of their blood.

Maybe I just had sex on the brain. It'd been a while.

John's blood streamed down the needle and oozed into the patch of cells already cramping the screen. Without a pulse to meld them together there was little natural movement, but again the needle whisked back and forth, blending like an artist on a palette.

"Same as before," the preacher said. "No change, y'see? No reaction. No rejection. Both the same kinda blood."

Cut back to the smirking preacher, only now he had a guest. Seated and frail in a chair beside him, looking even less healthy – more zombified – than usual, was

John-Paul Rohare Baptiste, *filled with quiet serenity or incontinent senility, depending on your view.*

The crowd around me – predictably – went nuts.

The preacher bent down, fussed, muttered prayers, kissed the old git's robes, and eventually got the hell on with it and stuck a needle in the withered skin of the 'Human Prune's' arm. There were a few artfully displayed bruises clustered in the same area where the poor dear soul had undergone previous tests, making the audience cluck and sigh in sympathy at his selfless suffering. They all looked like makeup to me.

Whatever the truth, the preacher was eventually successful in drawing-off a spoonful or two of the holy man's divine fluids, and quickly returned to the microscope, syringe in hand.

The needle slid into the silent mixture of the acolytes' blood and immediately disgorged its own cargo, a slick of ruby covering over the rest.

The effect was almost immediate.

The cells intermixed. Knots formed. Colours darkened. Like some glue-smeared retraction, the whole bloody morass shrunk-down together, accreting and clinging, separating into dark nodules. It was like watching something perfectly transparent held over a flame warp and ruck into sharp new angles, forming nodes.

"What y'all are seeing," the preacher said, "is called clumpin'. It's what happens when you put the wrong kinda blood into someone. Now, all us O-negs, back before the Holy Wrath of Him On High – Hallelujah! – delivered The Cull upon our miserable sinner's world, you coulda' given our blood to just about any Tom, Dick or Harry. You do it slow enough, you get no reaction at all. Universal donor, brothers and sisters! Amen!

"But you try introducing something else into an O-neg

system, it's gonna react. It's gonna get to clumpin'."

Cut back to the preacher. Face serious, now, all fire and brimstone, sweat prickling on his brow.

" 'And I heard a great voice'", he hissed, " 'out of the temple, saying to the Seven Angels, "go your ways, and pour out the vials of the wrath of God upon the earth!"

" 'And the first went, and poured out his vial upon the earth; and there fell a noisome and grievous sore upon the men which had the mark of the beast; and upon them which worshipped his image!'"

The preacher wiped his brow, as if he'd been overcome then released from some powerful trance. I stifled a yawn.

"Revelations!" He yelled. "Revelations 16, one and two! The prophet foresees the wrath of God, claiming to death and damnation all them miserable sinners and heathens he's marked! Marked on the inside, brothers and sisters! Marked in their very blood!"

He took a deep breath, and in the pause I glanced across the crowd beside me. None of them could stand still; quivering, hopping from foot to foot, shivering in elation.

"Brothers and sisters," the preacher said, "the righteous Cull swept across creation and took from us the means to pursue our iniquities, our selfish agendas, our unholy wars. It took away our great numbers, our great technologies, our great civilisations – ha! Amen! – and left us only with our spirit and our faith. He spared only those without the mark – the O-negs – and all others have perished! Science tells it! The Lord-ah explains it!"

Extreme close-up.

"All were Culled – except one! One great man, whose purity was so great, whose vision so intense, whose strength was so indomitable, that he withstood the mark *placed upon his vile family of sinners, that he bore the pain of his ancestry with cheek turned, and was spared, alone in all the world, by the Lord on high!"*

A crash-zoom, crude and old fashioned, but just right for the intensity of the moment; slinking away from the preacher and straight onto John-Paul's face.

Smiling. Beaming.

Crowd goes wild!

I let myself out at the back of the warehouse whilst the cheers were still echoing about.

He should be dead, the old shit. He should have choked and died.

Oh, fuck, I know, it could easily be a fake. Who's to say they're cutting to that same microscope as the one in the studio? Who's to say it's not someone else's blood in the syringe? But I've seen the cockups, when the blood of the acolytes react weirdly because of this or that blood disease, or some other unusual condition. I've seen the episodes where they have to fetch replacements, or the preacher's used his own blood, or the microscope-camera fucks-up and they have to mix such massive quantities – live in Petri dishes – that the Abbot ends-up looking whiter than a sheet.

Always the same. Always the clotting and the clumping.

I've seen episodes where they've held up his birth certificate for the camera, focused hard on the 'A(Rh+)' box. His name was John P. Miller, for the record, before The Cull.

I've seen episodes where they've filmed his blood – exposed to the air – shrivelling and dying as the Culling virus withers it away.

It could all be a stunt. It could, but it wasn't. My instincts told me.

161

So how the fuck had the old shithead managed it?
Either way, it was great TV.

CHAPTER ELEVEN

We started seeing people – real ones, out in the open, slinking out of our way – as we approached our destination.

Evening came down like a curtain – sudden and soft – and the egg yolk sun sat on the encrusted skyline and punctured the milky haze just enough to blaze along every angle of that great slab of rock, that great blue-black monolith, that towered over the East River like a gravestone.

Once, it had been the Secretariat building; the administrative heart of the United Nations HQ, with the library and the General Assembly (a shallow curl of white concrete with a colossal bowling ball embedded in its roof) cowering in its sunless shadow; the whole complex pressed-up against the river like it was trying to swim to freedom.

As we swept nearer, I couldn't help noticing how many of the windows were broken; how vividly the great satellite-dish squatting beside the river had been painted.

Scarlet. A great scarlet 'O'.

Clergy territory.

I've always been a tad conflicted, as far as the UN went.

On the one hand, it's a pretty bloody obvious idea, isn't it? An organisation to get all the contrary fucks in the world *talking*, cooperating. It's what an American would call a 'No-Brainer.' And yeah, you could whinge at length about how, at the end, it had no power to speak of, how its hands were tied-up in red tape and corruption, how its goals were too vague or too elitist, how its unity didn't extend quite as far as everyone made out... but at least it was *there*. At least people could look at it and say:

"Check it out. There's *hope*."

On the other hand, I spent my entire professional life doing nasty secret things the UN had made illegal decades before, so chalk another one up to national disharmony.

Besides, there was a steaming crater where the White House once stood – along with everything else inside a ten mile radius – serving as cancerous testament to the UN's ability to mediate in a crisis.

I'm being uncharitable again. These poor fuckers must've been hit just as hard as everyone else when The Blight struck. It's not like you can calm someone down when their finger's on 'The Button', when the whole world's dying around you, when a mystery virus is in the middle of slaughtering 59 billion people, just by appealing to their bloody humanity. These are *politicians* we're talking about!

But still. It was hard to reconcile the dismal uselessness of the whole bloody organisation with the magnificence of its home.

On the approach, the people on the road were moving slowly; barely looking-up as we passed. One or two vehicles shunted along cracked streets, full of people with dead eyes and no words. I got that quiet chill in the base of my spine, like with the combat conditioning except colder, more logical, and let my senses fill-in the blanks.

Tear-streaked faces, eyeing-up the brooding edifice with fear and disgust curling their lips. Knuckles white.

Anger, resentment, terror.

Heads lowered, bodies resigned. Dejection and despair.

They had the look of people who'd come to see something; who'd travelled expressly for a sight, a vision, and were now wending their way home having seen it, heartbroken.

They had the look of pilgrims whose journey had been wasted. Misery tourists.

None of them were Clergy. None even sported the same brand as Nate. They wore Klan colours of a dozen different kinds, avoiding one another but united in the uniformity of their expressions.

And the vast majority were women.

"What's got *them* so pissed?" I asked Nate, as we took the last corner onto 1st Avenue. "I thought people *loved* the Cler..."

My voice just... stopped.

In the guidebooks, it was flags. A great arc of them, fluttering and proud, lining the approach along United Nations Plaza, one for each member-state. I used to wonder what happened every time someone new signed-up. Did they have to stick up a new flag? Re-space the others? Who determined the order?

It wasn't flags anymore.

Nate had warned me about this. The *Spartacus* moment. The forest of crucifixes.

The warning hadn't worked.

At one edge of the road there stood a tall truck with a cherry-picker, painted blue and scarlet in the Clergy's colours, and at the peaks of each immense flagpole, T-squared with crudely welded crossbeams, its grisly works hung down and moaned.

And bled.

And pissed.

And crapped on the heads of the crowd below.

Distraught lovers, I started to understand. Friends. Family. Unable to reach up to cut them down, eyed warily by the robed *fucks* with guns and vehicles and all the toys in the world, from the other side of the great razor-wire fence. Spike-tipped stanchions, scaffolds with heavy machine-gun positions, looping ribbons of barbed wire and more guns than I could count.

The United Nations had become a fortress, and it displayed its captured enemies with all the medieval subtlety of heads on gateposts.

"What did they do?" I whispered, as the quad chugged away to silence. One of the dangling men was screaming down at a face in the crowd, telling her to get away, to not see him like this, to go back home, forget him. Eventually the Choirboys took turns pelting him with stones until he shut up, then glared and sneered at the woman in the crowd, daring her to stop them.

They had a basket of rounded pebbles standing-by. I guess this sort of thing happened a lot.

Nate clambered off the quad and sighed. He looked jumpier than I'd ever seen him, hopping from foot to foot, nervous energy renewed, chewing his nails.

"Mostly rule breakers." He said. "Fight starters, thieves. Maybe tried to settle shit without appealing to the adjudicators. Skipped-out on a Tag. Who the fuck knows?"

Staring up at those men and women – stripped naked, black and blue, lashed to their poles with barbed cables, necks sagging, shoulders aching – I found myself too exhausted, too disgusted, to even bother asking Nate what the fuck he was talking about.

The crux of it had come through loud and clear.

"Anyone who pisses them off." I said.

Nate nodded, expression wary, and pulled his cap lower over his face.

An even larger crowd was gathered directly outside the gates. They had the look of a picket or protest, but stood in silent rows with arms lowered, a bulging semicircle of quiet indignation, staring in with eyes smouldering. Their gazes were lifted past the bored guards, past the barricades and silent vehicles, past the shanty-buildings clustered like barnacles around the base of the Secretariat. Here an even greater proportion were women, and when I let my senses slip into that subconscious state of information ravening – drinking in every tiny indicator around me, letting my old brain piece it together – I could almost taste their hunger, their sorrow, their desperation. They'd come here to reclaim something they'd lost.

"Moms." Nate said, fussing with the quadbike. "Come to see their kids."

"They get to visit them?"

Nate gave a grim little laugh and shook his head. "Hell, no. Mostly they just... stand here. A week, maybe two. Hoping for a glimpse, some sort of sign, I dunno. Something to show 'em their kids really *are* building that... 'New Tomorrow.' Make them feel better, maybe. Not so guilty."

"They ever get their wish?"

"Uh-uh. Whatever happens in there, it *stays* in there."

"But you used to bring them here. You must have seen the inside."

Nate shrugged. "Parts. Reception garage, fuelling pump. But I tell you this... the New Tomorrow looks kinda the same as the Old Today, and there ain't no hordes of happy kids rushin' about in *there*, either."

I stared across the scene for a long time, letting the misery infuse. Nate lit a cigarette and sat smoking, turning away with overblown discretion every time one of the guards happened to glance our way.

If I'd stopped, if I'd thought about it right then and there, I might have been surprised. For all his posturing, for all his fear and anguish at the Clergy getting their hands on him, here he was. Hadn't raised a word of protest, coming to this place. He'd walked right up to the outskirts of the dragon's den, and sat down outside with his new-found protector and his knightly armour lowered to his ankles.

But I wasn't thinking of that, right then. Call me dumb. I was thinking of the groans from the crucifixes, and the sobs from the mothers, and the silence from inside the compound.

And Bella, briefly. Thinking about Bella, when I should have been focusing on the mission. When I should have been concentrating on—

Don't you fucking give up, soldier.

Sir, no sir, etc etc.

"In London," I said, eventually, "they used to send out Catcher squads. Clergy goons. All armed. Lot of them were women... Maybe the bigwigs thought it'd make things easier. Woman's touch, that sort of thing.

"A lot of the people who survived The Cull ended-up well into the Church anyway. All those broadcasts, every Sunday. Never ceased to amaze me, but I saw it happen all the time. People giving-up their own kids, *shit*. Treated it like a fucking ceremony."

Nate blew a smoke ring. "I was there too. Remember? I seen it."

"Yeah. But did you ever see them with the people who didn't give-in so easy? The ones who... wouldn't let go. Hid their kids. Kept them safe. You ever see that? The Clergy used to call them 'selfish.' You believe that?"

He sighed.

"You ever see the Catcher squads?" I said, feeling strangely angry with him, wanting to press until he snapped. I couldn't work out why.

He shook his head.

"You ever see them kicking down a door, or shooting a screaming woman in the street, or dragging-off kids to the fucking airport and telling the parents they were *dead* if they tried to follow? You ever see that Nate? You ever see that shit, before they brought you over here to ferry the sprogs back and forth?"

He looked away.

The sun dipped below the horizon. A few fires were being built by the more enterprising segments of the crowd. The silence stretched on.

"It's different here," Nate said, after long minutes had eked away. There was... *something* in his voice. Bitterness? Guilt? "All the Klan shit, you know? It's what's *expected*."

"I don't follow."

"Choirboys keep the Klans in order. Oversee disputes. S'what the Adjudies are for. And they... they parcel out guns, sometimes food, sometimes water. And the drugs. They got so much of that shit in there..." he nodded to the Secretariat, and again that *something* in his voice "...it's coming out their fucking asses."

"So they dish it out to all the Klans? Why? Just for... for loyalty?"

"Cos in return they get the *tithe*."

I glanced around the crowd, the tattered clothes, the dirt-smeared tags.

"But these are just scavs. These aren't Klansmen."

"Right again. But they gotta do what the bosses say. They want to eat? They want to stay alive? They don't wanna get skewered on no territory-pole like a fucking shish kebab? Then it's easier to go with the flow. Hand over the youngsters. Believe they going someplace better." He sighed again, staring at the crowd. "You act like a good little scav, you give up your own flesh and blood;

you maybe get an extra ration, maybe a better sleepin'
pitch. Maybe you get promoted to Klansman earlier than
otherwise. And if you're smart, if you figure out that's
the way to the top, then the only way to do it is to... to
make yourself *believe*. You understand? Make yourself
believe it's *right*.

"Self-sacrifice, man. That's what the Klans *do*."

"Can you get inside there?" I said, suddenly tired of it
all, hungry to press-on.

He chewed on the smouldering dogend of his cigarette
for a long time, closed his eyes, reopened them, and
said:

"Snowman's chance in hell. Sorry."

We camped out on the plaza in front of the crucifixes
overnight, warming ourselves at an oil drum fire some
of the desolate women had built, and ate dog food. We
discussed getting inside.

Nate kept asking me why. Why the hell was I doing
this? Why the hell would I go up against the Clergy?

I didn't answer. It wasn't his business. Nobody's but
my own.

Nothing to do with anyone but me. Not Nate, not the
Clergy, not these scavs with their dead eyes.

Just me.

Good soldier. Good soldier.

Except that every time I looked at the building, or at
Nate, or at the sobbing mothers, I ended up thinking
of Bella; sat in that burnt-out pub in Heathrow, with
her bitter glances and don't-fuck-with-me face. Then
hunched over the controls of the plane, shivering and
sweating. Then dead.

Impaled in the middle of a mashed up plane.

By midnight, when Nate's voice was getting croaky from
explaining the ins-and-outs to me, when my eyes were

starting to droop and the stink of his endless cigarettes was all over me, I had a plan.

At two in the morning – give or take – a convoy of AVs entered the compound. Seven in total. Old military models, repainted in sky-blue with scarlet circles, covered from tracked wheels to pintle-weapon roofs in ablative shields and home-made deflectors.

In the lead vehicle, a tall man with a long face, a pale robe, and a strange cap stood with his arms folded, gesturing angrily in heated conversation with someone out of sight beside him. He wore scarlet sunglasses.

Nate almost popped.

"That's Cy," he hissed, shivering. "That's fucking Cy..."

The old man covered his face, lurking in my shadow like a terrified child, peering between his fingers.

As the lumbering machines took the final corner I caught a glimpse of Cy's companion, the unlucky receiver of his displeasure. I felt the skin prickle on my forehead, recognising the muscular man with perfectly white hair – bare chested – whose shoulders were criss-crossed with rank scars like a sergeant's stripes.

"The Mickey." I muttered. "That's the guy who saw us take the tunnel."

Nate moaned quietly, hopping from foot to foot.

The Klansman had a black eye, a foul expression, and a hateful glare reserved just for Cy. They appeared to be arguing, though if I know body language at all – and I *do* – the Mickey wasn't getting anywhere fast.

The Clergy've been tracking me.

Asking questions.

Plotting my movements.

It felt vaguely exhilarating. Almost a *pleasure*, to be hunted, to be second-guessed, to be looked-for but never found. Just like the old days; sneaking and scuttling in the shadows. Staying covert, staying secret. Doing what I'd been sent to do, then melting away.

Don't you fucking give up, soldier!

Sir, no sir! etc etc.

It was an effort to push down the shivery desire for action. I flipped the remaining blanket over the quadbike's body; trusting to the darkness to hide the confused shape. I needn't have bothered. Cy was barely conscious of his surroundings; so busy grilling his unhappy witness that he didn't so much as glance at the crowd.

When he'd calmed down, Nate hazarded that the convoy had returned from the airport. He said that coming home empty-handed wasn't going to help Cy's standing in the Clergy *at all*, and it stood to reason he'd bring a witness back with him. Evidence that he'd been doing his job.

Nate said the Church wasn't exactly renowned for being forgiving. Not towards guys who'd slaughtered entire companies of Choirboys, trashed functioning aeroplanes and rendered one of the three Clergy airports useless.

I told Nate: thanks for the good news.

He didn't mention how the angry-looking Cardinal would certainly also have noticed that *he* hadn't been amongst the dead. He didn't mention that the white-haired Mickey would certainly have reported an elderly black man clinging to a stranger, on the back of a clapped-out quadbike, entering the Queens Midtown tunnel.

He didn't mention that he'd just become an official enemy of the Church, right up there beside me, with the added epithet of 'traitor.'

But it was all over his face and heavy in his voice.

Somewhere deep inside me – somewhere petty-minded

and sadistic, which didn't really understand its own motivations – I *liked* that he was worried.

Something about him.

Oh yeah, one other thing:

As the last vehicle in the convoy growled its way through the razor wire fences, just before the guards slid the tracked walls back into place, a group of the women in the crowd broke free from the shadows and rushed the guards, sobbing as they ran.

The guards shot a few – almost perfunctorily, just to prove they *could* – but did their best to keep the others alive; clubbing at them with rifle-stocks and batons. I almost mistook it for mercy.

But at first light, as the sun broke over the sooty limits of the river, there were six new bodies dangling and shrieking at the tops of the flagpoles, and three more turning black on a pyre inside the gates.

They were called the Red Gulls, though in defiance of all naming-logic their headquarters were black. *Very* black. Black in the same way the ocean is damp.

The whole thing was built of wood, laid down over shattered concrete. Cut and fixed lumber, crudely planed and inexpertly joined, sealed with sinuous rivulets of tar and vomit-patterns of wax, draped in layers of black bin-liners. Ultimately the whole thing looked not so much constructed as congealed; spreading out in a great glossy puddle like a drying cowpat.

Just as Nate had warned, the far perimeters were a tangled morass of razor wire, crude trip-alarms and grotesque territory-markers with picked-clean skeletons skewered at their peaks. It was almost embarrassingly easy to slink past.

The whole wretched thing stood near the heart of Central Park, set to one side of what had once been the great lawn, and where the twisted trees loomed out of the dappled sunlight they seemed to tangle and grow *into* the weird construction, as if its boundaries had little meaning. As if it intended to spread as far as it could, without human aid.

I worked my way towards a knotted entrance on the quietest face, using the shadows of the tree trunks and my own raggedy camouflage to avoid the traffic heading in and out in all other directions. To the south of the park the Clergy ruled absolute, so it didn't surprise me in the slightest that of all the scavs and muscular Klansmen striding out on their business – red feathers rising like spines from their scalps – hardly any did so in this direction. The guard at the door looked positively catatonic.

I opened his neck from the side – punching in and cutting forwards – oozing from the shadows before he could even call a challenge. I dumped the body on a natural shelf above the doorway, formed by a crook in a mouldy tree, and oozed inside like a ghost.

I *love* this shit.

Prowling. Slinking like an ethereal fucking tiger. Corridor by corridor, beaver-like nest chambers crossed in a doubtful blur, shadows adhered-to, every passing footstep used to mask my own.

It was beautiful.

The Red Gulls were the biggest Klan in the city, besides the Clergy itself.

This was important to my plan.

Years ago they'd put down a concerted coup by some long-gone uptown gang calling itself the NeverNevers, who thought they could take a crack at the Choirboys' power-base. Ever since the Gulls had been John-Paul's most favoured underlings. Permitted to spread through territories on the Clergy's own doorstep they were gifted with all the best weapons, all the choicest scav and all the craziest narcotics.

Maybe the boost made them sloppy. Like a spider invading a rabbit-warren, I was deep inside the labyrinth of sleeping chambers, food-stores, scav-holds and moonshine stills before the so-called 'guards' even became a problem. At a thickset corridor intersection Gulls stood posted at regular intervals (they might as well have pinned-up a sign saying *'you're near something important'*), and for all the adrenal shivers and subconscious hunger for violence I was forced to consider something a little more subtle.

So I put my head down and walked past them, confident as you like.

Just another scav.

For the record, this sort of scam works more often than you'd think. Trust me on this. Afghanistan, Peru, even once in North Korea... You put you head down and walk like you're *supposed* to be there. Doesn't matter what you look like, where you're going.

Note that it doesn't work *all the time*.

Like for example when you're just passing the last red-feather-wearing wanker in the row, stepping out into the sweaty cavern at the heart of the rickety palace, and some despicable little piece of *shit* somewhere starts shouting about the south entrance being unguarded.

And then, a beat later, about poor old Crocksy lying with his windpipe torn all to shit.

Situation like that, suddenly *everyone's* hefting a gun. Suddenly everyone's wondering who the guy that just walked past actually *was*. Suddenly everyone's on edge, and shouting, and running up and down, and the whole fucking place is *shaking* from the noise.

The shutters came down in my head.

The old brain took over.

I stepped into the cavern and cut a hole in the face of the guy shouting at me.

Didn't stop. Heard him screaming on the floor. Moved on.

Another guy running my way, pistol gripped tight, calling for help. Stabbed him in the stomach, lifted upwards under the ribs.

The way to a man's heart...

His pistol-arm stuck out under my shoulder, already going limp, so I hooked a finger under the trigger-guard, beside his own, and took out the next suicidal motherfucker in line. Forehead splatter. Red froth on the air. Singed gull-feathers.

Something inside me, howling in joy.

I helped myself to the gun, letting its owner empty out his guts on my shoes. Echoes still flapping in the air. Shocked faces and sprinting legs. Stop for a situation recon.

Know everything
Cover the angles.

It was an audience chamber, like a medieval throne-room. Hordes of scavs and favoured women rushing out by other exits, hooting and spronking. Up the steps of a raised dais stood a succession of lieutenants and ranking Klansmen, each one in colours more gaudy than the next. Feathers, beads, bare skin with crimson tattoos, gull-feet headdresses and hands heavy with Uzis, AKs, machetes.

At the top sat a big fucking guy in a chair. He looked sort of startled.

I smiled at him.

First step. Ducked under a messy punch designed to slow me down whilst the other goons got themselves loaded-up. Used the numbers against them; kept the greasy little shit with the knuckleduster between us.

Told him: "Scuse me." Put a knife through his ribs (felt the blade notch – *shit*) and spat pistol fire over his collarbone, taking out the obese sod with a Kalash' two steps up. Then turned and kicked – boot to the throat of the punk behind. Scamper three steps higher in the muddle of limbs and shouts. No one wants to risk a shot. Too many bodies packed together.

No one but me.

Shot a lanky youngster holding a .44. Probably would have broken his wrist anyway.

The ranking Klanners moved in, boxing me off from the honcho on the throne, shoving and snarling, letting space open-up for weapons to bear.

I let the knife play random patterns, spun behind the guard of a dog-faced woman with a fucking *sword* in her hand (amateur!) and hit step number four.

Shot out the knees of the biggest feather-wearing arsehole of the lot. Wasted another two rounds on his ham-hands when he smirked at the pain in his legs and tried to open up with his cute machine pistols anyway.

Time ticking by.

Ammo all gone. Bitch with a sword hacking at air.

Space blurring.

I shifted tack, rushing the downed giant and using my momentum; stamping on his shoulder to vault up (bloody Hollywood antics – amateurish! Pathetic!), and pushed him down the slope on the rebound, toppling like a bowling ball towards the indignant youngsters at my back.

Satisfying shouts of alarm and pain as the steps cleared

behind me.

I came down on top of the last goon, the last guard, the right hand man. Small but fast, wiry as shit. My landing was messy; knocking us both down, tangling and tussling on the floor with knives pressed together. I felt a blade-tip kiss my cheek and angle up towards my eye. Ignored it. Pressed in towards his sides; a slow squeeze against the resistance of his arm, forcing him back, knife entering like a slow-mo javelin.

I stamped on him as I stood, and blinked the blood out of my eye.

And there was the boss. Seated. Eyeing me.

Impassive, the cool motherfucker.

"Who," he said, and everyone else had gone still, and nobody wanted to shoot me because they'd hit *him*, and everything stopped, and the silence was thicker than the noise had ever been. "The *fuck*. Do you *think*. You *are*?"

So I slapped him playfully on his big forehead, and shouted: "Tag!"

Fun for the whole family and all part of the plan.

CHAPTER TWELVE

The Tag went back a year or four.

The Tag was one of those little things the Clergy put in place as soon as it was obvious no other motherfucker was ever going to big enough to kick them off the top spot. The Tag was... a tradition. A ritual, if you want. A way for the robe-wearing arseholes to take charge of every dispute, every promotion, every powerplay.

Above and beyond all other things, The Tag was *entertainment*.

The way Nate had explained it to me, sitting in the dark outside the United Nations was:

"You're a chicken. You spent your whole goddamn life afraid of the wolves. What you want right now is freedom. Get away from the meat eating shitheads. Spend some quality time without carnivore assholes watching your back.

"But you know what? What you want *so much more* than that, is to have a go at being a wolf *too*.

"Tag's how you do it."

The Tag was a pretty simple concept, all things considered. A tough sort of justice: survival of the fittest with a lopsided twist to favour the overdog. I guess when you're living in a pit, the rules *need* to be as nasty as everything else, which is scant comfort for the underdog.

That'd be me.

In a nutshell:

One man, or woman, challenged another. Rules varied from here to there on the nature of the challenge, but generally you're looking at punching, slapping, kicking, hair-pulling, whatever. Something publicly humiliating; an affront to the challengee's dignity. He or she was permitted to defend themselves by any means – as if in self-defence – up to and including muscle-bound lieutenants with machetes, machineguns and magnums.

Heh. For all the good it did.

But as soon as the challenge was *made*, everything stopped. No more violence allowed. Break the rules and the Clergy Adjudicators would be down like a ton of bricks.

The challenger was escorted away, told a place and time, and left to prepare whilst the disgruntled VIP who'd been tagged set about assembling a hunting party.

Five people. Any weapons, vehicles or gadgets they wanted, which amounted to whatever stuff they could get their hands on.

Five people, drugged to the gills, with territorial knowledge on *their* side and not a scruple in sight.

At the allotted time the challenger and the hunting party were placed in position, normally beneath the gaze of a thunderous crowd. In a world without TV, *this* was the Superbowl.

The challenger was stripped of all guns, tools and blades. An electrical tag was pinned beneath his skin (joyously provided by the friendly neighbourhood Clergy), and with all due ceremony, gravity and cheer, he was told to fuck off and get running.

The hunters were released five minutes later.

When you initiated a Tag, there was only one rule worth knowing:

Stay alive for two hours; you've won. Everything that belonged to the loser now belongs to you. Power. Privileges. Property. Rank.

I got the impression it didn't happen often.

And just for the record, just to make the whole shitty thing even more wonderful, it was overseen from start to finish by representatives of – take a wild guess – the

Apostolic Church of the Rediscovered Dawn.

The cleverest thing I'd done – and if I'm honest it wasn't until afterwards that Nate explained why it was such a smart move – was to wade-in heavy and cause some serious collateral along the way. At the time I'd done it as a path-of-least-resistance thing: I wanted to get to the boss, his goons were in the way – *QED*.

But no. I'd got lucky. It turned out that killing a Klansman in the normal course of life carried an immediate penalty of 'Oh-God-Make-The-Pain-Stop-Please-Please-Please' death. It was supposed to prevent gloryhunters from killing their way up to the top without effort, to stop disgruntled scavs getting mutinous around their overlords, and to deter internal arguments from spilling-over. It worked too – most of the time – and the only ones exempt were the Klanbosses themselves.

Which meant I'd accidentally carried-off a neat spot of playing the odds. If I *won* the Tag I'd *be* the new Boss, and they couldn't hold me accountable for all the chop-socky I'd caused en route. And if, Nate said, I *lost*, then it didn't matter then either.

I scowled. "How come?"

"'Cos you'll be dead anyway."

I'd crippled, killed or incapacitated more of my potential hunters than seemed fair or decent. I'd wiped out the Klanboss's top dogs in one fell swoop. I'd left him with an untested rabble to try and catch me, and put the fear of god up them at the same time. They'd seen what I could do. They'd hesitate, I hoped, to corner me alone.

And, frankly, I needed every advantage I could get.

All this just to get into the UN building. It had better be fucking worth it.

They kept us waiting until ten o'clock. It meant that when things kicked off, the two hour limit would expire at midnight. I guess they thought it was more dramatic.

I wasn't about to complain. It gave me the rest of the day to sleep and prepare, whilst *they* – the Gulls – scuttled about like headless chickens, conspiring and scheming, treating the wounded and carting-off the dead.

All through the day, Nate kept a nonchalant sort of 'watch' while I kipped, nestled up in a bed of dry leaves beneath a footbridge, on an out-of-the-way path in the park. He shuffled off once or twice to chat to the little knots of Red Gull scavs living in bivouacs in other parts of the greenery, keeping himself out of sight of any Clergy passing through, and seemed to be warming to the role of information gatherer. I like to think he saw himself as a duellist's 'Number Two', preparing for his benefactor's moment of pistol-waving tribulation... but frankly behind his open face and warming smile it was fucking impossible to work out *what* he was thinking, let alone what historical-romantic notions he was dreaming-up.

He mumbled a lot, just under his breath, and had started to sweat too much.

All very weird.

As I slept, I dreamed of the signal on the computer in the Vauxhall Cross building – the glowing word PANDORA, beaming bright. I dreamed of Bella impaled on her spike, shouting at me to stop being so selfish and *think*, dammit, about what she'd told me. I dreamed of Nate, laughing, and John-Paul Rohare Baptiste, dancing through it all like a daddy-long-legs, battering himself against polished glass to reach the shining light outside.

The light was red, and *sticky*.

I dreamed of somebody else too, but the face I should

have memorised years before had become a fuzzy collection of features in my mind, and the figure dissolved the instant I reached out to grab it.

Nate woke me at eight. He'd caught a couple of rats off the banks of the stagnant Turtle Pond and sat cooking them, not once complaining at doing all the hard work, rambling away blithely on the events of the day, apparently not troubled by whether I was listening or not.

I was.

He said the whole territory was in uproar. He said the scavs were all but hysterical at the news of what I'd got up to that morning, and it was a toss-up as to whether said hysteria was based on delight or disgust.

He said no one had ever heard of a Klanboss getting himself Tagged before. He said already the other tribes in the area – the StripLims to the east and the Globies up on the edges of Harlem – were choked with gossip and book-running. Already barter-wagers were hot business all across the Island, he said, and scavs from Klans he'd never even *heard* of had been showing up in the En-Tees all round the edges of the Red Gull patch, to stand about and murmur in low voices about the 'Big Tag', hoping to catch a glimpse of the action.

He said it was big news.

"You, *ah*..." He coughed awkwardly, and twitched. He looked unwell. "You sure you wanna do this?"

I told him, of course I did. How the hell else was I going to get into the UN building?

"Yeah, yeah... Yeah." He coughed again. "Only, *ah*... That Cardinal asshole, Cy. He was up here 'round noon." His voice shook.

"Did he see you?"

"You think I'd be talking to you if he did? Shit, no!

Stayed well outta his way. You live in En-Why any lengtha time, you get good at making sure folks ignore your ass. Like... There was this one time I got stuck with..."

"Nate." I interrupted the tangent before it got started, troubled by his uncomfortable manner. Even in the midst of his most enthused ramblings, he'd never seemed quite so twitchy. "You were saying. About Cy."

"Yeah. Sure. H-had himself a little chat to Scrim, that's all. In-depth, man. *Intense*."

"Who's 'Scrim'?"

Nate looked at me like I was stupid. "Motherfucker you tagged. Top dog."

"Fair enough." I poked the rat in the fire. "Stupid name, but fair enough. So what did our friend Cy have to say for himself?"

Nate shook his head, eyes rolling weirdly. "Pass. No way was I getting close enough to hear. But you want me take a wild stab, I'd say he's keeping an eye. Knows it's you. I mean, shit, it don't take a genius! Raggedy-assed stranger shows up at LaGuardia, goes through a pack of Choirboys like a razor. Next day you got witnesses see the same guy heading through Queens on a quad. And *next* day, Mister 'Nobody-Knows-Who-The-Hell-He-Is' not only gets himself balls-deep in the Red goddamn Gulls, but slaps a challenge on Big Scrim.

"You think Cy ain't gonna make the connection? C'mon! He *knows*. He knows it's gonna be *you* out there tonight."

"But you said this shit is sacred, right? You said nobody else gets to interfere."

"And that's the truth. But that don't stop our pal the Cardinal from helping the odds. Clergy got themselves every killing toy in the world holed-up over there." He nodded east, towards the unseen slab of the Secretariat.

His hands were shaking. "They got every brand of... of *chem* with a name, and twice as many without.

"I hate to say it, *most* guys, running a Tag, they got less hope than a snowball in hell. But *you*...? Up against the Gulls? And them tooled-up by the Choir?

"Shee-it!"

I let this sink in.

"I see," I said.

Ten o'clock. I stood and waited, tensed, beneath a canopy of spindle-fingered trees. Beside me the stagnant water sucked at the south bank of the Turtle Pond, on the fringe of what had once been 79th street and was now a crippled lane of rubble; its tarmac long since plundered for the construction of the Gulls' shanty nest.

I'd filtered out the noise of the crowd by now, but the force of it was still there at the back of my head, nudging against my concentration. I'd spent an hour flicking through my tattered map, and a series of notes Nate had gathered from the scavs nearby; all of them covered in spidery descriptions that didn't help at all (*'gud rats!'* and *'watr mostly clean'*). I had a vague idea where I'd go. I wasn't stupid enough to let myself believe I had a plan; that I was *ready*. In situations like this, there's no such thing as 'ready'. There's just people who can wing it, and people who can't.

I let the instincts take over, like shrugging on an old coat; patched and frayed and stinking, but so comfortable you can't imagine ever taking it off.

Vehicles rumbling nearby. The five Gulls glared at me, weapons bristling in every direction. Four blokes, one woman. That same crazy chick who had the sword before, but the others were just faces. Muscular, armoured-up, ready to play. All except Big Scrim. *He* stood out; encased in flashy sports gear and rubber body-armour, holding the Clergy's tracker-device like a novelty TV aerial in the back of an open-top jeep.

Everywhere I looked, Clergy.

Clergy guns. Clergy AVs. Cardinal Cy whispering to Scrim, his four goons cross-armed behind him, pointing and directing, throwing glances my way beneath hooded eyelids. Silent communication between us, crackling like static.

Twat.

The crowd gets noisier. Arms slap against my shoulders, people shout and laugh, something painful digs beneath the skin of my neck.

The tracer.

Stay calm.

Breathe.

Are you ready, soldier?

Sir, no sir!

Well done, son. Right answer. Now get goi—

A flare went up.

I ran.

Trees whipping past. Branches scraping cheeks already sliced and puffy from last night's mêlée. Legs pounding like pneumatics.

It's almost a joy to open-up. All cylinders. Let go. Feel the burn.

Know everything.

Cover the angles.

Their advantages: Speed, local knowledge, the tracker in my neck, more guns than a survivalist all-comers WorldCon and enough drugs to make a pharmaceutical multinational look like a primary school chemistry kit.

So. One thing at a time.

Get off the track. Confound the vehicles.

I took the verge beside the street at a vault, darted through more trees; heading for the dark blot of stone ahead. Heading west, I think, over slimy husks of rotting trunks. Something man-made looming between the boles. An escape from the preternatural chaos of the park with its forested wilderness. Too many shadows here. Too many unknowns.

I paused for a second, shaking my muscles down, taking the time to stretch whilst I caught my breath, then onwards. Up steps greasy with lichen and mould, past knots of scavs hoping for a good view, clamouring in the shadow of a colossal building. The poor buggers recoiled and ran when they saw they'd got their wish, terrified I'd bring-down the Gulls on their viewing spot.

A second flare went up behind me – blood red and baleful – and I stumbled without pausing through a shattered doorframe into a great emptiness.

It took my eyes a while to adjust, and as I groped the echoes of my clumsy movements suggested a vast void all around me; the tinkling of broken glass and crunch of rubble underfoot. Shapes swam into focus. Button-like eyeballs regarded me. Brass signs and red ropes.

A fucking great elephant, staring down. Someone had snapped off its trunk.

AKELEY HALL OF AFRICAN MAMMALS

...a banner read; plucked out of the shadows in my peripheral vision by the overstretched blur of the instinctive training.

Trust your perceptions.

Don't think. Just react.

Trust yourself.

Go!

Reality swam and reformed, and I'd barely noticed myself rushing up stairs that folded back and forth in concertina ribbons, up the sides of a great hallway, passing glass cabinets crammed with taxidermy's greatest trophies and fossilised impressions screwed to walls beside plastic plaques.

Engines growled in the distance, rushing nearer, audible through crack-holed windows, arched and medieval. Raised voices.

Fuckers.

On the fourth floor a frieze of limp connections and cable-like structures swam together in my mind to form great prehistoric beasts: fleshless and comical in their gawky poses, tangled amidst steel supports and gaudily-coloured waxwork models.

In my state of mind, adrenalised to hell and incapable of rationalising through the tsunami of reactions, finding dinosaurs on the fourth floor of a vast building did not seem worthy of remark. Just another bunch of dumb bastards, wiped out before their time.

Up here, scav kit was everywhere. Blankets and cushions concealed lazily between titanic ribs, small piles of combustible rubbish pulled off the displays, heaped in odd corners for tinder and late-night fires. Beside me a glass cabinet containing rows of fossilised teeth had been partially shattered; torn away from the wall, left jagged with razor panels incised. On the other side of the room someone had used the Apatosaurus as a toilet, and the whole chamber was thick with flies and dust.

Voices spiralled up from the great hall far below, shouts and curses followed by the conspicuous silence of people being quiet. I peered cautiously over the rim of the balcony, hoping the radio marker didn't provide a vertical reading. Sure enough, ghostly shapes moved in the light-dappled lobby; oozing from cover to cover with the exaggerated care of those who think their enemies are close.

Cat and Mouse. Rule number one:

Don't be the mouse.

Sir, yes sir etc etc.

So I picked up the remains of the cabinet with all the care I could muster, winced at every tinkle of fragmented glass, and pitched it with a roar over the balcony's edge.

The snarl took on a violent life of its own in the acoustic void of the stairwell, modulating musically with the xylophonic traumas of the cabinet.

Someone below reacted fast. The poor sod.

Automatic gunfire stitched the open stairwell with muzzlefire and noise, and then nothing but glass. Like champagne. Like watery froth, dazzling.

Shattering.

Tumbling.

Slicing.

The sound was shocking. A calamitous crash that resounded in every dimension and shook the air.

Then nothing but silence.

Then screams that bubbled away into gasps, as whoever was underneath the cabinet rustled off their jagged little coil. Then more silence.

Then just the moans of shocked survivors, cut to shreds.

And the soft sound of me, running like hell.

I'd stopped twice on the way down from the dinosaur exhibits. The few fractured shards of rationality still spinning inside my head had decided I was inside a museum, and the one thing museums *always* have is an enormous floor plan in every corner.

That was stop 'Number One.'

In a display of the Woodlands Indians, in the far western wing of the third floor (within easy sprinting distance of a stairwell which – I was reliably assured – led down to the side exit on West 77th street), I crouched and bled.

This was the result of stop Number Two.

Thick rivulets down my spine, oozing under the hem of my trousers and down the backs of my legs. Didn't matter. I was in control.

Taking my time. Calm. Breathing well.

The sensible savage.

I think somehow, somewhere inside, I felt *indignant*, too. Like: *how dare these fuckers chase me? How dare they? How dare they outnumber me?*

Me!

It was a useful emotion.

This was *home*, in a way. Worming through the darkened corridors of an embassy in some exotic place, waiting for the moment to strike. Lurking, stalking, closing in.

Or letting *them* come to me.

This time the arseholes came mob-handed. They'd closed on the tracker beacon with admirable speed, slinking along open corridor corners to avoid ambushes, sidestep-by-sidestep. I could hear their progress with practiced acuity: three together on point then another (a softer tread, probably the woman) taking rearguard.

Only four. The other one was staked-out in the lobby, crushed and sliced-up by the glass cabinet. Twenty minutes into this nasty little game, and one fucker down already.

It would be dishonest to pretend I wasn't enjoying

myself.

I could hear them beyond the last corner of the twisting hall.

"Strong signal," one grunted, voice terse. "Directly ahead. Other end of the room."

An arm blurred in the shadows.

Something small flying, bouncing, rolling, then—

Light and smoke and noise, and three heavy figures springing-out to let rip into the phosphor distraction. I couldn't even see the weapons; only feel the drumming of the air, the epileptic nightmare of endless automatic muzzleflare, and the quiet smugness on the bright faces of the attackers.

They were standing so close I could almost have touched them and, for the record, they were shooting in completely the wrong direction.

I waited until they'd walked further into the room. The one with the tracker grunted in satisfaction, claiming the marker was stationary and they *must* have hit me. They took up swaggering stances before the darkened 'Iroquois' display – now reduced to shattered plastic and crumbled wax – and took a few more potshots into the rubble, just to be sure.

Behind them, I ducked out from beneath the cosy chickenwire-supported wigwam of the Ojibwa tribe (never heard of them) and ghosted back along the empty corridor.

Divide and conquer.

The woman stood with her back to me, pressed into a pool of darkness, nervous at the cacophony her comrades were throwing-up from round the corner. She had a mini-Uzi in each hand – compact little toys with folded stocks and extra-long mags – and the pale curve of her neck was perfectly caught by the dim moonlight of the arched windows, like a ski slope. Waiting for an avalanche.

Carefully, using swaddled fabrics I'd stolen from my pals in the Ojibwa, I palmed the long shard of glass I'd used to slice the electric tag out from the skin of my shoulder (stop number two, remember?), I'd hidden it carefully amongst the dummy-display of the Iroquois, letting the morons walk right past me.

Some people might call that 'cheating'.

Don't you fucking give up, soldier!

Sir, no sir etc etc.

Cat and Mouse. Rule number two:

Even the biggest cat picks-off mice one by one.

The woman had the good grace to die quietly, and she'd even warmed-up the grips of my two brand new Uzis. That's consideration for you.

Half an hour later, the others were getting frustrated.

I'd left the museum and headed south, careful not to double-back on the park. This whole lightless neighbourhood was their turf, and the more advantages I could give myself, the better. Right now that meant staying out from the moon-dappled weirdness of the trees, hugging the right-angles and solidity of the West Side.

I turned off down 74th and found a tenement block; took the fire escape up to the top floor and bust my way inside as quietly as I could. Still no sounds of pursuit – and after all why *should* there be? The marker pressed under my skin was their only ace; and now that was nothing but a bloody shard of circuitry in the pocket of a mannequin. It was almost tempting to sit out the two hours here, reclining on the unscavved sofa in some long-dead New Yorker's grotty little apartment.

But.

Think. Cover the angles.

But other people had surely cut out the trackers before.

The fuckos must have a Plan B.

But.

But if they have the marker, couldn't they just claim victory anyway?

'Proof of kill'?

But, but, but.

And the biggest shitter of them all:

The End.

By midnight I had to present myself to a member of the Clergy. That's how it finished. That's how they knew who'd won or lost.

They'd given me a perfunctory description of places I could look: slums on the En-Tee border zones, territory markers down to the south, Clergy-run checkpoints. With each item on the list, spoken through softly clenched teeth by the pale-faced Cardinal Cy, I'd cast a quick glance at Nate – hiding in the crowd, face shadowed inside a hood. He'd simply shaken his head, over and over.

The Clergy weren't going to make this easy for me. They wouldn't be waiting to shake my hand, tell me well done. If they *were* waiting at all, it was with a bullet.

Think it through.

Cover the angles.

Which just left the park. Right back to the start. Presenting myself to the crowd and the bastard Cardinal himself, standing up there on the podium beside the turtle-pond with his four hulking Choirboy guards and his stupid ruby-red glasses, to *show* I'd done it.

Easy as that.

Big Scrim and his two remaining goons, they knew it

as well as I did. They knew I'd be scurrying out from the undergrowth, back in the park, at five minutes before midnight. And that meant all they had to do was wait.

Shit.

Cat and mouse. Rule number one.

So I plundered anything useful from the apartment – an out-of-date band-aid for my shoulder, a vac-sealed packet of salami on a shelf, a couple of rusty kitchen-knives in plastic sheaths, and went out to find them. Followed the sounds of engines rumbling. I took the rooftops where I could; a raggedy tabby going arm-over-arm, pouncing across alleyways and ghosting up empty fire escapes, leaving a trail of terrified scavs, their sleep disturbed by a prowling monster.

I found the Gulls hunched in the back of the biggest AV, far below the roof ledge of a fire station. Voices rose from below the closed hood, and I worked my way down with the utmost care; letting go of everything, letting something unevolved and primitive – but so much *better* at this shit – swim to the forefront of my mind.

I climbed down to meet them. An ape with Uzis.

At the foot of the building an alleyway cut out onto the main street, and there I nestled myself into the bricks, unfolding the stock of one of the tiny guns to give myself at least a fighting chance of hitting something.

I could see them clearly, shadowed by the moonlight like patches of cut-out card.

I could hear them.

Both of them. Two guys.

So where's number 3?

Scrim was busy, bent down over the scrawnier of his two warriors. Jacking a hypodermic needle into the other man's neck, holding him tight in a vicious headlock as he grunted and pleaded. I found myself entranced, all but forgetting to poise myself for that critical moment, that perfect shot.

"You fuck! You stay *still*. You *fuck*!" Scrim kept up a volley of abuse, squeezing the plunger with a sly grin. "You gonna *help* us, boy. You gonna *find* that limey shit. You gonna track his *ass*."

The little man jerked his head and finally pulled away with a howl. Scrim watched him, smiling quietly, clambering down to the driver's seat.

The man shivered for a moment, sweat prickling along his forehead. I held my breath, wondering what weird shit Doctor Scrim had prescribed, what narcotic treats the all-conquering Clergy had handed-over to help their pet Gulls finish me off.

The little man grunted. Frowned.

Then...

Changed.

He sat up. His head moved a little too quickly. Darting, like a bird's: from position to position with no intermediary movement. He drooled. He closed his eyes.

The thing inside me, the primitive 'self' in control, gave a little grunt of recognition.

The little man *sniffed*.

And licked his lips.

Scrim plucked something silvery-red from his pocket and dangled it above the man's nose. He tilted his head to taste it like a wolf on a scent, lapping at it, smearing it across his cheeks, then closed his eyes.

Scrim re-pocketed the tiny shape. Didn't take a genius to figure what it was.

The tracker. The tracker covered in my blood.

I shivered, despite myself.

The little man smiled. Sniffed again. Pointed his finger.

Opened his eyes.

Moaned.

Stared right at me.

Fuck.

I was already running, I think, though I didn't realise it. Engines growling to life behind me, a voice shouting "There! There!", radios crackling in some distant world.

I heard someone say, through thick static:

"Yeah. Roj that. Got him."

And then the sniper *shitbag* on the roof above, the third Gull, who'd been waiting like an angler poised over bait, waiting for the dumb psycho to try and turn the tables, opened fire and blew my fucking ear off.

Things rushed past without shape. Everything seemed to throb; the whole world bulging in time to the pain inside my head.

It hurt like a bitch, and I hadn't even had the time to poke and prod at it yet; to see how bad it was. In the mean time I was letting myself get good and freaked, imagining the worst.

I think I could still hear okay, though frankly nothing much came through except the throbbing and the engines. *Always* the engines. It felt like they'd been chasing me forever, though I guess it was more like an hour. Maybe more. I'd stop and look at my watch, if stopping wasn't tantamount to getting dead quickly.

The *me* doing the thinking – the instinctive snarling primate bastard I was taught to *let out* in situations like this – howled and yelped at the pain, fighting to scratch at the torrent pouring down my neck.

The *me* inside – rational, detached, cold, keeping the monkey-man in control... He *loved* it.

Such focus!

Such *sensation*!

Don't you fucking give up, soldier!

I ran like a steam train. Like a bloody Duracell bunny, with an amphetamine volcano up its furry arse. Like an animator's run-cycle stuck on a fast-forward loop. The same movements over and over, with a background cyclorama tumbling by and nothing but the *throb, throb, throb* to accompany the slapping of my feet. Puddles. Cracked tarmac. Weed-strewn sidewalks.

What I'm getting at is, I ran like a *robot*. Never tiring, never *feeling*. I ran until I was sure my heart would pop, and smiled through frothing teeth and kept going.

Fuck it, I kept thinking. *Fuck it all.*

Down tight alleyways. Over dumpsters, through drifts of shitty litter. Sharp corners. Over wire fences and down labyrinthine passages. The vehicle-roar came and went, bashing and smashing at intersections, voices raised in curses.

Hot breath, burning my lungs.

The AV couldn't keep up. It kept trying to double-round, to sneak ahead; headlights blazing then jerking off on some random course. They might have had some luck, if I hadn't been a contrary bastard. If I hadn't been changing my mind about what direction to run every five minutes.

The third man had a bike. Some suped-up Japanese travesty, whining like a prepubescent dragonfly, and *he* had no trouble sticking to me; negotiating alleys too tight for the four-wheeler. I took him down circuitous switchbacks and wide avenues, letting the skittish scavs confuse him, hiding behind dark corners and doubling-back every time he scorched past. Earning ten minute respites here and there, curled-up in dark rooms with terrified squatters moaning beneath soiled sleeping-bags. But he was good. Give him his due; he turned on a penny and came straight back the instant the sniffer-freak on the AV caught the scent, headlight tracking like a laser-sight, rubber squealing.

It would be fair to say – in fact it would be a royal bloody understatement – that I got fed up with him. The bike was enclosed like a sleek little turtle with riot-shields and bullet-proof plex; caroming off angled walls that should have unseated him, slipping through the oil drum fires I pulled-down in my wake like a galleon through fog. And yeah, maybe he couldn't shoot me through the balustrades of shielding; but it worked both ways, and every time I found some perilous vantage point – dangling from a low-hanging escape ladder, peering like Oscar the Grouch out of a scav-nest dumpster – to open up with the Uzis and riddle him with lead, all it achieved was to let him know where I was.

He was trying to make road kill. Exhaust me, flush me out in the open. Re-curved scythe-blades on the bike's front mudguard, ankle-breakers poking like twisted spokes from both wheels.

He was running me down, and he was fucking *good* at it.

So eventually what I did was: I stopped running.

Stood in full view.

Waited.

(Took a moment to glance at my watch. 23:13hrs, yank-time. *Not out of the woods yet, boyo.*)

He came round the corner like a flaming bullet, and pulled-up with unnecessary flashiness, propping himself on the far leg so I couldn't even blast open his knees.

Cautious little cocksucker.

I willed him to get on with it before the AV caught us

up.

He laughed behind his dusty shield and shouted:

"Getting *tired*, little limey?"

I opened fire. For all the good it did.

He gunned the whiny engine like every mosquito in the universe shouting in unison, blurring tyres snagging at the floor with a smoky blast of inertia, and came for me.

Bullets punching worthless craters in the glass.

Laughing.

Closing the gap.

Scythe-blades looming.

It was all deeply melodramatic. I rolled my eyes, took three steps backwards – down the flight of stairs lurking in the moonless shadows directly behind me – and lay down.

He didn't see *that* one coming.

"The fu–?"

The stupid little prick went hurtling over my head, angled in mid-air, hit the wall of the subway stairwell, and just sort of...

Came apart.

No flashy fireballs or smoke-drenched detonations. Just a noise like a big cockroach, cracking under a swat, and a *lot* of debris.

He was gurgling nastily when I walked away – like maybe he'd broken his back or something – and I should probably have put him out of his misery.

Paint me bothered.

The AV found me fifteen minutes later. The scrawny little freak doped-up on whatever military-grade tracking drugs Scrim had dished-out – clung to the roof like a surfer, rapping on the glass and snarling inarticulately, directing the Klan boss's crazed steering. Again with the sodding circling-round, slipping along too-tight alleyways. It felt good to begin with. Rushing past their clumsy attempts to get ahead, disappearing into the shadows to clamber up on this or that fire-escape, pausing to catch my bearings, trying to head back towards the park. It was time to begin the home-run.

It took me a fair old while to realise they were herding me. They were smarter than I thought.

I came upon an office block – nothing special; redbrick and shattered windows – with a door hanging open on a narrow stairwell. Sick and tired of the growl of engines, I rabbitted up the first few flights without any trouble, pausing to vomit discreetly before pushing myself onwards. Somewhere near floor five – or maybe six – a particularly large scav wearing Gull colours tried to axe me in the head, yelling for me to get the hell away from his wife.

There was an inflatable sex-doll on the floor next to him, but it didn't seem like the right time to point this out. I shoved the Uzi up his nostril until he got the message and backed off, then carried on upwards towards the roof whilst he noisily comforted his wife' below.

On the roof, I puked again. The throbbing in my ear was jacking about with my sense of direction, and it didn't help when the moonlit city put itself together bit-by-bit inside my topsy-turvy bearings.

I was so far west of the park I could see the tiny fishing punts on the Hudson, beyond the tangle of docks and quays spread out below me. Taller buildings rose to my left and right – faint lights glimmering inside where innocent scavs struggled to get by with some semblance of a *life*.

It was actually sort of beautiful. If it hadn't been about

a mile in the wrong direction I might have paused to appreciate it.

There were no roofs to leap across to here. No secondary stairways to scamper back down.

And, if I'm honest, no energy to go on. The thing inside me curled up and went to sleep, exhausted, and left me alone. Only human. Outnumbered and outgunned.

Trapped.

"Fuck." I said. "Fuck fuck fuck."

From the open door I heard the huge scav shouting again – "My wife! Tha's my fucking *wife*!" – then a sharp little gunshot to shut him up.

Footsteps up the stairwell.

Time for the endgame.

CHAPTER THIRTEEN

Interlude

If he was honest, Hiawatha wasn't nearly as bemused as he felt he should be.

Or rather, as he felt Rick *should be.*

The name change had only been cosmetic at the beginning. Just a... a symbol of his willingness to embrace all the weirdness, to get stuck-in, to do as the Sachems asked. To drop all the moping angry-native-kid-trying-to-be-white crapola and cuddle up to the Old Ways, like a brand on his soul that said 'On A Mission'.

But it was purely temporary – always had been – and that was the point. When he got home he'd still be 'Rick'.

If. If he got home.

But then again, Rick wouldn't have sailed through the peculiarities of the last couple of days without feeling at least uncomfortable, whereas he – Hiawatha, whoever-the-fuck-he'd become – was taking it all in his stride. The sights and sounds, the little excursions into foggy dreamworlds, the blending of reality and legend.

At the back of his mind Rick ranted and raved about cod-mystical tribal bullshit, whilst at the forefront – in the driving seat – Hiawatha shrugged, listened carefully to the messages on the wind, passed a critical eye over the runic algebra decorating the stars, trailed a finger in bubbling brooks and paid close attention to the splinters of light – and the codes they inferred – on the surface of the water. He didn't even need to keep stopping to smoke dope any more. It was like he'd prised his brain through a sideways gap and – now that it was there – it could stay as long as it wanted.

The cynical part of Rick's mind told him he'd turned into a big dumb stoner expressing the classic idiocy of a drugged-up moron who suddenly decides everything is significant and the whole world resonates on some profound metaphysical level. If he'd been fully in charge, rather than just a morose little echo of a former voice, he would have rolled his eyes.

Hiawatha didn't give a rat's ass.

Hiawatha had suddenly decided everything was significant and the whole world was resonating on a profound metaphysical level.

Overall, Rick/Hiawatha was kind of messed-up in the head.

Out on the road the dream-visions were at least straightforward. Talking trees, rumbling skies, fluttering crows, yadda-yadda; the sort of stuff the tribal myths were packed full of. But here in the city things were different. None of the Haudenosaunee legends spoke of buildings that shuddered like horses dislodging flies; of smog-palls becoming faces and hands; of rats seething from clogged sewers to become corkscrewing whirls of smoke; of tenements making love by starlight – balconies locked together like slippery tongues – and skyscrapers cutting great intestinal scars across the belly of the clouds, where blood and shit oozed into the rain, and huge thunderbirds pecked at the wounds like vultures.

It was kind of cool.

The silver needle in his back pocket hummed to him.

The coloured smoke had brought him here. Just like out on the road; revealing the pothole that wiped-out Ram. All across the suburbs, through spaghetti-like turnpikes and graffiti-plastered tunnels, across the George Washington Bridge then down through the eerily silent West Side, it had hung above the city like an electric net; green and purple, narrowing itself down to a single column of hallucinogenic smoke. He discovered he could see it twice as well when he looked away, concentrating on the corners of his vision; like an optical illusion his brain tried to conceal whenever he stared directly at it.

It took him down Broadway, through Harlem and Morningside, places he'd heard of but never visited. A small part of him felt like he'd missed a chance; like the bustling human ratraces he used to see on bygone TV shows were lost forever, and when finally he'd got his dream and escaped his small-town roots to do what every youngster always claimed they would – leave for the big city – he'd arrived five years too late.

In the middle of a goddamn ghost town.

And now here he was, cross-legged on the roof of a colossal parking lot, in an unfamiliar part of an unfamiliar town, with the dark sky rippling like an inverted ocean, the moonlit streets pulsing with curious colours and stranger sounds; and the twisting column of smoke focusing down to a sliver of light above his head, before winking out.

Making him wait.

As ever.

As midnight approached engines growled below him, and he looked down with a sort of foggy indifference. He'd been hearing the distant chatter of gunfire on and off, but given the ungentle look of the city he'd dismissed it as 'not my problem', and even then hadn't been entirely sure whether it was a true sound or just another backflip of his brain. But now, glancing over the street side canyon, he could see a bulky armoured vehicle slipping to a hurried halt outside a low office block, and knew not only that it was real and solid, but that it made him shiver and his *blood turn sluggish.*

The car had been painted half-heartedly – a smear of messy red along both flanks – but from Hiawatha's vantage the redecoration couldn't hope to disguise the undercoat. The glossy skyblue sheen marked on the thick roof with a wide scarlet 'O'.

Clergy.

Here.

Hiawatha rushed to his bike to snatch-up an appropriate weapon, acting on automatic, scrabbling through pistols and automatics like a chef tossing salad. Finally his hand closed on a rifle – some crow-blasting farmer's friend, no doubt, stolen from a deserted homestead somewhere by Ram and his cronies – and raced back to the edge: just in time to see the AV's two occupants disappear into the office block.

He swore out loud.

And then he saw the man.

The man with green and purple fire tangled above him. With a great bird hovering over his head and wolves slinking past his legs. With rivers and grasses flowing in unreal ripples from his booted feet.

With one ear a tattered mess, with blood all down him, with rags on his back and an Uzi in each hand.

"You'll know him," the Tadodaho had told Rick. "You'll know him when you see him."

Everything stopped.

The man stood on the roof of the office block, opposite and below Hiawatha's own vantage point. He looked like he was breathing heavily, sweating buckets, bleeding from a dozen cuts; but even as Hiawatha watched the man seemed to force-down the exhaustion, eyes closed, face calm. When he reopened his eyes he was almost a different person, moving with predatory grace, stepping to the shadows on one side of the door.

A little part of the old Rick muttered: "Jedi, man..."

In his swirling dream-vision, Hiawatha watched the man change. Become something different. A puma-king of lank fur and subreal shadows; a primitive shade; a Walking Instinct. Reality kept adjusting around him; slowing down, jarring, highlighting its dangers and hazards, blazing along the edge of anything that could be used as a weapon, streaming into dark corners that offered cover, snaking in silvery beads along potential escape-routes, ambush points, blindspots...

Hiawatha realised with a start he was seeing the world as the stranger saw it, and shook his head in annoyance, wanting to watch the spectacle unclouded by the druggish haze.

Out on the rooftop, the two goons from the AV bundled through the stairwell door together, hands full of blades and barrels, and everything went crazy.

The stranger sort of... blurred. Maybe he kicked the door, or slunk around in front before it was fully open. Maybe he duck-sneaked across the open hatch, below the aim of their guns, and darted-in towards them before they could react. Maybe he took them on the full, twisting sideways between outstretched gun arms with fingers locked and lunging.

Hiawatha couldn't say for sure.

An arm jerked, a leg flicked-out. The scrawny goon shrieked and fell, the bigger man raised his gun—

Hiawatha gasped and struggled with the rifle. He'd save the stranger. He'd keep him alive! He'd—

Except the goon was already disarmed. Bleeding from his nose. A kitchen-knife up to its hilt in the soft meat of his leg.

He looked more pissed than hurt.

The stranger turned. Ducked. Flexed. Impacts raining on the swarthy thug, boots lashing out in balletic patterns. The smaller goon was back up now, pistol firing twice in the wrong direction, the stranger twist-turn-kick-duck-pouncing, then the little guy was back down again, all but launched off the roof; gun tumbling out into space.

Hiawatha sighted the rifle back on the big guy, adrenaline roaring, desperate to do something, to take part... But the stranger was too fast.

Didn't need any help.

He took the two shitheads apart like a surgeon, and when they both rocked back on the floor – disarmed, disoriented, slow like glaciers fighting fire – he scooped a single tiny Uzi out of his pocket, aimed it with the minimum concentration, and blew their surprised expressions right open.

The whole fight, from start to finish, took about five seconds. Hiawatha discovered he was still aiming at the dead goons and let his shaking arms relax by degrees.

"Fuuuuuuuuuuck." he hissed.

Which is when an enormous naked freak, bleeding from a hole in his chest, tore through the remains of the door with a meat cleaver in one hand and a limp sex-doll in the other, screaming for revenge upon the murderer of his wife.

The stranger had his back to the colossus. Taken by surprise. Unprepared.

Even he couldn't move that fast.

Hiawatha blew two new holes through the fat man's ribs, smiled a secret smile, and melted away into the shadows of the parking lot before the stranger even knew what had happened.

He wondered if he should go over. Tell the poor guy who he was.

What he was doing here.

What he wanted with him.

"Not time yet." The sky told him. The needle sang in his back pocket. "Not time yet."

Hiawatha followed the stranger at a discreet distance. He seemed to be in a hurry; vaulting into the thugs' AV and tearing off into the east. Hiawatha stayed out of his sight, letting the signs and portents – the roiling purple fire – guide the throb of the Harley's progress; grumbling internally about relying on hippy bullshit to guide him.

It felt a lot like cheating.

Half an hour after the rooftop struggle, at the edge of a great blocked-in wilderness, encircled by dead trees and stagnant swamps – Central Park, he assumed – he deserted the Harley in a quiet alcove and ambled out across the browning lawns. He'd done his best to conceal it, but the whole area seemed to be crawling alive with knots of raggedy-looking people, and no amount of security was ever going to stop a truly determined thief. He searched his feelings for a moment or two – still not quite sure if he was seeking divine solutions, subconscious rationality or plain old trippy make-believe – and decided he wouldn't be needing the trike any more anyway.

(The defining moment in this decision was a fat bear, made entirely out of smoke, waddling past with a claw flicking dismissively towards the vehicle.

"Hope you're right," Hiawatha said. If he'd been in a more rational state of mind, he might have felt slightly dumb addressing such an obvious figment of his imagination. As it was, it not only seemed utterly natural, but far more real than the mundane shit going on around it.)

He shouldered the sack of guns he'd taken from the general store, and followed the flow of the crowd.

Somewhere ahead, in a copse of spindly trees, a great cheer went up. It seemed to hang in the air. Hundreds of hands clapping, voices laughing and shouting, and a single booming tone raised above the others. The rodent-like people nearby seemed to be gravitating towards it, sticking to little groups of two or three for as long as possible, then awkwardly mingling as the numbers locked together. Hiawatha saw luminous tags hanging above each one's head, wrapping ethereal chains and brambles around each neck. He understood without knowing how that these vision were brands declaring each persons' ownership. Each to a different tribe; like the Beaver-Lodge tattoo on his own left shoulder, but far harsher – symbols not of familial ties but of property, like a name tag sewn into valuable clothes. The peoples' cautious movements marked them out as rivals, awkwardly picking their way into someone else's territory at the mercy of their curiosities, unaccustomed to mixing.

Hiawatha began to understand this was unprecedented. A crowd like this; a gathering like this. Hopeful glances traded between bitter enemies, slaves electing a new master...

In his mind, there was a blanket of gold hanging above the park.

It was all deeply peculiar.

Every now and again a better-dressed man or woman – most in red, with feathers pinned in their hair – would point and shout accusations, snarling "you fucking Globies get outta the park!" or "Gulls only! Gull scavs only! No fucking Mickies! No fucking Strips!" Their shouts meant little to Hiawatha, and went mostly ignored anyway. Eventually the crowd just surged around them, and they wandered off, forlorn, towards the edge of the park, casting hateful glances back towards the source of all the cheering.

He began to catch snatches of conversation as he picked his way through the trees, letting the cheers grow up around him; feeling the excitement of the hordes. But what little he overheard seemed nonsensical at best, and he scowled and forged on through the storm of random commentary.

"...figures he told 'em if they wasn't with him, they was out on they fuckin' ear, man..."

"...got fresh rat here, fresh rat, barter for clothing, barter for burns... fresh rat..."

"...says any 'n all welcome. Never seen nothing like, man, and I bin here years..."

"...wassa wassa wassa fucking Liiiiimey? Never hearda no Liiiiiimey..."

"... sent the rest to tear down the territory poles... got plans, he says..."

"...rabbit meat and rats, rats and rabbits, get 'em while they're hot..."

And so on.

On the shores of a truly revolting pond (which formed a great miserable face in Hiawatha's mind, moaning plaintively for aid) he found the stranger; stood on a ramshackle podium built of logs and sheets, set-up in front of a great ghastly building that sprawled across the lawns like a living ooze.

He also found the largest crowd he'd ever seen.

In the ravages of his memory – from a time before his mind was prised open by the expedient application of mystical mumbo-jumbo and hardcore perception-altering pot, from a time even before the great Cull – he remembered concerts he'd visited, student rallies, great gatherings where all personal differences were thoughtlessly disregarded in the shared reverence of a single band; a single demagogue, a single voice.

This was like that.

But more so.

The stranger spoke surprisingly softly. He had the look of a character unused to such attention; far better suited to the quiet application of force in secret, covert places. Hiawatha guessed that under other circumstances the man would have passed for utterly unremarkable. A forgettable face, cropped hair, a physique neither tall nor short, vastly over inflated or ultra-weedy. Just a guy with a crazy accent and a hopelessly British manner, whose words managed nonetheless to silence a crowd thousands strong.

If it hadn't been for the blood drying in thick streaks down his cheek, the matted tangle of gore-splattered rags on his back – once patched in every conceivable colour, now stained to a uniform brown-grey – and the glossy rifle hung nonchalantly over his shoulder, nobody would have looked at him twice.

"Where," the man said, into a silence as deep and dark as the sky above his head, where the QuickSmog oozed out of the stratosphere, "are the Children?"

Hiawatha shivered.

No, no... scratch that.

The whole fucking crowd shivered.

As he stood there, playing the reaction like a pro, the stranger was patched-up and fussed-over by an elderly black man wearing the most ridiculous clothes Hiawatha had ever seen. It was all part of the spectacle, he supposed; holding an ever-growing host spellbound.

"I don't see them. Do you?" The stranger glanced about theatrically. "Look. Look at you. Not a single kid in the

whole place."

Here and there people muttered, but whether in anger or fear Hiawatha couldn't tell. The bright stars above the crowd – figments of his imagination, he was pretty sure – had turned to an angry scarlet, pulsing along with Hiawatha's own heartbeat.

"I'll tell you where the kids are, shall I?"

He smiled, almost paternal, just a little too sweet to be genuine.

"They're sleeping. Just over there." He nodded off to the horizon, to the south east. The crowd muttered just a little louder. "Like little angels, they are. Come from all over the world, the dears. Sleeping-off a hard day of... of dutifully learning their scriptures. Preparing for big things. Getting ready to... lead the world into a new age of glorious civilisation. Right? That's right. That's where they are."

He sounded sincere. It was hard to believe he was being sarcastic, hard to believe he was forming dangerous words, but the crowd were off-balance. What was this? Rebellion or respect-paying?

And then the stranger leaned down low to the front rows, dipped his head so he was staring from beneath grimy eyebrows, and shouted so loud that everyone jumped.

"Bollocks! Fucking bollocks!"

Hiawatha didn't know what bollocks were, but he got the gist. Everyone got the gist.

"If they're locked away," the stranger growled, "in that... that fucking prison, why don't we see them? Why do they never come out? Didn't you people ever stop and think? Didn't you ever smell a bloody rat?"

Somewhere near Hiawatha, a couple of rows to his left, a woman started crying. It was a mystifying reaction.

In any other place, at any other time, he would have expected the crowd to rise-up against the sanctimonious prick giving them a dressing-down; to react with fury at the open-blooded accusations.

But no. No, this crowd was a chastised kid. A naughty child who knew it deserved to be punished.

The stranger rung his hands together. "Didn't you ever... Didn't y..." his voice tailed-off, lost to the frustration. He stood silently for a moment, and Hiawatha wondered if he'd run out of energy, if the anger gobbling him up had overtaken him.

But:

"Fuck!" He shouted. "Fuck – come on! Even if those shits-in-dresses are telling the truth, even if your sons and daughters are hidden away in there, don't you tell me you're happy. Don't you tell me you handed them over with a... smile and a fucking song in your heart. Don't you tell me that!

"No, no. You gave them up because you were told to. I get it. Because... because maybe if you said 'no' they would've just been taken anyway. Because you're nobodies. Because the shits in the Klans with the... the guns and the drugs, they said that's what you scavs do. That's what you're for. Right? And maybe you told yourself over and over it was for the best, that the kids would be going somewhere better, somewhere more hopeful... But people, I don't believe that. And I don't believe you believe it either.

"Here's the truth, ladies and gents. These people... these fucking scum..." and here the stranger raised a crooked finger towards a line of men stood at the back of the podium, held in place by scrawny scavs with knives and guns "–they've.

"Stolen.

"Your.

"Children."

Silence.

Thick, heavy, accusatory silence. On the stage the hostages shuffled their feet and traded glances. Scarlet eye-rings hiding furtive fear and the first glimmerings of tears. One of them – the scrawniest, whose face was contorted not with fear but with hatred – wore ruby-red sunglasses, as if to protect his eyes from the moonlight's glare.

Their robes had been stripped away, their weapons taken.

Neo-Clergy, fallen from grace.

Hiawatha almost snarled with joy to see them so humiliated.

And then, as had happened in every crowd since creation began, the prerequisite asshole at the front opened his mouth.

"For the glory of the New Dawn!" Came a shrill voice; a scrawny man in stained rags leaping up and down, stabbing a finger towards the podium. He had a scarlet tattoo around his left eye, and a pistol raised in his right hand. "Your selfishness betrays you!" he shrieked, drawing a bead on the stranger. "Your wickedness shall..."

He never got the chance to fire. A blade snick-snackered in the crowd somewhere behind him, hands reached out to snake around his neck and his arms, and within an instant the mob had swallowed him up and closed over him. His cries went muffled, then tailed-away into silence. The crowd's head twisted, as one, back towards the stranger.

He sighed.

"Any other morons?" He said, letting his eyes rove, like a teacher peering across a rowdy classroom. "Any other stupid bastards? Anyone else thinks their kids are better-

off cuddling a bible instead of their own flesh and blood? Anyone else want to tell me they did the right thing? They like it how it is? The Klans and the killings and the fucking Tags? Anyone else want to tell me they believe the Clergy?"

He was almost shouting. Voice hoarse. Anger dribbling over his eyeballs and into his words.

"Because, people, they're building us all a better tomorrow. Remember? That's what they say. And wouldn't it just be the best thing in the world to believe them? Wouldn't it just be so easy to shout 'hallelujah!'? To pray every night and... go with the flow? To feel like you did the right thing, letting them take your kids? Wouldn't that be the dog's-sodding-bollocks?

"Too right it would."

He spat on the floor. He took a deep breath.

And he drew a long knife out of his pocket.

The crowd stopped breathing.

"But believing it – really and truly, I mean – in your guts, people. That's a tough call. That's a tricky business. And I'm going to go out on a limb here, and say I really don't think there are many of us who do. Not really. Not deep down.

"So let's find out. Let's cut the crap."

He smiled.

"Let's see how many of you really love the Clergy. Let's see who's willing to stop me."

And he turned to the line of men, those captive Choirboys stood behind him, and he smiled.

"I came here from across the ocean," he said loud enough for everyone to hear but aimed directly at the hostages. "It was hard fucking work, let me tell you. But I came. I didn't let them stop me, your pals in London, though they tried. I had to kill all sorts of people on the way. And all

because I wanted to ask you a question, matey, face-to-
face. Nice and simple."

He leaned down towards the first goon.

"What I wanted to ask you, is:

"Where are my children, you kidnapping psychotic
indoctrinating pieces of cancerous shit?"

The goon stared at him. The goon spat in his face with
a sort of doing-it-by-the-script doggedness.

So the stranger cut out his throat.

The crowd made a noise. Not quite a cheer. But definitely
not a scream of horror.

The man went down, his legs shivered and thrashed,
blood oozed, and in Hiawatha's eyes something dry and
unpleasant fluttered up from the corpse to lose itself in the
spreading QuickSmog.

The stranger turned back to the crowd. No one made a
move. No one breathed.

Hiawatha could see the lie. He could see the red taint
of dishonesty hanging above the stranger, glittering and
mewing like a mutant cat. This man, this unstoppable Brit
with his boring face and his quiet voice, he had no interest
in the scavs gathered in Central Park. He didn't care one
bit about punishing the wicked. He couldn't give a damn
for doing the right thing.

All he had was an agenda – whatever the hell it was
– and Hiawatha could see, burning bright in his third eye,
that this man would do anything to get what he wanted. He
would lie about an abducted family, just to make a crowd
of allies empathise with his anger. He would slaughter his
way through as many hostages as it took, to show them
they didn't need to fear the Choirboys.

He wouldn't stop until he got his way, and whilst
Hiawatha couldn't bring himself to admire such apathetic
selfishness, such casual manipulation, it just so happened

that the Limey bastard's goals and his own were – briefly
– aligned.

So he smiled, and started to clap.

And the whole crowd picked up the applause.

Later, the second goon went the same way, though
his resolve left him as the stranger's question went
unanswered and the knife blurred upwards towards his
throat. He cried out wordlessly, gurgled, then dropped.

The fifth man in the line – the wiry one with the thick
glasses, whose aura seemed to crackle with an orange
edge – shouted something to the two remaining thugs.
Hiawatha caught the words 'reward' and 'heaven', and
could imagine the rest.

The town goons sprang forwards, rushing the scavs who
held them at gunpoint, shouting and snarling as their
naked flesh rippled in time to their meaty swipes. The
black man with the bandages dived to the floor, hands
over his head; the stranger shouted – more angry than
surprised – and the scavs opened fire.

The crowd shuddered. Muzzlefire lent the whole drama
a lightning-storm animation, and between freeze-flashes
specks of blood appeared across the faces of the crowd.

When it was over, when the gun smoke cleared and
the scavs were cooling-off and the crowd was in uproar,
four naked goons lay bleeding on the stage, and the
rat-like bastard with the sunglasses was gone, pushing
his way through the recoiling crowd, through trees and
undergrowth, shouting and laughing all the way.

The stranger swore. Loudly.

The crowd swore with him.

By four in the morning it was no longer a crowd. It was
an army.

It was a tired cliché, but that didn't make it inaccurate. As Hiawatha watched, buffeted by awe and abstraction, he could think of no better description:

It was like a tidal-wave.

The captured AV went first, followed by the smattering of vehicles the stranger had liberated from the Red Gulls. As their new de facto leader he was more than entitled to requisition them for his own ends, but a gutsy minority of the Klansmen had reacted badly to the idea of throwing-off the feudal yoke and rising-up against the tyrants, and had holed-up inside the Gulls' base to stop anyone getting in.

In the end, the stranger had had to kill pretty much all of them.

Hiawatha had stayed out of the way. It wasn't time yet. He'd sat to one side, beneath the great boughs of old, dead trees, and listened to the spirit-voices whispering mournfully inside them. As the first fires started burning deep inside the Gulls' lair, he had taken the stick of blacking-paint from the bottom of his pack, and began to slowly mark his face, chanting quietly to himself, feeling the silver needle in his pocket chiming-along with his words.

Afterwards, when the armouries were opened and their bounties distributed, the crowd didn't wait for the dawn. It was like a crusade; a great wedge of people, shifting together along empty streets, swelling as they went. A magnetic pull.

And on the edge of the city, in Hell's Kitchen, squished up against the black waters of the East River, they faced the United Nations building, and advanced.

He – the stranger, the man whose name no one had bothered to ask – went first. It was all deeply medieval. All deeply mythic. But as the crowd roared as one and the *vehicles gunned their engines and the guards inside the compound shouted and shit themselves, it felt right.*

The AV ploughed through the main gates of the UN headquarters like a harpoon through whale meat, bullets rattling off its sides; slivers of shredded steel and tangled barbed-wire thrashing in its wake. Even as it sat steaming in the forecourt, dents opening-up across it, the Clergymen in the guard-nest were realising their mistake. Betraying their positions in the darkness with tapered candles of muzzle-fire.

The second wave of vehicles thundered through, guns firing. Sandbag-packed nests ruptured, grenades tumbled from heavy-launchers and choked out red-black plumes of soot and smoke and people dying. Somewhere up on the roof of the Secretariat a heavy auto opened fire – thundering its payload down into the crowd – but at such a range and in such darkness its accuracy was far from perfect, and the spooky trails of tracer-fire stitched themselves neatly through panicky Clergymen as evenly as rioting scavs. Eventually someone had the presence of mind to order the ceasefire, and the artillery fell silent.

In odd corners, fires took hold. Sparks billowed and roiled, and beckoned with tongues of white light at the crowds waiting in the shadows, eyes gleaming. It was like an invitation.

The horde swarmed from the streets, in every hand a weapon, in every mouth a scream, and everything went straight to hell. Gunfire above grenade-blasts above human roars above dying screams above engine purrs and the horrified gasps of unprepared Clergymen.

Cy had forewarned them, maybe. But still. But still.

Yeah, *Hiawatha* thought. Just like a tidal wave.

It surged and boiled, fuelled by years of bottled anger. It lapped against the walls of the compound and spun in eddies of violence. Whirlpools with isolated Choirboys at their centres, screaming out as the mob circled and slashed and shot. It frothed at its edges; the glowing foam of muzzleflash and the warm spume of impact-craters, spitting dust and mortar and blood.

The AV gave up the ghost in a spectacular fireball, fuel-tanks finally punctured, hefting itself in warped fragments off the crowd to spin lazily in the air; but by then the crew were well clear, and its messy end served only as a distraction to the true violence, close and personal and vicious. In dark corners men and women pushed blunt blades into robed sides, struggled muzzle-to-muzzle to bring poorly-tended pistols to bear on the thugs who had terrorised their worlds, beat and battered with crowbars and tyre-irons at the tattooed faces of the pious pricks.

"Where are they?" They screamed. "Where are the fucking children?"

Not much of a battle cry, but it worked.

Hiawatha stayed at the rear. Oh, not through cowardice – the spiralling dreamhaze had done away with that – and he lent his aid where he could; firing with a calm accuracy into Clergy lines where the other scavs hooted and panicked, picking-off stragglers in their grey robes with a savage sort of joy. He felt like all the Sachems stared through his eyes, and laughed and giggled and passed-around the beers with each new kill. The Haudenosaunee, it would be fair to say, did not much like the Clergy.

But no, no, that wasn't his major role, here. He worked his way carefully along the edges of the mêlée, eyes darting, dreamsenses spinning; seeking out the stranger.

"Almost time, now..." the wind said, hot with the breath of fuel-fires and roasting skin. "Almost time."

The purple cloud ran like a thread through the crowd, and Hiawatha realised with a start that the stranger had snuck away. He'd got what he wanted, access to this barbed-wire compound, and had left behind the agents of his aid the instant they'd ceased to be of any use. It was cold and brutal and logical, but it had worked.

The trail led into the Secretariat.

Hiawatha skidded on blood, marvelling deep-down at the raw apathy of a man who could bring about such wanton violence in the sole pursuit of... of what?

He stepped into the gloomy building, and went to meet his destiny.

CHAPTER FOURTEEN

I couldn't help smiling. The heat coming up from the fires, the smell of unpleasant things cooking, the acid stink of gun smoke.

Yeah. Let it out. Let the grin break through. *You're so close. Enjoy. You deserve it.*

Then with the guilt. Screams and blood and desperate people cutting chunks out of each other, just because I told them to. Just because I needed to get past those big fucking gates. I lied to them. Worked them up like a sculptor hammering clay.

Monster. Manipulator. Don't you care about anything? Don't you—

Then with the irritation *at* the guilt.

You trained for this. This is what you DO. This is who you ARE.

Round and round and round.

Fuck it. Fuck them all.

Don't feel guilty.

Look at what you did. Enjoy *it.*

From the third floor, looking down through the Secretariat's shattered mirror glass, it was quite a sight. Barely visible in the darkness, the undulations of the throng could easily have been mistaken for a gloomy sort of fog; wafted about by contrary breezes, lit internally by wyrd lights and wil-o-the-wisps; all of it sped-up by a factor of ten and replayed to a BBC Sounds Of War effects tape. Now and then something solid differentiated itself from the mêlée – a moonflash along the edge of a blade, a torn strip of pale robe, an effervescent burst of cranial fluids. Little details, like individual brushstrokes discernible within a completed painting.

They didn't last. Big, crazy spectacles have a way of homogenising like that. Little by little everything was sucked inside; reabsorbed by the heaving, living, collective amoebic monstrosity that was the crowd.

"Jesus," I muttered, not really thinking.

Being stuck in a fight on ground-level, that's a messy, brutal, untidy sort of shit. No time to think. No time to gauge the way it's going. Just act, react, dodge, stab, duck, shoot. Gunfire ripping from left to right, contrary angles of devastation, panicky shouts and thoughtless responses, friendly fire.

But from above...

Oh yes. From above you get a pretty good idea of why generals get to be such arrogant arseholes. Why politicians don't talk about individuals, just 'the people'. Why the guys who make decisions – the top dogs, the head honchos – get to be sadistic fucks with no concept of human expenditure whatsoever. From above, it's all... *neat*. Tidy. Like playing war games with over expensive models, rolling dice to determine movements, accuracies, wounds.

Nobody ever rolled a dice to determine how many sobbing loved ones each dead model leaves behind. How much the poor bastard suffered before he was removed from the playing table.

It takes a funny sort of brain to see a crowd of people, and mentally note them down as a 'diversion'. 'Cannon fodder'. 'Acceptable losses.'

Guilty as charged.

Again with the guilt.

Something exploded down below, and lit them all up. Just for a fraction, they were *people*. Different faces, contorted in anger and pain and fear. Individuals, locked together. All unique.

For just a fraction, fat with guilt and empathy and all that other bollocks, I wasn't the cold-hearted manipulative scheming *fuck* I thought I was.

Then the light faded and the mob coalesced in the shadows, and I was back to enjoying the spectacle, congratulating myself on getting inside the Secretariat without a scratch, being *me*.

"You... *ah*... You don't want to go help 'em?" Nate rumbled from somewhere behind me. He'd followed me up here like a puppy dog. He looked even worse now, twitching and sweating and jerking. I couldn't be bothered to ask what was wrong. Not when I was this close. Not when nothing else mattered.

I ignored him.

The fight was all but over anyway. Still a few pockets of resistance. Clergymen scrabbling behind improvised cover to mow down scavs in their dozens, stuttering cones of perfect light drizzling lead into onrushing walls of black rag and snarling flesh. The bodies piled up like human ramps, twitching and groaning, but there was more to come, more plugging the gaps, more stolen vehicles blasting away with heavy weapons.

Little by little the Choirboys were becoming isolated; cut-off from buildings, rounded-up in coils of the mob and gradually ringed in, hemmed, set upon.

None of them went quietly. And after the first few who tried to surrender were torn apart – limbs wrenched clean-away, eyes put out, scalps sliced off and ribs broken – none of the others bothered to fall on the scavs' mercy. They'd seen the look in their eyes. The excitement, the primal joy of being caught-up in... in *something*.

The pack-instinct. That old-brain thing, rustling inside my head, howling to go and join its brothers. But no mercy. None of that.

One or two of the Choirboys sang hymns as their ammunition ran out and the crowds seethed forwards. Mostly they didn't get past the first line.

There were fewer robes out there than I'd expected.

Where are the others?

I turned away. Pretty soon the big, spectacular part would be over and the scavs would be slinking inside the buildings. Kicking down doors under the auspices of finding their lost children; secretly yearning for nests of resistance, dorms piled with sleeping Choirboys, easy targets.

Let them.

Oddly enough, the Secretariat itself was almost deserted. On floor after floor the plush offices of another time – structured with the all the ergonomic ingenuity of too much money, in broad stripes of grey and beige and airy spaces and comfy sofas and padded swivel-chairs and blah blah *blah* – sat silent; deserted. It reminded me, in a homesick sort of way, of Vauxhall Cross; my base for the past five years, where once the SIS had controlled its agents all across the world, keeping fingers on the pulses of foreign threats, adjusting and prodding regimes they didn't like, sneaking about with a distinct absence of Martinis, pithy one-liners, Q-Department gadgets and obscenely horny chicks.

Well. Mostly.

The difference was that the offices back in London had a dangerous sort of mystique lacking here in the Secretariat. Sharper edges, maybe. Deeper shadows. Tight corners and internal windows. *Em-Eye-fucking-Six*, the place said. *Don't you cock-around with us.*

The Secretariat just looked like an expensive software corporation.

Still, at least it felt *lived in*. Most of its airy floors had been comprehensively violated. Desks and waiting-sofas used as sleeping palettes, walls covered in neat lines of devotional graffiti (*Book of Revelations*, mostly, which I guess is sort of *de rigeur* amongst insane apocalyptic cults). I figured the Clergy used them for sleeping dorms, store-rooms, pantries, whatever.

Which sort of begged the question: Where *were* they all?

The battle outside was still raging, still going strong, but there was no way in hell the scavs had overrun every last Choirboy in this place. It was *enormous*.

So where *were* they?

Nate and I had bumped into a few of the little shits on the stairwell on the way inside. Mostly they were sprinting down from above, guns and heavy packs stowed on their backs and crooked beneath overladen arms, and I'd been obliged to shoot them as they came clattering down the last flight without waiting for them to arm-up. I'd be discreetly ashamed, if I could be bothered. No; more worrying was the reason for the sudden evacuation. These grunts weren't dashing off to join the defence of the outer gate, or form a second layer of repulsion. They were getting *out*. All possessions carried; scampering off through the vast lobby (now strewn with military netting and a blotchy mural of John-Paul) and out, towards the wide shape of the General Assembly Building.

Something was going down.

I couldn't give a flying fuck.

On the third floor we came across a shattered desk covered in telephone switchboard pins, and I rummaged through piles of discarded paperwork whilst Nate stood watch with that same nervous foot-to-foot hop. Amidst crumbling cards and files I found, finally, a yellowing printout of floor designations. Thirty-nine levels; thirty-nine busy little worlds dedicated to 'World Peace'.

A spray of stray bullets knocked out the windows beside me. Kind of ironic.

'32-35', the printout said. 'SCI/TECH RESEARCH ADMINISTRATION,' with a list of departmental names as long as my arm and the telephone extensions of each. Someone had ringed one of the entries in green ink, with the bored assiduousness of someone who was tired of being asked for the same department over and over.

Towards the end, I guessed, as The Cull turned the city outside into a ghost town, the phones would never have stopped ringing.

Fl 34. Ext 34033. Epidemiology.

"Right," I said.

"You found what you been looking for?" Nate grunted, trying not to look too interested. He'd been pretty good so far, I supposed, at not asking out loud what the hell I'd dragged him into. He'd got his payment. He'd got his protection, and a little sliver of fame as the guy who's with the stranger. He was doing *okay*, and the Clergy hadn't tried to kill him yet.

But you could see it in his eyes. The curiosity was killing him.

I wondered if I should take him with me.

But.

Something not quite right...

Still that sensation of disquiet. His eyes twinkled over his soggy dogend, his teeth sparkled with every smile. He cooked a fine rat. He told a fine story. He looked a clown and acted a clown, and his shaky-handed approach to medicine had saved my life at least twice. Nothing to dislike about the guy, right?

Right.

But no. No. *Something not right.*

Something besides this new twitchy, sweaty routine he was going through, something besides the weird behaviour since yesterday.

A little tentacle of memory uncurled. A voice cut-through with exhaustion and inebriation, curdled with heavy breathing and fresh sweat.

Bella.

I only knew her a couple of weeks. Planning for the airport, mostly. Getting provisions, working out where to hit, how to get through, who to target. Mostly.

Except the one night we got smashed on whatever brain-killing homebrew the local survivors had been cooking up in their bathtub stills. Lost track of our conversation.

Ended up fucking on the bar in the abandoned pub we'd been using as home.

Even off my face, even after five years of hardcore celibacy, even in a world as careless and repercussion-free as this one, the guilt!

Didn't matter, in the end. We fell asleep all cuddled-up on the trapdoor behind the bar, and as I dozed-off I got confused and kept kissing her forehead, like she was someone else. And she started telling me things. Stuff I hadn't asked about, hadn't expressed any interest in. Stuff I barely bothered to listen to.

When she was finished there was a long silence, then she said:

"Doesn't matter. Not your problem. But that's why I'm going."

Back on the fifth floor of the United Nations Secretariat building, with people shouting and dying outside, I turned to Nate and said:

"Go help the others. Find the kids. Look everywhere."

He stared at me like I was mad. Half relieved, half terrified.

"But..." He waved a hand, searching for the right words. "*Why*, man? Ain't like you *care*. Ain't like you expect 'em to *find* anything. Why the sudden ch..."

Doesn't matter, she'd said, sweat making the grime on her face streak and run. *Not your problem.*

I snapped. Just a little.

"Fuck*sakes*, Nate! Just fucking... Just..."

His eyes bugged. I looked away.

Took a breath.

"Just... Just go help them, will you? Please? I'm going upstairs. Might be dangerous. Just give them a *hand*."

Outside, a fireball licked at the edges of the building and blew-in the rest of the windows, letting in the screams from outside. Nate grunted.

I started to climb the stairs.

From the thirty-fourth floor I couldn't even see the fight outside. This high up, the green-glass windows were all intact, and I couldn't hope to angle my vision down to the base of the tower without bashing my head in the process.

I was sweating heavily, by the time I arrived. Not a good sign. Since The Cull robbed us all of a functioning power grid, elevators had been a survivor's wet dream. Judging from the lack of empty food cans and discarded sleeping-mats, very few Clergy goons had taken the trouble to come this high. Even the walls were mostly free of nonsensical graffiti, and any plundering of office supplies appeared to have been more a matter of overturning desks and causing a mess, than looking for useful stuff. If I'm honest, as I climbed the stairs I was quietly entertaining the suspicion that sooner or later I'd come across floor-after-floor of children, packed together in tiny bunks, poring over mass-produced bibles and reciting the day's lessons like good little acolytes.

Bella's words, getting to me.

"Not your problem."

It's a funny thing, convincing a horde that something was a lie whilst dimly suspecting it might just be true. I guess, deep down inside – *maybe* – there was a little bit of me expecting that the scavs *would* find their kids. Behind the carefully maintained disinterest, behind the rock-solid focus on my own goals (*Don't you fucking give up, soldier!*), it was lurking there like an irritating little piece of humanity.

The looks in the eyes of the women, standing outside the gates last night.

The way Malice rocked her child to sleep in the midst of the Wheels Mart, knowing she had four more years before the little mite was whisked away.

The edge in Bella's voice.

Was it so unlikely that they'd find them, after all?

Why did the Clergy *want* the kids, if not for their grand future-shaping scheme? Why fly the little buggers in from overseas, from all over the bloody world, if not to train them in the ways of the Lord, to fill their heads with destiny-based-bollocks? It's not like the Clergy were running a secret sportswear sweatshop, or mass-producing child meat pies...

No. They *had* to be here somewhere, somewhere inside the compound, hidden away.

But not here. Not a soul. Just the dim moonlight through thick plate glass, a morass of overturned desks and stalwart filing cabinets, and endless silence.

I started searching.

Once or twice I heard voices from the stairwell, torches wobbling in the gloom, puddles of hard light wafting past walls and windows. I froze every time, hands reaching for the M16, convinced they'd followed me. They knew what I was after.

Then they went clattering past – upwards – and were lost to the endless silence. I half-wondered what was on the roof that was so bloody important, then rammed my head into another heap of cluttered files and forgot all about it.

I found it forty minutes later.

Tucked away in a chrome cabinet (locked, but fortunately not bullet-proof), inserted between vile-green separators like the most unimportant thing on earth, rammed between bulging files marked PAL-, PAM-, PAO-, PAP-, it was a slender, unremarkable thing. A faded project-report, listing funding allocations, resources, classification levels, diplomatic passes, locations, and personnel.

I had to sit down.

Take a breath.

Look away. Out across the dark landscape and that brightening patch of sky to the east, promising – eventually – a new sun.

Then I looked back and re-read the title:

PROJECT PANDORA

It made me shiver, which is quite a thing to admit when you've spent most of your adult life killing people in secret.

I rifled through the loose sheets inside like a man possessed, fingers trembling, spilling useless documents and paper clipped photographs. It all seemed like it was happening to someone else.

I found the name I was looking for near the back.

Vital statistics. Origins. Code numbers. Re-assignment location.

There was a photo pinned to its rear.

I stared at it for twenty minutes.

The sun edged higher.

And then abruptly I was ready to leave, and stuffing the papers into my pockets, and staggering upright, fighting the shivers, and casting my eyes across the photos I'd dropped, stopping to retrieve my rifle, and—

Oh shit.

And there he was. Staring at me. Pictured in black and white, a decade or two younger, smart in dress-uniform and sergeant's stripes, smiling with officious intensity at the camera.

JOHN P. MILLER.

Lacking only for a vast white mitre, a snowy robe, and an exaltation to the Lord on his lips.

John-Paul Rohare Baptiste.

Why the *fuck* was *he* in the file? What the hell was *he* doing *th*—

Snkt.

This is a sound I have heard many times. This is a sound I am acquainted with intimately, and have been responsible for creating in the vast majority of cases.

This is the sound of a semi-automatic pistol being armed, in close proximity to someone's head.

The head was mine. The pistol was Cardinal Cy's.

"Fuck." I said.

"Yeah," he said.

Nobody moved.

"How did you find me?"

"On the way up. Heard a shot. Took it nice and slow."

Opening the filing cabinet. Bugger.

Still the same, strange voice. Little stammered bursts of thought, tones just a *touch* too high for comfort.

"Given us a chase. Haven't you? Troublemaker. Caused all sorts."

"What's on the roof?" I said. Stalling. It didn't matter. He had no reason to keep me alive now. Just showboating. Just being curious. Just playing with me.

"No concern." He said. "What you looking for? Up here, huh? What's got you into this?"

"None of your business," I deadpanned.

He punched me in the kidneys, giggling horribly and as I went down I made it look *good*, cried out, and staggered, and threw up my hand to ward him off, letting the photo of John-Paul flap about, and—

—*and in the confusion sneaked my other hand onto the Uzi in my pocket, and*—

—and the gun was back on my scalp, only this time I was kneeling.

"Fuck."

"Hands. Lemee see. On head."

He giggled again. Not right in the head.

I did what he said. The Uzi clattered to the ground beside the photo of John-Paul, and somewhere behind those impenetrable red specs I guess he snatched a glance.

"That who I think?"

"Yeah."

"Looks young."

"Yeah."

"What you doing here?"

"Looking for something."

"What?"

"Information."

"What information?"

"You really want to know?"

"What information? Fuck! What information?" The muzzle jabbed against my temple.

I sighed.

Tensed.

"I'm after the location of a secret UN funded research-team sent to find a..."

And I struck. Always mid-sentence. Always unexpected.

Turned. Arms swiping across the pistol muzzle. Knocking it to one side.

He got off a shot – angry and loud and shocking in the silence – and the muzzleflash vanished in the wrong direction, and I was standing and snarling, and then wrestling with the gun between us, and *oh fuck oh fuck oh fuck...*

He was laughing.

He was stronger than me.

The gun came up slowly like the sunrise outside, like a perfect black 'O' opening to swallow me, and I pushed and fought and put everything into it, and—

Don't you fucking give up soldier!

Sir, no sir! Etc etc.

—and it still wasn't enough.

Hooked a leg behind his knee. Tipped us up. Rolling on the floor. Grunting, dribbling, spitting, sweating. The cords in his neck stood out like ropes, and still he wasn't going to stop laughing, the bastard, still he was giggling like his sides had bust.

He took a hand off the pistol, and for a second I thought I'd won. Redoubled my efforts. Forced everything I had into snapping his wrist.

But it made no difference, and he was still laughing,

and he was still stronger than me.

With all the time in the world, he picked up my own rifle in his spare hand – fat fist wrapped round the muzzle – and hit me so hard on the head that my teeth rattled, my lips went cold, my eyes burned with a sudden whiteness then faded back to an awful half-gloom, and the sound that reached my ears shivered around inside my empty skull like an endless echo.

Still laughing. Standing over me, gun in hand.

Still laughing in between telling me he's going to shoot off my kneecaps and let the Abbot have his fun. Spitting on my forehead. Warm rain.

Still laughing when he aimed the pistol and took a breath.

Still laughing when the blurred shape that had been creeping up behind him for the past thirty seconds – tall and dark, dappled with stripes and patches in blue and red – swatted his wrist to one side, ignored the spastic misfire of the pistol, and jabbed a hunting knife so hard into his skull that it slid inside with a *crack* and stayed there.

And *then* he stopped laughing, the shit.

Which is about when I lost consciousness, and went skidding off into my own head.

From somewhere, the sounds of engines. *Big* engines. A *lot* of engines.

People were shouting ("They're going! They're getting out! Stop them!"), guns were chattering like woodpeckers in a distant forest, and two voices were arguing.

"Fuck were you *doing*?"

"You mind your *business*, man! The hell are *you*, anyways?"

"What's in the pack? Hey! Hey, I'm *talking* to you!"

"You back *off*, Tonto!"

"What did you call m..."

And so on.

Oh, and an ugly throb of motorised *something*, slinking off into silence.

...thrpthrpthrpthrp...

I didn't even bother opening my eyes. It was all too much trouble.

"I had a kid." She said. "That's all."

She was beautiful, I suppose, in a stretched-out way. Gangly almost, but not clumsy. Not my type, but I could appreciate her. With little beads of sweat catching the fire on her compact little breasts, and her legs sort of wrapped over-then-under mine, any man could.

The sex had been... okay. Nice.

A little awkward, maybe. Heart-not-quite-in-it, but... yeah. Nice.

"They took her last year. Just turned five. I hid out for months, moving about. Eventually some small-town fuckwit sold me out for a bottle of meths and a new shirt. I kicked his bloody teeth in, when I could walk again."

I pressed my nose against her hair. It smelt of dirt and damp and woman.

Oho, the guilt...

"You're lucky they didn't kill you," I said. "The Clergy. Not big fans of tithe-dodgers."

"Nah." Her shoulders shrugged against my chest. "Why bother? Another woman left alive, another baby-machine to spit out more brain-dead bible-thumpers."

Then quiet. She was a deep-breather and didn't fidget quite as much as—

As some people do.

"Who was the father?" I said, trying to sound interested. In truth the guilt was eating me up, chewing on my stupid prick-controlled-brain and cursing the nettle brandy (or whatever the hell it was) I'd been drinking all night.

Not that I wasn't interested in what she had to say, exactly. Just that I'd heard it – or something like it – a hundred times before. Just that I had my own worries.

Shit, five years since The Cull it was still a selfish motherfucking world.

"No one," she said, and her voice said otherwise. "Just some... guy."

"Before The Cull, right?"

"Yeah. Year or so. Prick." She sighed and nuzzled her way backwards until her bum was squidged up against my groin, and pulled the blanket we'd found tighter round herself "Seemed like he knew everything, at the start. Smart guy, capable. Knew everyone.

"You get to feel like you're safe with someone like that. You know? I mean, Jesus... I was only... what? Twenty one? Living on the street. Spoilt rotten as a kid, I was. Ponies, swimming pools, four-by-fours, you name it. Thus the flying lessons. Got bored of that too. Same as anything."

I was already tuning out. I know, I know. I'm scum. "I only got halfway through uni," she said, building up momentum for an entire bloody life-story. "Had a bit of a... hiccup. Took a look at myself. All the money, the materials. Probably got a bit too far into the whole student thing, if I'm honest. Just kind of... backflipped. Dropped off the radar. Wound up on the streets, getting by. That's where I met Claystone."

"That's the father?"

"Yeah. And then the baby came. A-and... and give him

his credit, you know...he hung around. Brought in some money, once in a while. Knew who to ask, get favours. Fingers in all sorts of pies. We got ourselves a little place, no questions asked – proper little family. Even tried to clean ourselves up. Stop using, y'know?"

I tangled a finger through the ringlets of hair next to her ear, then realised what I was doing and stopped. All these little betrayals, all these guilty little things.

If she noticed, she didn't show it.

"Then The Cull."

"He died?" I said.

She laughed, bitter.

"No. No, he didn't die. Stuck about for a while. Just long enough to see little Shayla hit one. Went out every day for food and togs, came back... now and then.

"Then one day he just didn't come back at all. Left a note. 'Couldn't handle the responsibility'. Prick."

More quiet.

"Sodding cliché, ain't it?" She said. I jerked back awake, realising I'd been slipping off.

"What?"

"Single mother, whingeing on."

"Yeah. Maybe. Though it's kind of different when you can't just nip to the local supermarket for nappies."

"Exactly. Anyway." She shrugged again. "We survived. Me and Shayla."

"And Claystone?"

"Pfft. Saw him about, once or twice. Heard about him all the time. Everyone knew Claystone. He worked for everyone, sooner or later. Had a way of... of finding the best groove. Like... things got tough, he knew a comfier slot. Gold fucking medallist at living an easy life."

Her voice dripped bitterness.

"But he never came looking for me. Vanished, eventually.

Wound up in the river for all I know. All I care.

"Prick. Prick! Well shot of him."

Somewhere outside the pub's shattered windows, a fox loped by with its weird baby-scream call. Bella shivered.

"You know what it's like, when your whole world is focused on one thing?"

I scowled, uncomfortable with the thought. "Yeah." *I decided.* "Yeah, suppose I do."

"And then six men in robes come one day and take it away from you, and kick the crap out of you into the bargain, and put things in your mouth, and tell you to behave and do what you're told, then scuttle off into the night. And then you hear that thing – that... that centre of your universe – get loaded aboard a plane and fucked-off to Yankland.

"What then, mate? What do you do then?"

I didn't answer.

We lay like that for a long time, and I could tell from her breathing she wasn't asleep.

Eventually she mumbled:

"Doesn't matter. Not your problem. But that's why I'm going."

I was already asleep, and heard it only on the fringes of a dream.

I woke up, and almost shat.

There was a face about a foot from my eyes; curved nose sharp like the edge of a scimitar, mouth tugged down at each corner, lost across a jutting chin to a network of weather-lines. Its hair – long, perfectly dark – was trussed-up in loops of red and yellow PVC-tape, so it stood upright like a tower then spilled down on either side to box me in.

From the hairline to the bottom of the eye sockets, the man was black. Not just Afro-Caribbean black, but *black* like ink, pressed-up tight against dark eyes that shimmered inside their puddle of shadow. But below the eyes – face bisected in a straight horizontal line across the bridge of the nose and down each angular cheekbone – the man's skin was tanned a ruddy red. He looked savage. He looked terrifying.

He looked like an ancient God of war (or rather, how I assumed an ancient God of war might look, never having met one), and in the fuzzy moments of half waking, with my whole head throbbing from the sharp pain in my scalp, I remembered the wax figures in their diorama displays in the museum, and wondered if one of them had come back to teach me a lesson for using him as a decoy.

The only detail that somewhat spoilt this scowling character's prehistoric spectacle, was the head-to-foot biking leathers in blue, black, red and white.

"He's awake." The effigy proclaimed, rising up and away from me. At a distance, he stopped being the most terrifying thing I've ever seen, and became a young man wearing face paint. I relaxed my sphincter.

"What? You *what*?" A familiar voice. I felt myself smiling, happy at the note of familiarity in the midst of all this oddity. Nate appeared on the edge of my vision like a man possessed, pushing the boy aside and stooping down to poke and prod at me. He was no longer sweating or shivering; a total transformation that left him grinning massively and mumbling to himself.

"Ow," I said, as he pressed his crinkled fingers against my temple. He did it again.

"Miracle." He said, grinning, cigarette hanging off his bottom lip. "That's what it is. Damned miracle. Asshole all but opened you *up*."

He tittered to himself.

I picked myself up slowly, fighting the urge to vomit every inch of the way. My head felt like a meteor had hit it – or possibly a speeding elephant – and judging by the dry tightness of my cheek it was appropriately blood-splattered. Added to the bandaged remains of what had once been an ear, the slashes and scars across cheeks and forehead, the aching wounds – messily fixed-up – in my left arm, right shoulder and nape of my neck, I imagined I was starting to look just as patchworked as my coat. One of these days, I decided, I was going to have to find a functioning shower.

I tottered to my feet, lost the battle with my gyrating inner-ear, and barfed like a trooper. I was hungry enough to consider asking someone for a spoon.

Nate watched me cautiously, like he expected me to fall down any second. His pupils looked even bigger than usual, pushing against the bright whites of his eyes, and he was clinging to a red plastic box – like a power drill case – like it was a lifeline. Where he'd got it and what the hell it *was* were queries I never got around to asking. My surroundings swam into focus, and my senses came online.

The prevailing sound was: engines.

I was back at the Wheels Mart. The same raggedy little tent, by the looks of it, that Malice met me in before. Through the tattered openings I could hear the braying crowds and see the spastic danglings of the MC, shouting out his endless stream of nonsensical bid-acceptances. The smell of cooking meat underwritten by the heady chug of noxious fumes, the whooping and arguing of punters. It made my head hurt, if possible, even more than it already did.

"Brought you here in a *car!*" Nate whooped, doing a little dance. He was clearly on something. "Borrowed it, yes we did. Fucking Clergy, heh!"

"What... what happened?" I murmured, wincing at my own voice. "What happened to the priests?"

"Fucked off!" Nate sat down suddenly, cross-legged, and nodded like a flapping wing. "Trucks, hidden-away. Took-off all at once. You scared 'em off! City's free!"

Then he slumped against the wall of the tent with no warning and just... *switched off*, smirking. He dribbled a little.

High as a kite.

Hmm.

The young man in the leathers stood nearby, leaning against a tall wooden pole, arms folded; watching it all without movement. I found myself looking for the bow and quiver of arrows over his shoulder – hating myself – and dipped my eyes back up to his own to cover the up-and-down staring.

He didn't move a muscle.

"You saved me, huh?" I said, remembering the red and blue blur behind Cy, the knife cracking through his skull.

He shrugged. "You needed saving."

Nate *tsked* quietly behind me, then giggled again.

I held out a shaky hand to the boy, which he took with a suspicious sort of glance and shook firmly.

"Hiawatha," he said.

I nodded. "Pleasure. Want to tell me what you were doing on the thirty fourth floor of a hotly-contested building swarming with insane priests, Hiawatha?"

He smiled. Sort of. I don't think there was much humour there.

"Saving you." he said.

Uh-huh.

Which is around about when Malice came in. Different.

She looked bigger, for a start. It took me a while to figure she wore body armour beneath the black threads. Pointy football-pads over each shoulder, skateboarding shields on elbows and knees, and a bloody enormous anti-stab vest that made her look like a samurai. Guns and knives poking from belts and straps on every conceivable surface – and that *included* the baby's wicker support-cage, still humping from her back like a dorsal fin.

She looked like an ice hockey player who was too hardcore to bother with a helmet.

Oh, and someone had beaten the shit out of her.

"Still alive then," she said, not even bothering to make eye contact. She sounded disappointed, dumping an angular bag on the floor with a metallic crash.

"Uh. Yeah. Yeah, I guess." I tried to stop staring at her bruised face. "What happened?"

She rummaged industriously in a couple of crates nearby, then paused to glower at me. "Clergy happened, retard. You're a popular guy."

I suppose I should've guessed. Back before The Tag and the siege and all that, when Cy dragged the big Mickey-chief back to the UN with tales of the Limey psycho driving about on a clapped-out quad. Wouldn't have taken the Choirboys long to work their way back to the Wheels Mart.

I wondered whether she'd told them anything worth a damn.

"Sorry," I said.

"Skip it. We're ready to roll when you are."

"Excuse me?"

"We're loaded-up and ready. Awaiting your pleasure, your majesty. And payment, of course."

"Sorry, I'm... I'm not with you..."

"I *said*," Nate grumbled. "Didn't I *say*? Let him wake up, I said! Just goddamn wait! Let him decide himself!"

Malice ignored him, hooking a thumb towards Hiawatha. "Last of the Mohicans here said you'd want a ride. Long distance. Heavy protection. No expense spared."

Hiawatha stared at me.

"But..."

"North-west," Malice said. "That's what he told me. You saying he's been wasting my fucking time?"

She didn't look in the mood for games.

I groped in my pocket and felt the crumpled sheet of paper I'd taken from the Secretariat with its REASSIGNMENT LOCATION and the smooth photograph. Undisturbed, right where I'd left them.

I stared at Hiawatha.

"How did you know that?" I said, off-balance. "What's...how... how did you know?"

"Lucky guess," he said, then turned back to Malice, pointing a finger at the bag she'd brought with her. "That's mine."

"And?"

"They confiscated it at the door."

"And now I'm bringing it back Tonto. Keep your fucking scalp o..."

"No, I mean... I mean you might as well keep it. It's for you anyway."

He strolled over and kicked open the drawstrings, letting dozens upon dozens of glossy guns – rifles, pistols, autos, semis, weird spiky things I didn't recognise and antique bloody revolvers – spill into the dirt.

"Figure that'll cover the rental costs," he said, into the silence.

Malice gaped.

The *Inferno* was waiting for us outside.

CHAPTER FIFTEEN

The kid came too.

Right before we left, I had a half-hearted sort of attempt at talking Malice out of it. Over the roar of the fire-truck's engines (extensively tinkered with, a sweaty little man called 'Spuggsy' told me, to "purr like a lion on stee-roids an' go like a cheetah got a rocket up its ass"), I appealed to her sense of responsibility, reminded her we were taking the *Inferno* instead of some suped-up speeder because we might easily blunder into trouble, and finally had a stab at convincing her the little brat would keep us awake at nights.

It was pretty lame.

Malice just glared, scratched absent mindedly at the split lip the Clergy's goons had left her with – as if to remind me whose fault it was, and who therefore had no fucking right to be suggesting *anything* – then went back to loading ammo-belts into the truck's hold. I'd half expected her to be vaguely grateful – it was arguably thanks to me that the Clergy had been kicked out of the city – but evidently she either refused to believe the news coming out of Manhattan or was a grudge bearer of championship standards. She pretty much ignored me after that.

The kid, for the record, never even made a sound.

Ten minutes out of the Wheels Mart, as the solid wall of noise thrown-up by the engine started to normalise inside my head, the diminutive gunner who called herself 'Tora' – fast-talking, flirtatious as hell, mad as a box of badgers – leaned close to my ear and whispered:

"She left her kid behind once before. That's all. Rental mission just like this. Some moron trying to get to Miami,

I forget why. Figured we'd run into some crazies en route – 'specially with the DC *hole*, shit – so she laid out the responsible mother bullshit, left him behind. No *way* the Clergy gonna try collecting tithes inside the Mart."

"And?"

"And that's why she's only got *one* kid, 'steada two. And ain't a fan of the Choir."

Ah.

Still. Tensions aside, cramped and sweaty lack of comfort aside, snarling engine-volume aside, this was travelling in *style*. The *Inferno* slipped through New York like an icebreaker; stately and magnificent, oozing *don't-mess-with-us* torment and *explode-your-ass-muthafucka* intent. Weaponry on prominent display, promising instant overkill.

I kept catching myself wishing I could get out and have a look; standing in the street like all the wide-mouthed scavs and Klansmen, who bristled and hid as it slunk past like a nuclear armadillo. We wended our way in silence, across the meandering Triborough bridge – its girdered pillars flaking paint, flocked with hundreds of gulls that picked and squabbled over a dead sheep hung, upside down, for no appreciable reason – and skirting the edge of the Bronx on Highway 87, peering solemnly into a deserted wilderness that seemed to have been frozen in time. Cars packed together in cryogenic traffic-jams, skeletal shadows sealed within.

Now and then we passed territory poles – or the remains of them – and gaudy wall murals where the local gang wars were meticulously chronicled: long lists of names, each one crossed through where some other mob had taken over. At some point the internecine squabbles had ended, and some thoughtful soul had added a broad scarlet circle to the foot of each list; unquestionably proclaiming the *true* rulers, regardless of which banana-republic Klans they allowed to govern in their stead. Every time we passed such ownership tags a fresh round of spitting, swearing and tutting would circulate round the truck's interior.

That was about as close as we got to conversation, in those first hours.

There were eight of us altogether, not counting the baby. Malice drove, mostly; the wicker basket transferred to a special harness on the cab wall beside her. Even in the city, where she was obliged to take it easy to avoid vehicle wrecks and pits in the macadam, I could tell she wasn't about to make it comfortable on her passengers. She throttled where any sane person would have braked, skewed the machine at hairpin corners round ancient riot-control vans with their panels stripped off and their remains burnt to slag, and every time I stared in horror at her recklessness there was a savage smile on her face.

Great.

She never hit anything and the rest of her crew were entirely at ease. Eventually I stopped staring ahead and decided to take in the scenery, just as the Yankee Stadium went sailing by on my right. Gone, mostly – just a few shards of tangled black spaghetti at the heart of a splintered parking-lot continent – but the determined observer could just about make out the sagging segments of an aircraft's tail hanging over the edge of the burnt-out shell. I wondered what had happened, then decided I'd rather not know.

Someone had painted 'THICKER THAN WATER' in black tar across a fifty-foot expanse of the parking lot. I wondered if it would be visible from space.

Next to Malice, in the cab, was where Spuggsy sat. Well, reclined anyway. Lazed.

Slobbed.

Spuggsy, from what little I'd seen, wasn't much of an engineer. Granted, he had a gift for smoothing-out the most angular of mechanical kinks, though I couldn't help noticing his technique tended to involve hitting things hard with a spanner until they started making the right noises. He was short and plump, as bald as a cueball and sat there flicking lazily through porno mags with an expression of unconquerable boredom. His one concession to arousal was the copious sweat oozing off his chubby face, but given that it remained even when he *wasn't* browsing *Anal* Carnage, *Wet Domination* or whatever the hell it was, that didn't mean much. When he spoke it was with an enthusiastically sleazy good nature – like a mischievous schoolboy who discovered German hardcore before he discovered snot-eating contests – and I found myself liking him and wanting to disinfect him in equal measure.

The Cross Bronx Expressway petered-out in a fug of chipped road segments – mottled like they'd been in a firefight – and then the Hudson was below us, wide and shimmering and almost passable for clean. The George Washington Bridge stood just as solid and untroubled as always, as if this 'End Of Humanity' business was a passing fad by which it was neither impressed nor concerned. A couple of scavs had hanged themselves from the rails on one side (I like to think it was a tragic death-pact between lovers despairing of this cold new world... but it could just as easily have been a drunken dare) and a crowd of others was tugging them down as we passed by. Tugging a little *too* violently, actually, with knives and roasting-sticks in hand and a fat man building a campfire, waving-away the gulls like the unwanted competition they were.

Tora kept them covered from the pintle-cannons all the way past.

"Fucking *cannies*," she spat.

Tora was sort of weird. She came from Japanese stock she said – a heart-shaped face and dark hair (dyed deep blue at its tips), with a delicate sweep to the edges of her eyes and a nose like a button – and was one of the most mixed-up women I've ever known. Not beautiful exactly, but she knew how to move, had an attitude you wouldn't believe and could easily have flirted for her country. But it was *skewed* – the whole thing – like you knew somehow she was damaged; fucked-up deep inside, and everything she did was just a façade to create the impression of humanity. She used sexual friendliness like a battering ram. Like an act of aggression. Her arms were covered – wrist to shoulder – in thin little scars where she'd cut herself, and she sat in the dangling canopy above our heads – half poking-out to man the guns – singing a pretty song and carving new tally-marks into her skin. I asked her about it, later on. She shrugged and said:

"Why do you scratch when you've got an itch?"

"To make it feel better."

"Uh-huh."

I never found out what had happened to her – shit, maybe she was just born that way – but you could see it every time she looked at you, or spoke to you, or smiled. Like... just behind the veil, behind the spunky playful bollocks and cleavage-jutting body language, she was eyeing that scalpel and wondering just how deep she'd have to cut to make *all* the itches go away.

We bounced into New Jersey in a blur; Malice finally able to throttle-up all the way. Fort Lee, Leonia; names on crooked signs that drifted by without any sensation of reality. Just echoes of something that might once have had some significance, but now... Nothing. Skeletons on the edge of the road – picked clean – and blasted wrecks that jutted and trailed, forcing us to slow. Highway 80, place names fogging-by.

Hackensack.

Saddlebrook.

Elmwood Park.

At one stage Malice muttered something darkly to Spuggsy – spotting something ahead – who huffed and dropped his magazines then scrambled back towards us, poking Nike and Moto awake from their nest of sleeping bags and telling Tora to stand-by. The *Inferno* jinked hard to one side; overtaking.

It was strange to see another vehicle on the open road; but even stranger to see one so... *normal.* I'd expected dune-buggy gangs, flame-jobs, hotrods and... oh, I don't know. Nuclear-fucking-powered bulldozers, maybe. Skull-hurling catapults. Something a little more... *survivalist.*

Passing an HGV hauling a trailer marked *Cheesy Snax* was pretty surreal.

A couple of heads poked warily from the roof – guns arrayed cautiously towards us, just in case – and I spotted square slits in the corrugated sides of the container, bulging with naked flesh and squinting eyes.

"Workers," Tora told me, swinging in her harness. "'Burb klans. Scavs work the fields, different shifts going back and forth all the time."

"Dangerous?"

"To us? *Pfft.*"

But still, but still... It was tense, as we passed them by, and Moto stared back at them – through the square porthole above the rear gun mount – for long minutes afterwards.

Moto and Nike kept themselves to themselves, mostly.

The former was a well-built young man with startling white hair and an almost perfect face. I figured before The Cull he was maybe a model in cologne commercials, or a male escort, and he looked simply *wrong* – out of place, somehow – in the midst of all us raggedy bastards in the back of the *Inferno*. Actually, scratch that: he looked *almost* out of place. His one concession to chaos and ugliness was worn proud on his cheek. A mess, shredded and rippled in all kinds of gravely keloid contours, so that his lip and eye were all but joined by the matted tangle of scarring. He'd been whipped with barbed-wire, Spuggsy told me later with an indecent grin. Held down by a bunch of thugs and whipped carefully... lovingly, almost, by Nike. He didn't say why.

Towns went by. The QuickSmog came down, hid the distant rooftops and tree lined avenues, then went back up again.

Denville.

Roxybury.

Netlong.

Hills and gorge-blasted roads, the weak sun, the *Inferno* rumbling ever on.

That scar on Moto's cheek, I figured it was like a brand. Like some jealous tribal elder, maybe, defacing his young spouse to dissuade all thoughts of adultery. Maybe it was punishment. Some quiet misdeed, some jealous retribution. Fucksakes, who knows? The types of people out there these days, for all I knew Nike might have done it to *improve* the poor kid's face according to his own twisted tastes.

Either way, it was a mark – a signature – left by Nike, that said loud and clear:

Mine.

Moto said pretty much nothing to anyone except Nike

for the whole journey, and when he *did* it was quiet and deferential, and he turned his face to one side so that all anyone ever saw of him was the scar. He seemed quite happy. *They* seemed quite happy.

Love, huh?

Nike, by comparison, was tall and skinny, quite old, I'd guess, and a perfect gentleman in every way. He nodded and smiled, and passed the time of day, and traded dirty songs with Nate. Towards the end of the first day, when Malice swapped with Spuggsy for a kip, Nike chatted to me about what sort of state London was in. He told me how he used to be a teacher – American history – and collected model aircraft for a hobby.

Everything about him oozed calm, rational, intelligent, polite decency.

And then you happened to glance at Moto, staring like a devoted dog at the older man, face all fucked-up like that, and you *wondered*.

We stopped for a bite to eat on the freeway, just outside a place called Knowlton. Nate cooked, giggling and dancing annoyingly. The *Inferno* carried a heap of supplies as part of the cost of rental, and amongst the tins and rats there were three actual chickens and a genuine, freshly baked loaf of bread. If it's possible for your tongue to have an orgasm, mine did.

Mostly we sat by the fire – silent – though Tora stayed on the roof of the *Inferno*, keeping one eye on the road, and the man who called himself Hiawatha took it upon himself to perch, cross-legged, some distance away. He looked like he should have been meditating – communing with some indefinable infinite – but instead was smoking an enormous spliff and starring at the sky, nodding or shaking his head at random intervals. I still wasn't too sure what to make of him.

Earlier on, when all my questions were exhausted and his enigmatic bullshit responses were getting right on my wick, I'd got bored and asked him where he got the weed from.

He smiled mysteriously and said it wasn't just weed.

Moron.

"Surely," I said, with just a tiny guilty hint of pomposity, "there are more important things to be growing?"

"Yes," he said. "We grow them too."

I left him to it, after that.

It was around then that Malice decided she'd had enough sulking and sat down next to me, only slightly frosty. She offered me a flask of water.

"Ta."

"Your friend," she said, too quiet for anyone else to hear. She nodded towards Nate. He was picking gristle out of his teeth, fiddling with the red case he'd had with him ever since the Wheels Mart.

"What about him?"

"He okay?"

I scowled, glancing at him again for any obvious signs of damage. It occurred to me that in all the excitement and strangeness of beginning this weird journey, I'd barely spoken to him. Certainly I hadn't asked him if he was sure he wanted to come along. He just... *had*.

"He looks okay," I said.

"I *mean*... is he trustworthy?"

I stopped chewing and stared at her. Skin prickling.

I don't know why I didn't blurt-out "*of course he is*" straight away. I don't know why I didn't tell her he'd saved my life a bunch of times since I'd met him, had expected nothing in return but a few condoms and a pot of dog food, and was even more in danger from the fucking Clergy than *I* was. I don't know.

"Why do you ask?" I said, intrigued despite myself. Was she getting it too? That feeling. That *sense* of...

Not quite right...

"'Cause the motherfucker's been outta his tree all day on whatever shit he's got in that pack and he ain't slowing down."

I scratched my chin, brain flopping over. "There a problem with that?"

(Actually, there *was* a problem with that. Two problems. The first was, I hadn't noticed. Hadn't being paying attention. Too busy watching the road, watching the others in the group. Letting myself down.

The second was, where the hell did the sneaky old bastard *get* it from?)

"No," she said, wobbling the harness on her shoulders. "No, I guess not. Only he keeps staring at my baby. All the time. *All* the time."

I told her not to worry.

Highway 80.

We hit Pennsylvania pretty soon afterwards. It looked a lot like NJ.

Towns. No longer paying attention. Letting the names roll together, like some great American gestalt; an obese vehicle with a thousand names that used cheeseburgers for fuel and liposucked fat for tyres.

I get surreal when I'm bored, and *boy* was I *bored*!

Stroud.

Kidder.

Black Cross.

Out across the fields, unlikely contraptions wobbled and smoked and steamed; hybrids of a hundred combine harvesters tended by hordes of miserable locals. At one point a bunch of guys on motorbikes overtook us, not even slowing to stare or glare. They wore strange silver puffer-jackets and jauntily-positioned bowler hats, gunning Harleys with hair flapping behind them. Each vehicle had skulls bouncing in its wake, like cans tied to the back of a bridal limo, and a smattering of guns hoisted on its pillion.

Tora tracked them the whole way over the horizon.

Hiawatha, who hadn't moved from his corner since we came aboard, except to roll and smoke occasional joints, twisted his whole head to watch them go by. I wondered what he was seeing. I wondered how he'd even known they'd been there in the first place, when he wasn't sitting anywhere near a window.

Actually, there was a *lot* I wondered about that boy.

He said he came from a place that was once called Fort Wayne. He said, actually, it was just outside the city; the rolling plains of Ohio where the Haudenosaunee convened once a year, with all its scattered lodges coming together to plan and barter and talk.

He used long words that I'd never heard before and didn't understand. All the time.

He spoke with a natural sort of rhythm which was as off-putting as it was hypnotic. Like a mother reading a nursery rhyme or a poet picking his way through pentameter.

Like an evangelist, too. Like a mantra.

The weirdest thing was, every now and again there was a *crack* in what he said. Just a little fissure, a hint of something beneath. You notice that shit when you're me.

The voice changed, the eyes blinked. For a second or two he was just some kid; confused and wrapped up in something too big to understand, who didn't believe his own mumbo-jumbo any more than I did and had all the attitude of a scared young thing caught in the company of double-hard bastards. Too much testosterone for his own good, too much insecurity for his own safety.

I preferred him, in those tiny moments.

He said someone called the 'Tadodaho' had decided that my course and his were... well, he used the word "aligned". It seemed too weird, to me. I'd never heard of this guy and he already knew where I was headed, what area I'd be passing through, who I'd be up against.

Hiawatha said:

"It's all been seen. It's all been dreamed."

Enigmatic Bullshit.

Listen: I believe in moving fast, taking opportunities, focusing on what's ahead and getting the job done. I believe that anyone who gets in my way is dead. I believe in my own ability to deal resourcefully with any situation, and kill the fuck out of any stupid wanker who tries to stop me.

I believe in:

Don't you fucking give up, soldier!

I believe in:

Know everything.

Cover the angles.

What I *don't* believe in is Thunderbirds and dream-quests and voices on the wind and patterns in the sky, which is the sort of stuff Hiawatha talk/recited about right after he'd smoked one of his spliffs. Outside a town called Mifflin, as the afternoon wore on, Malice lost her temper and shouted at him to quit murdering her baby with his second-hand cancer gas. He smiled, shrugged, and blinked once or twice at the baby, like he was about to deliver some quasi-wise rebuttal.

Instead he just looked somehow... sad.

"Yeah," said the real-life-insecure-boy lost behind all that mystical arsebilge. "Yeah."

He climbed up to smoke on the roof, after that, and every time he went Nate watched him go, muttering and rolling his eyes, groaning in pleasure.

I caught him shooting-up, once or twice – sat in the dark corner at the back of what had once been the *Inferno's* pump-housing. *Hey,* I told myself, *as long as he's happy.*

But still. But still.

Lamar.

Boggs.

Lawrence.

Pine Creek.

Place names harder and harder to read with every mile. Eventually the sun slid like an old turd behind the hazy west and even the road signs – decorated variously in graffiti, dangling bodies and hungry looking crows – vanished into the ocean of dark beyond the *Inferno's* lights. At some unspecified moment, ducking and weaving between the mangled remains of some long-gone pileup, Spuggsy declared out loud the road was "covered in more shit than a nuthouse wall," and declined to go any further until it was light.

We pulled up and ate again, in silence.

Up in the hills, and across the landscape to either side, tiny embers of light shivered away, like fireflies. Families, maybe. Cannibals, psychotic mountain-men, diseased brain-dead mutants or whatever. But most probably just families – normal people, or as good as – trying to stay warm and stay together.

Poor fuckers.

I chewed rat and didn't think about it.

Somewhere nearby, Nate was singing a song to himself

and laughing after every verse. Totally wasted, totally out of his tree. It would have been funny – would have been endearing – if he didn't glance up every now and again, all casual, and stare at Malice's kid. I was noticing it now. The little hint of... what? Intensity, that visited his face in those moments.

I shivered again.

The crew slept in shifts. Two on watch at all times. Malice volunteered to take the last shift alone and I offered to accompany her. She shrugged, like:

Do what you want, asshole. It's your lack of sleep.

I dreamed of seagulls wearing robes, man-sized spliffs running up and down along the George Washington Bridge on little stubby feet, and of a great wound in the heart of New York; bleeding a fine mist of QuickSmog up into the air, where it separated into colossal blood cells that floated and wobbled like lava-lamp clouds.

I dreamed of Bella saying:

"*Doesn't matter. Not your problem. But that's why I'm going.*"

Then she flopped over in my arms, gave me a look of bored disinterest, and poked me in the rigs.

"*Hey,*" she said. "*Hey, Patchwork...*"

Malice, waking me up for the watch. I tried to conceal my hard-on.

"So."

"So."

"What's this all about?"

I scratched my manky ear through its equally-as-manky dressing. "Which 'this', specifically?"

She nodded out into the dark.

"Going west. Highway 80. Lake Erie. What's there,

patchwork man?"

I smiled.

"Probably nothing."

She thought about that for a moment. "That's a long way to go. Lot of trouble, for probably nothing."

We sat in silence for a minute or two, listening to the deafening silence of the world. It wasn't a cold night, exactly, but there was something... *shivery*, yeah, about such profound darkness. Like living in oil.

Yeah, we had a rifle each. And *yeah*, we could scramble inside and be manning Tora's collection of hardcore artillery within a second or two. But still, we were *tiny*. We were nothing. There were stars and sky and road and hills, and nothing else, and we were just parasites. Fucking *fleas* on the back of an elephant.

I told you already, I get abstract when I'm bored.

"Okay," I said to Malice, suddenly feeling talkative, catching her eye. "Long way to go. You're right. You mind if I ask you something?"

She shrugged.

"It might piss you off."

"Would that stop you?"

"Probably not."

"Then shoot."

I fiddled with the rifle, keeping my eyes fixed – uselessly – on the night. Somewhere far, far away I thought I could hear engines, a muted throb that died away almost instantly, and left me doubting my own senses.

"Let's say there's something you want," I said. "Let's say you... you had it once. Lost it. Want it back."

Her eyes narrowed, just a fraction. I wondered if she knew Tora told me about her other kid, and if she'd blow my head off for raking the past. She didn't look the type to enjoy in-depth discussion about personal tragedies long bygone.

I know the feeling.

"Let's say," she said, cold.

"Right. Now let's say you find out there's a chance. This thing, getting it back, it's... It's the world. It'll make everything better. It's *important* – and, shit... not just to *you*. To *everyone*."

She didn't move. I blundered on, forcing myself not to jump when a bird launched from some perch out in the dark, cawing noisily.

"Far as you know, it's gone. For good. And okay, that's a shitter, and you'd pay money for it to be otherwise, but what's done is done. You're a realist. You bottle it up, you put it away, you *get on*. You get by."

I could see it in her eyes, and in that quiet little instant we were so *the same* I could have reached out and touched her and felt my own fingers against my own arm.

The silence got a little thicker.

I stared at her. "And now suddenly there's a chance. One in a million. Defies all logic, as far as you know. No reason to *believe* it, no reason to give it headroom. But still..."

"*Just in case.*"

She swallowed, lips tight.

"How far," I finished, "would you go?"

Her jaw rocked back and forth once or twice.

"Long way," she whispered.

I nodded.

We sat.

We waited.

I smiled.

"You should go inside." I said.

She glared. "Pardon me?"

"You should go inside." I drew the knife from my belt

and passed her the rifle.

"And why the fuck would I do that?"

"Because there are two men approaching the truck from two different directions, and we're sitting ducks up here."

Even in the gloom, I could see her eyes go big. Disbelief, maybe. Surprise.

"They pulled up a mile out on motorbikes. Probably from that crew that passed by earlier on. Listen."

"But I don't h..."

"There. A twig. And another bird. Fucking *amateurs*."

She just stared.

"Don't worry." I said, and I smiled again because I couldn't help it, and I couldn't be bothered to stop. "I won't be long."

And I slipped off the edge of the truck and onto the concrete, panther quiet, and went out into the shadows with a savage joy.

Don't you fucking give up, soldier!

It snarled. It *burned*.

Sir, no sir! Etc etc.

When I got back Hiawatha was sitting on the roof, waiting, fiddling with something small and silver.

"You get 'em?" He said.

I wiped blood off the knife and stared.

Letting the humanity come back into me. Slowly.

Reluctantly.

First rule of stealth combat. Advanced training, third year:

Don't fear the predator in the dark.

Be *it*.

"I can see you," Hiawatha said, conversationally.

"Properly, I mean. All that... *conditioning*. All those changes. You're a wolf, mister Englishman. You know that? Inside your head. They made you a wolf."

The adrenaline was still up. Heart still going. Beast still *just* below the surface.

I spat on the ground. Couldn't be fucked with any more mystical bollocks.

Hiawatha smiled and said nothing.

"Who were they?" I said, not bothering to sound impressed or spooked-out or anything but bored. My hands were shaking with the desire to hunt and hurt, and this snotty little idiot was getting on my tits.

"Collectors," he said, after a pause.

"And they are?"

"They're... I mean..." He stopped and scowled, and I could see again the person coming through, the scared kid chipping-away at the 'Know-it-all Straight Jacket'. Then it was gone.

"They're scouts." He said, voice rising and falling in that same lilting chant. "Men of money and misery. Mercenary filth. Cells of aggression, unfaithful, unloyal, sent ahead of the crucified god and his robed horde to..."

"Cut the crap, yeah? Just tell me who they are."

He blinked.

And slowly, boyishly, smiled.

"Fuckheads." He said.

"Fuckheads. Right. And what do these fuckheads want with us?"

He shrugged.

"Clergy sends them, mostly. Or at least, that's where they get their shit. Trading with the Clergy. They... roam round. Outside of cities. Finding things the Church'll pay for."

"Things like what?"

"Like guns. Food. And... mostly... mostly kids." He looked away. Jaw tightening.

"Kids."

"Yep. No Klans out here, see? No loyal fucking scavs to hand over their own kin. Only the Clergy and the scum they pay, helping themselves. That's... that's what this is all *about*. You being here."

"I don't follow."

"I know. But you will."

I huffed and shook my head, too tired to push it. "Whatever. Doesn't explain what they want with *us*."

"No... But they came from behind, on the road. From the city, probably."

"And?"

And then the boy was gone, and fucking Hiawatha was back, smiling and staring and rolling his eyes.

"And perhaps this holy man, this John-Paul, this withered thing... Perhaps he knows where you're headed. Perhaps he sent word to slow you down."

"How the fuck would *he* know?"

I remembered the personnel file. The name. The photo. Cy, staring over my shoulder.

Hiawatha ignored the question and stared off into the night.

"Tomorrow," he said. "We'll find the rest tomorrow. They sent out these two to take us in the dark. Explosives, yes?"

I grunted, patting the pockets of my coat. There'd been four sticks of C4 on each corpse, with some surprisingly sophisticated remote detonators. Out in the dark, when the fat fucks had stopped shivering and bleeding and trying to shout with their windpipes torn-through, I'd helped myself.

"So if we're lucky the rest won't know we survived."
Hiawatha smiled and nodded.
We weren't lucky.

CHAPTER SIXTEEN

We hit Ohio first thing, and they were waiting for us.

Outside a town called Hubbard, rammed up against the edge of the I-80 like a gaudy reminder of a long lost time, was Truck World. Truck World did exactly what it said on the tin.

There must have been twenty or so vehicles. Vast things, these fuckers; like whales built for the road, basking outside a long derelict burgers-n-barf joint and a once snazzy truck wash. And not the poky little beasts we used to get in the UK either, but *monsters*. Bloody great behemoths with bulging engines and recurved exhausts, chrome snouts and brightly painted bodies. And yeah, they'd been grafitied and smashed up – what hadn't? – but they were still *awesome* to see, lined-up like that. Like hibernating ogres, waiting for a wake-up call.

I was still staring at them through the window when Malice hit the brakes.

Still staring when Hiawatha – who had his eyes closed – shouted: "Fuck! Fuck, they're *waiti...*"

Still staring when Tora – bless her cotton socks – opened fire with the Mk19 and everything went nuts.

The Collectors weren't stupid. Their two boys didn't come home to them with the dawn. They'd taken precautions – obvious, really – and big dumb precaution one was to block the road.

Truck World, when all was said and done, had represented one big sodding barricade on wheels. They'd strung them out across the interstate, those road-whales, two deep and three across, with no room to edge the *Inferno* past and no hopes of ramming through.

And the Collectors – leather junkies with artfully

matted hair and once-expensive sunglasses, silver jackets patched and frayed, bowler hats arrayed like a long line of tits, lounging back on purring choppers like middleclass morons who'd watched *Easy Rider* once or twice too often – they *swarmed.*

The day before, when the little gang went zipping by, there'd been maybe six or seven. Lightly armed. All mouth and no trousers.

Now there were twenty, easy, and as the *Inferno* squealed to a halt and Malice wrestled to reverse, swearing inventively as she went, the windshield blew in like a metaphysical fart, glass frothed through the air, bullets rattled like drumbeats on the firetruck's skin, and everything *shook.*

Bikes. Engines growling in every direction. Smoke-bombs and sound overkill. Voices whooping and shouting, closing in. Someone with a fucking boom-box, playing *Metallica* at double speed.

Thump-thump. The Mk19.

Thump-thump, then – distantly – the hard-edged crack of a detonation, tarmac spewing and smoke gushing. One of the bikes fell apart, lifting up and out on the rim of a fireball, and Tora shrieked like a joyful psycho, chugging-out lead with the autos whilst re-sighting with the grenades.

Nike and Moto opened fire, which meant the arseholes had surrounded us. Heavy *things* thumped against the walls of our dark little cell, and I found myself torn between the frustration of sightlessness to the rear, and confronting the ugly situation through the windows at the fore. The *Inferno* twisted and flexed on the road, three-point-turning under a withering storm, and every whirligig impression through the flying glass and shifting landscape was a scene of spinning rubber, gun flare and snarling faces with too many piercings. Nate started screaming – fucking junkie probably didn't even realise what was happening – and outside Tora found another target. Another shuddering clash of sparks and steel, and a scream lost to the rolling thunder.

But it wasn't enough, wasn't enough, wasn't enough...

One of the tyres exploded.

The *Inferno* pitched to one side, wobbled. Malice shouted. A deeper growl came out of the tumult and Spuggsy was yelling like a kid – "No! Oh no, no! *No!*" – staring through his window, eyes wide.

Then he was just...

Paste.

It was another juggernaut – though I didn't figure it out until the world stopped rushing backwards and the *Inferno* went back to standing still. They'd taken the opportunity as we crept sluggishly away from the blockade, firing-up the nearest HGV and ploughing directly into the cockpit; an acute angle that left the ramming truck speared on the *Inferno*'s jagged nosecone – driver chuckling insanely through shattered glass and bloody teeth, his ride mashed all to fuck and venting radiator steam into our cab – but it'd done its job. Spuggsy was crushed, with barely time to scream, and as the impact shunted us away he was a thing of fractured angles and limp bones, head lolling, skull slack, porn mags fluttering uselessly amidst broken glass.

And then footsteps. Heavy thumps on the roof. Collectors scrambling off the cab of their own truck onto the *Inferno*'s back. One hopped down onto the hood, sleek black auto ready to fill the interior with lead, but Malice calmly shot him in the forehead and watched him sag out of view.

Not enough. Not enough.

The baby started to cry.

Moto and Nike were firing continuously now, screams and shouts intermingled with stamps and boot falls on the ceiling, and Tora's dangling rig swivelled round and round like a drunken ballerina, spitting grenades and bullets at whatever target she fancied. She was shouting too, high voice clearly discernible above the racket – "Too many! Too many!" – and a world away Malice was fighting to restart the truck, its engine coughing uselessly.

"We're screwed," she said, quietly, calming the baby in a maternal little bubble of her own.

"Fuck that!" Tora wailed. "Fuck thaaaat!"

Thump-thump, thump-thump.

Bikes detonating. Men screaming.

Didn't matter.

Faces leering at windows, batons crashing against reinforced glass. I leaned out the window and emptied the last clip of the mini-Uzi into the fuel tanks of a dirty red Harley, smirking as the rider was shredded, his whooping comrades doused in burning gas, his bike reduced to a rubberised shrapnel-bomb.

But it wasn't enough.

Then Tora was just *gone*. Vanished upwards through her circular lookout, feet thrashing, screaming and spitting and calling for help. The voice was carried off, away from the truck, dwindling to an echo of a scream on the smoky air.

And then they came in.

Three of them. Bullet-vests under leather, hockey-masks over heads. A knife and a pistol each. Shock troops.

Repelling assault-squads. Kill the last one first.

Advanced training, year two.

He's the best. He'll send cannon-fodder ahead. Useless rookies.

He'll come last, wait 'til you're tied up.
So you kill him first.

Nice thought. But the *Inferno* wasn't a big space, and by the time bastard-number-three slid down the chute, I was up to my elbows in the first two goons.

Savage again. Reacting without thinking.

"They made you a wolf..."

Well woof-the-fuck-woof.

I killed Number 1 pretty quick. Only fired once – back on the M16 again – but the startled motherfucker grew a hole in his forehead and another in his cheek, knocking out his lower jaw and spraying us all, so I figured Malice was playing along too over my shoulder.

The second guy was luckier. Used his mate for cover, even held him up like a human shield – hand on the hem of his jeans – and pumped three panicky rounds into Nike's legs, hanging from the gun mount above, before I pushed up close and shot him through his buddy's throat. Even then he took his sweet time, bashing about, trying to get a bead on my head as he squirted from his neck and screamed like a bullhorn. I had to bash his fucking brains out against the heavy iron edges of the gun-mount above, and he stared at me – eyes burning, accusing; lips spitting and frothing – all the way.

Somewhere a great noise went up. Like... like an army of hyenas, all laughing at once. I had no time to think about it, no time to try and place it, no time even to notice – in any sense except one of pure instinct – that outside the *Inferno* the gunfire had stopped...

The third man to tear into our little space, the man I should have killed first, he was *hollering*.

Ignoring everyone.

Throwing down his gun in contempt.

And leaping onto Hiawatha with an inhuman scream.

"K-k-kiiilled *Sliiiiip!*" he growled, knife held above the boy's eyeball, wrestling and grunting and rolling. "Ffffucking *kill you!*" Beneath the Cullis of his helmet his face was a mass of festering wounds, skin scraped-clear, bloody welts from chin to brow, nose a smeared mess.

Hiawatha was babbling, eyes wide, tears on his cheek, both hands wrapped around the hilt of the blade, shrieking "Sorries" and "Pleases" and "OhGodDon'tKillMes". Human again. A boy, scared and lonely and pissing himself and—

And I placed the muzzle of the M16 against the man's head, feeling abruptly calm, and said:

"Hey."

He looked at me. I shot him through the eye. So it goes.

And then everything was quiet. At least, quiet*er*. As quiet as it *could* be with Hiawatha sobbing for his mother, Nike yelling and moaning, Malice's kid screaming like a dying cat, and my own heart pounding in my ears.

But no more gunfire. No more biker engines. No more grenades detonating or trucks rumbling towards us.

I stared out the window – through the crazy spider web shatter-patterns on what little glass remained – and saw why.

"Ffffuck," said Malice.

The Collectors had been scared off. I knew how they felt.

There was an army. Hundreds upon hundreds of men and women.

Guns.

Bikes. Cars. Horses.

They looked kind of pissed.

His Holiness John-Paul Rohare Baptise closed his eyes and kneaded his temples.

Inside his head a sealed gate was opening wide. Every time he stopped to think. Every time there was no distraction – nothing to stare at, nobody to talk to, nothing to think about – it was like... like stepping into a great bazaar, full of painful exhibits he'd never seen before.

Or... worse, like a labyrinth. Yes. That was it. The memories didn't come pouring out, exactly. He had to go in and explore, hunt them down, look for them. Afraid, tentatively digging into dark corners.

Never too sure what he'd find.

He'd always known there had been buried treasures. Always felt, instinctively, that for whatever reason his mind had shut him away, closed itself down to him. He'd called it, privately, a gift from 'Above'. A purification designed solely to plant him firmly in the Now and the tomorrow. Never concentrating on 'then'. Never looking back. It was as if everything that had existed about him, from before five years ago, had been stripped away in a rush of balefire. God had severed his past, he felt, because he was no longer a creature of history. His was a role of divine prescience. Shaping the world for the new dawn.

Why should he need a personal past for that?

And now this.

"Hmm."

It was all terribly confusing.

John-Paul Rohare Baptiste was remembering what it was to be something he hadn't been for a very, very long time, and it was giving him a headache above and beyond the state of near-intolerable pain he spent the majority of his life experiencing. The 'something' he was slowly remembering was:

Normality.

The car shuddered – just another pothole, probably, or at worst a car wreck being bumped aside by the snaking convoy – and he straightened out the crumpled sheets of paper in his lap. He supposed it could have been a coincidence... The English scum, the destroyer who'd come so close to finishing the Apostolic Church of the Rediscovered Dawn, rummaging about in old records... Coincidental that he'd just happened to find... this...

This.

This sheet. This crumpled personnel dossier with its clipped photograph and personal details, its family affiliations, service history, recommendations and citations.

One of the Cardinals had brought it to him. Found in some nameless file in some empty part of the Secretariat.

There was a story attached, he recalled – something about a struggle, a death? He couldn't remember. It hardly seemed important, now. Compared to this file, nothing seemed important.

John-Paul fingered the sheets and licked dry lips.

He'd always known his real name, at least. That had never been a shock. Back at... at the start, when he wandered into the city out of the west, alone and confused, filled only with the certainty of his own divinity and the exact requirements of his body in order to preserve it, even then he'd known. He'd had his birth certificate with him, hadn't he? Or... Or maybe he faked it? Maybe he...

Anyway.

Anyway, it didn't matter. He'd known he was John P. Miller, somewhere at the back of his skull. He just hadn't cared, until now. Didn't want to remember where the name had come from, who he'd been, what he'd done, what he'd been like as a person before he became more than a person; before he became John-Paul Rohare Baptise, Abbot of the greatest institution existing in the world today, architect of Tomorrow's Civilisation.

In a roundabout sort of way.

Another group of robed outriders swept past the limousine on his left. The driver was being boringly silent – probably star struck, the poor devil – and John-Paul found himself craving conversation, or distraction. Something of interest to stare at, perhaps, rather than the bland hills and blander roads of suburban nowhere. Something, anything, to take his mind off the sheet.

But no.

Sergeant John P. Miller. N.A.T.O liaison officer.
Assigned 4332/GGfT/332-099#1
PROJECT PANDORA.

It was a lot like watching a film. Like the trigger on a projector, immersing the viewer immediately in a cannonade of scenes, shots, impressions, memories. The only difference was, it was all inside his eyelids.

It all came right back to him, and for the fiftieth time he struggled with the desire to vomit. Soon he'd have to tell the driver to stop, to get the Acolytes up here, to prepare the Host.

It was a lot to take in.

And this, at his age. At his time of life. In his current state of health. Oh, was there no end to the tests he must pass?

He mumbled a prayer and tried to ride out the nausea.

He'd seen his empire shaken to its roots. He'd seen his fortress invaded by heretics and filth, his perfectly structured city ripped away from his grasp and – oh, worst of all – his link with the world denied to him. The great satellite dish on the banks of the East River, the great studios and broadcast suites his loyal children had pieced together inside the General Assembly buildings. The means of speaking to the world.

The means of reaching out.

Spreading the Good Word.

All of it taken away. Destroyed, ripped apart, trampled underfoot by the ignorance and hatred of those who could never hope to understand his Divine Plan; who were led by The Man. The Stranger. The...

The fucking Devil.

John-Paul muttered a second prayer, shocked at the crudity of his own thoughts. Perhaps, though, it didn't matter. Perhaps... Mm. Perhaps being reawakened to his past was no simple coincidence, but an act of the Lord in itself?

Yes. Yes, that was it.

His tribe was beaten, but not destroyed. His home was taken from him.

What better time to recall another place? A better place. A hidden place, where once he'd served a far lowlier authority than the Lord. A place with communications facilities of its own. With defences and secrecy.

A place to start again, and grow strong.

He found himself clenching his jaw.

And if, in the course of this Holy Exodus to new lands and new futures, he should come across that same troublesome bastard, that Limey cumrag, if that should occur – and the Collectors had been sent out to make fucking sure it did –

Then fine.

Fine. Whatever the Lord willed, of course, but... Yes. Mm.

If. If they met him...

There would be a reckoning.

Hiawatha was real again. Curled on the floor, shallow breathing, fighting tears and trauma, the dead Collector hunched over beside him with his brains leaking out.

This was how the poor kid must have been, before. Before he came all the way to find me, in a city he'd never visited, with a head full of mumbo-jumbo and a mission I still wasn't any closer to understanding.

It was like the whole thing with the psycho and the knife – the guy with his face scraped off – had been the last straw, and whatever weird-arsed personality he'd been hiding behind these last few days, inhaling it up through each of his sweet-smelling spliffs, it was comprehensively gone.

Thank *fuck*.

In the sudden silence after the fight, as we traded glances and worked ourselves over to find wounds and scars, as we eyed the horde gathered outside the truck with growing anxiety, Hiawatha wiped his eyes and started to laugh.

We all stared at him. Even Nike, crippled on the floor, fussed over by Moto (who clearly had never expected to be the one to do the fussing), looked up from his pain and misery in shock. Even Nate, curled in smacked-up otherworldly confusion, stared and muttered.

Hiawatha took one look out the window, grinning at the hordes of silent figures standing there. Just standing, staring. He smiled like he'd overcome constipation and shat a gold brick, then rummaged in his bag for the dope he'd been smoking and threw it with undisguised satisfaction through the mangled hole where Tora had been taken.

Like he didn't need it any more.

"We're home," he said. "We're fucking *home*."

"But. Uh. Hiawa..."

"Rick." He said, shaking my hand warmly. "My name's Rick. Everything's going to be fine now. Come on."

He wriggled up and out through the gun-perch. I glanced significantly at Malice and checked the load in the M16. Then I went after him.

"Careful!" Nate giggled, eyes rolling. "Injun's a... Injun's a fucking liability."

Junkie.

Hiawatha was down on the ground, walking away. I went to follow him, then stopped.

There was a man on the roof of the *Inferno*.

I don't know how long he'd been there. I hadn't heard footsteps since the Collectors fucked off, and he didn't look the sort to go *anywhere* quietly. The wind moved in his hair, and the beads under his ears, and the feathers on his shoulders.

Which was sort of weird.

Because.

(*what the fuck is going on?*)

Because there wasn't any wind.

The sky smiled.

"Welcome," he said. And his face moved as he talked in ways I didn't understand, and the skin beside his eyes was a red desert that shifted with continental patience, and his eyes sucked in the universe, and the great decorated robe he wore, furled like the wings of a bat, danced in my eyes.

Messages in patterns.

The smile on the corners of his lips.

The—

The walkie-talkie poking out of his cloak.

What?

It hissed.

The man looked away for a second.

"*kkk*... llo..?" The radio said.

This vision before me, this ancient God of plains and prairies, this magnificent man with skin like leather and whorls of black and white across the bridge of his nose, with a great feather-totem spread across his shoulders and a long war-club held in his hand, he shifted from foot to foot, and said:

"Uh."

"*kkk*...cking *talk* to me, asshole motherf...*kkk*... said, is he *there* yet?... llo?... *kkk*... oddamn food's nearly ready an..."

The man rolled his eyes and sighed.

"C'mon," he said, turning away with a despondent beckon, reduced abruptly from awesome Earth Deity to an old bloke with a crazy costume. "Let's get a beer before the old bitches get pissy."

The *Haudeno... Haudanosaw... Haw...* oh, fuck, the *Iroquois* weren't what I expected at all.

Listen: I'm English. Only exposure I ever got to indigenous life was a school trip to a Stone Age village when I was a kid, and a whole shitload of John Wayne movies. You ask me, a Native American lives in a wigwam, says "How" a lot, and has a name like Two-Ferrets-Fucking. I know, I know. It's despicable, stereotypical and downright unforgivable. But I yam what I yam.

Still, I was *ready* to be educated, you know? As the quiet tribesmen loaded us all into cars and trailers, patching up Moto as best they could, and swarmed around the *Inferno* in our wake, I was prepared to have my eyes opened.

Rick – Hiawatha, whoever he was – babbled the whole away about the 'new' Iroquois. About how, in a cruel post-Cull world, the Old Ways worked best. He said the people who'd come out here, they forgot all that bullshit we used to call 'society' and went back to the land. Back to basics.

Funny thing is, he sounded sort of bitter as he said it.

Rick told me it was a popular movement. Sure enough at least half the tribesmen around us – variously wearing scavenged trousers, leather jackets or woolly jumpers, all with beads and mouse-skulls and intricate tattoos decorating heads and faces – were whiter than white. It was funny to see them like that. Embarrassing, in a way; like being seen in public with a raging tourist who doesn't mind stopping to take a photo every five seconds, and wears a hilarious T-shirt saying something like:

I CAME TO LONDON AND ALL I GOT WAS THIS LOUSY STD

But they looked so earnest, smoking their cigarettes and hefting their guns, and they acted so friendly as we drove, that I kept myself from pointing and laughing. It was a struggle.

The point is, I guess I was ready to be... impressed. Stunned by the allure of this atavistic lifestyle. I was awaiting nomadic groups, great tribal fires, comfy lodges made of wood and mud.

Oh, piss... I admit it: I was expecting a *spectacle*.

Instead I got thirty caravans, assorted Winnebago clones, two dozen pickups and one of those prefab mobile homes, like a cheap Swiss chalet, on the back of a lorry. I almost choked. They stood formed together in a rough circle around the prefab, on the banks of a clean-looking reservoir, in the shade of a huge bridge carrying the I-80 to the opposite bank.

The old man who'd greeted me, who'd introduced himself as we clambered into the waiting car as a 'Sachem' named Robert Slowbear, caught my look of vague disappointment. He seemed to bristle.

"Just a mobile base," he said, defensively. "Not regular at all. We're a long way from home too, stranger."

"Yeah?"

He settled back and smiled. "You should see the lodges, Englishman. Fields giving crops. Herds of swine all through the forests. More people coming every day..."

Hiawatha muttered under his breath. "Caravans as far as the eye can see..."

Slowbear threw him a *shuddup, kid* look.

"You all live in the same area?" I said, intrigued by the vision of some sprawling trailer park in the middle of Indiana.

The Sachem shook his head. "No, no... The *Haudenosaunee* is a... a Confederacy, not a state. Settlements with the right to roam. Mostly they stay still... farm, raise livestock, fish... Others move with seasons. We come together, now and then. Trade news. Share stories and lessons."

"Party..." Rick murmured, slightly more enthusiastic.

Slowbear ignored him. "The means of living vary, stranger. That is my point. Does it matter if a man sleeps beneath a pelt or a... a *duvet*? In a wooden lodge or a... hah... a TrekMaster 3000? The circumstances by which he acquired items do not lessen their value. It is the *ways* that matter. The councils. The families. The beliefs."

I felt my fists tighten, just a tad. Bugbear.

"What beliefs?"

He met my gaze, and we held eye-contact for a long time, without any sense of threat or status. It was an extraordinary sensation.

"Consider," he said, pausing to slurp on a flask of something that smelt like lager. "What is unchanged?"

He passed it to me. It tasted okay.

"What do you mean?" I said, wiping froth off my lip.

"This... this Blight. The 'Cull'. Call it what you like. What *didn't* it affect?"

I wasn't in the mood for a guessing game. "Tell me."

"Ha. The world."

I scowled.

"Do the animals care?" He said. "Did the deer fall down and die? Or the crows in the trees? Did the soil turn barren, or the rains stop? Did the earth *care*?"

"I guess not. Unless you count the minor case of nukage..."

"I don't."

"Figures."

"The point is, why look to some... heavenly God? Some crucified idiot born of mortal man." He stretched his arms out wide and gestured across the fields and hills, the glittering water of the reservoir and the clear sun in the sky. "Isn't this *enough*?"

I gave it some thought. It was a cute speech. Tempting, even. But still...

"Sounds a lot like just another faith-specific boys' Club to me." I said. "You don't believe, you don't get to play along."

He didn't look offended.

"You must understand," he smiled. "It's not the tasks a man performs that defines who he is. That's just staying alive. That's just *being*. It's what sings in his heart as he does so."

Out of the corner of my eye, I caught Rick rolling his eyes.

"And what sings in these peoples' hearts?" I said,

only a *little* wry, gesturing around me at the beered-up white-man-Injuns with their polished guns and rattling pickups.

Slowbear smiled faintly, and took a long time to answer.

"Freedom." he said.

I stared at him. Worked my jaw. Thought about it. Said:

"Just another way of saying 'nothing left to lose'..."

We finished the journey in silence.

They took Moto away to be looked after and sat the others down to eat and drink. Pork, bread, freshly harvested vegetables, thick soups and wooden bowls of porridgey-paste and whiskey. I eyed it all longingly as Slowbear led me away. Nate tried to follow, shivering as he came-down off whatever he was on, but a couple of big guys wearing freaky blue masks politely told him to get some food in his belly, and steered him back towards the campfire.

I made a mental note to have a word with the guy. He looked like death warmed-up, and things had been far too crazy for far too long for me to find out what he was taking.

Where he'd got it from.

What the hell he was *doing*...

The big mobile home was a lot more impressive on the inside than the out. Someone had stripped out most of the dividing walls and blanketed the floor in a cosy mish-mash of cheap Persian rugs, animal skins, fur-coats and a thick pile of carpet off cuts. It was like wading through the shaggiest patchwork in the world, and contrived to give the structure an earthy, russet-brown air; helped along no end by the chipboard walls. Each panel was so industriously graffitied with a swirling combination of text, iconic drawings and childlike scribbles that each component ceased to have any meaning on its own, and became just a part. A raw *splat* of language, of *culture*.

I caught myself getting abstract again, and noted the thick pall of smoke in the air, the sweet-sour smell of something that wasn't just tobacco.

Ah-ha.

It was weird. It was like I'd stepped through the door of this whitewashed suburban kitschism and entered some magical beaver-lodge. Some ancient cave, or skin covered bivouac. It just happened to have a few more right angles than you'd expect.

Slowbear lurked at the door and waved me inside.

"Who'm I looking for?" I asked, irritated by the mystery.

"The boss." He grinned, and closed the door.

At the end of the hallway I came to a large chamber, where the windows were boarded-up and the high ceiling lost behind a canopy of drooping skins and weird shapes. Knotted ropes and dyed fabrics, a mournful cow-skull and a stuffed eagle turning on a string tied to the roof-joists. There was a very old man sitting beneath it, hunched over an electric fire, wearing a bland little chequered shirt with a brown waistcoat. His hair was almost white, and pulled back in a silvery ponytail that left his face uncovered; magnificently under lit by the glowing heat. Each line on his face was a fissure in a great glacial surface; ruddy-red but still somehow icy, like it radiated age and a slow, unstoppable determination.

There was absolutely no doubt at all that this man was in charge, in every sense, and despite the lack of gaudy costumes and outrageous symbols, I had to wrestle with my own desire not to dip my head.

He was smoking a pipe in the shape of a bear-totem. It

looked cheap.

"Please," he said, and waved to a low chair placed opposite him. I made a move towards it, not thinking, and hesitated. Call me shallow, but the memory of the food cooking outside and the hole in my stomach was more powerful than I'd expected.

"No offence," I said. "But is this likely to take a while? I'm fit to fall down, here."

And then I smelt it.

Rich. Gamey. Good enough to kill for.

Vegetable aromas mixed with the smoky emanations of the old man's pipe, underscored at all times by the unmistakable scent of cooking meat. I realised with a stomach-gurgling jolt that the chamber led – via an archway in the corner – into a kitchen, and from inside caught the shadow of movement and a fresh burst of steam and smoke.

I almost dribbled.

"It is on its way." The old man smiled. He had a kind voice, and spoke with the thoughtful enunciation of a man to whom English is a second language.

I sat.

"Who are you?"

"*Tadodaho*." He said. "You would say... Chief. Over all the *Haudenosaunee*. Over the sachem council."

"And why have you brought me here, Chief?"

He puffed on the pipe, letting white coils billow upwards with that curious slowness of silt sinking through water, but reversed; rising to the surface, lifting up to—

Abstract bollocks.

Hold it together.

"You are here for a talk with the highest authority within our great Confederacy." He smiled, rotating the pipe in nimble old fingers. "The *Haudenosaunee* have been waiting for you."

"You knew I was coming?"

"Yes."

"You sent that kid to fetch me."

"Yes."

"How did he know where to look?"

He held out the pipe.

"A better question is: how did he know *how* to look?"

I pursed my lips. Stared at the pipe for a long time, then slowly shook my head.

"No thanks."

Clear head.

Know everything.

Cover the angles.

If my refusal constituted some big bloody cultural insult, or whatever, the old man gave no sign; shrugging good-naturedly and continuing to smoke himself.

Eventually, as the silence was killing me and the desire to blunder through to that kitchen and go crazy was starting to hotwire my muscles, he sighed through eddying clouds and said:

"My blood is not like yours."

"Excuse me?"

"Blood, Englishman. Blood *types*. I assume you are normal? Type 'O'. Rhesus negative. Yes?"

It was fucking weird, I don't mind telling you; sitting there in that warm lodge with a genuinely creepy tribal mystic, listening to him go off on one about bloody pathology. Like a brontosaurus with an MP3 player.

"Well..." I said, a touch too sarcastic. "You'll notice I'm technically *alive*..?"

"Mm."

"Then *obviously* I'm O-neg... What the fuck *is* th–?"

"I, on the other hand, am not."

He stared at me. His face was still. And in his eyes, oh fuck, I could see, I could just *tell*:

He wasn't lying.

"You're...? I don't underst..."

"Nor do we. Not fully. I tell you this because it will help you to understand why we have brought you here. We know you have desires of your own. Agendas. It is our hope that ours might briefly... compliment your own."

I swallowed. My mouth suddenly felt dry.

"Tell me more. About the... about how come you're still alive."

"I cannot. I do not understand such things. What I know is that of all my people alive before The Cull – my *true* people, stranger, by blood and birth – less than one half perished. Regardless of blood type.

"This, we hope, is welcome news to you.

"This, we hope, will give you some hope of your own."

He knows.

The old bastard, he knows what I'm looking for...

But if he's right. If he's telling the truth, then couldn't it mean that—

—don't even THINK it! Don't even dare to hope—

—that there's a chance?

That I didn't come here for nothing?

I must have looked thunderstruck. Sitting there, mind back flipping. The Tadodaho was tactful enough to say nothing, watching my face, and when five old ladies magically appeared in the doorway to the kitchen, each bearing a wooden bowl, each bowl smelling like it'd come direct from an all-angels edition of *Masterchef*, even then my excitement at the feast couldn't quite sever my thoughts.

Some people. Some people lived through it, who

shouldn't have.

Look at these folks.

Look at John-fucking-Paul.

Wasn't it possible?

I started eating like a man possessed, nodding thankfully to each woman as they delivered venison, sweet-potatoes, beans, sour-bread... In the confused fug of my thoughts – made sluggish by surprise and smoke – I noticed the last of the entourage wore flowing robes of a particularly vibrant red and had a cute little radio-mic clipped to what passed for her lapel. I squinted, trying to remember why this was significant, but couldn't. I thought the group might shuffle out of the room as they'd come in, but they gathered instead in a huddle of smiling faces and crinkled skin behind the Tadodaho, and stood there staring at me.

"The men of the Church," the old man said, watching me eat, "have their own interest in our survival."

I scowled, wiping sauce off my chin. "Why?"

"We don't know. All we understand is that their Collectors come to our lodges every day. In greater numbers. With guns and bikes and metal cords. Every day they come, every day they steal away our people."

"They take your kids?"

"There are no children left to *take*, Stranger. They have... widened their attentions. Any Iroquois, by birth. Any redskin. Any who survived the Cull, who should not have.

"They are killing us, little by little, Englishman. And we would like your help."

I stopped eating. I hadn't expected him to wrap-up so soon, and it felt like every eye in the room was boring into me.

Worse, the eyes *shifted*. Swirled. I shook my head to

clear the sensation.

"And... and that's why you brought me here?" I mumbled, trying to stay focused. "To help you beat-off the bastards?"

The room suddenly seemed far less angular. Tapestries became rocky walls. The steam from the kitchen was an underground river, spilling through sweaty caves.

"Sorry." I said, shaken. "My fight's not with the fucking Clergy. They got in my way, I took what I wanted. End... end of story."

Somewhere, a million miles away, I felt the bowl fall from my hands and spill across my legs. I felt the room move sideways. I felt the skins drooping from the roof writhe and flex.

"We understand." The Tadodaho said. "We know. And do not think us so crude that we would attempt to convince you otherwise. You are a stubborn man, Stranger. We have always known it."

"Then... thuh... then why... brng...me here...?"

Slurring.

Not good.

Something in the food.

Drugged.

Panic.

"I told you," the old man's voice said, from far, far away. "You are here to talk with the highest Authority within our Great Confederacy."

"Buh... But..." Every word was a struggle. Every syllable a living beast that fluttered from my mouth and scuttled across the air, leaving trails of purple and green fire. "But we bin... bin *talking* alrrrrrdy..."

Somewhere out in the soup of my senses, the Tadodaho's face coalesced.

"Not me." He smiled. "Not me."

And then five shapes – five woman-faces that rippled like ploughed earth and swarmed with a host of stars and fireflies – bulged together around me, hooked soft fingers beneath the skin of my mind and dragged me down to the past.

CHAPTER SEVENTEEN

They're watching me, but maybe there's not much I can do about that just now.

They're in every detail. Flaws, mainly. Like when you remember something with such crystal-clarity that you know every line, every shape, every resonance...

...and then you look up expecting to see London's grey skies, and there's a face looking down instead.

...and then you shake the blood off a knife, or finish retching with the force of your anger, and the droplets splattered on the floor form eyes, and stare right at you.

These memories, they're full of rage and violence and weirdness. And the thing with weirdness is, there's always room for more.

Things keep changing. Time keeps jumping. There's a roar in my ears like I'm underwater, but I'm not scared. They're watching me – those withered Injun women – but so what? They're talking to me, too, and their voices are pretty, and maybe I'm talking back or maybe I'm not, but either way: they're in here with me. Spying on my past.

Back to the start.

Back to London.

After I got the signal, in the comms room of the old MI6 building at Vauxhall Cross, where I'd whored myself to the SIS for years and years, I sliced up some people good. Clergy. I don't recall how many. I was too focused.

We'd all seen the planes. Every rat-human crawling in the filth of London knew they were there. Blue-painted, marked with the red 'O' of the Church, going up, coming down. Why? Who knew. Who cared.

I went to Heathrow. My mind was a needle. Too angry

to speak. Too focused to negotiate.

PANDORA

PANDORA

PANDORA

Like a mantra, see?

Nothing would turn me. I'd impale anything that dared get in my way.

And I waited. Cut and slashed in the night. Hacked open necks. Cut off fingertips. Made grey robes run red.

Not because I hated the Clergy.

Not because they had anything to do with anything.

Not for any reason except they were convenient, and they had something I wanted.

Took me three days of torturing to work my way up to a Clergy-bastard of sufficient hierarchical power to be worth taking hostage. I think – I know – I stopped being me for a bit there. Let the animal thing take over too much. Let the rampage-instincts out of their box.

It was a weird time.

I made sure everything felt significant, everything felt like a step in the right direction, and by god's own piss it felt good. I let everyone I came across seem responsible, took it all out on them, mixed up the anger with the focus, just like they taught me in training:

Made it personal.

So what I did, back at the start, I strolled into the airport as bold as brass, with this pigshit priest under my knife, telling every gun-wielding arsehole who came near to back off or get splashed.

And this guy, this hostage, this high-up canon or whoever he was, he leaned down so the knife was pressed up against his neck... and he shook his head.

Slit-slat-slit.

Faith. That's what. Obvious really. Never take any

wanker prisoner who's prepared to die for his beliefs.

So bang went my clever-clever attempt to hijack a plane alone, which is all I ever wanted out of those child-stealing sadistic delusional fucks. Bang went my momentum, bang went my anger, bang went the feeling of progress, of inertia-less drive. The juggernaut rolled to a halt.

Cue running away, hiding, rethinking.

Cue a realisation or two: doing it alone wasn't going to work. Focus wasn't enough.

Enter Bella.

I found her waiting outside the airport, just standing and staring. Like she was shellshocked, maybe, except it looked like she'd been that way for years. Watching every plane, mumbling to herself. Waiting for something to happen.

I happened.

Cut forwards in time.

Bella telling me she knew how to fly.

Recon of the airport.

Preparing. Arming-up.

Getting drunk one night and fucking, and not caring except to feel the guilt, and letting down the shields for five seconds and discovering – holy shit – I'm still human after all.

Telling myself I didn't care what her story was. Listening anyway.

They took her kid.

They took a thousand kids. Every week, another load. Off across the ocean. Off to be with the skeletal bastard Abbot off the TV. Off to a better life, or a worse one, or who knew what, except that it was OFF.

Scared. Crying. Can't you just imagine them?

(The faces in the clouds are watching and nodding, and

saying yes we can, and wiping tears and telling me to get on with it.)

And then there was Bella, saying:

"Doesn't matter. Not your problem. But that's why I'm going."

And then the time comes and we make our move, and con our way inside, and kill our way further, and gather guns and steal drugs, and then it's sprinting across tarmac, and guns opening fire, and pain in my shoulder, and Bella dragging me up the steps, and then—

And then away. Stateside-bound.

And then the story started.

And Bella died in fire and pain and chaos.

And Nate and the city and blah blah blah.

"Doesn't matter," Bella told me, as we clung to each other in the dark. "Not your problem."

After everything she did for me. After she flew me and died for me. After she gave me back my humanity, and stuck a booster up my hope.

"Not your problem."

And all the others. The people of London who bartered and fed me, and said hello every day, and didn't care that I didn't say hello back. The scavs of New York, who died and cried and followed me, despite my lies, into the jaws of hell. The Iroquois, who sent their scared little envoy to watch over me, then saved me themselves on the road.

All of them. Children stolen away. Tears long since run-out. Dead inside, but still fit to help. Still fit to see hope for a better tomorrow. Still fit to smile and think the best, and do something good.

And here's me. Here's me pursuing my own goal and forgetting the rest. Damn the world. Damn every motherfucker alive. Ignore it. Let it happen. Be selfish, why not?

Nothing to do with me.

"*Not your problem,*" *she said.*

Well shit.

About time I made *it my problem.*

They were coming. So said the Tadodaho.

(Or, rather, so said the Matriarchs, who whispered and sighed in dark corners then told the Chief what to say and do. It amounted to the same thing.)

I didn't bother asking how they knew. Scouts, surveillance, divine-bloody-intuition, I didn't know. Or care. I'd just taken a lazy stroll through the psychedelic bullshit of my own mind, and if the weirdest thing to greet me on my return was the rock-solid assertion that the Clergy were *coming, here, en-masse,* then frankly it was a taste of reassuring normality.

They were following me, I guessed. We'd got past their psychotic Collectors, but it didn't matter. Their base in NY was overrun and they'd came pelting out here in my wake. Why?

Revenge?

Maybe. But it sounded like a lot of hard work to go to, just to kick the arse of the guy who'd rattled them up. So why else? Unless...

Unless they were going to the same place as me.

"What's the plan?" Nate said, hours later, when my head stopped spinning from its heavy barrage of hallucinations and synaesthetic memories. We were still sat at the fire between the caravans, watching the evening roll-in, just the two of us. Nike was laid-up in one of the 'vans, dosed out of his skull, and Moto refused to leave his side. Tora... Tora's body had been found near where the Collectors caught-up with us. I didn't like to ask what state it was in. Malice went and oversaw a quiet cremation outside the camp, and I'd figured it would be rude to invite myself along. She hadn't said anything, but there was an unspoken accusation in her eyes as she wandered off:

You brought us out here.

This is your fault.

I told myself I'd imagined it. I told myself they were all mercenaries who'd known the dangers, and it was a little late in the day to start complaining about the risk when two were already dead and one mangled to shit.

It didn't help.

So. Me and Nate. Warm and full of food (still chowing, in fact, on a second portion of everything to make-up for the stuff I puked first time round). And again the old bastard's jaw was lolling, cheeks pinned-back in a rictus-smile, pupils dilated big enough to turn his eyes inside-out.

"What's the plan what's the plan what's the plaaan?" He said, giggling, wobbling around like he was dancing to some silent beat. "Got any more burns? Need a burn? Needaburnneedaburn?"

I stopped chewing. Looked at him and shook my head.

I guessed... oh, sod it. I guessed now was as good a time as any.

I put down my bowl.

"Look at you," I said. "Nate. Seriously. Look at yourself."

"Eh?"

"You're bombed. You're off your face, mate."

It took him a while to react, and his smiling face crumpled like a hollow mountain.

"Am not!" He shouted, far too loud, standing and pointing. "Am fucking not!"

I just stared, getting bored. Eventually he sat down.

"We had a deal." I said quietly, slurping on more of

the homebrewed beer. He reacted jerkily, like he couldn't control his own defence.

"Yeah? *Yeah*, so?"

"So I paid you good scav and I kept you alive. Right? You were in pigshit up to your neck after the airport."

"I know that! Did I say I didn't know it? Fuck *you*, m..."

"And all you had to do in return was play at being a doctor."

I picked up my bowl again and spooned some potatoes into my mouth. Tasted good. Ignored the old man's rolling eyes and hurt silence.

"And... and I haaaave!" He yelped, like a kicked puppy dog. "Didn't I? Didn't I? I've done *good!* Patched you up over and over. You know it, you know it, you know it!"

I glared.

"Yeah. And Nike's in a Winnebago over there with his legs shot to shit, and you haven't lifted a hand to help."

Nate's lips moved. Searching for words.

"But... H-hold it, he's... but..."

"But he's not part of the deal? Is that it?"

"No! No, I just... I thought your, your Injuns here would take care and..."

"Some doctor, Nate."

We sat in silence for a long time then; darkness spreading above us, fire drooling embers upwards.

"The Secretariat." I said, eventually.

"Wh... What?"

I sighed, shaking my head. "Oh, nothing. Just thinking. Our little deal. Never seemed quite right to me."

"But... I don't understand. What's...?"

"You didn't seem to get much out of it, I mean. I was wondering why you were sticking with me, to be honest. Now I know."

He looked suddenly angry, thick sarcasm souring his

voice. "Oh, you know. You *know*, do you? The fuck do *you* know? You gonna make shit up and say you *know*, then you can kiss m..."

"The Secretariat. I sent you downstairs. Told you to go help the others find the kids."

His eyes went narrow. Chin jutting. "S-so?"

"So that's the only time you could've found that shit." I pointed at the pack next to his knees, unsurprised to see his fingers coiled securely through its handle. "Stole it from the Choirboys, didn't you?"

He almost exploded, hugging the bag to himself as he stood and shrieked, irrational and embarrassing. "The fuck's wrong with *that*?" He snarled. "The fuck's wrong with *thaaaat*? You saying, you saying I shouldn't *steal* from *them* assholes?"

"Course not. I'm saying don't steal shit that'll turn you into a prick. Sit down."

"Fuck *y*..."

"Or, don't steal shit that'll bring an army of motherfuckers chasing after you. Sit *down*, Nate."

"That's not why they're *comi*..."

"Or even better, don't steal shit when you're an ex-junkie."

Quiet.

He sat.

"Tell you what *I* think," I said, feeling sharp things moving in my words but not caring. Bella's face was swimming behind my eyelids, and for some reason it made me *angry*. "I think you never quit."

"What?"

"Back in London. You used to live there, you said. You said you quit, remember?"

He didn't say a word.

"I think maybe you were telling half a truth there, mate.

I think what actually happened is, the supply ran out. Tough call, getting smack right after The Cull." His white eyes dipped, firelight reflecting. "But then along comes the Clergy and tells you they can fix you up, sort you out. All you got to do is clear off stateside and look after some kiddies on the way through..."

"That's... wasn't *like* that..."

"And for a couple of years it's all gravy. Probably wasn't even smack they gave you, right? Some weird new military shit. Am I right? Even better. Double the high.

"Then some dumb English fuck arrives and screws the whole gig, and before you know it you're out on your ear. Right? Am I right?"

He was just staring at the fire, face closed-down. Nothing to say. Nothing to deny.

I noticed a stain on his trousers and wondered if he'd even noticed he'd pissed himself.

He swallowed and looked up at me. "I... I just..."

"Why should you stay with me? Oh, fuck, there was all that shit about me protecting your life, blah blah. Didn't buy it for a second, mate. But then we get to the Secretariat and *bang*, you've got right what you wanted. That big case right there. And I'm thinking... That's a *big* place. How did he find it? Unless maybe he knew where to look..."

"J-Jesus..."

"And *that* makes me wonder how you knew we'd be going to the Secretariat at *all*."

His eyes gave it away. In the end.

Flicked away from my face. A split second, no more, to the green sack hanging on my shoulder.

The penny dropped.

"The map..." I said, kicking myself. "Fuck. Of course. Of *course*."

I always knew he looked through my bag, back at the

start, as I lay dying on the tarmac. I assumed he'd lusted after the booze, the Bliss...

But no. He went straight to the map. The New York City map, marked with a bloody-red ring around the UN Headquarters.

"So you saw where I was heading... Right? And you thought... Well now... Maybe I'll just... *tag along*?"

I glanced up.

He stared.

"You didn't even have the guts to tell me the truth, Nate."

I wouldn't have cared, if he'd been honest.

I *don't* care, even now. Don't give a shit what he does to himself.

I just don't like being wrong.

He opened and closed his mouth like a fish.

"Parasite," I said.

I stood up and walked away.

I went for a walk.

Took a look around. Found Malice and sat down to talk and draw maps in the sand. Scheming. If she was pissed about the *Inferno* and the others, she didn't show it.

Around midnight I went and fetched Robert Slowbear, and he took me to the Tadodaho. I politely declined anything to eat or drink.

Around four o'clock the camp moved, all at once, across the great concrete bridge spanning the sinuous lake, and by six I was up to my armpits in cold water.

By seven we were ready.

They didn't keep us waiting.

The Meander Reservoir was a twisting strip of spilled water, dividing Youngstown from the green ocean of fields surrounding it. On the Tadodaho's map – an ancient and laminated thing, long-faded and well-worn – the lake was an obvious part of a chain, connected by creeks and ditches, that ran south all the way from Lake Eerie. It wasn't a huge watercourse, I suppose. Maybe five or six miles, tip-to-tip. It wouldn't have taken too long to go around either, if someone'd had to, but what was perfect about it was this:

The I-80, straight from New York, spanned the lake dead across its centre on a single, exposed, vulnerable and oh-so-deliciously-narrow bridge.

If ever there was a better place for an ambush, I would've liked to have seen it.

For the record, somewhere – deep down at the rotten core of my mind – I shouted and cussed at myself, waggling a subconscious finger at this daft display of time wasting.

Not my problem, it kept shouting. *Focus on the mission!*

And my response, my considered reply to this seemingly watertight argument, went something like this:

Fuck off.

The Clergymen came out of the QuickSmog on the horizon at dawn, and the sound of engines reached us long before we saw them. The air went electric.

There were three other bridges too – two smaller roads, a mile on either side, that forded the water at its narrowest points, and a larger bridge far to the south where the Ohio turnpike turned northwards, with no easy access or turn-ons. We could ignore *that*, at least.

At about the same time we heard the engines, the *Haudenosaunee* vanished. All of them, dipping out of sight without so much as a word. It was incredible to watch.

Vehicles bundled off rapidly to the west, to be parked behind knots of trees and dips in the road. Bikes were laid-down on their sides and covered with grass and leaves. Men and women lugging improbably huge weapons squatted on the banks to either side of the central bridge, and simply—

—*disappeared.*

One moment there was an army, hundreds strong, arranged silently along the banks of the lake, staring off into the fog. The next: nothing.

Well.

Almost nothing.

The *Inferno* had been dragged to the centre of the road on our side of the bridge. It was a sad sight, mangled and unsteady, lolling to one side with its cockpit torn open and its sides dented to hell. But the guns still worked, oh yes, and wedged-up on either side of it there stood a pair of Iroquois caravans, untidily blocking the road, holding it upright.

It looked like the world's crappiest blockade.

Rick – Hiawatha, whoever he was – had volunteered to man the *Inferno*. He'd done so with the chin-jutting defiance of someone too young to know better, trying to prove something; to himself, I guess. If it'd been down to me I would have told him to stop being a macho prick and leave it to someone more capable.

"Good." The Tadodaho had said. "Good."

The youngster opened-fire right on time.

Down in the shade cast by the bridge, covered in a loose mesh of twigs and brambles, I had a perfect view. Malice grinned openly to my left, and even Nike – sprawled in a mess of splints and crutches behind, with Moto mothering him wordlessly – chuckled to himself. Could've just been the painkillers, I suppose.

The bikes came first.

And went down like dominoes.

Outriders; scouting ahead of a far larger convoy that could barely be seen amidst the far fringes of the QuickSmog; Clergy corsairs with white helmets and dark robes, some on military bikes with sidecars containing Uzi-waving idiots, others sprinting ahead on powerbikes re-sprayed grey and white.

Rick exploded them one by one.

The shape of the road funnelled them naturally, drawing them together, bunching them like skittles. As they ripped onto the far span it was to be greeted by a wave – a *wall* – of lead and fire and shrapnel. They should have been more cautious. They should have looked ahead at the obstruction and taken their time, but no. Straight in. Still accelerating when the ordnance closed on them and the world shook.

Thunder and smoke and muzzle-flare, and two bikes skidding in hot rubber and screaming chrome, and torn leather and blood on the road, and the next idiots flipping head-over-saddle as they smashed into their fallen comrades, and *then* – only then – did the brakes slam on and the situation slow.

By which time it was far too late.

The kid aimed with only the vaguest accuracy. He simply poked a cautious head through the *Inferno*'s turret, steered the great mass of oiled death mounted there towards the far edge of the bridge, and held down as many triggers as he could.

It was like...

Bonfire Night. Or the Fourth of July, depending.

Or maybe just a war zone. Maybe just a field-spotter's

guide to hasty death.

The Mk19 lobbing its tumbling shells, spit-crack-flare-smoke; a brace of machineguns vomiting spent cases and angry tracers; dust and tarmac rising-up; splinters of air and rock tumbling; bikes shivering in haloes of sparks then dissolving – just *going away* – behind great balls of incandescence. The whole bridge shook with each grenade-flare, and underneath it all came the sharp ring of Rick's voice, shouting and laughing.

On the edge of the bridge, through curtains of hot smoke and fire clinging to shattered bodies and disassembled bikes, the blunt shadows of blockier shapes nudged at the edge of the QuickSmog. Beside me, Malice's face dropped. The rest of the convoy, perhaps.

If Rick had noticed, he didn't care. The Mk19 spat its last grenade then whirred on, empty chambers cycling uselessly, but the rest of the arsenal kept going. Throwing curtains of dust and sparks at the far shore, as if daring the knot of bikes that had turned aside and backed away to *come get some...*

Nobody seemed keen to oblige.

The blocky shape began to solidify; angular panels and reinforced glass, painted sky-blue in defiance of camouflage. I recognised the boxy nose of an armoured vehicle – some ex-military ground car or other, heavy with ablative plates and sensor-gear – and let my eye wander quickly to the gun in its rear. Autocannon. 25mm, maybe 30. Against a crippled fire truck with armour made of corrugated iron, frankly, it wouldn't make much difference.

The bikes zipped off in either direction, clearing a corridor. Rick's petulant salvo rattled uselessly off the AFV's hull, and after a second or two he allowed the guns to fall silent, uncertain, letting smoke waft across the bridge.

Everyone held their breath.

The autocannon opened fire.

A *lot* of fire.

Somewhere deep in the tedious equip-details drummed over the years into my mind, I recognised the sound. The angry rattle, the hollow retorts of heavy calibre shells thumping – *stamping* – against the *Inferno*.

M242 Bushmaster. 25mm chain cannon, 200 rounds a minute. Probably ripped from some heavy-arsed Bradley tank and installed messily, incongruously, in the rear of that stupid little AFV. The whole thing shuddered and shifted backwards with the recoil, brakes clawing at the earth, but it didn't matter. Didn't make a fucking spot of difference.

The *Inferno* simply *tattered*. The shells didn't dent the sides, they ripped them. Metal shredded like cheap fabric, panels peeling back in lacerated strips, exit-wounds worthy of cranial trauma that blasted an organic gore of shrapnel and slag through the blockade's rear quarters.

Only a matter of time before the fuel tanks went up.

And then Rick was running, hopping between geysers of fire and dust, leather trousers ripped and bloody where shards of concrete had jumped up to slash his ankles, and the gunner swept the cannon to find him – thunderous blasts picking apart macadam, drawing close to his heels—

—and he was gone, diving with a shriek over the edge of the bridge, lost to the waters below. The gunner turned back to his first target with a dogged sort of *well-I'll-be-blowed-if-I-don't-get-to-have-some-fun* determination, and finally – throbbing at the air like a stuttering bass – found the fuel tanks.

The *Inferno* tried to fly. A heavy jet of black flame

glommed from its belly, blew out its arse, lifted it up in a
halo of flapping damage and slammed it down, keening
on its side, to creak and vent fire.

"That's coming out of your deposit." Malice whispered.
I smirked.

From across the lake came an uproarious cheer, broken
and muffled by the fog, but *loud*. Wide. Spread-out.
Hidden there in the fog, waiting to emerge, were a *lot*
of people.

And onwards they came. The AFV jinking to one side,
making way for a lumbering colossus that might once have
been a truck-cab but now – via the careful application
of welds, armour plates and a fucking enormous dozer-
scoop – looked a little more like a medieval dragon, lower
jaw hanging open.

The Iroquois remained hidden.

Behind the hulking machine came others like it. HGV
cabs bristling with guns, AFVs plugging gaps, converted
civilian vehicles painted in the Clergy's colours and
distorted by weaponry, spikes, ramming-noses. It poured
from the QuickSmog like a tide of filth, like an armada
emerging from sea fog; robed figures standing at arms
on every surface. Behind it came the carriers. Vast lorries,
armoured but unarmed. Buses and coaches riding low
on their suspension, figures crammed behind mesh
windows. Plated limousines and SUVs, blue-and-scarlet
flags fluttering like a presidential cavalcade.

I realised, then, why the resistance had been so
lacklustre at the Secretariat building. Why so few
Clergymen were left to guard the gates, and why so many
ran, as we swarmed inside, towards the other parts of the
compound.

They'd known we were coming. Cy's timely warning,
spies on every street. They'd known we could wash across

them despite their sternest defences, and so they'd loaded themselves aboard a long-prepared convoy, and taken the only course open to them:

Exodus.

And now here they were. All of them.

I understood, abruptly, why the Tadodaho had brought me here. Why this moment was so important to him, and Rick, and the rest of the tribe. And more than that: to the scavs in the cities, to the people back home in London, to Bella – if she'd been here to see it...

To me.

A chance to cut the heads off the bloody Hydra, if you like. Not my business, nothing to do with me, not my problem, but still. Something I had to do.

The Iroquois remained hidden.

The dozer-scoop behemoth inched towards the flaming wreck of the *Inferno*, preparing to shunt it, and the caravans beside it, to one side. I wondered how big a threat the Clergy had estimated this curious little blockade to be, and sincerely hoped the answer was:

Not big enough.

The radio in my pocket hissed.

"...*kkk*... orth bridge..."

"Go ahead." I whispered, watching the convoy crawl cautiously forwards.

"...ot outriders up here... crossing now. Ten bikes, two AVs..."

A second voice cut in – the thoughtful tones of Slowbear:

"...ame here. South bridge. They've sent a lorry over as well..."

"Standby," I said, feeling the adrenaline coming up, imagining the two groups away through the haze, one on each of the smaller bridges, sneaking round to flank us. I saw them smirking and tittering, feeling oh-so-bloody-clever, mumbling bullshit about classic pincer movements, surprise attacks, blah-blah-blah.

I fished in my other pocket and handed a small black box to Malice, pointing to the top button. "The honours." I said. It seemed only fair.

She smiled, dipped her head with *faux* graciousness, and stabbed at the button.

The dozer scoop in front and above us hit the *Inferno*'s side and squealed in protest.

And then ceased to be the main event.

The light came first. Obviously. From both directions at once; a sudden flicker of white and yellow, pulsing across the entirety of the QuickSmog like a firework lost in the clouds, then building more focus as the first flash of the explosion gave way to a pair of dancing fireballs; one on each side, great pyrotechnic monsters that clambered into the air and dissipated into the mist.

Then the sound. Almost perfectly synchronised; two rolling thunderbolts that echoed and coalesced in the eerie fog, becoming a single sub-aqueous *roar*.

And then screams. Even at this distance, even separated by water and haze, the shrieks of the maimed and the groans of the dying. Ghostly. Haunting.

The Collectors had left behind their C4 and their snazzy little detonator when they tried to kill us in the night. It would have been rude to waste them.

"*kkk*... orth bridge... Got 'em... *got* the fuckers... bridge is down, bridge is down!"

"...owbear here, same for the south. Hoo-ee! Can't see for smoke yet, but they're not coming any further..."

The dozer-scoop shunted the *Inferno* like a casual distraction, bashing as it went into the side of the nearest caravan. The driver wasn't watching. I guessed he was staring in shock at the baleful firelight hovering on either side in the distance, or shouting into a radio, or just wondering *what the fuck is going on.*

Distracted, one way or another. Otherwise he might have noticed the cables. Iron cords, tied-off to the railings at either side of the bridge, each one carefully tensioned, leading in through the shattered windows of the caravans.

Each one holding aloft, in the stripped-out spaces inside, a dangling gallery of jam jars.

Each of which contained a single fragmentation baseball grenade, pin removed, trigger prevented from releasing by the glass of the jars.

Fort Wayne barracks, Slowbear had told me during the night. One of the few armouries that hadn't emptied its supplies into the Clergy's hands. Forget bows and bloody arrows. These Injuns were *packing.*

The first caravan shifted. Jerked against the other, like marbles colliding.

On both sides of the bridge, the cables went slack. A tinny sound of shattering glass filled the air, and maybe I was imagining it or maybe I suddenly went fucking *psychic*, but I swear to god I could hear the driver in that colossal sodding rig mutter:

"Aw, piss."

A second or two, with the echoes of the C4-detonations still ringing, and then:

Think Baghdad. Think Hiroshima. Think surface of the fucking *sun.*

It was big, and flashy, and I could feel the heat from my cover. Frag-shrapnel turning the air to razorwire, men somersaulting out of gunner-mounts on the cusp of the blast, flesh sliding off bone, fingers clutching at air then clutching at nothing. The lorry-rig pelted onto its spine, its nose upright, then crashed down in dust and death on the vehicles behind, bouncing in a way that something that big *shouldn't*. Driver and gunners alike screamed and died, sliced to ribbons; soot and black smoke washed over the top of the bridge and the tarmac *gaped* where the explosives had tripped. The caravans were gone. The *Inferno*'s shredded corpse was gone. What remained was modern art.

And finally the Iroquois rose-up from their cover, screamed like an operatic banshee, and let loose.

It would have been a massacre. We had them boxed-in. Exposed on the bridge, unable to back-out at speed. We had machineguns and grenades and autocannons. We had a couple of rusty old mortars that found their range after two watery explosions (by which time Rick had already clambered, panting, ashore, so no damage there) and a crateful of anti-tank rockets which all the Haudenosaunee had been clamouring to play with.

Above all we had surprise and stealth, and well-camouflaged men and women using smoke and shadows and patience. We had so much lead and fire raining down on those pricks that they never realised how much knifework went on, how much scurrying and slicing was taking place in the noxious gaps between packed-in vehicles.

I know. I was there. I was *doing* it.

It *would* have been a massacre. It started out just dandy. The Iroquois vehicles came tearing back up, the bikes slipped onto the bridge to sow madness and death, AVs and lorry rigs popped like fiery bubbles with each shrieking mortar-round, and *oh god yeah* it felt good. Malice and me with pistols and knives, scrambling over bonnets and under tankers, slipping grenades through open windows whilst drivers shouted and raged at the back-up, then scuttled off to listen for the *boom*...

Great times.

And fine, the convoy just kept getting bigger and bigger. More and more lorries oozing from the haze, trying to back-up, trying to manoeuvre in the madness. Fine, there were a lot more of the bastards than we expected, a lot more guns and psychos slowly getting their act together and returning fire. Fine, it would have been *messy*. But we *had* them. We could've *taken* them.

And then my radio hissed, and everything changed.

Malice and I were holed-up behind the vast tyres of an earthmover, waiting for the wanker in the cab to stop blasting our end of the bridge with whatever fat-shell cannon he was manning for long enough to sneak up there and blow his brains out, when Slowbear's voice broke through the maelstrom; tinny and tense.

"...ou there? Oh shit... oh shit... This is Slowbear! Are you there?"

"Yeah, here. What is it?"

Something bit at the rubber tyre next to me and made the whole vehicle shudder. Malice winced.

"The lorry! The... shit... shit... *kkkhh*... the lorry on the south bridge!"

"We got it, right?"

"Yes! F-fuck, yes, it's not that, it's..."

"Slowbear?"

"...t's full of children! You hear me?"

Malice's eyes bulged.

"...orries are all full of fucking *children!*"

It *would* have been a massacre.

We turned and ran back to our lines without another word, and as we strafed through optimistic fire streams I caught a glimpse of Malice's eyes, and the liquid glistening inside them. She'd left her baby with the Matriarchs in safety but still... it didn't take a genius to figure out what she was thinking.

It'd been her that pressed the button, after all.

A weird noise filled my head. Like an engine, but airier; filtered through the fog and the gunfire, distorted by the screams and shouts all around. I wondered if I'd damaged my ear more badly than I'd thought, then shook my head and stopped worrying. What, exactly, could I do about it anyway? I spotted the incline facing the bridge where we'd left Nike and Moto, and together with Malice I scrambled up the bank, forgetting all about the noise, concentrating on staying alive.

...*thrpthrpthrpthrpthrp*...

Nike and Moto were hunkered-down with five Iroquois holding shoulder-launchers. Nate was there too, watching, staying apart and looking shifty. I ignored him and he ignored me, making a show of staring directly upwards into the turbulent QuickSmog. It seemed to be getting worse. Odd bursts of fire snapped at the tops of the ridge, off-target but getting closer, and before I could take the time to work out *how* someone was keeping track with us, at this distance, at this elevation, we threw ourselves down into safety. Rick was standing below the grenadiers; sopping water and trying to catch his breath, dishing out the tank busters.

"Aim for the lorries..." he was saying, unable to keep the twinkle of testosterone-choked-male out of his eye. He'd done his part. He'd lured the fuckers into the trap. No wonder he sounded older.

Nike was already lifting himself gingerly into a sitting position, head above the edge of the ridge, tube to his shoulder, when Malice gathered her breath and shouted:

"No! Stop! Don't fire!"

The older man swivelled his head to look at her, brows furrowing.

"But wh..."

The hesitation almost killed him. A round caromed dustily off the ground beside his face, within inches of splitting his head. He swore out loud and let gravity pull him back down into cover, the rest of us tugging him along in a knot of shouts and grunts. When we'd got him back down to the bottom of the ridge Moto flopped-down next to him and clutched at his arm, horrified.

"Fuck..." Nike said, eyes wide. "Did you... fuck. Did you *see* that?"

And then his head really *did* split open.

Suddenly I was wearing him. Bits of blood and brain in my eyes, shards of bone stinging the exposed skin on my face. His body slumped and smoked, and next to it Moto's mouth went up and down like nothing made sense, like everything had gone dark.

How? My brain was screaming. *How did someone...? We're in fucking cover!*

Out in the haze, the noise again. An angry dragonfly-throb, cut through with a motorised grind.

...thrpthrpthrpthrp...

Moto's face had gone perfectly slack.

He picked up the rocket launcher. Malice scrabbled against his arm, trying to pull him off, and he hit her – hard – on the cheek. His expression didn't change. She fell; he turned. Rose to the top of the bank. Aimed.

And then everything went white and black, and I realised with a giddy sort of uncertainty that either the rocket had misfired, or someone had shot the launcher, and now – look – I was flying, and my hair was on fire, and everything hurt.

I landed and lay and didn't move. Staring straight up, as fire and smoke and chaos thundered all around me. I wondered if anyone else was still alive.

...*thrpthrpthrpthrpthrp*...

The QuickSmog billowed. Surged. *Boiled.*

And finally I recognised the sound. Finally I figured out how the fuckers had shot Nike, I figured out how come they'd been taking potshots at me and Malice ever since we scrambled up here. How they'd blasted Moto's launcher before he could even squeeze the trigger, and blew us all to shit.

Why Nate was staring straight up.

There were lights above me. Rockets zipping down in all directions. Iroquois screaming, vehicles exploding. A sniper rifle *krak-krak-krak*ing from on-high.

And as the pain in my ribs exploded behind my eyes, and I sucked hard to get anything resembling a breath, my last thought was:

Nobody told me *the fuckers had helicopters...*

CHAPTER EIGHTEEN

Rick could move his arms. Broadly speaking.

He'd never been in a 'copter before. Big novelty. The vibrations had woken him, he supposed. He'd always fancied going up in a chopper when he was a kid, but he'd never imagined it'd be like this. Lying in pain on a grille floor, feeling something sticky that was probably puke on his cheek, knowing full well there was a trio of Clergy-fucks standing nearby with big-ass Russian guns aimed at his head.

He had opened his eyes a moment ago. He was still regretting it.

They'd left the bay doors open. They'd laid him out right next to the damned thing, so his first sight was green fields and jagged hills, gushing past below.

A long, long, long way below.

Yeah. Big fucking novelty.

To be honest, he couldn't even decide if he really was awake or not. Even with his eyes closed again, lights kept dancing weirdly in front of him, odd sensations were shooting up and down his left arm, and every time he tried to concentrate on anything the world went grey and prickly. Eventually he came to the conclusion he must be concussed. Maybe brain-damaged. Maybe dying.

Whatever.

He cast his mind back to the battle on the bridge, and tried to sort out what had happened. He remembered diving into the lake. Swimming to safety. Finding the little knot of Haudenosaunee fighters – all from different lodges, none of them recognisable – and staggering over to get some help for his bleeding legs. He remembered the way they'd looked at him – looked up at him – and instead

314

of rushing round to check he was okay and pat him on the head, they'd pointed at the tank buster grenades and asked him:

What shall we do?

A couple of weeks ago he would've avoided the war painted pricks with their stupid clothes and daft ceremonies, and living-off-the-fucking-land, and 'Great Spirits' and 'Earth Initiates' and 'Ghost Dances' and yadda-yadda-yadda, and here he was: a leader.

Well then, he'd thought.

Might as well lead.

He remembered telling them what to do. Remembered the itch at the rear of his head, just like he'd felt back in NY, back when he was Hiawatha, except this time it was him in charge and that older, wiser, weirder voice consigned to an echo that he could attend or ignore as he chose. Best of both worlds.

He remembered the dull flicker of green and purple fire on the edge of his subconscious, and turning round on cue to find the Stranger sprinting up with that sexy black chick in tow, and that old guy Nike going splat, and the kid with the scarred face flipping-out, and reaching out to stop him, and—

And then something about light and fire, and pain.

And then confused blur-memories of a lot of people screaming and a lot of people dying, and men in grey and white laughing and shouting, and chanting in choral voices whilst guns chattered. And a radio hissing something about they're all fucking dead, they're all fucking dead, and a general retreat, and then the howl of rotors.

And that was about all.

Rick figured he'd been blown up. It certainly goddamn felt like he'd been blown up. He wondered how come he was still alive at all, and why these robe-wearing assholes were dragging him off to who-knew-where, rather than just... squashing him. He felt like he should be more scared than he was, but inside the sweat-lodge of his skull Hiawatha sat and played strange songs on stranger instruments, and everything was okay. Nothing hurt, except in the physical sense.

Which somehow just... didn't count any more.

Rick risked opening his eyes again, this time turning his head with a nauseous lurch to the other side, ignoring a muttered command from somewhere far away that might have been "stay still, fucko."

Yeah, yeah. Whatever.

He wasn't alone. Three other shapes, bundled side-by-side, head-to-toe, lay beside him. He kept his face down, focusing close through clouds of greyout blur.

All he could see of the recumbent figure directly next to him was a pair of boots. Muddy and bloody, fastened over tattered combats and the hem of a raggedy coat. Blazing, from the corner of his eyes, with a warm fiery glow.

The Stranger.

Beyond him was Malice. Her face was gone. Her skin was charred and burnt, her hair singed away in great bloody patches all over her scalp. If she was still alive, she didn't look it. Her eye was open. Unblinking. Staring straight at him.

Next to her were Nate's feet. Crazy red sneakers with army regs tucked into them, tied-together with a single loop of wire. He couldn't see past Malice's charred body to check if the old junkie was still alive or not.

All three lay, like him, on their bellies; arms twisted into the smalls of their backs, where pairs of black cuffs held them in place. Rick tried to move his own arms, unsurprised to feel a fresh tsunami of agony (all a million miles away, not worth worrying about) swarming along his left wrist. They felt impeded, sure, but there was something loose about the whole arrangement, a sort of dried, gluey stickiness rather than metal solidity.

Weird.

He tilted his head as best as he could, to peer down towards his own feet; hogtied, just like everyone else. Next to them, the Stranger was looking at him. Eyes open and alive, jaw clenched. Blood and flesh covered his face, and it was difficult to tell how much of it was his. They stared silently at each other for a moment or two, then the Stranger's eyes flipped downwards towards Rick's back.

Then back up again.

"Your hand's gone." He whispered.

"Shut the fuck up!" One of the Clergymen screamed, stamping hard on the Stranger's head and mashing one lacerated cheek against the grille. Rick barely noticed, exploring his own body with a morbid sense of certainty.

The stranger was right. His left hand. His left hand was gone.

Well, shit.

It felt like they'd bound it up, maybe. Rags or bandages, tied at pressure, holding the arteries closed. Then they'd slapped the same old cuffs over the top of it and left him to it, maybe expecting him to die from blood loss, maybe just not caring.

He could move his wrist. He could unglue it from the sticky mess of dried blood and pull it free from the cuff. And if he could do that, it meant his other hand – no, his only hand – would be free to move.

Hiawatha sang a new song. The wind against the back of his head, from that great drop beyond, tousled his long hair and whispered strange things in his ear. Something about... about a gift?

He shifted his weight, trying to determine if any other

interesting parts of his anatomy were missing. The pockets of his leathers had been chock-full of ammunition and handguns before the blast knocked him out, but now all he could feel about his person was a shitload of bruises and something tiny – sharp, but swaddled-up – in the zip-pocket on his ass.

The wind giggled.

The gift, it told him. Remember?

And then he knew what to do.

Poor kid.

Shell-shocked, I thought. *He's been blown up. He's woken-up dangling over an abyss surrounded by fanatic goons, and he's got a bloody hand missing.*

Shit, *I'd* be shell-shocked.

Outside, the green blur of land streaking past began to turn sooty and black. A sharp smell – like burning oil – filled the chopper, and above my head the three Choirboys muttered to one another, shuffling discreetly towards the open bay to see below.

The Haudenosaunee camp, I guessed, set-up far back from the war zone at the bridge. I couldn't see past the edge to whatever they were marvelling at, but I could imagine it. Blackened vans and charred wagons. The Tadodaho's weird mobile-home collapsing in embers and smoke. What else could it be?

We'd been roundly beaten; us plucky idiots with our ambush and our rebellion. Slaughtered and routed for our hubris. Taken prisoner. Taken away.

The smoke got thicker. I decided not to look.

Nor, evidently, did Rick. With the guards distracted his arms were moving slowly, gingerly releasing the swaddled stump of his left wrist from the cuffs and, thus freed, his right hand easing – *inching* – towards the pocket of his trousers.

What did he have in there, I wondered? What had the idiot-goons missed when they went through our stuff, rifling for weapons? What cunning escape plan was he cooking up?

"Lord Almighty," one of the Choirboys grunted, half reverential, half cursing, staring out into space, now almost completely choked with black smoke. The dancing light of flames lit his face from below, giving him and his comrades an eerie, devilish look. I imagined the tribal Matriarchs screaming as they burned. The Tadodaho coughing on the thick pall. Malice's baby, left in their care, breaking its silence and starting – briefly – to wail.

Rick drew a folded rag from his pocket. Manipulated it with careful fingers, unwrapping it millimetre by millimetre. The cloth fell away with a dreamlike slowness, and I discovered myself holding my breath; desperate to see what he'd squirreled away.

My heart dropped.

It was a silver needle. Long and sharp, barely thicker than a hypodermic, slightly distorted by its time in his pocket. Not quite the weapon of mass destruction I'd envisaged.

There was a time, once – somewhere in the Middle East, I recall, on business – when I got into some bad shit and found myself up against a knifeman with nothing to defend myself but a table fork. Don't laugh. This shit happens.

For the record, he perforated my right lung before I got close enough to stab him through his eyeball – and that was without having a bruised and battered body upfront. Without gun-wielding maniacs watching. Without sodding handcuffs. With a fucking *hand* missing.

Good luck, kid.

Rick was staring at me again, needle held concealed in his hand.

"Sorry." He whispered. Then: "Trust me."

And then he was moving. Sudden and unexpected, face contorted, hefting himself off the floor and onto my back, flexing his legs to get towards me.

"Fucking limey asshole!" He snarled. "Fucking prick! You said you'd stop them! You said you'd save us!"

"What? I hissed. "But..."

"*Kill* you, sonuvabitch! Look what they did! You said you'd stop them! Just fucking *die!*"

And then he was pressed over me, and his mouth was next to my neck, and *oh my god* he was *biting* me. Trying to rip out my bloody throat. I shouted and hollered – more confused than anything – and tried to shake my body to get him off. The guards were reacting slowly, turning back from their sightseeing in a chorus of curses and exclamations, throwing horrified glances up and over my shoulder to the bulkhead that led into the chopper's cockpit.

From where – cold and forced, like steel scraping cobwebs – there came a voice.

"What." It said. "The *fuck*. Is going on?"

Rick's teeth dug in further, but in an abstract section of my brain – not actively shrieking and demanding answers of this ludicrous situation – it occurred to me that by now he *could* have killed me if he'd wanted to. He wasn't even biting that hard.

The guards grabbed him and tried to wrestle him off.

And between us, in the secret concealed shadows of the ruckus, something sharp and tiny punched into the fleshy meat of my right buttock, buried itself there, and went still.

What the—?

And then Rick was gone, hauled away, severed hand squirting blood through its disarrayed bandages. The guards clung to rails and handles, bracing him, facing the owner of that cold, grating voice.

"Sir?" one said.

"Hold him," it hissed. I recognised it, sort of. It was sharper than before, more strained, like it'd been pushed through a filter of trauma and hate.

It can't be—

But it was. He stepped over me, dainty steps untroubled by the chopper's shuddering, and crouched down to stare directly into Rick's face.

The boy smiled. "I should've pushed harder, huh?" He said.

Cardinal Cy snarled.

The knife was still embedded in his head. From behind, I could see its ghastly angle, hilt decorated with antiseptic patches and freakish lumps of bandaging. It had gone deep. Deep enough to fuck with his brain.

It didn't seem to have slowed him down.

He put a hand – almost tender – on Rick's cheek. "Old man says... old man says. Bring troublemakers to him. Ones who caused all this. Fuss. Likes to tidy things up personal. Y'see?"

Rick spat on the surface of his red glasses.

"Mm." Cy smiled, wagging a finger. "Mm. Except, except, except. Never even *saw* you, did he? Doesn't even know. So. Maybe you're too much trouble, eh? Don't you think? Maybe I should tidy-up. Personally."

He twisted Rick's face to the side, hand digging deep into his cheeks and brow, forcing him down and round, making him stare out into the empty sky below the chopper.

I stayed silent. Wondered at the weird pain in my arse – the silver needle, I supposed – and watched. Waited for Rick's face to contort in horror as he saw the remnants of his tribe's war party burning away.

I couldn't have been more wrong.

"Lake Eerie." Cy said. "Know what I heard? Used to be... So much shit came downriver, man could almost walk across. Some years, surface caught *fire*. Believe that?"

He pushed Rick's head further down, forcing him out, smoke billowing round him, held up only by the arms of the guards.

"Course... nowadays, all sorts. Weird shit pouring in. Oil from them... big refineries up north. All deserted. Gas, debris, timber. You name it. And pal... No fucker left to put out them fires.

"Now, the old man. When he kills a guy, just got one way. But me? I'm understanding. Got *mercy*. So what it is... Giving you a choice. How to die.

"Three options. Number one. You drown. Number two. You burn. And number three. You fall from on-high."

The Cardinal put a hand on Rick's chest.

"Decide on the way down. Huh?" He said.

Rick said something in a language I didn't understand. His face changed.

Smoothed-out.

And then he smiled at me, and I cried out something wordless, and Cy pushed, and he was gone.

Below, wow!
Below, thunderbirds soared on fiery thermals. They keened and screamed as he fell, and squabbled to catch him.

And the trees sang and the wind murmured, and far

away buffaloes grunted moronic greetings, and he settled as light as a feather on the back of the greatest fire-crow of all. It laughed and laughed, and so did he, and in its eye was lightning, and as it rose across the burning lakes Rick-Hiawatha felt something dull and insubstantial continue to fall away from him: something heavy and clumsy and solid, which he didn't need anymore.

The thunderbird kept pace with a garishly-painted helicopter for a moment, then veered off into the smoke, heading for the sounds of the plains.

>

It'd end here. I'd figured that much out already.

Don't call it a hunch, or a spooky sensation. Call it reality. Call it there's-no-fucking-way-I'm-getting-out-of-here-except-dead-or-victorious.

Call it: I know when to stop chasing.

It would end on this green-and-brown splat of land, choked-up by curtains of smoke that hid the horizon and denied the mainland ever existed. It would end, for better or worse – probably worse – in the middle of a sludge-like lake, whole patches of which were flaming-away happily, with a trail of dead people behind me, a psychotic cardinal with a knife in his brain bearing a grudge, and a throbbing pain in my right buttock.

Way to go.

They'd chained me to a sign. Mottled and half-cracked where a small golf-buggy had toppled into it (and indeed sat there still, crumpled and rusting in the tall grass) it was the only thing to keep me amused whilst the world turned-on blithely around me, and I'd read it several times already.

It announced that in 1813 a bloke by the name of Oliver Hazard Perry kicked the shit out of a fleet of British ships on Lake Eerie. I'm paraphrasing. It was a minor engagement, all things considered, but had a knock-on effect that ensured that a year down the line the peace talks were in full swing. Eventually some bright spark decided a memorial to the guy in charge was exactly what was needed, and it only took a hundred years to raise the cash. This was considered a triumph of human persistence rather than a lamentable token of inefficiency.

The sign was obviously intended to enlighten any visitor unfortunate enough to find themselves stranded on South Bass Island, and was crammed with interesting facts regarding the construction of said monument. At any other time I'd have expected to see fat tourists clustered around it making "ooh" sounds and taking pictures.

Alas, today, there was nobody but me to enjoy the info-feast. Instead there were dozens of armed Choirboys – men and women alike – spreading out across the tiny arsecrumb of land to convert any locals from their savage un-Christian ways to—

—well, death, probably. As it happened they hadn't found anyone yet, though they continued to kick-in each mouldering door and holiday-home porch with optimistic enthusiasm. In the meantime I'd been left chained here with Nate – still not talking – to watch the two Clergy choppers ferry people from the shore. It was boring. It was boring and it was underscored by the imminent probability of my own death, which made it even worse. It was like these pricks had dug a hole in my stomach, told me to make peace with my maker, placed the gun against my head, then told me to amuse myself for a while.

As they dragged me out of the chopper I'd asked Cy what happened to the rest of the *Haudenosaunee*. He'd sneered and ignored the question. I couldn't work out if that was good or not. I couldn't work out if I cared.

The monument itself, for the record, stood nearby. I glanced up at it for the fiftieth time, on the off-chance it might be doing something interesting. Like so many military monuments it was basically a giant penis, cunningly disguised as a three-hundred-and-fifty foot Doric column with a bronze 'urn' (11 tons, you'll be fascinated to learn) in the place of a throbbing glands, which was constructed, apparently, to *inculcate the lessons of international peace by arbitration and disarmament.*

Which was odd, because to me it looked a lot like it had been built to inculcate the lessons of international one-upmanship, specifically by stating: *My Cock's Bigger Than Yours.*

A foghorn blasted nearby, and I watched with a minor flicker of interest as the clapped-out old ferry they'd found deserted at Port Clinton made its third journey towards us, this time bearing two blue lorries and a school bus, undoubtedly crammed with scared kids in white robes. Next to me Nate stiffened, reminded of the innocuous job he'd held down for two years before all this mad shit started with a plane crash and a—

No. No, hang on.

'Innocuous' my arse. He was driving kids to a prison, or worse. And he knew it.

I hadn't entirely made my mind up yet how I felt about Nate.

I leaned back against the pillar of the signpost and sighed.

The long and the short of it was: The Clergy had invaded a nowheresville island in the middle of the burning Eerie, *en-mass*, and were in the process of transferring their *entire* stock of idiots, arseholes, arsenals and initiates. Don't ask me why. Don't ask me what they expected to find here, or how they thought it would advance their march towards a new future. I didn't know.

All I knew was that this place, this island, this dull little shithole, was where *I* had been diligently trying to reach too.

That sheet of paper from the file in the Secretariat, remember? The photo.

REASSIGNMENT LOCATION, it said.

UN INSTALLATION SAFFRON. SOUTH BASS ISLAND, OHIO.

The tourist map they'd chained me to didn't mention any UN installations. That would've made it too easy, I guess.

I sighed again.

There seemed to be a lot of activity around the base of the column. I couldn't see clearly from where I stood, but it looked like a lot of figures were waving a lot of hands, pointing and nodding profusely.

There was someone in a wheelchair with them, and it struck me that every now and again the crowds' gesturing hands would freeze, their heads would twist to stare down, and then a fresh wave of nodding and scraping and bowing, in response to whatever the chair bound figure had said.

John-Paul, then.

The group disappeared behind the great stone column in an excited bundle, and I waited for them to emerge from the other side, pleased to be watching something mildly diverting. They never reappeared. They'd vanished.

"Huh." I said to myself. Nate glanced at me, briefly, as if maybe he thought I was about to talk to him.

I looked away.

My arse hurt. More specifically, my buttock hurt where a tiny silver pin had been rammed into it, and every now again I felt a fresh dribble of blood down the back of my leg. Every time I moved it stung, like it was worming deeper into the muscle, and every time that happened it made me think of Rick.

Tumbling off into smoke and death with a smile.

And that made me think of Malice.

Dumped, thoughtlessly, over the edge of the pier where the chopper landed, when one of the Choirboy crew bothered to tell Cy she looked like she'd croaked during the flight.

And that made me think of Bella.

And that made me think of... of something else.

And that made me think of all *sorts* of shit, which made the hole in my stomach burn and writhe, and my teeth clench, and my eyes sting, and—

You get the idea.

So I stopped thinking about the pain in my arse and ignored the voice growling – no, *shrieking* – in my skull:

Don't you fucking give up, soldier!

Dull, dull, dull.

The ferry docked. The trucks rolled off. Someone shouted at someone else.

Gulls wheeled overhead on smoky updrafts. A hundred miles south and east, a bunch of dead Iroquois were going hard in the sun.

The chopper headed back across the lake. Somewhere in the distance came a short burst of gunfire, and I figured the goons must have found a local or two after all. The chopper wheeled off on a new course, vanishing into the smoke.

Time stretched on.

My arse continued to hurt.

In my head, Rick continued to tumble backwards,

smiling.

Malice continued to sink and burn beneath the waters.

Spuggsy squished, Tora dragged off to be squabbled-over by human animals, Moto shot.

Bella screaming and thumping like a boneless doll against the insides of the pla—

"You think they'll kill us?"

Nate was looking at me. There was something like... *pleading*, in his eyes. Something that cut through all the shit, all the anger at how he'd used me, tagged along to get his fix, lied. Something that whispered frostily in my ear:

But didn't you use him too?

"Yeah," I said, not unkindly. "Probably."

I looked back at the monument. It was something to stare at, I guess. Didn't move, didn't change: just stood there, defying the wind, a granite prick raping the sk—

"Whoa," said Nate.

The monument moved.

At the top, the tip of the great upturned basilica creaked, squealed in protest, then opened.

"Well there's a thing," I mumbled.

It was like a flower blossoming. Petals rattling into place, unoiled pistons groaning deep inside the rock. Without being entirely sure when it changed from one to the other, I suddenly wasn't looking at an enormous phallus any more.

I was looking at a bloody gigantic broadcasting dish.

And then Cy was standing in front of me, sneering.

"Time to go," he rasped.

CHAPTER NINETEEN

With each new room, a new calamity of memory. A new disastrous, deadly (wonderful) explosion of sights and smells and sounds, bubbling-up from the past, like liquid pouring into a mould; taking its time to slip into the deepest recesses.

Or, like dust blowing free from a hidden treasure.

Like cataracts dissolving.

His Holiness the Abbot John-Paul Rohare Baptiste allowed his minions to wheel him through the great, secret facility beneath South Bass Island, saying nothing, and felt his memories slither back one by one. They gathered pace the deeper he went, with each new level, each new string of concrete walls, each new dim light fixture that flickered and illuminated as it sensed movement.

Until eventually he remembered it all, like it had just been yesterday.

He'd arrived here, on the Island, five years ago: angry and bitter. It was below him, he'd thought. A man of his experience – of his record – sent to keep an eye on a bunch of backroom nerds.

Sergeant John P. Miller, the reassignment form had said. NATO Liaison Officer.

It should have said: fucking nursemaid.

But still the facility had been a pleasant surprise. Hidden away beneath the monument, below vaults supposedly for the Lake Eerie dead – in fact crammed with generators and feeds from the solar panels above – down creaking elevator shafts and plunging stairwells. Always the drip-drip-drip of condensed water.

Oh-so-very exciting. Oh-so-very impressive. It almost made up for the ignominy.

Here and now in the present, his assistants wheeled him past doors marked LAB#1, LAB#2, LAB#3...

He didn't like using the chair – it created the wrong impression – but it'd been an exhausting journey from the city and he wasn't as spry as he was. He was forty nine years old. He looked approximately seventy.

This was living with anaphylaxis. Constant pain.

This was living with AIDS, and more drugs than he could count administered by Clergy-doctors who'd have their testicles ripped-off and fed to them if they breathed a word to anyone.

This was three anti-coagulation shots every day, and antihistamine solutions three times a week.

This was the AB-Virus, eating his blood cells every second, staved-off only by communing with the divine.

This was living by numbers.

This place, it'd been a nuclear bunker once. So his superiors told him. Secondary or tertiary governmental; an alternative to the presidential chambers beneath Washington and NY. Somewhere safe to rule an irradiated country. Somewhere cosy for a ragged government to sip clean water and make comforting addresses.

The whole thing had been converted at short-notice to the requirements of the UN team. Dormitories and armouries stripped-out, curious equipment shipped-in for days on end. 'Project Pandora', they'd called it. An international attempt to stop the virus in its steps.

Out loud, as his wheelchair squeaked its way down the ramp to the sub-third floor, he mumbled:

"When all the evil spills out, there's still a... glimmer of hope..."

Pandora's box.

His chief minder must have heard him. An effete man named Marcus, good for very little but wheeling a chair and kissing arse, he gave John-Paul a concerned glance and crouched down to address him, unintentionally condescending. John-Paul approved of ignorance and ineffectuality. The soldiery were all very well; the cardinals and their units served a purpose, but one couldn't trust them. They were too full of their own ideas. Too focused.

"Your holiness?" The man said softly. "Did you say something?"

"Mm? No, no..." he closed his eyes and let the memories absorb him again, enjoying the concern on the man's face. "Everything's fine, Marcus."

He remembered wondering, at the time, why they'd sent the team here. Why not to some scholarly lab in New York? Why not out in the open?

And then the riots had started. They'd listened to the news every day before work, gathered together in the social-room. Riots and police actions and union strikes, and embassies closing-down at a rate of knots.

Then the diplomatic wrangling.

Then the rumours of Def Con escalation.

Then the standoffs and false alarms and real-actual-genuine-fear-of-Armageddon type talks, and suddenly everyone was living in a bad disaster film, and Sergeant John P. Miller became very very grateful indeed that his superiors had sent him deep underground.

Even then, he'd been bored out of his brain. The team's progress was just so slow.

No – correction: the team's progress was non-existent. It just happened to take them forever to find out how impotent they were.

Outside the world went to hell in a handcart, and inside... inside test-tubes clinked and microscopes whirred and men and women in white lab-coats made fussy notes with fussy biros. A lot of them had families. A lot of them looked unwell.

More rooms glided past the wheelchair, now circuiting the fifth level. COMMS, RESOURCES, the door names went, RECORDS, STUDIO, ENGINEERING...

The place was enormous. He remembered thinking that, too, all those years ago. Far too big for the research team. They'd set themselves up in their little corners and got on with it, and with nothing to do but file reports that said 'NO PROGRESS' he'd taken to wandering, exploring, poking in the dark.

A mothballed war room, with its displays darkened and tactical consoles disconnected.

A water purification plant.

A dozen storerooms marked NON-PERISHABLE. All empty.

And the communications room. And the broadcast suite.

And the Presidential Address studio. Plush red and blue walls. Elegantly draped flags. TV cameras jacketed in plastic wraps and rubber covers.

That was it. That was what brought him back here, now. In the flash of a triggered memory – those records unearthed from the Secretariat, presented to him by Cardinal Cy even as the doctors fussed over his bleeding skull – he'd remembered the place, the resources, the cameras and broadcasting equipment and security.

And as the exodus convoy had slipped away from the overrun UN headquarters – lost, futureless, despairing – that crumpled file from all those years ago had been like a bolt from the heavens. A sign. In that perfect instant he'd known, clearly and immediately, where to take his Clergy to find safety and security.

It was perfect. An island with its own tiny airstrip. Easily defendable. Perfectly secure quarters for the luminaries of *the sect. Plentiful housing for the soldiery and devotees. Vast holding-rooms below ground where anything could be conducted in secret and silence. Airports a mere spit away in Cleveland, Toledo, Detroit...*

And the studio. It couldn't be any better.

Halfway down the main hallway of the fifth sub-level a priest stood waiting, dressed strangely. He wore not robes but overalls – oil-stained and heavy with tool pockets – but in deference to his spiritual allegiance they were pale grey with a scarlet circle on the breast, and the same pattern tattooed over his left eye.

Marcus waved towards him with an introductory nod. "Chief Engineer Maclusky, your holiness."

"Mm. Yes? Yes?"

The man dipped in a bow that combined deference, religious awe and sphincter-tearing-terror. John-Paul resisted a smirk.

"Studio's up and running, your holiness. Cameras work fine. Shocking, frankly, but then again they built this shit to last and I guess we can't be surpr..." The man stopped. His eyes snapped wide as his brain caught up with his rambling and noticed what it'd just said. "Uh... E-excuse my French, your holiness, i-it's n..."

"Please go on, child."

"W-well, uh."

"The cameras"

"Yeah, yeah, well... they ain't maybe as advanced as we're used to, but..."

"That doesn't matter. We can find new ones, eventually. As long as we can broadcast."

"Yeah, yeah." Another mad little bow. "The dish needs some tuning – but no problem. Up and running whenever you want it."

"Good. Very good. One hour."

The man's eyes bugged out again. 'Whenever you want it' clearly hadn't included 'right now.'

"One h...! B-but..."

"That's a problem?"

"B-but... uh, no. No, your holiness, no. It's just... I assumed you'd want to wait for Sunday. H-how will people know we're going to be broadcasting?"

John-Paul treated the sweating man to a look that contrived to inform him his assumptions weren't worth a scrotumful of diseased spunk, then broke into a friendly little smile.

He liked to keep people off-balance.

"Aha." He said. "The people aren't my first concern, my child. The Cells need to know we've moved. London, Paris, Moscow, Beijing... All those little mini-churches, happily ferrying the Divine Initiates to LaGuardia. What will they do, I wonder, when they get there?"

The terrified man shook his head. He dripped.

"No, no. What we need is a message of reassurance. Just to... let them know where we are. Where to re-route. A permanent broadcast. A loop. You can manage that, I trust?"

"W-well, yes, I should think that would b..."

"Good. One hour, then. I believe I will be feeling rather stronger, by then."

The wheelchair squeaked on, and left the engineer behind. John-Paul hummed to himself.

At the end of another corridor, round a pair of sharp right angles, was one final doorway. It was marked:

DETENTION.

His smile dipped.

Here.

Here was where it all began.

It made sense, he supposed. A nuclear bunker, containing

dozens of important personalities and their families, all crushed together for an extended period. It was inevitable, perhaps, that tempers would fray. Behaviour would slip. A wise precaution, then, including somewhere to let troublemakers cool-down. To keep them out of harm's way.

Another aide opened the door, infuriatingly casual, and John-Paul felt cold prickles shivering across his entire body. Didn't they know? Didn't they understand?

Here.

It began here.

Five years ago, this was where it happened.

The research. The virus getting inside. The first symptoms. The discovery of the trend – the O-negatives unaffected, the antigens revealing their secrets – and the broadcast to the UN to let them know. Then the luckiest ones shutting themselves away, fearing the anger of the dying. The place was supposed to be airtight. How did the disease get in? Who was to blame?

For just a little while, the place became... hell.

There were gaps in what he remembered. Something a little like insanity had gripped the bunker, for a time. But here in this room he'd let God touch his blood, and let his memories swallow themselves up, and let purity cleanse his bitter soul; and then there was nothing... nothing at all... until he staggered out of the haze and into New York, to claim his destiny.

It was a curious sensation; returning.

They wheeled him into the dull little chamber, stepped formally aside and let him see.

The prisoners.

He smiled. He smiled with a vicious little glimmer of glee at seeing these fuckheads, these arch-devils, stripped of their clothes and humiliated, beaten and captured. He stared with an imperious smirk at their exposed genitals and the bruises criss-crossing their bodies. He sneered and smiled and tittered quietly. He was smug and arrogant and self-righteous, and the best thing was: he didn't care.

"Leave us." He told the aides. "Wait outside. Someone find Cardinal Cy. He'll want to watch, I think."

They were smart enough not to argue, leaving in a silent gaggle of grey and white. John-Paul called out to Marcus as he reached the threshold.

"Y-yes your holiness?"

"Prepare the equipment, Marcus. Hurry back."

"The... the cameras?"

"No, Marcus. The other equipment."

"Oh... oh, y-yes. Of course." The young man swallowed, blinking. "Where would you like to... uh..."

"Here, Marcus. Right here. I shall... commune... with the Lord before we broadcast. I will perform the miracle, I think. People must see that all is as it should be."

"I understand, your holiness."

"See to it."

"Y-yes, uh..." he lingered, shifting his weight awkwardly.

"What is it?"

"The... the communion. Would you like me to fetch an... an initiate?"

John-Paul stared at him for a moment or two, then broke into a wide smile.

"No." He said. "No, Marcus. My friends here are all I require."

And he smiled up at the prisoners, and Marcus scraped and kowtowed his way through the door. It swung shut with a heavy clang behind him.

And then there were three.

His Holiness the Abbot John-Paul Rohare Baptiste

*turned to face the pair of bruised fucks who'd caused him
so much annoyance, and said:*

"Blessed are the children."

"You what?" I grunted.

He smiled.

My arse, for the record, continued to hurt.

The detention room was a boring cube with a grille-
fronted cell set into each of the three walls unoccupied
by the door. Rather than sling me and Nate into the cells
themselves – oh no, that would've allowed us all sorts of
unfair luxuries like being able to bloody *sit down* – Cy
and his goons had cuffed us with our hands behind our
backs to the front of the grilles themselves, then taken
great pleasure in stripping off our clothes and covering
us from head to toe in foul smelling antiseptic powder.
The upshot was that we were standing there buck-naked,
stinking like necrotic kippers, unable to either turn, sit
or slouch without dislocating our shoulders, and now
faced with an unlikely audience with a chair bound old
git with a gargantuan hat.

My top ten surreal moments had a brand new highest
entry.

"The children." He repeated, watery little eyes
glimmering. "Blessed, blessed, blessed. Mm. Yes."

He twitched and giggled.

I exchanged a silent look with Nate. Whatever
unspoken enmities might exist between us, this overrode
them all. I looked back at the mummified vision and
chose my words with care.

"You," I said, "are mentally diseased."

Nate moaned quietly. For the fifth time he tried to
reach out with his foot towards the red case on the floor,

the same pack he'd been lugging about ever since the raid on the Secretariat. Cy had positioned it carefully next to our discarded clothes with a gleeful sneer, ensuring it was *just* out of Nate's reach.

Glancing now at my companion, in this light – with none of his daft costume-clothes to cover him – I could see the needle marks, the collapsed veins, the train track bruises of a lifetime. He was sweating. Coming down again.

John-Paul Rohare Baptiste barely even looked at him, sitting directly before me and jerking strangely to some silent beat. He had eyes, as they say, only for me.

"They called the prophets insane," he said quietly, like he was talking to himself. "They called the apostles madmen."

I shook my head and looked away, more *disappointed* than anything. All this grief, all this bloodshed, all this *struggle*: caused by an incontinent chimpanzee in a squeaky chair.

"They had a point." I said.

The first shock was: his frailty. On the telly, during those annoying bloody broadcasts, he looked old, true enough. He looked old and calm and maybe a tad doddery, like a friendly old boy who'd had his share of an eventful life and more besides. He looked like the sort of human raisin who'd fall asleep halfway through his favourite soap opera but could shout and rant with the best if someone mentioned 'The War'.

He looked, in other words, like an old man with a lot of life left in him.

In the flesh, in that cold detention room, under strip lights that strobed *just* too fast to notice, he was a cheap zombie special effect from an art-student B-movie. Skin so paper-thin you could make out the veins beneath the surface, hands so withered they looked like finger bones dipped in molten plastic. His eyes were set so far back in his head the sockets looked like volcano calderas, ready to bubble-up with pus and rheum.

Nice image.

This close up, under these lights, without the benefit of makeup, he *wasn't old*. He was *sick*.

I remembered the photo I'd seen inside the Secretariat. The NATO Staff-Sergeant, sat with an expression of quiet seriousness, staring into the camera. Forty, forty-five years old, well-groomed, no-nonsense.

The man before me hadn't got older. What had changed about him had nothing to do with age. It was simpler than that.

He'd just... *withered*.

He saw me staring.

"The Lord has sustained me." He said, like he could read my thoughts. With one hand he reached down to pluck a long coil of rubber tubing from a pocket on the side of the chair. "The Lord has shown me the Way."

"The Lord has taken a shit in your brain." I told him.

The second shock was: his smile.

It wasn't friendly. It wasn't pure. It wasn't the beatific expression of extreme serenity that basked in the studio lights every Sunday in the weekly broadcast. What it was, was:

Fucking vicious.

"The Lord has given me life in the midst of death. He has scoured the world with plague and fire, and wiped away those who bore his mark, and only I – whose blood runs with impurity – have been spared by his hand. The Lord favours me, Englishman, and in the hour of my greatest need – when the arch-Satan stormed at my door – he has delivered me from evil."

"The arch-Satan?"

"The arch-Satan."

"That'd be me?"

He smiled again. He smiled and underneath the God-talk, underneath the brimstone bullshit, I think maybe I saw...

—yes, I'm *sure* of it—

...a rational man staring out. A rational man who knew the truth.

A rational man who wasn't such a nutter after all.

Just a great liar.

"What happens to the children?" I said, suddenly exhausted. My body ached. My head hurt. Felt like it always had. I couldn't be *bothered* any more – not with any of it. With my own journey, with the goals I'd picked-up *en-route* like a travelling orphanage, with the whole twisted plate of crap this stupid bloody journey had become.

Don't you fucking give up, soldier!

Training. Secret Intelligence Service. MI6. Drill Sergeants screaming and yelling, shattering conventional wisdom, plumbing the depths of each grunt's soul for reserves of anger, for animal resilience, for the snarling shadow-lurking wolf loping about in the pits of the mind.

"The children?" John-Paul said. "Oh. Oh, yes. Oh, I see..."

Don't you fucking give up, soldier!

Blah, blah, blah-the-fuck-blah.

Not your problem, said Bella, and I believed her.

"That's it, isn't it?" The little man sniggered, chair squeaking. He carefully fitted a bung to one end of the rubber tube and drew back the fabric of his sleeve. A plastic canula, stoppered-up, sat in the crook of his

340

elbow, lodged deep in the vein underneath. "That's what it's for. That's why you came to get me." He looked pleased with himself.

I scowled. "Come again?"

"A little boy, was it? A little girl? Hmm? Did I... Did I *steal* one away from you? Some little blonde slut, eh? Some filthy little brat with his finger up his nose?

"Came all this way, did you, English? All this way to get back your kiddiewinks?"

Slowly, lip twisting, he fitted the tube to the end of the canula and pushed.

"Think you're the first, do you? The first disgruntled daddy to come get his brat?"

I could see the way his brain was working. It was logical, I supposed. It made sense. It was the same lie I'd told the scavs in Central Park; the same idea of aching loss, borrowed from Bella and Malice and all those others, who'd surrendered or deserted or *handed over* their own children.

It was the best rational reason for someone – someone like me – to do all that I'd done.

To clamber over piles of bodies. To cross oceans. To lock horns with the great Church.

It was so wrong it was funny.

"No." I said. "I don't have children. Never have."

The old man's eyebrows furrowed together. He stopped fiddling with the rubber tubing, let it hang loose in his hands.

"Then... but. Then *why*? Why did you come after me?"

I laughed, and I admit it must have sounded manic. Even in my head, the stupidity was too much to bear. The arrogance. This dried-up old lizard, this piece of desiccated skin.

He thought I'd come all this way for him. He thought this thing, between him and me, was *personal*.

"I didn't." I said in-between chuckles, which grew thicker and damper with each breath, until my eyes fuzzed with water and I could barely see. "You silly old twat. I didn't."

I said:
Listen.
Her name was Jasmine Tomas.
She was... she was more beautiful than a new moon reflecting off a perfectly still sea. She was so beautiful I spouted corny old movie bullshit like that all the time, and I could get away with it and not get even a little bit embarrassed. She had skin and hair the colour of coffee – one with cream, the other without – and curves in all the right places. When she laughed it was too loud and made people look, but they always looked then smiled, because when she laughed it was like... an infection. Like everyone caught it straight away.

We disagreed about almost everything, but we disagreed in a weird way. Like it meant we thought just the same as each other, but would go hammer and tong to disagree over details. Ha. The colour of wrapping paper. New music. Pretentiousness of art. We couldn't start a conversation without arguing. It was great.

We loved each other so much it scared the living fuck out of me.

An aide came shuffling into the room, then, as silent as death. He didn't speak. He wheeled a medical stand before him carrying a small steel machine with a glass front and a system of tubes dangling below it. I ignored him. I carried on talking.

A week before Jasmine Tomas moved into my flat, she told me to get rid of all the photos I'd taken of her. This was six years' worth. She said... she said when we lived together all our photos should be of both of us, or neither of us.

She said that sort of thing a lot.

The thing about Jasmine Tomas was, it would be easy to mistake her for a romantic. It would be easy to be fooled by the things she said, the gestures she made. And then just when you figured you'd got her pegged she'd switch on the footy, or tell a sick joke, or come home from work with stories of scalpels and infections. One time, I cooked Jasmine a stew. I mean, fuck... my job was to go overseas and kill stuff. I don't cook. Still, it turned out okay, you know? Cheese, leeks, you name it.

So I took the lid off the stew when she arrived – wearing the purple-and-blue dress with the earrings I got for her birthday – and oh god I wanted her, and everything was just perfect, and the first thing she said was:

Looks just like the inside of a gangrenous leg.

And then she laughed too loud, like a drain, and I laughed too. I couldn't help it.

The aide took the end of the rubber tube John-Paul had fitted to his arm. He slotted it neatly onto a spigot on the side of the steel machine, and turned towards me. He avoided my gaze.

My arse hurt. I kept talking.

He pulled a needle out of a plastic wrapper, and came forwards.

The first time I met Jasmine Tomas, for the record, she was teaching a group of wankers with too much testosterone about biohazards. All part of the training. She'd been seconded to the MOD from some governmental research-team or other – had more letters after her name than an episode of Sesame Street – and there she was, stuck in front of a room of leering arseholes who spent far longer staring at her tits than at the projector presentations she brought along. So... a few of those same arseholes dared another arsehole to ask her an embarrassing question about the dangers of sexual infection during fieldwork, and she didn't skip a beat. Told him she'd examine his infected areas after the lecture as long as he promised not to leak pus on her, then kept on talking over the top of the laughter.

I was the arsehole. I went and apologised after she'd finished. She took it well.

A week later we got dinner, then coffee, then the best fuck I ever had.

Three years later I was still killing people for 'Her Divine Majesty's Government', only now I was looking forward to the weekend just like every other guy, bored of his job.

Jasmine Tomas was my weekend.

The canula was in my arm, somewhere. Fitted to the tube that was fitted to the machine. I couldn't see behind my back.

My arse continued to hurt.

The aide flicked a switch with a devotional smile towards his master, then stood with his back to me, fussing over the machine.

And the tube – oh fucking hell I understood – the tube that led from me to the machine to John-Paul, it filled with blood like a long thermometer; red mercury bulging upwards.

My arm felt warm and cold at the same time. A prickling sensation. Pins and needles, killing my cells, spreading across me. And oh Jesus fuck shit I got it, I got it you withered old bastard, and I felt sick and weak and faint, but I kept talking because it's all I could do.

I said:

Listen.

I was never really designed, you know, for the romantic thing. Wasn't sure how to do it, I guess. But then nor was she, so we got on fine. Squabbled and sniped and smarmed our way through it all, awkward as you like. Never happy for long, but never sad for long either. Fuck fairytales. Fuck 'perfect'. We loved each other like nobody else, and that's enough.

So she decides to move in. I asked her, she said yes. The thing is, she works all day every day and I'm... out of the country. Business trips. Frequent flyer, blah-blah. So we figure we'll see more of each other if it's all cosy. All domestic. No need to schedule it every time.

Then the disease started. You remember? Right at the very beginning, it was just... some new thing. Nothing to worry about. They sent me to the East, to... Well. It doesn't matter where or why. I got back and Jasmine Tomas was supposed to move in that week, and all I got was a bloody text message telling me we'd have to postpone.

She'd been reassigned. Couldn't say where. Couldn't say why.

So I waited.

And the world died around me.

John-Paul just stared.

With my blood pouring out of me, filling him up like a greedy mosquito, bringing colour and warmth to his shrivelled face, he just stared and listened. He groaned once in a while, like a man in the throes of passion, and it made me feel sick to imagine him balls-deep in someone, grunting like a pig.

I felt sick in a lot of ways.

The world wobbled around me. Nothing was the right shade. Greyness was creeping out of every corner, and stinging the insides of my arms. My eyes rolled. My arse hurt.

I twitched my fingers behind my back, certain now that the aide was too busy watching the machine to turn around. I worked with all the speed and focus I could muster as everything slid away into bloodless limbo.

I kept talking. I kept fucking talking.

It was all I could do to cling-on. To stay awake. To stay alive.

I said:

I did some digging. Pulled some strings at the SIS; found out what she'd been sent to do. Where she'd gone, even.

UN mandate. That's all I got. Reassigned to a secret location as part of an international research team. Supposed to find a cure for the AB-virus.

'Project Pandora,' it was called.

John-Paul looked up.
And moaned, softly.
My fingers moved behind my back.
My arse stopped hurting.
Blood moved on my hands.

I said:
Listen.
Everybody died.
Jasmine Tomas, who I loved in that old movie way... I never heard from her again. Not for five years.
People died and lay on the streets, ambulances rushed back and forth, the world shat out its own guts and sat there like Elvis, poised on a toilet, dying by degrees.
I went back to Vauxhall Cross. I checked her records. Blood-type AB+.
As good as dead.

John Paul wasn't listening any more. Not so you'd know it, anyway.

His eyelids fluttered and his lips twisted in a smile, and I could see the strength filling him up, my own blood giving him life, turning him back into that man in the photo, the man on the TV, the calm and peaceful saint.

He communed with God through the medium of my fucking blood.

Blood-type O, rhesus negative. Safe to transfuse into anyone, more-or-less. Not quite good for him, not quite recommended. Risk of anaphylactic shock if conducted too fast, but still, but still...

My fingers twisted.

My body slumped. My brain started to slip away.

Something clicked quietly behind me.

I said:

For five years, I didn't exist.

I was just... alive.

And then one day the machines in the SIS comms-room chattered to life, and the correct passwords slotted into place, and the power fluttered through the consoles, and in a string of exchanged information a single word rushed-by.

'PANDORA.'

And a voice said:

"Are... Are you there?"

And it's a long shot. And maybe it's coincidence. Maybe it's fluke.

She should be dead. I know that.

But...

But you listen to me, you fucking leech. You listen to me, because you're still alive and you should be dead, and so nothing in the whole world – you hear me? – nothing, no one, no fucking old reptile or his gang of delusional pricks, would stop me from finding out.

So here I am.

And John-Paul Rohare Baptise smiled, like he'd been catching-up on what I was saying, and his eyes weren't sunken any more, and his lips were red, and he said:

"Mm, yes. Yes. Here you are. And... hah... And maybe you aren't the arch-Satan after all. Maybe you didn't come to get me, eh? Maybe I just got in your way? That's it, I think. But it doesn't matter, you see? No. No, it doesn't. Because here you are, and here you die."

And I smiled despite the weakness. Despite the nausea. Despite the rushing in my ears.

"It won't be as perfect," he said to himself, eyes closed, rapturous, "as a child. A child is perfection. The communion is... perfection. Yes. Mm."

His eyes opened.

He looked right at me.

"But you'll do. For today. It's only fitting. After all the trouble you've caused, mister. It's only fitting that you make a donation."

I smiled and I dropped the handcuffs to the floor by my feet, and the sliver of metal that was buried in my arse tinkled from the lock – the lock it had helped me pick – to the floor.

And John-Paul Rohare Baptise was opening his mouth to protest, to shout for help, to cry-out in baby like shock, but it wouldn't do the old fucker any good, because my fist was already in his face and his teeth were already shattered, and I was already moving onwards and head butting the aide and cracking his nose, and he went down quick and quiet, and I was turning back to the groping old bastard with my knuckles bare and bloody, and this time I didn't stop until he was silent on the floor, and lying in his own juice.

Scratch that:

My juice.

And then I pulled out the tubes from my arm, and threw up like a trooper.

CHAPTER TWENTY

When Cy came blundering-in fifteen minutes later, things were a little different.

I wasn't naked any more for a start.

"You wanted me, your holin—?" He started.

And stopped.

I tried to imagine how he must have seen things, in that cold moment when we all froze and stared at each other. But I didn't know him, and could only guess what his brain *did* in moments like this.

Would he have fixated on the blood? There was certainly enough of it about: great thick pools, already congealing, from where Nate's shaking hands had tried to puncture the comatose aide's artery with the crude transfusion tube. Third time lucky, in the end.

Or maybe Cy's eyes, hidden away behind those stupid shades, went straight to his Lord and Master? The great Abbot John-Paul, slumped on the floor with his teeth smashed out, whimpering as consciousness came slinking back.

After I'd cut Nate free, as the old junkie staggered and whinged and gagged, he told me I needed more blood – quickly. I'd wanted it from the Abbot – take back what he'd stolen. It seemed only fair.

But no, no, no. Nate had shook his head, eyes unfocused, shivering in need of a fix, telling me no. The old man had a different blood type.

"'Member... 'member the TeeVee show?" He grumbled. "'Member the clumpin' cells? Clots inside. Wrong type. One way only."

So he'd swapped the tubes and let me leech off the spindly little aide instead. I would've felt bad, if I had the energy. If I gave a flying fuck.

So John-Paul was still lying where I'd left him, moving slowly, scrabbling in the blood. Was that what Cy saw first, when he stepped in?

Or was it me? Maybe that was it. Instant fascination. The English *bastard* who'd blown-up his airport, who'd wiped-out his unit of grunts, who'd run rings round him in New York, who'd almost executed him following the Tag, who'd led the army that ejected his gang from their base, who'd held his attention as an honest-to-god Red Injun snuck up and stabbed him through the skull, and who'd beaten-up the withered old man he worshipped.

I guess you couldn't blame him for being a tad grumpy.

Was that what he focused on, as he came marching in? Me standing there, looking and feeling like I'd died, wanting nothing more than to curl up and sleep for a year, letting my body adjust.

No.

Fair enough, the freaky shithead pulled a gun on me the second he appeared – quicker than I could see – but his heart wasn't in it. He wasn't going to shoot.

No. What Cy looked at as he stepped inside was this: Nate's bag.

"Ah," he said. "Hm."

"K-kill... kill them..." The Abbot groaned from the floor, bent double. "Look what... they did..."

"Yes, holiness." Cy said, voice flat, not even looking down. "Get out now, sir. I'll deal with it."

And so the Abbot John-Paul Rohare Baptiste, spiritual head of the Apostolic Church of the Rediscovered Dawn, turned his back on the arch-Satan and wobbled away on his hands and knees, trailing blood. The door swung closed behind him.

And then it was just me, and Nate, and Cy. And a gun.

And Bella saying:

Not your problem.

"Well, now," said the Cardinal.

Nate was a wreck. Sweat poured off him. The effort of dangling there off the cell bars, then thinking straight long enough to hook me up to the whitewashed aide, must have finished him. He could barely stand, snot and tears and vomit decorating his face. I wondered how long it had been since his last fix. Certainly since before the battle by the bridge. I wondered what sort of weird-arsed home-made shit he'd been chasing anyway.

"Nigger looks like death," said Cy, grinning.

Nate swayed where he stood. "J's... Jus' need my... my..." He blinked, trying to focus. "Medicine."

A lot happened at once.

Nate lurched towards the red pack with his arms outstretched, gurgling from his guts upwards. Cy moved even faster, gun shifting to freeze the man on his spot. He had the sense to stay.

And I took my chance.

Pounced.

Fists raised. No *way* he could turn back to cover me in t—

—*fuck, he's fast*—

The pistol muzzle sat on my forehead. Cy smiled.

"Now." He said. "Just you back up. Back up there."

I didn't move.

"Limey. Limey, you hear?"

I worked my jaw. "I hear you."

"You back up. Or the nigger gets shot."

"Not me?"

"Hah. Not you. No guns for you. Not 'less you make

352

me."

I didn't move. Didn't care.

Let him go for Nate.

(But—)

No buts.

(But he saved my l—)

No excuses. You know the rules.

Don't you let yourself owe anyone anything.

Don't you fucking give up, soldier!

(Sir, no sir, etc etc.)

Let him do it.

Let him try.

The second the gun moves, he's mine.

Cy said: "Don't say. Didn't warn you."

And then Nate was on the floor, and a gunshot hung in the air, and the stink of guns and the shock of movement, and the pistol was back against my forehead – hot, singeing my skin – before I'd even tilted forwards.

Too fast to see.

He, I decided, *isn't natural.*

Nate screamed. His foot was a wreck. Bones poked at fractured angles from a fragmented red sneaker, fountaining blood and singed fabric.

"Back up." Cy said again, and still the grin. "Back up. Or next. His face."

I backed up. Nate's screams turned to moans, then whimpered away. Cy kept the gun aimed squarely at me, sidestepping around the growing slick on the floor, squatting to his haunches beside the heavy case. The muzzle never wavered. The dagger-pommel poked from his head like a rubber cock, and I bit-down on the cheap joke in my mouth.

"Didn't have time," he said, smiling like a Cheshire cat, "to grab my own. Back at the Secretariat. Shit, Limey...

You shoulda seen the stashes. Junk coming in from all over. Collectors collecting. Scavs bartering. Even had us a team of geeks. Geeks *making* it. New kinds. Mixing it like fuckin' *artists*."

"Drugs?" I said. The word sounded... *naïve*.

"Best currency." He licked his lips and rummaged in the bag, not even looking. "'Cept for God. Heh. 'Cept for kids."

He withdrew a sealed hypoderm. Bit the rubber flange off the needle and spat it away.

The gun didn't waver.

"Put it to good use. Trickled it out. Some to Klans, some overseas. Let them know who's boss. See? Rewards for good boys. Sweeties for ignorant masses. Heh. Manna from heaven. Always kept the best shit for ourselves."

His stupid syntax was pissing me off. "Until the ignorant masses rose up and kicked your arse, you mean?"

"Uh-uh." He shook his head. "'Til this nigger stole it." He kicked Nate's ruined foot, drawing-up another round of tortured screams.

Then he lifted the hypoderm to his neck, still staring right at me, punched through the skin and squeezed the plunger. His whole body went tense, cords straining.

"What is it?" I said, morbidly fascinated, watching the liquid vanish inside him.

His lips peeled back.

He hissed, like a boiler reaching critical mass.

Then grunted.

Then he yanked out the needle with a girlish giggle and chucked it away, letting it smash on the floor.

"The fuck knows?" He said, voice abruptly smooth, body moving with a weird liquidity. He stood up straight and peeled off his glasses, ignoring the tiny dribble of blood hanging on his neck. "Gave up reading labels years back."

His eyes were almost red. So bloodshot that they bulged, capillaries swollen and angry, pupils dilated to swallow dark irises that brooded at the heart of hot, insane scarlet.

It took me a moment or two to find my voice.

"Good to see there were no adverse effects, mate."

He giggled and winked. It looked painful.

"Now then," he said, moving slow. "You recall the Secretariat? You recall before the Injun arrived?"

"What about it?"

He grinned. And then carefully, letting me see what he was doing every step, he tucked the pistol away in a holster inside his robe and cracked his knuckles.

"Let's... pick up. Hm. Pick up where we left off?"

The first lunge was almost too fast to follow. Maybe I was still groggy.

Maybe I was just too slow.

It didn't matter, really. I knew it'd be a feint before he'd even started, and was ready when he blurred left-right-left – confusing and showy – then sent a foot arching down towards my shins.

Looking flash, playing dirty. Trying to break my ankle, the arrogant fuck; that or push me backwards, keep me on the defensive, box-me against a wall.

Best form of defence is –

I stepped forwards, through and under his guard. Took the force out of the kick with a sideways swipe of my right hand and rolled with the weight, down on one knee – letting fists strike uselessly at the air above my head. My left hand snapped palm-open, thrust forwards with a tiny snarl on my lips.

There's no word for what happens when you hit someone as hard as you can in the balls. It's like... it's like somewhere between a crunch and a squelch. It's like hard-and-soft altogether, and you can barely do it without wincing in sympathy.

What I did was: gripped.

Fact: it's possible to kill a man this way.

We must've stood like that for a second or two. That shocked sense of calm after a flurry of blows and kicks too quick to be handled intelligently. You just *react*. You just *let it flow*.

I waited for him to crumple.

And waited.

And looked up.

He winked again, then laughed.

And then his fist was slow-mo-ing and my cheek was all white light, and I was on my back, and the world came back bit-by-bit.

He stepped back and shook his arms, like an athlete warming up. Like there wasn't a great bloody stain oozing through his robes around his crotch.

"Round two." He giggled, every muscle shivering. "When you're ready, limey."

Fuck.

I stood up carefully, overplaying the grogginess. Hamming it right up. I swayed on my feet, waving him forwards with the punch-drunk bravado of an amateur. Trying to be *clever* about this... He was quicker and stronger and meaner, but if he was as dumb as he *looked* maybe I could—

Now.

And he was on me again. Expecting it to be easy; an elbow thrown out at my cheek as he spun past, a low leg orbiting at the edge of the curve. I took the elbow in both hands and wrenched, letting his weight overbalance him, chasing him down so the roundhouse arced uselessly. I fucking *pummelled* him, knuckles mashing on cheeks and lips, knowing it did no good but enjoying it anyway, leaning my arms on his chest as his back hit the ground, forcing the air out of him and feeling his ribs crackle, then planting both fists in his guts.

Hard.

Trying to get the shithead bleeding inside. Emptying him of oxygen. Playing it carefully, thoughtfully. Not a brawl but an amputation, not a fight but a fucking *dissection*. He coughed blood and tried to lever himself up, sucking back air, and I broke his nose with a smile and kept hitting, sat astride him; pounding away until my fingers felt broken and my arms ached from wrist to shoulder.

Intelligent application of force.

Yes.

Yes, you *fuck.*

Controlled violence.

Thwap

Thwap

For Rick. For Malice and the others. For Bella, you *shit.*

Yes.

For Jasmine.

I took him apart, little by little, and no brain-surgeon was *ever* as precise as me in that glorious flurry of aggre—

Snuk

My fists stopped moving.

Cy smiled through teeth smeared with bloody spittle, gripping my hands in mid-swing as if he'd caught a pair of tennis balls, then sat up in a single continuous movement and nutted me on the bridge of my nose. Something snapped.

Fact: It's possible to kill people like *this* too.

I went over backwards. A fist in my eye helped me down. Warmth spattered off my lips and chin.

And I lay there panting as he dragged himself out from beneath me, and stood with no obvious aches or pains, spitting the blood away and clearing each nostril with a viscous rasp of snot and gore. He rolled his head as if he'd fallen asleep in the wrong position; jumped up and down in his spot once or twice, then gave me a great, bright smile.

"Let's go." He said.

Fuck.

It took a long time to pick myself up. Every inch a mountain. Every movement a defeated consolation.

I couldn't win. This... this *thing* wasn't even human any more. With his veins clogged-up with freaky narcotic shite, nothing would work. Clever fighting. Precision and stealth. Fuck it. Fuck it all.

I've seen guys on PCP. I've seen guys go psycho on Yaba crazy medicine. Twenty bullets, major organs shredded. Doesn't matter. Takes the body longer to realise it's dead than it takes to kill whoever's killing you.

Cy was worse.

Cy soaked it up then smiled sweetly. He didn't rush. Didn't race to squish me before the wounds caught up on him. He just...

Enjoyed it.

So what happened was, my brain went away.

The conditioning shivered somewhere deep, unflexed like a great squid-thing, untangling from the murk. I'd held it down too long. Let it grow in the dark.

It took a hold of me and blurred-away all those insignificances, all those useless extremities of thought and intelligence. Sharpened me as it blunted me down.

The trainers at the SIS would have been proud.

Good little soldier. Good little killer. Good little machine.

The wolf came out from its shadows, and its eyes glowed in the gloom, and I stopped thinking. Let the instincts take over.

Don't you fucking give up, soldier!

Sir, no sir, etc etc.

And this time when he rushed me I was already hitting him, and when he scooped at the air to knock me back I was ducking into his belly with a knee, and when he snarled and spun and kicked-out I *let* him, and enjoyed the pain in my hips because it meant I was *close*, and *hungry*, and I lamped him so hard in the ear that the skin on my fist popped.

Chased him down to the ground.

Snapped his shin with my boot.

Took out his eye with a finger.

Caught a hold of his jaw as it flapped open and yanked down so hard something shattered and tore.

Grabbed a handful of his neck and balled my fist 'til the skin broke and the cords underneath moved in my hand.

Punches raining on my face.

Like I care.

And I locked my fingers round his throat, bloody and slick and crackling down deep, and *squeezed*.

His eye bulged and bled. He gurgled.

And then the gun was in my face.

The wolf loped away.

Cy's lips twitched into something like a smile.

I sighed. "You said no guns. Not for me."

"N't...*nk*... n't less... yuh... *made* me..."

His finger tightened on the trigger.

And from the corner of my eye a black hand reached out from nowhere, gripped the tall cock-like handle poking from Cy's head, and *pulled*.

It made a noise something like a champagne cork.

He rustled as he died, and a soupy sort of stuff oozed out of his skull, and Nate – shivering on the floor with the knife in his hand, foot still pulsing blood – grinned his pearly grin and said:

"'nother... 'nother one you owe me."

It was strange.

To have come this far for a *maybe*...

To have fought and killed and cut my way across... shit, across half the fucking world, on the strength of a feeble radio transmission and the half-a-chance idea of someone who *should* be dead *not* being dead.

To have shut myself off, to have *sliced* across any prat who stood in my way, because:

If John-Paul can do it, maybe Jasmine can too...

I'd come a long way. Following the voice in my head every step. Listening to its orders. It told me not to give up, and I didn't. It told me to know everything, and I had. It told me to cover the angles, and I covered them. Though it left me bloody and broken and knackered, I fucking did as I was told.

Right?

My head hurt, and the world spun around me. I giggled.

The voice, the voice. That was it. At the end, when the time came to find some things out, to finish it, the voice told me not to get distracted, to do the job, to stay focused. It told me:

Not your problem.

I wondered if I'd done the right thing, taking the syringe from Nate's bag. It made the world... different.

I giggled again.

I stood outside a room on the fifth sub-level of the South Bass Island UN Bunker complex, and shivered, trying to concentrate. Things were happening, somewhere. People running, voices raised, footsteps clattering and guns being armed. Right now, nobody was paying me much attention, which made a refreshing change. Earlier-on, as I staggered out of the detention room with my eyes watering and my head spinning, a couple of guards had got lucky and noticed the red patches soaking through my stolen robes. I'd lifted them from the Clergy aide on the floor, whose blood was currently filling my veins. It had seemed elegant, somehow. Like... regardless of whether the damp patches came from him or me, it was all the same thing.

Haha.

Should that be funny?

(The two guards who'd spotted the blood hadn't thought so. I tried to explain it as patiently as I could – not even slurring much – but they kept on telling me I was stoned, and asking me who the fuck I was, and poking me with their fingers. It got boring quickly. I like to think I left them alive – just – though to be honest I can't say I was subtle about it.)

The point was, I was free to roam. And right now I stood outside a door, on the deepest level of the complex, and stared in confusion at the sign.

COMMS

This was where it came from. The transmission. The word PANDORA. The voice. This is where she sent it. I could almost *taste* it. Could almost reach out and pluck her from the air, and remind myself of all the guilty sensations that time had stolen. The smell of her hair. The slant of her nose. The exact shade of her eye.

I could remember them all. Ish. But memories are like regrets, they linger and haunt you, but they *evolve* with time. They lose their edge. Become idealised.

I wondered, in some quiet giggling abstraction, if I'd even recognise her when I saw her again. Then my brain reminded me she was dead – *must* be. Had been for five years.

Idiot. It said.

All this way, for nothing.

Without even realising it, I'd placed a hand on the door handle and begun to push. And that, really, was all there was to it. Inside this room I'd find out. Had she been here? Was it really her that sent me the message?

I felt like a pilgrim who never expected to *get* to his shrine.

I relaxed the pressure on the door and stepped back. The air was full of light. Hallucinations turned my brain upside-down; twisted synaesthetic confusions swapping sounds for tastes, musical tones for physical feelings, emotions for colours.

Scents for light.

In the detention room, the syringe I took from Nate's pack had been marked: SNIFF.

I recalled a time that seemed long ago, and a chase through city streets, and a big man in red injecting another man with... Well. With something that made him a little less than human. That sharpened-up his senses. I recalled being pretty fucking impressed, at the time.

And now here I was. A wolf in the true sense.

And I turned away from the Comms Room with my

nose in the air, and followed a pulsing trail of light-stink that moved and shifted like electrified neon, because maybe it *wasn't* my problem, and maybe it *wasn't* part of my mission, and maybe no one would care but *me*–

–but some things need to be finished, whether it's your job to finish it or not.

Jasmine could wait.

She'd waited five years.

I found John-Paul Rohare Baptiste in a room decked in red and blue velvet, with flags hung-up behind him. The country they signified was dead.

It had been easy, closing-in on him, down bunker tunnels and twisting corridors, with lights shimmering before and behind me, sniffing the air.

He smelt of me.

He was sloshing with *me*.

He was talking as I stepped quietly inside, through a door marked:

STUDIO

"...and... and so I'm putting this message on... onna loop..."

He was swaying unsteadily. Face all busted-up – cleaned of raw blood but clearly bruised – eyes crossed. He was holding himself upright on the barn doors of an old TV camera, staring deep into the lens. The red light was on.

"...we've... had some troubles. You c'n... c'n see from my face, I think. But... h-hallelujah! We have prevailed, my sons and daughters. God's righteousness has... has shone through. We have been sorely *tested*, and faced down the... the evil of ignorance. We have endured our great Exodus, and in the... in the process have found our 'Promised Land'. My children... we have been found *deserving* of glory."

There was nobody behind the camera. Nobody behind the glass window in the control-booth set to one side. Not any more. Not since I stopped-off to say hello.

It had been impressively soundproofed. John-Paul hadn't even noticed.

There was nobody listening to him. Nobody except me, and the world.

What was left of it.

"I send out this message to say to you all: do not be alarmed. We have moved, as God's will has dictated. But our mission remains steadfast. We must build a brighter tomorrow. We must open the eyes of the children! *Amen.* Mm. *A-men.*"

His eyes rolled and closed-up; communing with the divine. His withered face creased in a perfect smile.

"And... and so I say to you all, continue to send me the architects of the future. Continue to bring me your sons and daughters. Bring them to Cleveland, and Toledo, and we will reveal to them the paradise we are building here.

"We will take them and raise them up, and... a-and... *ah...*"

His voice tailed off. His eyes fluttered open.

I pushed the silver pin a little harder against the frail skin of his neck. He hadn't even heard me approach him. Hadn't been aware I was behind him, looming like some great fucking bat, until the sliver of metal was pricking his throat.

The sliver Rick gave me. Buried in my own flesh.

John-Paul gurgled.

The red light continued to burn.

"Wh... who... who's there?" He said, not daring to move.

"I'm the Holy Ghost." I said. "I move in mysterious ways."

"Y-you! You would... you would commit this sin before the World? Y-you would expose your evil?"

I leaned down until I was close to his ear, senses alive with the drug, tasting his fear. *Enjoying* it.

"I will if *you* will." I said.

"Wh... what d... do you m...?"

"The children, Abbot. You were about to tell us about the children. About how you 'raise them up.' That was as far as you got. Why not... *tell* us about that?"

"B-but... But I..."

"Now, now. The world watches, your Holiness." I pressed harder with the pin. "Let's not scrimp on details."

And so he told them.

He told them how he'd survived. He gibbered and snotted and cried as he went, and he dressed it up in holiness. Didn't matter. Still came across like a desperate man polishing a turd.

It wasn't murder, he said, it was the Touch of God. It wasn't blood, it was divinity itself.

Listen: people might be a little short-sighted when confronted with miracles. And okay, maybe humanity has a hole in its common-sense where the idea of deity sits nice and firm. Maybe there's something to be said for the infuriating fucking gullibility of mankind, but here's the thing:

You can only push it so far.

I think the message got through.

I think what they heard, out there, clustered round TVs for weeks to come, as the message looped and re-looped over and over, was *not* a divine prophet delivering words of hope and purity...

...I think what they heard was a wretched little freak, explaining with patience and politeness how he'd stolen the blood of a thousand kiddies, how he'd convinced the world of his perfection, how his acolytes had flocked to serve him, just to fend-off the virus that was killing him.

He told them that there were no 'marks.' No angels pouring out their vials onto the earth. Nothing. Just people with a particular type of blood. Whole ethnic groups, with genetic traces that he neither understood nor cared about, but had nothing to do with the wrath of God.

He told them that the virus was just that: a virus. Biological. Predictable. It killed certain people and left great swathes of others alive. The O-negs. The Native Americans. Eastern Asians. Australian Aborigines. He told them he knew this because he'd been with the group who found it all out. They'd seen what the virus killed and what it spared, and they'd failed utterly to find out how to stop it. They'd hidden away down here in the bunker until the virus caught up with *them* too, and there was a time of madness and... and things he couldn't remember, and then...

Then he was reborn as John-Paul, the Holy.

Stealing blood to stave-off the virus. Whole transfusions of O-neg, to replace the juices the Blight guzzled every day. Injections of plasma from Iroquois captives, to plant whatever genetic armour they possessed deep inside him.

He told them *everything*. Then his voice went quiet and his face went slack, and he told them that children were better than adults.

Purer, he said.

More perfect. Like drinking the blood of an angel.

More beautiful.

And...

And when they were weak from blood loss, he said, when the Light Of God was in them...

They never said "no" to *anything*...

He went on and on and on, and when he was done I patted him on the head like he'd done well, pushed the silver needle into his jugular so the blood went out of him like a balloon losing air, and when he was on the ground I stamped on his head with a noise like a cockroach crackling.

And there were choirs of angels singing, and shafts of light, and the warm gaze of divinity to assure me I'd done well. But then again I was hallucinating like a motherfucker, so I ignored the whole stupid show and told myself – one way or another – I'd made the world a slightly better place.

"Architects of tomorrow." John-Paul had said.

Heh.

Sometimes architects have to tear down before they can build-up.

CHAPTER TWENTY-ONE

Predictably, the place was in uproar. Things were moving too quickly now, cascading towards a shit-littered abyss before anyone could even prepare for the fall. I wondered why. I wondered what was going on. I wondered why I couldn't give a damn.

Tangled cords of scent-trails braided and split apart in the air of the bunker; a three-dimensional map in the hallucinogenic chambers of my mind that documented fear and panic and confusion. Men in Clergy robes sprinted along corridors, rushing up tangled stairwells and queuing five deep at the cavernous elevators. Somewhere high above, on the first or second sub-level, shouts filtered downwards. Everyone seemed to be ignoring me.

The drug made me giggle. Or maybe I just felt like it. I don't know.

With my senses on overdrive – whole body *thrumming* to some internal beat, like an iron butterfly flapping great wings inside my chest – it was all too much to bear. The noises and smells and sights. Eventually I stopped paying attention, turned away and just... *walked*.

I found myself, eventually, back outside the Comms room, and slumped to the floor on the opposite side of the corridor. Just staring. Wondering.

Was she here, once?

Did she... did she die here?

Where are the bodies?

I killed some time picking lumps of brain and bone out of my boots.

The drug was doing something to me. Not just hotwiring my senses and overloading my brain, but picking away at parts of my mind, doing something insidious and unwelcome. Something that involved the wolf, somehow. Something that tugged at the upper layers – those useless skeins of civility and rationality – and went nestling *below*, into the 'Old Brain', into the scratching suspicions of the subconscious and paranoia.

Something *gnawed* at me. Something that had been gnawing for a long, long time... Something I'd noticed and disregarded, or ignored without concern. Something that had been clanging and shouting to grab my attention, formless and silent; beginning to piece things together moment-by-moment, to build me a message.

To show me something.

It had to do with Bella, I think. With something she'd said.

Doesn't matter. Not your proble—

No, not that. *That* was solved, now. I'd *made* it my problem. For her and Rick, and the crew of the *Inferno*, and the scavs and citizens and misguided klansmen and *everyone*, I'd made it my problem. A regular little hero. But that wasn't it.

My brain itched.

What else?

What else did she say after we'd fucked, in the pub outside Heathrow, as we lay on the barrel chute and I curled my fingers through her hair, thinking of someone else? My Jasmine. Thinking of my Jasmine and feeling guilty and dirty and wrong, and not evening listening to what the poor girl, poor little Bella, was saying.

Further along the corridor, a hurrying Choirboy limped towards me, hood-up, a red pack slung over his shoulder, with a medical stand used as a support. I knew it was Nate without even looking around. The drug made him smell of sweat and fear and chemicals.

And guilt.

What?

"T-that you?" He said. "What you doin'? We gotta get out of here."

I stared at the door of the Comms Room. Was I ready for it yet?

Instinctively, I felt it should be the *last* thing that I did. It should be the last mystery to be solved. I should get everything else out the way first.

Don't you get distracted, boy.

Don't you let things slip.

Know everything. Cover the angles.

"Just thinking." I said.

"Yeah? Well... well you do it and *walk*, man. Crazy *shit* goin' on." He leaned down and waved frantically at the other goons, face buried in the folds of his robe. I didn't ask where he'd got it. "They saying... they saying the Abbot's *dead*. You know 'bout that?"

I shrugged.

"They saying there's boats out on the lake. Circling round and round. They saying one of the choppers been knocked-out. They saying it's the... Hau...Howdenoh..."

"The Iroquois?" I said, barely interested.

"Yeah! How the fuck'd they do *that*?"

I shrugged again. *Good for them.* Wouldn't have been difficult, I guessed. Impossible to invade the island, but easy to prowl the lake. Sneaking about, exploding a lorry or two, taking down the choppers from afar. No big undertaking, for enough people.

I wondered how many survived the fight by the reservoir. How many of them got away because Cy and his shitheads were so busy collecting me and Nate.

I wondered if the Tadodaho had planned it all along.

Who knew?

Who cared?

I imagined Malice's baby, gurgling on the distant shore, listening to the fireworks.

I cared.

How annoying.

Nate tried to pull me upright. I shook him off.

"C'mon!" He burbled, eyes bulging. "N-now's the *time*! We can... we can slip away, maybe. Huh? In the confusion, you know? It's your *show*! 'S what you *do*, man! We gotta... we gotta look out for each other!"

I translated in my head. It was almost pitiful.

You've got to look after me! I saved your life! Protect me! Protect me!

He tugged at me again, staring off down the hallway.

"Ain't no fucking *way* Nathaniel C. Waterstone's gonna die here today..."

And there it was.

I stared at him. He was struggling out of his robe, yanking the eye patch out of his pocket to cover the tattoo, muttering under his breath.

"Nate?" I said.

"Huh?"

"What's... What does the 'C' stand for?"

He stopped with the robe looped round his neck and stared at me, like I was insane.

"What?"

"The 'C'."

"The fuck you wanna..." He rolled his eyes and shook his head, like he'd decided to humour the mentalist to hurry him along. "Stands for Cassius. Why you wanna know?"

"Like... Cassius Clay?"

"My pop's hero. S'where they got the name."

The pieces slotted together.

I should have seen it before.

No more mysteries. No more excuses.

And finally Bella's little voice in my head, saying over and over *not your problem, not your problem*, that voice had an answer from the wolf, its eyes glowing in the dark.

Problem solved. It said.

"Nate."

"Huh?"

"We need to talk, Nate."

"Shit, man – it can *wait*! We gotta g..."

"You remember I called you a parasite?"

He went quiet, then nodded and waved it away.

"Yeah. Yeah, I remember. Forget it, man. It was a... tense time. No need to apologi..."

"I wasn't going to, Nate."

"Wh... what? Oh."

"I was right. You *are*. You *are* a parasite." My voice was cold. I couldn't change it for the world. I was on autopilot.

Not your problem, Bella said. I shushed her gently and looked up at Nate.

His mouth formed words, trying to find something to say. Clergymen shouted nearby.

"L-look. Fucksakes! I... Listen, you got something to say, okay. O-*kay*. But you do it when we're out of here, huh? Or we both die right n..."

I pulled Cy's gun on him. His eyes bulged. He looked angry.

"What the... what the *fuck*, man? Are you out of your fucking *mind*? I saved your *life*, Limey! I saved your goddamn life, like, *ten times*! I got shot in the goddam foot, man. Don't you point that thing at m..."

"Nate."

"Don't you poi..."

"*Nate*. Listen."

He listened.

"You're good at favours, Nate. Good at finding people to take care of you."

"Now hold o..."

"No. Be quiet." I armed the gun. It sounded like bones scraping. "You told me you went over to England in the eighties, right? Got taken out there by your exec-bitch? Lived the life of Larry, blah blah. Cushy sort of arrangement. Right."

"Look, this ain't the t..."

"Then you fucked her pal and screwed it up."

He sighed. Looked down.

"Bummed your way around. Attached yourself to people. Yeah? Did the bare fucking minimum to make yourself *useful*. Got taken *care* of."

He wouldn't look me in the eye.

"Same as later on. You told me so yourself. The Clergy showed up, offered you a job. Nice and cosy, safe as houses. And who cared if the job was ferrying kiddies to get themselves sucked-dry? Huh? Who cared? You just pretend like you don't *know*."

The look in his eye told me: *he knew*.

"Oh, and there was the smack, too. You forgot to mention that. You told me you got clean back in London. Maybe you did, for a while. Must've been too good an opportunity, right? When these robe-wearing pricks showed up with all the skag you can shoot?

"Bare minimum effort, maximum reward. Easy life."

"L-look. It's... it's not like..."

"It was the same when *I* showed up. Shit, Nate, don't look at me like that. I know. You see this psycho Brit, all fired-up – who cares about what? – and he can make sure you don't get *dead*, and he can lead you back to the supply, and all you've gotta do in return is patch him up when he needs or wait for him to die."

"Don't you gimme that," he hissed, real anger in his voice. "Don't you act like I used you. You done the same! You lied to all them scavs. You had yourself a goal, same as me, and you used any motherfucker you had to to get it."

"That's true, Nate. Thank you for that." I smiled, cold fury doing something sharp to my belly. "I'm not a very nice piece of work either."

He nodded. Like he'd scored a *point*. "Well then."

"Except, the thing is, Nate... Responsibilities."

"What?"

"We've all got them. Don't always benefit us, but they're there. You think I gave a shit if John-Paul lived or died? Had nothing to do with me. Just got mixed-up in this. But I tell you what, Nate: I *finished* it. Too many people died on the way not to. Too much at stake."

"Make your point Limey."

"The point." I worked my jaw. Sighed deep. Saw Bella's face. "The point's name, Nate, was Shayla."

He stopped breathing.

Looked up.

"H-how... how did you..."

"She would've been, what? One, when you ran. Shit, you even left a note... 'Couldn't handle the responsibility', Bella said. Rare moment of honesty there, Nate."

"You... you know B-bella..?"

"You latched onto *her* too, didn't you? Nice young thing, bright as a button, rich family. I mean... there's you, out on the streets, no place to live, and here's this stupid kid. What an opportunity..."

"Y-you... you shut the fuck up, now..."

"Made her love you, right? Used her money. Got her hooked on shit and right up the duff. Then just when the cons outweigh the pros, just when there's a kid in the picture, off you toddle. Off to the Choirboys, waiting with their job. Off to the U-S of A. Something like that?"

He was glaring, now. Wondering whether to run or punch me.

"Malice kept wondering," I said, "why you wouldn't stop staring at her kid.

"Guilt, right?"

The gun was heavy in my hand. I sighed.

"Bella helped me get here." I said, voice tighter than I'd expected. There was something like a choke rising in my throat. "She's dead now."

"How long have you known who I was?" Nate said, quietly.

"I think..." I scowled, looking inwards. "I think from the beginning. Heh. Maybe I *am* like you, Nate. Maybe I ignored it because you were useful. Was only just now, sitting here, that it all clicked.

"'Claystone,' Bella called you. Nathaniel Cassius 'Clay' Waterstone. Small world."

"Small world." He muttered. Almost a whisper. Then: "How's... How's the girl?"

My jaw clenched.

"That's just it, Nate. That's what I meant about responsibilities. Y'see, that girl, that little Shayla... she turned five last year."

Nate's eyes bulged. He saw it coming.

"They raped her mummy and dragged her away, screaming, to an airport just outside London."

"Oh... oh god..."

"They loaded her onto a plane with a dozen more, all crying, and shipped them to a shitty little airport outside the Big Apple."

He moaned, knees giving way.

"And you'll never guess who was waiting for them, with a kind word and a silly costume, to ferry them off to see a nice old man."

"...no no no no no..."

"Bella told me... Bella told me it wasn't my problem. I wonder if she knew you'd be waiting there, at the other end?"

Tears oozed out of his eyes, falling in thick blobs to the floor of the corridor.

"I wonder if she knew I'd *make* it my problem?"

His lips parted.

"Wait. please! Just, w..."

And I shot him in the head, through the centre of the tattoo over his eye, and watched as smoke coiled up from the hole.

Then I stepped into the Comms room with a clear head.

Her diary was there.

The goons had moved it all to one side. Bits of old detritus, files and notes and sheets. Enough paperwork to keep anyone busy for months. They'd swept it all aside and got-on with preparing the place for John-Paul. On the TV above the control board the withered old man died, mid-confession, over and over again. Stuck on a loop.

Her diary was there.

I almost didn't see it. Almost mistook it for just another book of notes, more tedious laboratory results to be communicated back to New York.

I bought her that diary. It was just... just this stupid

thing. An idea for Christmas, one year. We gave each other notebooks, wrote down all our thoughts, everything we'd done, all the stuff we'd seen and said... then swapped them back at the end of the year.

Seems daft, now. It's not like I would've been allowed to write down half the stuff I got up to.

But hers... Hers were always full. Fat with notes.

My heart almost exploded. *Her* handwriting. Neat little letters, unjoined, in neat little columns. Page after page. Different pens, different colours. Dated at the top, and always the same beginning:

My darling.

My eyes went fuzzy.

She'd been here. She'd been here once, but how long ago?

My fingers were clumsy, suddenly. Pages stuck together, paper tore. I scrabbled through the tears and shakes to the last pages, blinking at each date in turn.

Towards the end, she'd started using a page per week.

Then per month.

Space was running out, as the back cover nudged closer. I didn't read a word, just let my eyes dance from date to date, not understanding, flicking further and further back.

The last two entries were separated by six months.

The last one—

Oh...

—the last one was made three months ago.

I was on the floor, then. Not understanding. Lights in front of my eyes.

Panels clicked and lights flickered on the consoles. My head swam.

This room. This was where she contacted me. This was where the signal started.

This was where my journey began.

And the greatest revelation of all, the one that all the others presupposed, but that somehow took far longer to settle; that blew them out of the water one by one and left me curled in a ball, head in my hands, teeth grating together, choking on dry sobs.

She's alive.

Oh, god.

She's alive.

Above ground, the Clergy ignored me. In my robe I was just another figure, and they had more than enough to be worrying about.

Wailing and screaming at the death of their master.

Hunting for Iroquois warriors, as their rusting ferry was sabotaged – listing in the water – and distant rumbles shook the island.

Some were taking over-optimistic potshots at the canoes and rowing boats just visible though the smoke, dodging between flaming patches of scummy liquid. The rest were just sitting, watching, waiting. They'd all seen the broadcast. They all knew.

It was over.

Soon, I'd swim out to the Iroquois in the boats. Nudging aside fiery drifts and scalding slicks. Maybe the *Tadodaho* was expecting me. Maybe I'd get medical treatment and food and thanks for my help.

Maybe not. Who cared?

I took the diary and the papers, bound-up neatly in a folded pile. I stepped past arguing clerics and screaming soldiers, and let the world turn-on around me.

She's alive.

The sun was setting. Through the settling QuickSmog

it was a distant spotlight, misted and artificial, and by its waning glow I read through the final pages of my lover's life.

Find me. The last page said. *Come and find me, my love.*

The fires of Lake Eerie burnt around me, and the sky choked-up with smoke and haze, and I flicked through pages and found—

Yes. There.

—found where to go. Found where to find her.

And smiled.

Don't you fucking give up, soldier!

Sir, no sir.

THE END

SIMON SPURRIER is an award-winning writer of novels and graphic novel fiction. He's worked extensively for the UK's talent-factory title *2000 AD*, has published novels with Abaddon, the Black Library and Black Flame, and has won a series of accolades and prizes for screenwriting. He's worked as a cook, a bookseller, a BBC Art Director and a film student. He lives in London because the night sky is a far better shade of green there than anywhere else.

coming
February
2007...

Now read a chapter from the first book in
Abaddon's exciting new series...

PAX BRITTANIA

UNNATURAL HISTORY

Jonathan Green

COMING FEBRUARY 2007

ISBN 13: 978-1-905437-11-5

ISBN 10: 1-905437-11-0

£6.99 (UK)/ $7.99 (US)

WWW.ABADDONBOOKS.COM

CHAPTER ONE

On the Origin of Species

The night Alfred Wentwhistle died began just like any other.

The cold orb of the moon shone through the arched windows of the museum, bathing the myriad display cases in its wan blue light, enhancing the blackness of the shadows and giving their time-locked occupants an even more eerie and sinister quality. The electric street lamps on Cromwell Road were a mere flicker of orange beyond the panes of glass.

Alfred Wentwhistle, night watchman at the museum for the last thirty-six years, swept the polished cabinets with the beam of his spotlight, gleaming eyes, hooked beaks and outstretched wings materialising suddenly and momentarily under the harsh white attentions of its searing bulb. The beam's path was a familiar one, the repeated motions of a never-ending ballet rehearsal of strobing light. And the winding path he took through the miles of corridors, halls and galleries was a familiar one too, the same route taken every night for the last thirty years. It was the course his predecessor had taken and taught him when he was a boy of barely sixteen, and when old Shuttleworth had just two months to his retirement, having trod the same path himself for the last fifty-four years.

There was never any need to change the route he took. Night watchman of the Natural History Museum at South Kensington was not a demanding role. Alfred carried his truncheon and torch every night but he had never had need of the former in all his years in the post, and he no longer really needed the latter either. He could have found his way around the galleries on a moonless night in the middle of a blackout with his eyes closed, as he used to like to tell Mrs Wentwhistle with a chuckle. He simply carried the spotlight through force of habit. There had not been one break-in in all his thirty-six years at the museum. And apart from the infrequent change of the odd cabinet here and there or the moving of an artefact every once in a while, the familiar layout of the museum had changed little in any significant way since the arrival of the *Diplodocus carnegii*, ninety-two years before in 1905.

But Alfred Wentwhistle enjoyed his job and it gave him great satisfaction too. He delighted in spending hours amongst the exhibits of stuffed beasts and dinosaur bones. Of course, you could experience the real thing now, with the opening of the Challenger Enclosure at London Zoo in Regent's Park, but there was something timeless and magical about the fossil casts of creatures that amateur archaeologists, who had effectively been the first palaeontologists, had taken to be evidence of the existence of the leviathans of legend such as the dragon or the cyclops.

Every now and then, undisturbed by the presence of the public, Alfred took pleasure from reading the hand-written labels explaining what any particular item was, where it had been collected from, who had recovered it and any other pertinent information the creator of the exhibit had seen fit to share. After thirty-six years there were not many labels that Alfred had not read.

And he took great satisfaction from knowing that he was playing his part to keep secure the nation's – and by extension the Empire's and hence, in effect, the world's – greatest museum of natural history. Even though there had been no challenge to its peaceful guardianship of Mother Nature's myriad treasures since he took up his tenure, Alfred Wentwhistle was there, every night of the year – save Christmas night itself – just in case the museum should ever need him.

Every now and again he would come upon one of the museum's research scientists working late into the night. They would pass pleasantries with him and he with them. They all knew old, reliable Alfred and he knew all of them by name, but nothing much more, and that was how they all liked it. Over the course of thirty-six years, he had seen professors come and go – botanists, zoologists, naturalists and cryptozoologists – but some things stayed the same, like the Waterhouse building itself and its night-time guardian. Alfred knew his place. The scientists were highly intelligent and erudite luminaries of the museum foundation and he was merely a night watchman. It was enough for him that he was allowed to spend hours enjoying the exhibits on display within. Nature's treasurehouse was what they called it; Sir Richard Owen's lasting legacy to the world.

Alfred's slow steady steps inexorably brought him back into the central hall and to the museum entrance, just as they always did. He paused beneath the outstretched head of the skeletal diplodocus to shine his torch on the face of his pocket watch. Five minutes past, just like every other night; regular as clockwork.

He looked up, shining the bright white beam of his torch into the hollow orbits of the giant's eye-sockets. It stared impassively ahead at the entrance to the museum and saw 20,000 visitors pass between its archways practically every day. He heard the tap of metal against metal, caught the glimmer of light on glass flicker at the corner of his eye, and it was then that he realised one of the doors was open.

There was no doubt in his mind that the door had been locked. It was the first thing he did upon coming on duty. Having had the keys handed over to him by George Stimpson, his counterpart during the daylight hours, and bid his colleague farewell, Alfred always locked the main doors to the museum. Should any of the scientists or cataloguers be working late and need to leave after this time, Alfred himself had to let them out and then would always lock the door again after them.

No, there was no doubt in his mind that something was awry this night. Pacing towards the doors he could see by the light of his torch where the lock had been forced.

The sound of breaking glass echoed through the silent halls of the museum from an upper gallery.

There was something most definitely awry. For the first time in thirty-six years, something was wrong. His museum needed him.

Turning from the main doors the portly night watchman jogged across the central hall, his shambling steps marking the full eighty-foot length of the diplodocus to the foot of the main staircase.

Once there he glanced back over his shoulder and up at the grand arch of the first floor staircase, at the other end of the hall over the museum entrance. Above him carved monkeys scampered up the curving arches of the roof into the darkness, amidst the leaf-scrolled iron span-beams. The sound had definitely come from somewhere up there, where the museum staff's private offices were located.

Putting a hand to the polished stone balustrade and taking a deep breath, Alfred Wentwhistle started to take the steps two at a time. At the first landing, where the staircase split beneath the austere bronze-eyed gaze of

Sir Richard Owen, he turned right. Hurrying along the gallery over-looking the central hall and running parallel to it, passed stuffed sloths and the mounted skeletons of prehistoric marine reptiles, brought him to the second flight of stairs.

Here he paused, out of breath and ears straining, as he tried to work out more precisely where the sound had come from. In the comparative quiet of the sleeping museum he heard another sound, like the crash of a table over-turning. The noise had come from somewhere on this floor, away to his right, from somewhere within the western Darwin wing.

Alfred turned into this series of galleries, passing beneath the carved archway that read 'The Ascent of Man'. He quickened his pace again as he came into a moonlit gallery of cases containing wax replicas of man's ancestors. They stood there, frozen in time, in various hunched poses, every kind of hominid from *Australopithecus* to *Homo neanderthalensis*. His sweeping spot-beam shone from bared snarling teeth, glass eyes and the black-edged blades of flint tools.

On any other night, as he had on any one of a hundred other previous visits, Alfred would have paused in this gallery to examine the specimens and their accompanying explanations once again, telling of the evolution of Man from primitive ape. He would have been just as fascinated and amazed as he had been the first time he had read of *The Origin of Species* and learnt of the incredible story of the human race's rise to become the most powerful and widely proliferated species on the Earth, and beyond.

When Charles Darwin had first proposed his hypothesis of the origin of species, natural selection and the survival of the fittest, he had been derided by the greatest scientific minds of his day and denounced as at best a charlatan and at worst a heretic. For he had spoken out against the worldwide Christian Church and its core belief that God had created all life on the planet in its final form from the beginning of time.

And with the re-discovery of the lost worlds hidden within the jungles of the Congo, atop the mesa-plateaus of the South American interior and on lost islands within the Indian Ocean, others – many of them churchmen – had come forward to challenge Darwin's claims again, vociferously supporting the supposition that because dinosaurs and other prehistoric creatures still existed on the Earth in the present day, the idea of one species evolving into another was ludicrous. And the debate still raged in some persistent, unremitting quarters.

But over a hundred years after his death, Darwin had been posthumously exonerated of all accusations of bestial heresy and scientific idiocy to the point where he was practically idolised as the father of the new branch of science of Evolutionary Biology, and had an entire wing of the Natural History Museum dedicated to the advances made since he first proposed his radical ideas in 1859. In fact there were scientists working within that field now, in this very museum; men like Professors Galapagos and Crichton.

On many previous occasions Alfred Wentwhistle had found himself wiling away some time gazing into the faces of his evolutionary ancestors, his reflection in the glass of the cabinets overlaid on top of the pronounced brows and sunken eyes beneath. On such occasions he had wondered upon Darwin's legacy for the human race and what implications such an accepted theory might have for Her Majesty Queen Victoria, in that it presumed that the British monarch was ultimately descended from the apes of ancient aeons past. But there was no time for such musings now. As he hurried passed the exhibits on this occasion, and turned into one of the numerous secondary galleries of the Darwin Wing, he barely even registered the frozen apemen locked within their glass cages.

The familiar smell of camphor and floor polish assailed his nostrils. Moonlight bathed the gallery with its monochrome light from skylights in the ceiling. The place Alfred found himself in now was one in which examples of animals from the orders of mammalia, reptialia and amphibia had been arranged so as to clearly show the evolutionary path Man had followed from the moment his Palaeozoic ancestors had first crawled out of the primeval swamps to the present day when he bestrode the globe like a colossus, the human race covering the Earth and the nearer planets of the solar system with all the persistence and perniciousness of a parasitic plague.

It was off this room that some of the scientists had their private workspaces. A number of doors on either side of the gallery stretching away before him bore the brass name plaques of the great and the good who worked within the museum, busily unravelling the mysteries of Evolution and Nature's – or God's – predestined plan for mankind.

He could hear clear sounds of a struggle now. In the beam of his spotlight fragments of glass glittered on the floor of the gallery before one of the frosted glass-paned doors, looking like a diamond frost on the first morning of winter. The flickering glow of an electric lamp cast its light into the gallery from inside the office before suddenly going out. There was a violent crash of more breaking glass and furniture being overturned.

He would certainly have a dramatic tale to tell Mrs Wentwhistle over his platter of bacon and eggs the next morning at the end of his shift, Alfred suddenly, incongruously, found himself thinking.

As the watchman neared the invaded office he noticed vaporous wisps of smoke or some sort of gas seeping under the door and a new smell – like aniseed, with an unpleasant undertone of gone off meat – made his nose wrinkle and made him instinctively hold back.

The door suddenly burst open, sending more shards of glass spinning into the gallery, clattering against the arrayed display cases. The figure of a man burst out of the office and collided with the aging night watchman. Alfred reeled backwards as the man barged past him. He couldn't stop himself from stumbling into a case containing a family of Neanderthal waxworks posed around an inanimate fire. The torch fell from his hand and its bulb died.

"Here, what do you think you're doing?" Alfred managed, calling after the man as he sprinted from the gallery. He was holding something about the same shape and size as a packing box in his arms. But the thief did not stop, and before Alfred had even managed to regain his balance he was gone, disappearing into the main hall of the Darwin Wing.

Alfred's heart was racing, beating a tattoo of nervous excitement against his ribs. In all his thirty-six years he had never known anything like it. Adrenalin flooding his system, he was about to give chase when something reminded him that the thief had not been alone in the office. Alfred had heard more than one voice raised in anger as he had approached and there had been definite signs of a struggle.

Cautiously, he approached the darkened doorway of the office. The rancid mist was beginning to dissipate. The soles of his boots crunched on the fractured diamonds of glass. He could hear the sound of the thief's feet pounding on the polished floors of the museum as he made his escape. But from inside the pitch black office-cum-laboratory in front of him he could hear a ragged breathing that reminded him of an animal snuffling. Then, suddenly, there was silence.

Alfred took another step forward.

"What the devil?" was all he could manage.

In an explosion of glass and splintering wood something else burst out of the office, ripping the door from its sundered frame as it did so. The night watchman barely had time to yelp out in pain as slivers of glass sliced his face and hands as he raised them to protect himself, before a hulking shadow of solid black muscle was on top of him.

Alfred had a momentary impression of thick, matted hair, a sharp bestial odour – a rank animal smell mixed in with the aniseed and rancid meat – broad shoulders and a blunt-nosed head slung low between them. There was a flash of silver as the moonlight caught something swinging from around the thing's neck.

He had never known anything like it, never in thirty-six years.

And then, teeth bared in an animal scream, its hollering cry deafening in his ears, fists flailing like sledge hammers, the ape-like creature attacked. Feebly Alfred put up his arms to defend himself but there was nothing he could do against the brute animal strength of his attacker.

It grabbed Alfred's head by the hair so violently he could hear as well as feel clumps of it being ripped from his scalp. And then, in one savage action, the enraged beast smashed his skull backwards into the Neanderthal display case. With the second blow the glass of the cabinet shattered and Alfred Wentwhistle's world exploded into dark oblivion.

For more information on this
and other titles visit...

**Abaddon
Books**

Dreams of Inan

A KIND OF PEACE

Andy Boot

Price: £6.99 ★ ISBN: 1-905437-02-1

Price: $7.99 ★ ISBN 13: 978-1-905437-02-3

TOMES *of the* DEAD

DEATH HULK

Matthew Sprange

Price: £6.99 ★ ISBN: 1-905437-03X

Price: $7.99 ★ ISBN 13: 978-1-905437-03-0

SNIPER ELITE

SPEAR OF DESTINY

Jaspre Bark

Price: £6.99 ★ ISBN: 1-905437-04-8

Price: $7.99 ★ ISBN 13: 978-1-905437-04-7